Shining City on a Hill

Book Two

Fanning the Flames

Karen Edmonds

Cover design by Benjamin Devey
Layout by Julie Larsen

Shining City Publications

ISBN 978-0-578-72524-6

To pilgrims, pioneers and patriots past,
present and future

Aux États-Unis, *pays de ma naissance*
To the United States, land of my birth

A la France, pays de mon éveil
To France, land of my awakening

Preface

Fanning the Flames is the second book in the *Shining City on a Hill* series. Using a mixture of historical and fictitious characters and events, *Shining City* recounts the manner in which the cultural, political and religious revolution known as the Protestant Reformation led to the founding of the United States and freedoms enshrined in the U.S. constitutional system of government.

During the 15th and 16th centuries, the translation of the Bible from Latin to the common languages of the people laid the groundwork for an epic struggle for freedom of conscience, in a world that demanded conformity of thought. As bourgeoning numbers of people pushed against the doctrines and practices of the Roman Church, both Church and state worked together to persecute unrepentant heretics with charges of heresy, burnings at the stake, beheadings, torture, imprisonment, and deprivation of property.

Beginning in the 1600s, organized groups of Christians began to flee to the shores of North America. Decades later, freedom of speech, religion, assembly, and a multitude of other freedoms became enshrined in American law, heavily influenced by the struggles of the Reformation.

Five hundred years after the events in *Shining City on a Hill*, when storm clouds of antagonism to Christianity and threats to freedom of conscience once again cast an ominous shadow over the world, the tragic and triumphal stories of those who stood firm against shackles of tyranny for adherence to conscience is a poignant message, for central to the American founding is the concept that freedom comes from God.

For most of America's history, the country's Christian foundation has been celebrated. However, more recently, especially in academic, left-leaning political, media and entertainment circles, the country's European immigrants in general are branded as ruthless conquerors. Along with an effort to delegitimize the American founding is an effort to delegitimize the government which sprang from that founding, putting at risk cherished and hard-won freedoms. Buried somewhere between truth and propaganda is the backstory of those who fled to the shores of the New World for religious freedom. They, and generations after them, believed God led them out of bondage, as He led the children of Israel out of Egypt.

John Winthrop, the leader of a Puritan group who fled from England to the Massachusetts Bay Area in 1630, exhorted the colonists to let their virtuous manner of living shine as a city on a hill to the rest of the world. It is from Winthrop's sermon, "A Model of Christian Charity," that the idea of America as a city on a hill originated, and from which the title of this series is taken.

What's Historical and What's Fiction?

Fanning the Flames makes every attempt at historical accuracy and draws heavily upon real-life figures and events.

Christopher Wade and Nicholas Hall were actual historical figures, but nothing is known of their daily lives except that Wade was a married linen weaver and Hall was a bricklayer. A search of genealogical records and a trip to England's National Archives revealed no lists or names of family members for either character; therefore, I used creative license to build a story based on the times in which they lived. The end of their lives is a matter of historical record.

Fanning the Flames

When thou passest through the waters, I will be with thee;
and through the rivers, they shall not overflow thee:
when thou walkest through the fire, thou shalt not be burned;
neither shall the flame kindle upon thee.
Isaiah 43:2
King James Bible

September, 1545

———

London

He came for me. Oblivious to the frenetic crowd milling back and forth past her on Cheapside, Anne replayed her previous night's encounter with Christopher, savoring each delicious moment like a sweet confection. *He showed up at the church. Offered to walk me home. Blew out the lamp. Put his arms around me and kissed me. He kissed me!* With her hand on her chest she took a deep breath, feeling her heart flutter within her chest cavity. *He said my taffaty tarts were the best he's ever tasted...gave me a comb he bought for me in the Kingdom of France...promised he would always come for me. He called me "Milady!"*

Oh, to be alone on a mountain top where she could shout for joy at the top of her lungs.

She and her Aunt Victoria passed a silver store, where a handsome salt cellar in the display window caught Victoria's eye. While Victoria stopped to admire it, Anne continued forward, bobbing along with the crowd.

"Anne, wait!" Victoria waved her arm. "Anne Cooper!"

Anne spun around. A hunchbacked older gentleman, keeping his eyes on the uneven cobble to avoid tripping, stumbled into her. The basket full of apples he carried on his elbow scattered across the street. Folks sidestepped left and right, casting annoyed jeers at the clumsy old man. With a profuse apology, Anne attempted to gather the apples while Victoria wove through the crowd to catch up.

"Forget it," the old man said, waving Anne off. "They're bruised beyond eating. Looks like the mistress'll be making applesauce, it does."

"I'm truly sorry," Anne repeated. She fished three pence from her purse and extended her hand. With a grunt, he wrapped his fingers around the coins, slipped his basket on his elbow and limped forward, keeping his eyes ahead on the crowd rather than on the ground.

The mishap gave Victoria time to catch up. She took Anne by the elbow and declared, "The lad you were with last night—'twas the Wade lad, wasn't it? I looked to eat a taffaty tart for breakfast and found the basket empty. You two must have had quite a time of it."

Fearing a lecture, Anne nudged her elbow free and resumed walking. Victoria noticed a bounce in her step, as if she were dancing to the music of the street criers.

"Buy my fine wash balls," called a petite woman with dark circles under deep-set eyes. "Wash balls. Buy my fine wash balls." On her head, she balanced a basket of Castile soap balls scented with a variety of herbs.

"Come, glasses, glasses, fine glasses." The elderly glass vendor's jowls jiggled, while his moustache danced up and down with his cry.

"Hot codlings, get 'em fresh, hot codlings." The obese, middle-aged woman with bushy grey eyebrows and long chin hairs stood in the same place every Saturday, on the corner of Cheapside and Bread Street, looking like she'd rather be somewhere else.

"Rosemary and bays, good maids, rosemary and bays, penny a bunch." Unlike the codling peddler, the woman selling herbs bubbled over with youthful enthusiasm.

The tantalizing aroma of cinnamon infused central London's air. Anne took a long, slow breath. "Chestnuts roasting—what a delicious fragrance," she remarked. "Where is it coming from?" With a joyful glance in all directions, she sang, "Isn't the city lovely this morning? The weather can't decide whether it's late summer or early fall."

"Yes, the weather is lovely indeed, and the smell of those chestnuts is making my mouth water. We'll have to stop and get some. Now, about this lad…"

With a quick turn and a sheepish grin, Anne conceded. "Very well. Yes, 'twas Christopher Wade. I already know what you're going to say. You'll tell me Father sent me here to get away from him; that Father will disapprove; that I'm making trouble for myself. And you would be correct." She stepped sideways to dodge a woman pushing a cart filled with vegetables. "But I don't care." A devil-may-care attitude possessed her, and she liked it.

"Mat for a door! Buy a mat for a door." The wiry-haired adolescent peddler brushed against Anne's arm and continued past.

"We could use a new mat." Anne stopped in her tracks and snapped her fingers. "Lad!" The young man turned, his eyes lighting up at the prospect of a sale. "A mat, if you please." He approached, and they stepped to the side while he lifted an assortment of mats from their perch on his back and laid them in front of her.

"Take your pick. For a door, is it?" She nodded, trying to avoid gawking at his severely mottled teeth. "A fine one, this is." He pointed to a mat that was solid green.

"What do you think of this one, Victoria?" Anne pointed toward it with her toe.

"I rather like it." Victoria cocked her head, admiring the color. "A new mat would brighten up the kitchen."

After Anne handed the vendor two groats, he picked up the green mat and handed it to her with a tip of his hat.

"G'day, maiden. Godspeed."

She tucked the mat under her arm with a nod. "G'day to you, lad."

"Now, about that Wade lad," Victoria persisted as they continued forward. "Stop avoiding my question."

At the mention of his name, Anne's body tingled. *Wade.* He came for her! She steeled herself for a lecture as they continued along the street. A firm hand on her shoulder stopped her.

"Look at me," Victoria demanded. Expecting to be greeted with a scowl, Anne turned to see a broad smile brighten Victoria's face. "How did you do it? Two lads courting you—you could have your pick, and both of them are mad about you. I must say, when I left you last night, I retired to my lonely bedchamber a bit envious."

Anne's jaw dropped. With a shrug of her shoulders she stammered, "I don't do anything."

"I suppose you don't know how pretty you are." Victoria searched her niece's friendly hazel eyes framed with long, brown lashes. "The lads can't help but notice."

"Christopher caught my fancy the first time I saw him," Anne confessed. "'Twas at Market Square in Dartford. I noticed him looking at me, but two bullies interfered—John and Edwin. They mocked him mercilessly, but he didn't give up. One of the bullies, John, courted me before he went off to Cambridge, proud as a puffed-up peacock. Still, Christopher refused to give up. My father treated him mercilessly because of his father's Lollard sympathies, but..."

"He didn't give up," Victoria interjected.

"Correct," Anne smiled. "When Father sent me here, I all but lost hope. Yet, here he is. He never gives up."

"A third lad vied for your attention? By Jove, how do you do it?"

"At the time, 'twas only John and Christopher."

Victoria smiled at Anne's modesty. "It appears the male species flocks to you two by two, as the creatures did Noah. No wonder Matthew sent you away." She searched Anne's eyes. "What about Nicholas? The banns were read in church. Everyone knows you're betrothed. What will you tell him? 'Twould be scandalous for anyone to see you with Christopher now."

A low moan escaped Anne's lips. "I haven't decided. 'Tis happening so quickly. Do you have any suggestions?"

"I think it best to be honest. Better to lance a wound so it can heal, than allow it to fester."

"But I don't want to hurt him."

"Hurting him can't be avoided," Victoria replied.

Watching a young couple pass by, arm in arm, Anne sighed. "I suppose you're right. 'Tis not that I don't care for Nicholas, you understand."

"Of course. And since you asked my opinion, I believe you owe it to him to tell him as soon as possible, before he finds out some other way. Would you like me to accompany you to Smithfield? I'll stay a safe distance away."

Anne kicked at a loose cobblestone, biting her lower lip. "I suppose he has to find out sometime. Thank you, Victoria."

With a reassuring pat on Anne's shoulder, Victoria sighed, "I still don't understand how you do it."

"'Tis not all fun and games. Look at my predicament."

"'Tis a predicament I might like to have."

Anne stopped in her tracks, her eyes wide. "You? You entertain thoughts about such things?"

Victoria's coy nod answered her question. "Do you promise not to laugh if I share something with you?" A twinkle danced in Victoria's azure eyes that erased the sternness the former nun sometimes exuded.

"Of course."

"On Midsummer's Eve, I kept some of those rose petals for myself."

"You didn't!" Anne studied her aunt's expression, for the first time seeing Victoria as more than just a displaced nun. She was a woman in her own right and actually quite stunning, with an ivory complexion and coal-black hair that accentuated her blue eyes. The somber demeanor Anne had grown accustomed to Victoria wearing seemed to be softening of late. Now Anne understood why.

Victoria laughed. "I'm still waiting for 'he that will love me' to come after me now."

They discussed virtues and vices of bachelors at Honey Lane Parish until they arrived at Smithfield.

"I'll wait here." Victoria patted Anne's arm. "Good luck."

Anne moistened her lips with her tongue, took a deep breath and strolled toward the poultry stall, stopping once to glance over her shoulder for reassurance. Victoria nodded. Pressing forward, Anne scanned the stall for a sign of her betrothed and discovered him hovering over a bin of chicken feathers. Fighting back a sense of overwhelming dread, she trudged up behind him and tapped him on the shoulder. He flinched and turned.

At the sight of her, his face lit up; then, his eyes narrowed as he scanned the market. She recognized the look well, for all the workers had it. It was fear of Master Barnard. Nicholas rubbed his bloodshot eyes before fixing his penetrating gaze on her. Afraid he might see straight through her, she averted her gaze to her patten shoes.

"Where have you been? I was all over the city last night. A night watchman even helped me look for you. I've been sick with worry."

She shrugged her shoulders. "I'm sorry." The corner of her mouth twitched.

He frowned. "Is something wrong?"

Looking past him, she stammered, "It's…I don't know how to say this."

Barnard Johnson materialized from nowhere, wearing the scowl that comprised as much a part of his everyday attire as his jerkin, breeches and feather cap. With a warning glance at Nicholas, he scolded, "I don't pay you to conduct personal affairs, lad. An honest day's work for an honest day's pay."

Nicholas opened his mouth to respond, when Anne interrupted him. "'Tis my fault." She took a step toward Barnard. "I had to speak with him."

As if she weren't there, Barnard persisted, "To work lad, to work. There's more work to be done than there are hours to do it."

"Yes, sir." Nicholas rolled his eyes as Barnard hurried toward a hunchbacked man with silver hair who had leaned against a post to rest. "I'll call on you after work," Nicholas whispered, turning back to the bin. She offered a weak nod. Christopher planned to call on her as well, but how could she explain with Barnard on the prowl?

Just as Anne turned to leave, a familiar voice called her name. Waving an arm high, Christopher trotted toward her. Nicholas glanced over his shoulder. Her heart sank.

"Another?" Barnard turned in his tracks. Smirking, he watched as Christopher, with the exuberance of a playful puppy, threw his arms around her. Red-faced, she glanced at Nicholas.

"What are you doing?" Nicholas demanded, glowering at Christopher.

Christopher turned to Anne. "You haven't told him?" The panic in her eyes answered his question.

"What haven't you told me?" Nicholas demanded, his eyes combing over Anne, then Christopher.

"Yes, pray tell!" Barnard shuffled closer and seated himself on a wood crate, looking like he had just scored a front row seat at the theater. A mild breeze rustled the ivory feather in his cap while he tapped his fingers on his thigh.

Anne froze. She hadn't anticipated an audience.

Victoria hurried to her niece's side. Breathless, she blurted, "Did you tell him?"

"Tell me what?" A profound frown sank Nicholas' countenance.

Averting her eyes to a white chicken feather stuck to Nicholas' boot, Anne mumbled, "Christopher found me last night."

"Why didn't you tell me?" They were Nicholas' first words to Christopher in days. "You knew when I came to work this morning and didn't say a word."

"I was too groggy." Christopher cast a sideways glance at Anne.

"Where were you last night?" Nicholas asked Anne. "I looked everywhere. I feared the worst."

Averting her gaze like a scolded puppy, she confessed, "I went to the church to do some soul-searching. Christopher found me there." Several seconds elapsed. Her spellbound audience leaned forward as she whispered, "I didn't expect to tell you this way, in front of a crowd, but I—I can't marry you."

The color drained from Nicholas' face.

Barnard stood. Pointing a finger of scorn at Christopher, he barked, "How can you do such a thing to this lad—and in front of all these folks?" After fishing two shillings from his purse, he offered them to Nicholas. "Drink's on me. Take the rest of the day off." Turning to Christopher, Barnard scolded, "Before you go this evening, finish his work and yours." With an icy glare at Anne Barnard pranced away, the feather on his cap billowing in the breeze.

Nicholas studied the shillings in his hand, his eyes vacant.

"I don't suppose you would still like to call on me this eve, so I can explain?" Anne felt ridiculous the moment she uttered the words.

With the zeal of a tortoise, Nicholas untied his apron strings, pulled the garment over his head, folded it neatly, and set it on the crate where Barnard watched the spectacle moments earlier. "That won't be necessary." He put the coins in his pouch and looked one by one at Christopher, Anne and Victoria.

Victoria stepped forward, raising her hand to pat his shoulder.

He stepped back. "Thank you, but I need no pity."

Anne watched with a lump in her throat as he trudged away.

Bordeaux, France

"Go, Bijou. I see the estate, through the trees."

Thomas clicked his tongue and kicked his exhausted palfrey onward across the wet clay ground. Frigid rain saturated his wool hose and seeped into his riding boots, making his feet cold and numb. Perspiration mixed with rain ran in rivulets down the mare's dappled grey coat. A thunder clap shook the ground. The horse stumbled over a small crevice, throwing Thomas sideways. Threading his fingers through her coarse, black mane, he pulled himself upright.

"There's the vineyard. Come, my lady, run!" As if sensing the urgency, Bijou put her ears back and picked up her canter. When he reached the three-foot-high stone wall surrounding the DuBois estate, Thomas slowed the mare to a trot and whispered, "I hope we aren't too late." With a bluster and a flicker of her ears, Bijou twisted her neck to snag a mouthful of wet grass along the base of the wall. "First you have to get me there," he scolded, tugging on the reins. "Then I'll give you fodder."

A glance at the front door of the main dwelling sent Thomas' heart into a freefall. His father-in-law, François, stood in the doorway, engaged in a lively conversation with a cassock-clad priest. The clip-clop of Bijou's hooves momentarily diverted their attention, but the two men quickly returned to their discussion.

Thomas slipped off his mount, tied the reins to the branch of a chestnut tree in the front yard, and jogged to the door, water sloshing uncomfortably between his toes.

François DuBois greeted his son-in-law with a furrowed brow and a befuddled expression. He held up a hand, signaling Thomas must stay quiet. "The Father is looking for my daughter. She's missing. Could I speak with you later?"

Sensing that he must play along, Thomas responded, "Yes. I beg your pardon."

François swept his arm in the direction of the stables. "Behind the house, you'll find an empty stable, with water and grain. Feel free to refresh your mount there."

Feeling the priest's probing glare on his back, Thomas led Bijou around the house to the stables where François boarded his four horses—Jeanette's white jennet, a dappled Percheron plow horse, and two chestnut palfreys used for riding. At the sight of Bijou, one of the palfreys whinnied and pranced about the stable. Chafing at the reins, Bijou lifted her head and whinnied back while Thomas tightened his grip and led her inside an empty stable. A tap on his shoulder made his muscles stiffen.

"I saw you coming up the road." Jeanette kept a nervous watch on the side of the house.

Exhaling his relief, Thomas removed the bridle, gazing into his mother-in-law's red, puffy eyes. He pointed toward the front of the house with his nose. "Why is Father Berger here?" he whispered, hanging the bridle on a hook.

Pacing back and forth next to Bijou, Jeanette whispered, "The bishop sent him. We had no idea Charlotte was studying with a reading group in Bordeaux. She said nothing about it when she showed up here—only that you were traveling, and that she feared being home alone."

His cheeks reddened. "I've been on the road a lot, it is true."

"Did you know about the reading group?"

Thomas nodded, dusted the horse hair off his cloak, and waited for Jeanette to follow him out before he closed the stable gate. "One day," he explained, "she slipped and told me. Someone informed the authorities about the group. I was away the night they conducted a house-to-house search. Charlotte barely made it out before they reached our place, I am told."

Jeanette wagged her head. "Why didn't she tell us the truth?"

"She's afraid. That's why I haven't insisted she come home." Twisting the tip of his moustache, Thomas surveyed the vineyards around the house. Satisfied that he and Jeanette were alone, he continued, "Where is Charlotte now?"

"In the cellar. When she saw the priest coming up the road, she said she needed to look for something, and begged François to keep her presence here a secret."

"Where are the children?"

"With her."

François emerged from the side yard, his face pale.

"Is he gone?" Jeanette's voice wavered.

"Yes, but they'll be keeping an eye on us, I'm sure." With lips pursed, he hissed out the tension bottled inside and laid his hand on Thomas' forearm. "You showed up at an unfortunate time."

Massaging the back of her neck, Jeanette complained, "What will we do? She won't be safe here."

François frowned. "Reading foreign tracts, meeting to study heresies—these things are forbidden. Father Berger drilled into me, in no uncertain terms, that harboring heretics is a grievous offense—as if anyone could forget, with King Francis doubling down on the unfortunates."

Jeanette stopped pacing to face her husband. "How did you respond?"

"I promised him my full cooperation."

"I have to speak with her," Thomas said. He started toward the back door.

Tugging his elbow, Jeanette demanded, "What will you say? She has nowhere to go."

"I'll think of something." Thomas jogged toward the kitchen door with Jeanette close behind, while François peeked around the side of the house. The distant sight of a black-clad figure walking the muddy road to Bordeaux assured him his family was safe for the time being.

Inside the kitchen, Jeanette stammered, "Do you know how cruel the authorities are?" She reached for a towel to dab at the moisture pooling in the corners of her eyes. "They're worse than swine." Thomas looked at her blankly. With the toe of her shoe, she pushed aside a straw mat next to the cupboard, wedged her fingers under the trap door and heaved.

"Mamie!" The sound of Gabrielle's voice drifted up the stairs.

"I'm here." Jeanette crouched at the edge of the cellar opening. "Come up. Our visitor is gone."

Gabrielle pounded up the stairs and into the kitchen, her face brightening at the sight of her father. "Papa!" she squealed, running to Thomas's arms.

"I missed you," he gushed, squeezing her and kissing her forehead.

Resting her chubby hand against her father's cheek Gabrielle begged, "Can we come home with you?"

Brushing a strand of hair away from her mouth he replied, "Maman and I will talk."

Ashen-faced, Charlotte emerged, cradling Anatole. Jeanette reached for her grandson. He nestled into her arms and stuck his thumb in his mouth. With his free arm, Thomas pulled Charlotte to his side. She buried her head in his chest, while Jeanette and François watched helplessly.

"Gabrielle, come with Mamie. I made some fresh cookies." Jeanette extended her hand to her granddaughter with a knowing glance at her son-in-law. Eager for a treat, Gabrielle released her grip on her father's neck and slid down to the floor.

Thomas led Charlotte by the hand into the guest chamber. The tortured look in her eyes added to his already overwhelming guilt for confiding in Father Berger. "We must talk," he said, his voice low. "They're on to you now. There's no escaping their watchful eyes if you stay here."

Several seconds passed in silence. A teardrop splashed on her shoe, and then another. "What have I done?" she choked. "What have I done to you, to the children? I didn't see this coming when I attended the group. I wouldn't have gone." Her eyes searched his. "Please believe me, if I had it to do over again..."

Thomas swallowed his ugly betrayal. "One thing is certain," he said stiffly. "We can't change what has already happened. We must look forward."

Dark doubt saturated her eyes. "Look forward—to what? There's no safety here. There is no safety in Paris; they're after the reformers in Meaux. They slaughtered the villagers in Mérindol. Is that the fate that awaits me? To die at the sword, to have my children ripped from my arms by soldiers, only because I want to read and discuss the words of Jesus?" She trudged to the window and gazed out, suffocating in a cloud of despair.

He moved behind her and rested his hands on her shoulders. "La Rochelle is a possibility. Your people have strong numbers there." He felt her shoulder muscles stiffen.

"My people?" she choked, spinning around to face him. "What do you mean, 'my people'? You are my people—you, our children, my family and friends in Bordeaux." After pacing in front of the window for several seconds, she stopped to glare at him. "You say 'my people,' as if we who study Calvin's ideas are a breed of strangers, of a different race than you. They're your people as well, flesh and blood like you." She stopped to wait for a reaction. He stared past her, stone-faced.

"I meant nothing when I referred to them as your people. But you must admit, they're different—dangerous. Just look at you. You're a fugitive in your country, as I was in mine. Perhaps you should flee to England."

She glared at him with daggers in her eyes.

Desperate for an escape, he blurted, "Let's discuss this over a goblet of wine."

She scanned the landscape that cool autumn nights had transformed to a palette of yellow and gold. "How can you think of wine right now?" she snipped. "La Rochelle isn't as safe as you might think. A year ago, King Francis wrote to his lieutenant at Poitou and told him to double down on the reformers. A group of them was forced to stand in front of the church there, in bare feet and clothed only in their nightshirts, holding a tapir. Their choice was to recant or be punished. That's not all. A priest—I believe his name is Soulier—informed on some souls who were then rounded up, flogged until they bled, and ordered to not speak at all of heretical doctrines under pain of burning. They were banished. All at La Rochelle, which you think is safe."

"I'm thirsty," he repeated. "Are you sure you wouldn't like a drink?" She thrust her hands upward in frustration as he left the room.

Alone in the chamber, she contemplated her options. Many were fleeing to Geneva, but Thomas wouldn't survive there, surrounded by folks he considered enemies to his faith. Asking it of him wouldn't be fair. She imagined raising her children away from the climate of persecution and hostility darkening her homeland. It was a sweet thought.

Thomas re-entered the room, clasping a goblet of wine in one hand and a couple of cookies in the other. He offered her a cookie.

"Aren't you listening to me?" she groaned. "I can't think of food right now."

"I only thought you might like one."

"I was thinking about Geneva while you were in the kitchen, but you would be miserable there—wouldn't you?"

Without acknowledging her comment, he said, "I feel drawn to La Rochelle. A truffle merchant I worked for in Sarlat had dealings with reformers there. It's not too far from Bordeaux, Catholics still practice there, and your peo—the hereti—folks who study Calvin—are numerous there as well. I think we would both be safe there for the time being, if we're quiet about our convictions."

"But what is to keep them from hunting réformées in La Rochelle, as they did in Mérindol?"

"We'll find no guarantees anywhere. If we went to Geneva, how would I make a living? No one would buy my carvings. They're all reformers."

She plopped down on the green silk bedspread and picked at a callus on her middle finger. "I doubt they're all reformers," she mumbled. "I do know staying here isn't an option. Someone will show up here again, looking for me. The priest probably admonished the neighbors to keep a lookout. I wouldn't be surprised if he bribed them with indulgences."

Bribed with indulgences. Thomas swallowed his guilt along with a sip of wine. "You're absolutely correct. We must make a decision and act quickly."

Dartford, England

Elizabeth readied the room and sat on a stool next to the bed, awaiting Father Garrett's arrival. Across a small table at the foot of the bed she draped a white linen cloth, and placed a crucifix with a candle on either side. The table also accommodated a small dish of plain water and a flask of holy water, along with a linen towel. She'd just placed a cloth over her husband's breast when the priest knocked. After covering her head with a scarf, she picked up a burning candle that had already been blessed. Finally, tucking her rosary safely out of sight under her chemise, she crossed the room, opened the door and bent down on one knee.

"Come in," she said, her voice wobbling.

Father Garrett offered a somber nod. "Peace to this house."

"And all who dwell therein," Elizabeth whispered. "He's unconscious." She choked back a sob. "I must get word to Christopher. He needs to know. Christopher's name was the last word on William's lips before he closed his eyes."

Father Garrett licked his lips and wiped them on his forearm, as if he were wiping away the bitter taste of administering rites to a heretic. He made his duty more palatable by imagining that his services were for Elizabeth's sake, not William's, wondering how she'd coped all these years under the curse her husband brought upon his household. William's passing would be a blessing, whether she realized it now or not.

"Did he request unction? Or do you believe he would have, if he were conscious?" The priest knew the answer, but he asked out of respect for Elizabeth. Lollards were nothing if not blindly obstinate; that Garrett knew well. William Wade was nowhere near asking for rites from the Holy Mother Church, deathbed or not.

"I'm sure he would have, Father. And 'twould bring me such comfort to know he received unction before his passin'."

William heaved.

Elizabeth rushed to his side. Taking his hand in hers she pleaded, "Stay with me." Heartsick at his skin's pale, translucent glow she squeezed his hand tightly, as if holding on might keep his spirit earth-bound. His eyelids fluttered. "Don't leave me," she choked. "Don't leave me alone, with our son out wanderin' who knows where." She laid her cheek against his sunken chest, adding her tears to his perspiration-soaked nightshirt.

Father Garrett waited for a sign of recognition on William's part, but saw none. "He has the look of death upon him. I'll anoint his head and pray for him. But I can't offer him the Eucharist, as I have no way to tell if he's penitent."

Elizabeth let William's hand slip from hers and backed away, ceding the bedside stool to Father Garrett. The priest pulled a small ampulla of sacred oil from his leather sack. He placed a drop on William's clammy forehead and muttered, "Through this holy unction, may the Lord pardon thee whatever sins or faults thou hast committed."

William's eyes fluttered open, glazed and faraway, as if he were looking through a window into another world. "Christopher," he whispered, his voice cracking.

"His heart is broken," Elizabeth sniffled. "I wouldn't be surprised if a broken heart led him to his deathbed."

Father Garrett put the ampulla back in his pouch and set the bag on the floor. "I'm not sure you would find Christopher in London, amongst the thousands who dwell there. You do realize your son isn't likely to see his father alive?" He stood, motioning for her to take his place on the stool. She sat down and stroked her husband's cheek with her forefinger.

"Of course, but my son must have news of his father. William has a brother in London. Nathan would know Christopher's whereabouts. I'm sure of it."

"I could ask if any parishioners have plans to journey to London."

Elizabeth wagged her head, doubtful anyone would assist a Lollard's wife. Changing the subject, she whispered, "I would like some time alone with William, if it please you."

"Are you sure you can fare well enough on your own? I'll call on someone to sit with you, if you would like. I'm sure Amy would be pleased to."

She shook her head. "On the morrow, perhaps. For now, I would like to speak with him alone."

"Very well." Garrett placed a hand on Elizabeth's shoulder. "If you should change your mind, call on me."

"Thank you. I will. You'll see yourself out? I'm loath to leave his side."

"Don't trouble yourself." Father Garrett made his way toward the door and reached for the handle. He turned, struck with one last item he felt it imperative to mention.

"Elizabeth, about the Bible William had in his possession…"

Elizabeth glanced over her shoulder. "Yes?"

"You burned it in fire, did you?"

She turned away, her ire raised. Gazing at her beleaguered husband, she understood what he had been trying to tell her all these years. The wolves had gotten him at last.

"Yes, Father. 'Tis burned to ash." She didn't bother to turn around.

The priest grinned at the fireplace. "Then you may go forward at last, without the stain of Lollardy over your household."

As soon as the door closed, she buried her head in her hands and sobbed.

Bordeaux

"We can't thank you enough for helping our daughter," François DuBois said, with a vigorous shake of Father Maubert's hand.

Jeanette nodded in agreement with her husband. The candle in her right hand flickered as a cool, brisk breeze swept across the fields surrounding the estate, the yellowing grass undulating in waves of homage to the wind. A rooster crowed, signaling that parting time must be hastened.

Father Maubert smiled. "And I cannot thank you enough for the wine." He referred to three barrels of François' finest merlot resting in the wagon bed. "The priests in La Rochelle will be very happy to taste it. Keep us in your prayers. We should arrive a week from today."

Jeanette blew the candle out. "We'll pray for your safe arrival."

Charlotte kissed her mother lightly on each cheek. "You'll manage with the children? They can be a handful."

"Don't worry," Jeanette whispered, squeezing Charlotte's gloved hand.

"They'll be fine for a few weeks, and they'll be more than ready to see you when we bring them to La Rochelle for All Saints' Day. I'll try not to spoil them too much." Jeanette studied Charlotte's attire—a black, veiled hat and black robe. "I think the disguise will keep you safe. Folks will believe you're in mourning, and with Father Maubert delivering wine, it will be enough to distract them." It appeared to Charlotte her mother was trying to convince herself.

"Thank you, Maman. And I'll return your mourning dress when you come next month."

Gabrielle threw her arms around Charlotte's legs, while Father Maubert looked on in sympathy. Charlotte picked up her daughter and with a tight squeeze admonished, "Be a good girl, Gabrielle. You'll come to be with Maman and Papa soon. But for now, you get to stay and play with the horses and enjoy Mamie's cookies. Maman loves you." Sticking out her lower lip, Gabrielle gazed up at her mother with puppy-dog eyes. Charlotte smothered the child's face with kisses before passing her to Thomas. Turning to her parents, Charlotte sighed. "I'm relieved Anatole is asleep. Give him a kiss for me every day."

"I will." Jeanette forced a smile.

"We must be going." Father Maubert surveyed the horizon. "For the safety of us all."

After kissing Gabrielle on the cheek Thomas passed her to François, reassuring his wife's parents he would do everything in his power to keep Charlotte safe. François and Jeanette backed away, while Thomas held the reins for Charlotte to mount her mother's jennet. Next, Thomas wrapped Bijou's reins around his right hand and hoisted himself onto the mare's back.

"You'll manage without Jolie?" Charlotte studied her mother's sad eyes.

Jeanette nodded. "We have the palfreys. Remember, be sure to wear the veil any time you stop to talk to anyone. Wear the mourning clothes until you know you're safe."

"I will," Charlotte nodded.

"Are we ready?" Father Maubert's tone took on increased urgency.

Thomas tightened his grip on the reins, awaiting the signal. Father

Maubert clicked his tongue to start the caravan, pulling a small cart with the wine barrels and the few possessions Charlotte acquired while staying with her parents. Charlotte followed, her black clothing a stark contrast to the white jennet. Thomas was last, sitting tall and straight in the saddle, looking regal in his hooded leather cape and riding boots. Charlotte turned to wave to her family one last time, her eyes moist.

Rays of sunlight peeked above the eastern horizon, illuminating the sky with flaming cascades of orange. Jeanette dabbed her eyes while the rest of the family waved good-bye. Charlotte swallowed the lump in her throat and steeled herself for the journey ahead.

Outside La Rochelle

"Whoa, girl." Thomas pulled back on Bijou's reins, stopping to focus on two riders in a gallop toward them, capes wafting about their shoulders. As one of the approaching horses whinnied, Jolie danced sideways. Charlotte white-knuckled the reins to keep her from bolting forward.

"It looks like we have unwelcome company." Father Maubert's jaw stiffened.

A bone-weary sigh escaped Charlotte's lips. "We're almost to La Rochelle. I pray we have no trouble." Five days of travel—the past three in wet, grey weather—left her nerves frayed. She watched Thomas stiffen in the saddle as he studied the two men on horseback.

"Marshals. Veil your face," he warned. Taking a deep breath, Charlotte slipped the veil over her head.

"I'll handle it." Father Maubert waved his right hand high in a friendly gesture. As the marshals slowed their horses to a trot, water from the saturated ground splashed up around the animals' hooves. Maubert removed his hat with a polite nod.

One of the marshals, his face and physique more boy than man, prodded his dappled gelding closer. His greedy eyes studied Charlotte. A shiver tickled her spine.

"Heading to La Rochelle?" he demanded.

He continued to stare at Charlotte while waiting for a response. With bowed head she closed her eyes, not daring to blink them open for even a second, despite a gnawing curiosity about what the marshals looked like.

"Yes." Father Maubert fiddled with his hat, volunteering no additional information.

Pursing his lips, the officer demanded, "Where are you from?" Charlotte felt her heart flip-flop in her chest cavity as the officer glared through her veil.

"Bordeaux," the priest replied, clicking his horse one step forward. "We're on our way to La Rochelle with this wine—a gift for my frères at the monastery." His hand waved toward the wagon box.

With a hand on the hilt of his sword, the second officer inquired, "How can we know it is wine in the barrels?" A middle-aged man with bushy gray eyebrows, he dismounted to approach Father Maubert. The officer carried himself with an ambivalent air, giving off the impression he would rather be somewhere else.

"You clearly see they are wine barrels. What else would be in them?"

Charlotte marveled at Father Maubert's calm demeanor.

"Are you carrying any written materials?" The officer's gaze moved from the wagon bed, to Charlotte, back to the priest.

Maubert shook his head. "You may shake the barrels, if you wish. You'll hear the liquid."

The older marshal approached the cart. First checking the wagon's contents by shuffling a box here and tapping a box there, the marshal placed his hands on one of the barrels and rolled it back and forth. He cast Father Maubert a sheepish glance.

The priest nodded. "Go ahead, try the other two."

He shook his head. "I apologize, Father. You understand, King Francis sent orders to his lieutenant in Poitou to root out heretics in the region. They're spreading like the pox. We're hunting a book peddler who smuggles forbidden materials to réformées in the region. Books from Geneva are expressly forbidden, but they keep finding their way in, nonetheless. Did you pass a man along the way carrying a pack, or did anyone try to sell you books?"

Father Maubert turned to Thomas. "Did you notice such a man along the route? I don't recall anyone fitting that description."

Thomas shook his head. "We've passed very few folks, save for a few pilgrims on their way to Compostela." As an afterthought, and to remove any doubt about his loyalty to the Mother Church, he added, "I carve and sell pilgrim souvenirs."

Unimpressed, the marshal on horseback prodded his horse a step closer to his fellow officer and said, "Tell them about the reward."

"Reward?" Father Maubert raised his eyebrows.

"Ah, yes." Resting both hands against the cart, the marshal on the ground explained, "One-third of the property of anyone who purchases Lutheran books will be yours, if you will divulge their names."

"A most generous reward." Father Maubert scratched a mole on his chin. "I'm presently not aware of anyone who has purchased or sold such books. Have you managed to find informers?"

With a wag of his head, the marshal replied, "They're a stubborn lot. One peddler had every bone in his body dislocated, yet he refused to betray the names of those who bought his books. He was burned in Paris. What a spectacle these fools make!"

Beads of perspiration formed around Charlotte's hairline. Unbeknownst to Thomas or Father Maubert, her French Bible and a tract written by John Calvin lay hidden at the bottom of a crate in the wagon.

"Pray, remind me which materials are forbidden, and I'll keep an eye out." Father Maubert stood up straight and kicked a wagon wheel.

"Anything by Wycliff, John Huss, Luther, Zwingle, or Calvin. Watch for forbidden titles—what are they?" The marshal glanced up at his partner on horseback.

The youthful officer unwrapped his hand from his sword and combed his long, thin fingers through the coarse black hair of his stiletto-style beard, pensive. "We seized some in Saintes." He thought for a moment and snapped his fingers. "Yes, 'Commandments of God,' 'Life of Jesus,' 'Psalms of David,' and Bibles in which Paul's epistle to the Romans contains the words, 'We are justified by faith, not by works.'"

"I'll be on the lookout." Maubert glanced at Charlotte, relieved that she continued to keep her head down and her eyes closed.

The marshal on the ground stepped forward and cracked his knuckles. "I feel to warn you, Father, the heretics are dangerous. They hold secret conventicles at night, in caves and grottos, and practice every manner of lewd behavior imaginable—things forbidden in God's commandments. I have it on good report they eat their own young. The devil works in darkness, of that there is no doubt."

Charlotte almost choked, hoping the veil concealed her expression of outrage.

"I've not heard of these things, I must admit." Weary from lack of sleep, Father Maubert rubbed his eyes with his fists. "Are you sure they're not malicious rumors?"

"No. The heretics are plotting to overthrow the king and institute their own rule. They must be stopped—exterminated, in my opinion and in the opinion of many others."

"Thank you for the warnings." Father Maubert signaled his growing restlessness by tapping his fingers on the wagon rail.

"We must all work together to eliminate the threat." The marshal slipped his riding boot into a stirrup and placed his hands on his palfrey's withers. Charlotte felt a surge of hope until the officer pulled his foot from the stirrup and turned again toward the company. "Father, as part of my duty, I should inspect the contents of the crates in your wagon. I apologize for any inconvenience."

"Of course." Garrett promptly dismounted. Holding her breath, Charlotte stole a glance at Thomas. His face was pale.

Father Maubert pulled the marshal aside. With their backs turned, the two men conversed for what felt to Charlotte like the longest minute of her life. She offered a silent prayer for protection, holding her breath while the marshal backed away from the cart with his eyes fixed on her.

"I regret your loss, Madame," he offered, then turned to Father Maubert. "Thank you for your cooperation, Father, and may you have a safe journey to

La Rochelle. Be on the lookout for heretics. Remember, a third of their property will be yours if you inform authorities of their names and whereabouts."

"Thank you." Father Maubert nodded, making the sign of the cross. "Godspeed."

The marshal mounted his gelding and with a click of his tongue they were off, the pounding of hooves resonating in the air as the officers pursued their journey southward. Father Maubert, Thomas and Charlotte continued in tense silence until a safe distance separated them from the inquisitors.

"Father," Charlotte piped up. "I'm curious. What did you tell the marshal?"

Maubert pulled his horse to a stop and turned in the saddle with a mischievous grin. "I told him you're grieving the loss of a son and daughter and asked him to proceed gently."

She wrinkled her nose. "But my children are alive and well."

"Yes. But are you not grieving that you left them behind in Bordeaux?"

Charlotte glanced over her shoulder at Thomas. He winked. She smiled and whispered, "Thank you, Father."

A cluster of stone dwellings outside the ramparts of La Rochelle came into view, along with a smattering of grazing sheep and cattle. From a distance, the buildings and animals looked like toys. The sight of La Rochelle, with its growing reputation as a gathering place for réformées, gave Charlotte a surge of hope.

October, 1545

———

The Roman Road between London and Dartford, England

"Marry! I never imagined I would travel to London, not in my wildest dreams, I didn't." The cadence of Elizabeth's voice wobbled up and down with the bobbing of the horse-drawn cart. Her fingers had grown numb from holding on to the sidewalls to steady herself. "Spent most of my life in Dartford, and never fancied myself going there. Thank you for squeezing me in at the last minute."

Straining to hear, Matthew Cooper took a moment to process her words before shouting a reply over the clip-clop of his draft horse's hooves. "'Tis no bother at all. Just a matter of shuffling a few things—and children—in the cart. Off to see your brother-in-law, are you?"

She let go of the cart rail to tighten her wool cloak around her. No sooner did she clench the front of her cloak when the right front cart wheel hit a dip in the road and bounced her sideways, slamming her into Nathan Cooper. He grumbled under his breath.

"I beg your pardon," she gushed, her cheeks flushed with embarrassment. With a sideways glance at her he pulled his hood over his head and returned to his trancelike state, his chestnut brown eyes staring at the road passing under the cart. Dartford had disappeared behind the undulating landscape, leaving mostly heather and gorse bushes—along with an occasional lizard—to occupy his eyes.

She reached for the rail and, with a grunt, steadied herself to a sitting position. Straining to speak more loudly than was comfortable, she replied,

"Yes, I'll be seeking out Nathan Wade. I do hope to find him. Otherwise, 'twill be a heap of trouble for no good purpose."

Over the noise of pounding hooves, squeaky cart wheels, and rattling contents in the wagon box, she gave up on having a pleasant conversation. Retreating into her own thoughts, she wondered what prompted Matthew—one of William's most ardent adversaries—to accept Father Garrett's invitation to help her make a trip to London. She'd almost turned him down. William would roll over in his grave if he knew she was traveling with Cooper, but getting in touch with Christopher outweighed any other consideration.

"Father, I need the jakes," twelve-year-old Maria blurted in a pained voice, as if she'd waited too long.

Elizabeth cast the girl a reassuring smile, struck with how much Maria resembled her sister, Anne. Same nutmeg hair and green eyes, and all knees and elbows. The girls must have taken after their mother, for Matthew Cooper's eyes were brooding black-brown, and his hair cast-iron, peppered with grey.

If Matthew heard his daughter, he showed no sign of it. Maria fidgeted and grimaced with each bump in the road. Not wanting to embarrass the girl, Elizabeth remained tight-lipped until she could no longer tolerate Maria's pained contortions. Leaning close, she whispered, "Perchance he didn't hear you. Would you like me to get his attention?" Blushing, Maria shook her head no. "'Tis no shame, lass. You needn't suffer." Maria wiggled and nodded.

Elizabeth's satisfaction at helping turned to dismay when she realized the situation presented two equally inconvenient choices: shouting loudly to get Matthew's attention, or fumbling her way across the wagon to get close enough for him to hear her.

She elbowed Nathan. "Your sister needs the jakes. Tell your father, would you?" He pulled his head further under his hood, like a turtle retreating into a shell. "Get on, lad," she persisted, firm but kind. With the speed of a sloth, the adolescent pushed himself to his knees and stood, weaving his way across the wagon box while he used crates and barrels to steady himself. When Nathan reached his father, he glanced back at Elizabeth. She mouthed, "Go on."

A hearty "Whoa!" let Elizabeth know Matthew got the message. He turned, admonishing Maria to make haste, as a full day's travel lay ahead. Maria scrambled over the edge of the cart and scurried behind a gorse bush. The travelers sat quietly for several seconds until John broke the silence.

"Are we almost to London, Father?"

"We've barely left Dartford, lad. See the sun in the sky?" Matthew pointed above the eastern horizon to a white circle barely visible through thick, grey clouds.

"Yes," the lad nodded.

"I want to see, Father." Maria emerged from behind the gorse bush and ran toward the wagon. She took hold of Elizabeth's extended hand and scrambled over the edge.

Matthew waited for his daughter to settle in. "When the sun is over there," he pointed to the western horizon, "we shall be close to London."

"I can't see the sun at all," Maria complained.

"Right there," Matthew pointed. "See the white circle in clouds?"

Squinting toward the eastern sky, Maria exclaimed, "There it is!"

Elizabeth found Matthew's interaction with his children bemusing. This wasn't the harsh man she'd come to loathe. She wondered if the grief of losing his wife before he moved to Dartford accounted for what she considered his abrasive behavior. Too much sorrow could make a person's heart shrivel, just as too much heat could wilt a plant—that she knew from personal experience. Perhaps she'd been hasty in her judgment of him.

He glanced at Elizabeth from the corner of an eye, a faint smile turning the corners of his mouth upwards. She didn't recall ever seeing him smile before. It gave him a rather pleasant appearance. Her face felt flushed, despite the nip in the air.

"Are you well, Mistress Wade?" The question came from Maria. "Your face is pink."

Elizabeth placed the palms of her hands on her cheeks and stammered, "Yes, I'm fine, thank you."

Smiling, Matthew chirped, "Are all of you settled?" He waited for affirmative responses before clicking his tongue. At a hearty shout of, "Ho, Blanche," the horse stepped forward, recommencing the journey toward London.

As the road passed under the cart, a pleasant sense of anticipation filled Elizabeth's breast. The gentle brush of a hand on hers interrupted her thoughts.

"Thank you for telling Father." It was Maria.

"Why, 'twas nothing." Elizabeth offered Maria's hand a gentle squeeze. "Can I let you in on a secret?" Elizabeth whispered. Maria nodded. "I had a daughter. She would be your age now. Oh, she was such a precious babe."

"Where is she now?" Maria inquired, her brows drawn.

"'Tis difficult for me to speak of, so it must be our secret. It pains me when folks ask, so I keep it private and rarely tell of it."

"I won't tell. I promise."

"'Twas Market Day. She fancied playin' at the riverbank, so William—my husband—left her behind the church to make mud cakes while he set up his linen cart. Other children were there, and their mothers agreed to keep watch on my Isabelle. But—my poor babe!" Elizabeth stopped, tears pooling in her eyes. "Alas, she wandered into the river to follow a coot with her chicks. Happened in the blink of an eye. These things happen with imps—you turn your head for just one second, and… she wasn't yet four years old, and couldn't swim."

Maria wasn't sure how to respond to the tragic story, except to share her own misfortune in return. "I fell into a vat of water when I was three, but father plucked me out just in time. It had eels in it; father was keeping them fresh for sale."

"Oh, dear child. I'm glad he saved you." Elizabeth patted Maria's hand.

"Me too." Maria's countenance darkened. "But I lost my mother."

"Oh, dear. I figured as much," Elizabeth replied, "as I've never seen you with a mother. Pray tell, what became of her?"

"She died birthing my sister," Maria sniffled. "My sister died too."

"My Jesus, have mercy. Let me pray for you." Elizabeth crossed herself and uttered, "Mother of sorrows, pray for us."

Wide-eyed, Maria asked, "You hold to the Pope's church?"

"Let's keep that as another secret between us, shall we?"

Maria nodded. "Father prays as you do. We pray that way at home."

"I'm pleased to hear it." Elizabeth glanced over her shoulder at the back of Matthew's head and felt a strange sensation, like a tiny feather tickling the inside of her bosom.

"I wish you were my mother," Maria whispered.

Elizabeth felt an ache in her heart—for Maria's loss and her own. Not sure how to respond, she patted Maria's knee, offered a weak smile and said, "I fancy we'll become good friends on our journey to London."

Maria smiled. "It would please me very much."

"It would please me as well," Elizabeth whispered. "Yes, it surely would."

London

Christopher watched Anne glide through the kitchen, his eyes aglow with admiration for her quiet, graceful demeanor. She'd set the table with two each of Victoria's finest plates, mugs, and pewter teaspoons. With the fire poker, she pushed coals around the kettle, then stopped to listen as water for their tea sizzled and popped against the sides. Next, she leaned the poker against the fireplace and placed a basket of fresh taffaty tarts on the table, shooting him a quick glance with twinkling eyes. The tantalizing aroma of lemon wafted past him.

Almost reluctantly, he broke the silence. "Thank you for having me over this evening. Nathan and Lucy will welcome a break from me, and I needed something to look forward to after a day with that bloodhound. Barnard watches my every move. This morning I sneezed, and he glared at me. I half expected him to growl, 'I'm not paying you to do that'."

Anne reached for a potholder on a hook next to the fireplace. "It was a good night to have you over. Victoria is at a church social with a man from the St. Mary Le Bow parish. Michael Fairchild's his name. He's an usher."

Christopher let out a hoot. "Victoria is out with a suitor?"

"Yes, and very happy about it, at that. At any rate, you know Master Barnard sees Nicholas as a hero and you as a villain. Perhaps you should look for work elsewhere. 'Tis not the best of times to be looking, but it's worth the try." She lifted the kettle of boiling water from the fireplace with a potholder and carried it to the table, beads of perspiration dampening her forehead. "Does Nicholas speak with you at all?"

Christopher studied his reflection on the plate. "He won't even look at me."

Berating herself for the wedge she created in Nicholas and Christopher's friendship, she took a deep breath, summoning courage to make a suggestion that she had a hunch Christopher would reject. "Pin makers are always in demand. 'Tis not the best of jobs, but it might do until you find something better. Would you like honey in your tea?" Dreading his reaction, she held her breath.

"Yes, two spoons, please." He frowned into his tea. "Pin maker, Anne? Do you jest?"

"'Twould be temporary," she said, finally letting her breath out. She made her way to the fireplace to return the kettle. "Just until you find something more suitable. It could lead you to making artisan pins. Well-made pins are beautiful and command a high price. There's no shame in that." She fetched the honey from a small cupboard and returned to the table.

"Average pin makers earn only enough to purchase a daily loaf of bread. The thought of working all day in deplorable conditions for a measly loaf of bread…"

"Very well, then," she snipped. "Continue with Nicholas and Master Barnard. But don't come complaining to me." She stirred honey into his tea, brooding.

Miffed at her curt manner of speaking, he tapped his fingers on the table to register his displeasure. "'Tis not as if I have no other skills. You're suggesting I grovel. Is that all you see in me—a lowly pin maker?"

With a roll of the eyes, she stopped stirring. "Of course not. Jobs are scarce, and if we're saving up to marry, any money is better than none. I meant no insult. It's just that I would rather marry sooner than later. Wouldn't you?"

Blowing on his tea bought him a few seconds to craft an answer. "I'd marry you today, if I could. The truth is, I've been wondering if my father would take me back. I could have been a weaver in my own right by now." He stretched his hands in front of him and turned them palm side up, then palm side down. "It tortures me to be stuck in dull labor, knowing my hands can craft fine linen. I plunge these hands every day in the blood and entrails of beasts, while I'm treated no better than a beast. But to think of these fingers making lowly little pins. What a waste of my skill and ambition."

"You could look at it this way." Anne eased onto a stool across the table from him. "Were it not for pins, the whole of England would be stark naked. Now, wouldn't that be a dreadful sight?" She watched a smirk cross his face. "So you see, pin makers are very important—they hold the realm together."

He sipped his tea. "I'm happy you can see humor in the situation. But you're not making me feel any better."

Forgetting her manners, her mouth full of taffaty tart, she replied, "What would prevent you from going to Dartford to ask your father's forgiveness? Get yourself established there, and I'll join you after you're settled."

He shook his head. "You're forgetting something."

"What is that?"

"Your father. He'll never approve of me."

She swallowed hard. "Then what business do we have speaking of marriage? If finding suitable work and saving money weren't enough of a challenge, we also have my father to contend with."

Christopher wagged his head. "'Tis like crossing the sea. One wave after another."

"But the seas do calm, and the sun shines," she declared, hoping to interject a bit of cheer into the dreary conversation.

"Yes, and sailors best appreciate those times, for they never last. Another storm is always lurking on the horizon."

"But," she countered, "without the wind and waves, the ship would never make it across the deep."

"Do you think we can overcome the tempest that is your father? I can't imagine how." Christopher blinked at the tablecloth, his eyes clouded with doubt.

"Truthfully, neither can I." Anne took a long sip of tea to wash down her pastry. "But if our union is meant by God, there has to be a way. I'll pray for a way to open."

"While you're at it, pray for me to find suitable employment."

"I will. But you must pray too."

He smashed a crumb under his thumb and then studied it. Pray? He hadn't the slightest idea where to begin.

"You do pray?"

The conversation was beginning to make him feel like a heathen. "I—well, I prayed when I was on the masthead. But I haven't thought much of it since." His face reddened.

"How would you feel if you had a son who spoke to you only when he was in trouble? I think it must please God when we pray to Him in all seasons."

"How do you know these things?"

She shrugged her shoulders. "Deep in my heart, I've always known them. I wager you know them too, somewhere within your breast. Perhaps you've forgotten them along the way, or buried them because you were angry at God."

Angry at God? Her words startled him. He'd never thought of himself as angry at God—but he hadn't much contemplated his thoughts one way or another. In truth, he'd spent the past several years trying to escape the subject. He glanced at the door.

"Seeking a way out?" she said.

"Does nothing escape your notice?" He tapped the handle of his teaspoon on the table, staring at the wall behind her.

"Forgive me. I tend to be too pointed at times." She reached across the table and placed her hand on his. "I'll pray for my father's heart to be softened toward you."

"And I'll hope your prayer is answered." He gave her hand a squeeze and squinted toward the kitchen window. "'Tis getting dark, and Lucy is tired of my coming in late." He stood, thanked her for the tea and added, "I'll give some thought to going back to Dartford. Perhaps it would be the best prospect for us—except for that small matter of your father."

"If God can part the sea, as he did for the children of Israel, he can soften my father's heart." She accompanied him to the door.

Leaning down to kiss the tip of her nose he whispered, "I'll rely on your faith. On the morrow, Milady."

"On the morrow, Milord."

After she closed the door, he ambled down Honey Lane toward Nathan's house, a brisk autumn breeze tickling his nostrils with the odors of chimney smoke and musty leaves. A myriad of questions vexed him—foremost among them, the insurmountable obstacle of Matthew Cooper. He tugged Nathan's door open and stepped inside with a gasp.

"Christopher! By my troth, 'tis you at last." Her expression rapturous, Elizabeth propelled herself forward and threw her arms around him. Matthew Cooper watched from a corner, stone-faced, with his three children standing in a row beside him.

La Rochelle

"I see an inn, there." Holding down the wind-whipped black veil with one hand on her head, Charlotte pointed to a two-story stone building up ahead, enclosed within a three-foot high stone wall. To welcome visitors, a sign painted with a galleon and the words *Le Rochelais* creaked in the wind beside an iron gate in the wall. "Please, let's stop and see if they have room for us."

Father Maubert tugged on the reins and waited for Charlotte and Thomas to pull up beside him, eyeing the sinking sun on the western horizon. "I've stayed there many times. It's comfortable, and the innkeeper is a friend. What do you think, Thomas? Shall we continue into the city, or inquire about a room here?"

Thomas pointed to a formidable wall of dark clouds approaching from the west. "At this point, I would be happy for a roof over my head and a good night's rest."

"Very well. *Le Rochelais* it is. Perhaps the innkeeper will know a place you can rent in La Rochelle."

Charlotte veiled her face. Upon reaching the gate, Father Maubert dismounted and peered through the slats to a gangly, gaunt priest helping a young stable hand groom a white Percheron. The priest looked toward the gate, a smile of recognition brightening his expression. He set a horse brush on the stable fence and took long strides toward the three travelers. The gate screeched on its hinges as he pulled it open.

"*Mon frère.* It's been too long." Removing a wide-brimmed hat, he embraced Father Maubert while gazing, wide-eyed, over Maubert's shoulder at Thomas and Charlotte.

"Father Chaussée, it's my pleasure." Maubert stepped back and examined his friend from head to toe. "You're well, I hope?"

Morose, Chaussée replied, "The truth is, I've been better." He scratched the tip of his long, thin nose before rubbing the bald crown of his head.

Leaning forward, Maubert responded, "Oh? What is troubling you?"

Father Chaussée hesitated, studying Charlotte and Thomas through narrowed eyes.

"It's safe to speak your heart," Father Maubert assured, with a glance at his traveling companions.

Chaussée lowered his voice. "The persecutions are increasing. Do you find this to be true in Bordeaux?"

Maubert nodded. "Yes, it's the same all over the kingdom."

Charlotte strained to hear the conversation, while Thomas watched a red squirrel bounce along the stone wall with an acorn in its mouth.

"The king's edicts are getting more severe," Chaussée sighed. "He expects all of his subjects—not just officials—to report suspected heretics. The réformées are deemed guilty of sedition, of treason against God and king. Did you know he took away their right to appeal? He wants them tried and executed as quickly as possible."

The squirrel jumped from the wall to the top of the gate behind Father Maubert. Startled, Maubert scrambled forward, almost stumbling over his own feet. Upon seeing the animal, both priests chuckled in relief.

"You're not afraid of a squirrel, are you?" Chaussée winked.

Maubert massaged the goosebumps on his forearms. "I suppose the king's paranoia is contagious. He thinks they're plotting to overthrow his rule. Did you hear of the slaughter in the south of the kingdom a few months ago?"

"At the village of Mérindol?"

Maubert nodded.

Chaussée rested his shoulder against the gate with a heavy sigh. "The shame of it! Soldiers descending upon a peaceful village, in the name of God, slaughtering, pillaging, raping! They cut down trees, smashed homes, destroyed gardens, took prisoners, and left the few survivors to wander, destitute, without a crust of bread. A few years ago, I wouldn't have thought King Francis capable of instigating such butchery. He's proven me a poor judge of character."

"He shows no remorse, and the sad tales keep coming. Did you hear about the young Lutheran in Paris, a shoemaker's son?" Father Maubert shifted his weight from right foot to left.

Father Chaussée eyed Charlotte's mourning clothes and wondered who passed away before returning his attention to Father Maubert. "I don't recall hearing of a shoemaker's son, but I've heard of countless others—printers, booksellers, weavers, students. We have enough tragic tales here in our own province to keep us conversing well into the night. But tell me of this shoemaker's son."

"Only twenty years old, he was. They cut his tongue out, as they've been doing of late. The 'heretics' must not be allowed to speak to bystanders, as you know, for their words rouse the hearers to sympathy." He shook his head. "*Words*, Father—think of it. The powerful have armies at their command, yet they fear the power of words uttered by simple folk! What does that tell you?"

Father Chaussée was glad to offer an opinion, for he had already given the matter considerable thought. "It tells me words of truth are their greatest threat—but the price of speaking the truth can be dear, as these unfortunates learned for themselves."

Father Maubert watched an apple tree sapling bend under the force of a strong wind gust. "This lad in Paris knew the Bible better than the clergy who condemned him, an unforgivable crime in their eyes. The executioners covered his head in sulfur, and—" the priest swallowed hard, "he showed no fear, but boldly gave the signal to his executioner to move forward. Twenty years old, and such courage. Can you imagine?"

"I'm unworthy to latch his shoes." Chaussée drew a line in the dirt in front of him with his toe.

A loud clap of thunder drew all eyes to the approaching storm clouds. A crow attempting to fly in a westerly direction hovered in place above them, unable to master the invisible force.

Charlotte glanced at Thomas just in time to watch him slap both hands over his cap to keep the wind from whisking it away. She leaned close and whispered, "I hoped it would be safer here. I don't like what I'm hearing."

"What is that?" he asked.

"Haven't you been listening?" Thomas shook his head.

"I fear they'll stop at nothing but extermination," Father Maubert said.

Thomas glanced at Charlotte. She raised her eyebrows.

Chaussée nodded. "They're investigating La Rochelle's Master of Schools. I predict his excommunication. But you didn't come to speak of these dismal things. I see that you're traveling with companions?"

"My friends here—Thomas and Charlotte Nix—are looking to move from Bordeaux to La Rochelle. Her parents sent along three barrels of fine wine for me to offer the brethren here in La Rochelle, as I see fit. Perhaps you and I should keep it for ourselves?" he teased. "After all this talk, I could use a good drink."

Eyeing the barrels in the back of the wagon, Father Chaussée smiled. "Your timing is perfect. A group of brethren from Saintes are spending the night here before starting for their village tomorrow. They were sent to do God's work." His voice dripped with sarcasm. "They've been hunting for heretics."

Charlotte's heart sank.

"Have you lodging for the three of us?" Maubert asked.

"Yes, I have a large chamber available. Come, I'll have my stable boy groom and feed your horses." He waited for Thomas and Charlotte to dismount and led them through the gate. "How many days have you been traveling?"

"Today makes five," Maubert answered.

As they made their way across the grassy yard to the stables, Father

Chaussée turned to Thomas. "What is your occupation?"

"I carve and sell pilgrim souvenirs, mostly for those traveling the Way of Saint James," Thomas replied. "But I pray you, don't hold it against me."

Chaussée cast a concerned glance at Maubert.

"He's harmless," Father Maubert assured.

They reached the stables, where the stable boy was combing the Percheron's belly. The boy's head barely reached to the horse's chest.

"Marcel," the priest called out. The boy looked up. "Please comb and feed the horses for our guests here. Give the animals a clean stall and fresh water."

"Yes, Father." The boy laid the horse brush on a crate and trotted toward the visitors.

Chaussée turned to Father Maubert. "I'll help you unload your possessions. They won't be secure in the yard all night." After a few seconds' hesitation he added, "The priests might steal them." The two clergymen guffawed and slapped each other on the back.

Charlotte leaned to her husband and whispered. "It's some sort of humor among priests, I suppose."

"The flavor evokes—I struggle to find the words." Thomas lifted his gaze to the dining room's beamed ceiling as if he were communing with heavenly messengers. "This alone—this bowl of beans—was well worth the journey of thirty leagues to get here." He visually caressed the steaming bowl of fava beans, sausage and tender morsels of duck flesh, then looked across the table to Charlotte and Father Chaussée. "You know those rare moments when you taste something so excellent, so exquisite, you will never forget where you were when it happened?" His audience indulged him with chuckles and nods.

"Within this bowl I experience a garden at the harvest…the comfort of a warm bed on a cold winter morning…the merry crackle of a fire in the hearth. And the aroma—'tis the fragrance I hope will greet my nostrils when Saint Peter welcomes me at heaven's gate." He raised another scoop to his nose and inhaled deeply. "Ah. Mine is a feeble description. I'll just give up and enjoy it."

"I don't think you've ever looked at me the way you look at the cassoulet," Charlotte teased.

Father Chaussée beamed. "Your compliment gives me great honor, although to call it a mere bowl of beans—why, I would consider it an insult if you knew better. It's like calling a peacock a chicken. *Cassoulet*, my friend."

"Cass-ou-let." Thomas forced every syllable.

"There are no words, so unlike my husband, I won't even try," Charlotte inserted. "The cassoulet is nothing short of divine."

"I told you, you were in for a treat." Father Maubert lifted a spoonful of the hearty stew to his lips and blew steam away. "You'll have no better cassoulet anywhere. And Charlotte, your father's wine is the perfect accompaniment."

"I'm pleased that you like it," she nodded.

Father Chaussée disappeared and returned with a loaf of crusty rye bread. Thomas broke off a piece to soak up the rich broth, infused with duck confit, onion, garlic, celery and fresh herbs. He popped the entire piece of bread into his mouth and wiped the broth dribbling down his chin with his forefinger. Licking his fingers, he exclaimed, "By Saint John's bones! It is so good!" The entire company laughed.

"It's an old family recipe." Father Chaussée leaned against the table sporting a crooked grin. "I'm flattered at your praise."

As he dipped a second morsel of bread into the sauce, intent on picking up a cluster of tender fava beans along with it, Thomas watched three cassock-clad men appear in the spacious dining hall and make their way to the long table where he, Charlotte and the priest sat dining. Father Maubert slipped from the bench and dropped to his left knee. Father Chaussée and Thomas followed suit. Charlotte veiled her face and knelt down.

With bowed head, Father Maubert uttered, "Your Excellency." Bishop Charles de Bourbon extended his right hand. Father Maubert, Charlotte and Thomas each kissed the amethyst-studded gold ring on his fourth finger.

"Please," the bishop said. "Be seated and enjoy your meal. Father Chaussée's cassoulet is without equal, no?"

"It's divine," Thomas nodded, returning to the bench.

"Father Maubert, what brings you to La Rochelle?" The bishop seated himself a few paces away from the priest, on the opposite side of the table as Charlotte wiped the perspiration from her palms on her skirt.

"Two things, mostly," Maubert replied. "I'm bringing a gift of wine from Bordeaux, and I hope to help this man," he pointed to Thomas, "make contacts to establish himself in the souvenir trade. He's an excellent carver. He perfected the craft in England, before our neighbor to the north outlawed pilgrimages. As one who is loyal to the mother church, Monsieur Nix came to France where he could freely pursue his faith and trade."

"Excellent," Bishop de Bourbon nodded. "But La Rochelle is a gathering place for heretics, and perhaps not the most fruitful place to sell souvenirs. Have you considered Saintes? It's on the Way of Saint James."

Thomas guessed the bishop to be in his early thirties. He mused that the abundant wavy hair atop de Bourbon's head stole its growth from the man's meager mustache and scraggly goatee. Small lips and a Roman nose accented De Bourbon's delicate visage. Rather melancholy, charcoal-brown eyes gave him an ambivalent air.

Father Chaussée had just placed three steaming bowls of cassoulet on the table in front of the three clergymen and started back to the kitchen when Father Maubert shouted after him, "Father Chaussée, are the barrels of wine in the kitchen?"

"Yes. Shall I offer it to our guests?"

"Please. Let's have generous servings for all. It's for just such an occasion that I brought the wine."

Father Chaussée disappeared into the kitchen and returned with three of his largest goblets filled with red wine. He positioned them in front of the bishop and two priests, and went back to the kitchen for a loaf of bread. "Let me know when you need more wine," he said upon his return, placing the steaming loaf in front of his patrons. "You may have as many refills as you would like."

He crossed the room and placed a thick oak log on the fire. Smoke billowed from the fireplace. Charlotte covered her mouth with her sleeve, while Thomas buried his mouth and nose in his elbow.

"The oak is a bit damp," Father Chaussée apologized. He pushed the log further into coals and blew on it, using a stick to adjust its position and coaxing it until it ignited.

After offering grace, the bishop and two priests conversed in low voices.

Straining to hear, Thomas seized a break in the conversation. "What brings you brethren here?" he inquired.

Bishop de Bourbon straightened. "Fathers Jacques, Antoine and I came on church business."

"Oh?" Thomas replied, hoping the bishop would offer more information.

The bishop pushed his goblet to the table's edge. Father Chaussée promptly disappeared to the kitchen and returned it full. After guzzling half the goblet while Thomas watched, the bishop wiped his lips and smiled. "Superb. You brought three barrels, did you say?"

"Three indeed, Your Excellency," Father Maubert answered. "Please, take advantage. It won't keep, and you'll be lightening my load for the return trip."

The bishop downed the remainder of merlot in his goblet and pushed the vessel forward.

"The two of you as well?" Chaussée inquired. Jacques and Antoine guzzled their wine and slid their goblets toward Father Chaussée. He retreated to the kitchen and re-emerged with the goblets filled.

"And you?" Chaussée turned to Thomas, Charlotte and Father Maubert.

"None for me," Thomas answered.

Charlotte shook her head.

Father Maubert put his hand over his goblet.

As a king cobra slithers out from a basket to the music of a snake charmer, Father Jacques' tongue emerged, coaxed out by the wine. "We caught our prey," he boasted. "I'll never forget the look on their faces when we showed up at their secret conventicle! The damned devils caught in their orgy of heresy!" He kept talking while he dipped a morsel of bread in his cassoulet. "They fancied that a seaside grotto in the dark of night would keep them hidden—but secret works of darkness will always come to light. God will accomplish his work. We see that he is on our side. They fell like rotten fruit into our hands." He popped the bread into his mouth and chewed sideways, like a cow chewing its cud.

Antoine chuckled, the crackling firelight making shadows of his eye sockets. "I wish you could have seen the look on the schoolmaster's face when I showed up, unannounced, in the middle of his instruction. You would think I caught him in a liaison with Jezebel—the pale face, the startled expression. He began stumbling in his words, this 'master' of instruction, suddenly ba-ba-ba-ing like a child learning to speak."

Jacques patted him on the back. "Well done. Now that we turned them over to the authorities they'll be flogged until they are bloody, and banished as they deserve. You did make clear, if they continue in their heresies, they'll be sent to the fire? We must make a strong example of them."

"Yes, I made it very clear. One of them had the nerve to invite me to his home to break bread. I, of course, refused his offer, and later informed the deputy inquisitor of the man's attempt to bribe me. Apparently, this tactic has been successful with some lieutenants—a cloak and a loaf of bread to purchase favor."

"Did you confiscate the forbidden books and pamphlets?" de Bourbon asked, studying the fire's reflection on Antoine's wine glass.

"Yes, I ordered them to be gathered into crates for burning. And I assured the schoolmaster he would join his books in the fire unless he recants and turns away from this iniquity. I'm informed many more heretic writings are stashed in the city, however. We've made only a small dent."

"That is my understanding as well." A vacant look darkened the bishop's eyes.

"Is something wrong, Your Excellency?" Antoine's eyes narrowed.

"The wine isn't sitting well with me, I suppose." Folding his arms across his chest, de Bourbon appeared mesmerized by the fire.

"We've done our duty, have we not?" Antoine inquired.

"Yes, you've done exactly as instructed," de Bourbon replied flatly. Stifling a yawn, he excused himself. After proper respects were paid him, the bishop disappeared up the stairs, the somber mood he infused into the room leaving with him.

"May I get you anything else?" Father Chaussée asked the remaining guests.

"I've had too much already." Thomas patted his stomach.

"Nothing more, thank you." Charlotte wiped her mouth with her serviette, wishing she could will herself to a safe place, away from the inn filled with heretic-hunters.

"More wine, if you please." Father Antoine pushed his goblet forward.

After refilling it, Father Chaussée stoked the fire, taking care to find a dry log. He dragged a stool screeching across the floor to the hearth and seated himself in front of the fire.

"Your hospitality has exceeded my expectations," Thomas remarked, towing his stool across the room to join Chaussée. The other men followed, Jacques and Antoine with their goblets in hand.

"You were speaking of the réformées in La Rochelle." Thomas popped a piece of bread and a morsel of goat cheese into his mouth, watching light from the flames flicker on the faces in the dimly lit room. "Are there many?"

Jacques swirled the wine in his goblet and took a long drink before setting the empty goblet on the floor next to his stool. "We have it on good word they're building an army here. The king is rightly concerned, as are the church fathers. If we don't stop them, they'll overthrow the kingdom."

Listening quietly from the table, Charlotte felt her chest tighten.

"La Rochelle is a port city," Father Chaussée explained, his eyes fixed on a flame leaping heavenward and sending sparks flying. "Merchants from the north countries provide books and pamphlets to the réformées—merchants from Amsterdam, Germany, England and such." Charlotte imagined the excitement of meeting reformers from other countries, and of holding in her hands written words to water the seed of God's word sprouting within her bosom.

"Foreigners are part of the problem," Antoine opined. "But to me, it is more than that. These rebels have also sprung up in Meaux, and Paris, and in the south of France. They're everywhere, weaving a secret web, despite efforts to extinguish them."

"Have you finished your work here?" Thomas probed.

"For now," Antoine replied, "but we'll be back to instill fear, to stop the spread of these fools who follow Luther and Calvin. We have plenty of priests and lieutenants on the watch here, and a reliable group of everyday folks who can expect a handsome reward for informing on heretics."

Charlotte tiptoed out the great hall and up the stairs, relieved to escape the suffocating conversation. Only Thomas noticed her departure.

London

"Mother?" Christopher gawked at Elizabeth, then glanced over his shoulder in disbelief at Matthew and the children.

"You look as if you've just seen Saint John risen from the dead." Elizabeth stepped forward.

"By Jove, that's an understatement. I might have expected Father to come, but—where is he? How did you make the trip?"

"Your father—" The words caught in her throat.

Immediately, Christopher knew.

"Your father has gone to meet his maker." She bit her lower lip. "Matthew came to London to pay Anne a visit. He was kind enough to make room in his cart for me. You remember Anne?"

Did he remember Anne? Was she serious? Christopher shot a quick glance at Matthew, anticipating a negative reaction. "Of course I remember her. In fact, we've been spending a lot of time together." Matthew raised an eyebrow. "But tell me about Father. What happened?"

Elizabeth swallowed hard. "'Twas a horrible fever. At first, I thought he simply caught cold, until he made a quick turn for the worse. Seemed like the sweatin' sickness, but no one else in town had it. We tried cool baths and the wise woman's potions, but he wasn't a whit better for it. In the end, the best I could do was keep a cool cloth on him and try to keep him comfortable. 'Twas horrid to feel so helpless."

"Did he suffer terribly?"

"He was ready to go; said he'd endured sufferin' enough for two lifetimes. But—mind you, I don't want to add to your grief, but I think you should know—your name was the last word on his lips."

The color drained from Christopher's face.

"He held hope until the very end that you would come home, come back to Dartford and take over the weavin'. 'Tis not too late—you could come back now."

A familiar angst rose in Christopher's breast. "They hate me in Dartford, as they hated Father. How would I get along as a weaver, when half the village is against me?"

"'Twas not you they were against, 'twas your father. It pained me to watch you take the brunt of it, but I think you would find things different now."

Matthew stepped forward. "Your mother is right. I, for one, would like to apologize. I treated you as though your father's views were your own. It wasn't fair of me, and I beg your pardon."

Suddenly juggling three balls at once—the loss of his father, an apology from Matthew, and an invitation to return to Dartford—Christopher fanned his face with his cap and muttered, "I need to step outside for a moment."

Nathan waved a hand to stop him. "I don't wish to speak out of turn, but your mother could use your help in Dartford. You've struggled to get a footing in London. Weaving will earn you the money you need for your nuptials and help your widowed mother as well."

"Nuptials?" Elizabeth and Matthew blurted it out in unison. Maria's mouth fell open. Nathan and John snickered and elbowed one another.

Wishing he could slip out of his skin and run, Christopher resolved to stand firm. "Anne and I have discussed marriage. But to be honest," he looked Matthew squarely in the eyes, "I doubted I would ever gain your approval. In fact, we spoke of you just before I came here tonight."

Matthew folded his arms and leaned back against the wall. "I came to London to check on my daughter's well-being, not to give my blessing to a marriage."

Breathing in short pants, Elizabeth plopped onto a stool. "And I came to bring you news of your father's passin'. This is a surprise."

Nathan spoke up. "May I suggest you all join Lucy and me for supper tomorrow eve. 'Twixt now and then you'll have time to digest this evening's news. Anne and Victoria must certainly join us."

Lucy stepped forward, clasping her hands together. "We would be delighted to have you all," she beamed. "How about six o'clock tomorrow eve—which, it just struck me, happens to be All Hallows Eve."

Matthew responded first. "We have nowhere to be, other than to visit Anne. If she can make it, six o'clock will be fine. May I send you word in the morning?"

"Of course," Lucy nodded.

"Christopher, Elizabeth?" Nathan waited for an answer.

"If Anne can make it, six o'clock it is," Christopher answered.

"I have nowhere else to be," Elizabeth chimed in.

"We'll plan on six o'clock, unless you tell us otherwise in the morning." Nathan stepped back, removing himself as smoothly as he'd inserted himself.

"We'll be on our way, then." Matthew glanced at his children.

The Cooper family filed out, leaving an uncomfortable silence between Elizabeth and Christopher. After inviting Elizabeth to make herself at home, Nathan trailed Lucy up the narrow staircase to their bedchamber. The upstairs floor creaked as they crossed to their room.

"That leaves just you and me." Elizabeth broke the silence. "How is London treatin' you?"

"Well enough, I suppose," he replied, staring straight ahead. Elizabeth waited for her son to offer more details, but he remained tight-lipped.

"You found Anne. I'm happy for you." She patted the stool next to her. Christopher declined her invitation to sit. "You're to be married! Mercy me! Before we know it, I'll be a grandmother!"

"Please, Mother, slow down. I'm not betrothed yet," Christopher corrected her. "Matthew would never give his consent." After brooding for several seconds, he added, "I mean no disrespect, but I'd like some time to collect my thoughts. Perhaps we could catch up on the morrow?"

"Of course, dear." She gazed into his face with wonder, as if she were beholding her newborn infant for the first time. "I thought I would worry myself to an early grave. Not a day passed that I didn't pray for your safety and prosperity." Her words softened his heart; he felt he deserved to be scolded for running off the way he did. "What I wouldn't give for your father to see you now, as I'm seein' you."

"I wish I could go back and do things differently," he muttered. "As it is, I can barely take in tonight's turn of events."

"Get your rest, son. God bless." She leaned over and kissed his cheek before padding up the stairs to her bedchamber.

Christopher sat down in a daze. Too weary to sort out his jumbled thoughts, he picked up the candle on the kitchen table, made his way up the stairs and slipped into his nightshirt. After blowing out the candle and slipping under the covers, he realized he'd forgotten something. Slipping out of bed onto his knees, he pleaded for the seas to part.

"Lucy, by my faith, the spiced pears are delicious." Elizabeth licked a residue of sweet, pear-flavored syrup from her lips. "A perfect endin' to a fine meal. And you must tell me how you seasoned the baked carp. 'Tis the best I've ever had. Did I taste cloves?"

"Yes," Lucy smiled, "as well as salt, mace, prunes and butter. 'Tis simple, really. Do you have a good fish market in Dartford?"

"Why, yes." Elizabeth flashed a coy smile at Matthew. "Matthew is a fishmonger."

"Is that so?" Lucy turned to him. "You must provide the lady a fine carp, and I'll see to it that she has the proper seasonings."

"As long as she invites me over to sample it." Matthew flashed a mischievous grin.

A sideways glance from Anne told Christopher they were thinking the same thing. Not two months had passed since William's burial. What sort of man pursued a widow so soon after her husband's death?

Nathan, who had been unusually quiet all evening, spoke up. "Christopher, have you given any thought to taking over your father's weaving in Dartford?"

Christopher pointed to his mouth and finished chewing a large chunk of spiced pear before answering. "'Tis not much of a decision. To be frank, my father was losing customers faster than he could gain them. I see no wisdom in jumping aboard a sinking ship."

Elizabeth shook her head in protest. "Please trust me—your father was a good man, but his views drove folks away. If he'd just kept quiet, we wouldn't have had half the trouble. 'Twill be a whole new start for you. And you're good at it, Chris. I'll give your father that—he taught you well. God gave you talent, and a father who nurtured you along. You should put it to good use."

Matthew dabbed pear juice from the corner of his mouth with his serviette before inserting his opinion. "She speaks the truth. I've a good feel for the folks of the village who were upset by your father's leanings. Pardon my forthrightness, but he was all too vocal. Unless you're the same, I don't foresee you having problems. And Dartford needs a good weaver. We've had a void since your father passed."

"You should listen to them, Christopher," Anne inserted. "Could it be worse than making pins?" The dismayed look on Christopher's face told her the comment would have been better left unsaid.

"Pins?" Elizabeth's jowls quivered. "Have you had to stoop so low?"

"There's a pin shop next to Smithfield," Christopher explained, his chest tight. "My former boss, Master Barnard, provides the bones the pin makers use to shape the copper wire. He knew the owner and got me the job. Believe me, he was happy to see me go."

"Pin maker," Matthew uttered, looking like he'd just been slapped. "My daughter wants to marry a pin maker?"

Christopher's heart skipped a beat.

"Come back to Dartford," Matthew persisted. "Trust us."

"I couldn't leave Anne." Christopher spoke with finality, intent on ending the pestering.

Matthew set his spoon on the table, folded his hands in front of him, and stated matter-of-factly, "Bring her with you."

Searching Matthew's eyes, Christopher wondered if he had heard correctly.

"Bring her with me?"

"Bring me with him?" Anne's eyes danced.

Matthew nodded. "You've fancied my daughter since we moved to Dartford. I can see that time and distance haven't changed your affection. Or yours?" He glanced at Anne. She averted her gaze to the table. "I won't stand in your way." Christopher's greatest obstacle in life leaned back with a smug smile and folded his arms across his chest.

The words *parting the sea* popped into Christopher's mind. He laid his hand on Anne's and blurted, "What ever became of John Whitfield?" Anne gave him a puzzled look.

Shifting on his stool, Matthew took a deep breath. "He went to Cambridge and took up with the Lutherans—an absolute embarrassment for his father. Such a waste of potential." Christopher watched the muscles around Nathan's mouth tighten as Matthew continued, "He came back to Dartford and started meeting with your father and other like-minded folks to study heretical writings. The lad has quieted down of late. I suppose he either found some sense or got scared."

Christopher squeezed Anne's hand, hoping the clammy perspiration on his palms wasn't off-putting. "Mister Cooper," his voice cracked, "I would like to ask your blessing for Anne's hand in marriage. I'll take good care of her. You have my word."

"Oh!" Victoria jumped up from her seat. The unexpected outburst startled Elizabeth into knocking over her ale mug with her elbow. Lucy rushed to get a towel to sop up the spill, while Victoria continued to gush, her hands clasped in front of her, "The rose petals on Midsummer's Eve. They worked their magic!"

"No, Auntie," Anne said, shaking a finger. "If the rose petals had worked, Nicholas would be here in Christopher's stead."

"Nicholas!" Turning to Christopher, Elizabeth declared, "I had forgotten, you came to London together. What became of him?"

"Nicholas and Christopher had a duel, of sorts, for Anne's hand," Victoria interjected. "You should have witnessed it."

"He's not pleased with me at the moment. He works at the Smithfield market and avoids me like the plague."

To Christopher's surprise, Matthew extended his hand across the table. "I give you my blessing."

Elizabeth danced her way around the table to the newly betrothed couple with the gracefulness of a woman fifty pounds lighter. With one arm around Christopher's neck and the other around Anne's, she pulled their heads together and exclaimed, "Welcome to the family."

After the excitement settled, Matthew spoke up. "For Anne's dowry, her mother had many household things that I saved. I've been setting aside some of my profits for her as well." Christopher nodded, his eyes bright, as Matthew continued. "Does this turn of events change your mind? Are you sure you won't consider coming to Dartford to start your married life?"

Christopher shook his head. "Anne and I discussed it yesterday, before we knew you were in town. The question kept me up tossing and turning last night." He saw a shadow of disappointment darken Anne's countenance. "I can't go to Dartford—not now, anyway." Perusing the somber faces around the table, he offered an apology. "I'm sorry to disappoint so many folks."

"Would you consider working for me?" Matthew pressed. "I can always use an extra hand."

Christopher let go of Anne's hand and tapped his fingers on the table to release some of the pressure he was feeling. "My concern isn't the type of work I would be doing, but rather my very presence in Dartford. But before I turn your offer down, may I take some time to consider it?"

"Of course. I'll be in London another day or two."

Anxious to lighten the atmosphere, Elizabeth piped up, "Do you all remember, tomorrow is All Hallows? I would love to attend services while in London."

"I thought to attend at Saint Paul's Cathedral tomorrow," Matthew replied with a glance at Elizabeth. "Would anyone care to join me?"

"Lucy and I plan on attending our own parish at Honey Lane," Nathan replied. "But thank you for the invitation."

"I'll attend Honey Lane parish as well, Father," Anne chimed in. "We have wonderful services—not to take away from Saint Paul's, of course."

"The Anchor Tavern in Southwark is calling me," Christopher teased. Anne cast a reproving glance in his direction. "I jest," he winked. "Where Anne is, I will be. And you, Mother?"

"Saint Paul's? I would forever chide myself if I missed the chance."

Matthew folded his arms across his chest and leaned back. "'Twill be the goodwife and I, then, along with Nathan, Maria and John. Nothing compares to Saint Paul's. You'll see."

Christopher studied his mother's behavior, befuddled. She appeared happier now, he thought, than she ever did while his father was alive. Was she relieved to have William gone? He pushed the thought away. It was too irksome to consider.

"It's been a wonderful evening." Nathan stood slowly, the popping of his knees prompting giggles from the children. "Lucy and I are happy we could be present for Anne and Christopher's betrothal."

"Yes," Lucy agreed, rising from the table. "What a joy to see two young folks starting out."

Victoria laid her serviette on the table. "We'll be on our way while it's yet light outside. Thank you for the meal. It was delicious."

After he stood and motioned for his children to join him, Matthew turned to Elizabeth. "I'll be by for you at seven-thirty tomorrow morning. The mass starts at eight o'clock."

Elizabeth's heart fluttered. "Thank you, Mister Cooper. I'll be ready."

As Christopher made his way to the door to bid the guests farewell, three words danced through his mind: *the sea parted.*

May, 1546

———

La Rochelle

"Have you heard, the head master of schools is being excommunicated?" Charlotte turned away from the fireplace, white-knuckled from her tight grip on a cast-iron kettle handle. She carried it to the table taking slow, measured steps.

Thomas lifted his nose, sniffing the air, and seated himself at the table. "The food smells delicious. What are you cooking?"

"Just a pottage and some bread. Nothing fancy." She positioned the kettle on a round clay disk. "Are you avoiding my question?"

He interpreted the sharp, impatient edge in her tone of voice as a growing lack of submission to his male authority in their marriage. "We knew it was coming," he snipped. "A teacher can't canker innocent minds with reformed doctrines and expect no consequence. Frankly, I'm surprised he wasn't caught and punished sooner."

She turned her back to him and rolled her eyes. "Anatole! Gabrielle!" she shouted. Thomas pictured a donkey braying. "Put your toys away and wash your hands. It's time for dinner." The children groaned.

"But Maman, I'm not hungry. I want to keep playing with my poppet." Gabrielle's favorite toy was Charlotte's as well, for it kept the young girl occupied for long periods of time. It was a wooden doll Thomas carved to resemble a lady of the court that Gabrielle named Antoinette. Charlotte had stitched three changes of clothing for dress-up.

"You may play after supper. Put her in the toy box. Up, up." Charlotte scooted her daughter along. Gabrielle stood Antoinette in the toy box and placed the clothes alongside her, then skipped to the water pitcher and basin. Stretched on her tiptoes, she struggled to reach the pitcher. Thomas jumped up to help her, pouring water over her hands as she moved them back and forth. He patted her hands dry with a towel.

"Anatole!" Charlotte snapped. The boy was busy pushing a wooden horse around a castle he stacked from wood blocks. If he heard his mother, he showed no sign of it. "Into the toy box," Charlotte shouted, moving next to him to supervise. Anatole balked. "Now! If you mind Maman, you may play after dinner." Anatole flung his arm through the castle and sent blocks flying, then folded his arms, scowling at his mother.

"Did you see that?" She cursed under her breath and narrowed her eyes at Thomas.

"He's frustrated. He's just being a boy." Thomas met her glare. "Perhaps if you were more patient…"

"Perhaps if you corrected him," she interrupted. "Does nothing bother you? He disobeys me and…" At the sound of an ear-piercing shriek, she clenched her teeth and jumped into action.

"*Mon Dieu!*" she cursed, jerking her son up by one arm. "Stop crying and put your toys away!"

"Why are you braying at us? Hee-haw, hee-haw. That's all we hear anymore." Thomas felt an unexpected glow of satisfaction after he said it.

She cast daggers at him with her eyes, picked up Anatole's toys, and slammed them into the toy box. Next, she swept Anatole in her arms and plopped the young boy in his highchair. Gabrielle looked sideways at her mother and scurried to her place at the table, afraid of becoming the next target of Charlotte's ill humor. Charlotte ladled a small scoop of pottage into the children's bowls, followed by a more generous portion for herself and Thomas.

"Shall we say grace?" She plopped down on the table bench, swatted a few damp strands of hair away from her eyes, and glowered at Thomas while he wondered if demons possessed her.

After clearing his throat, he bowed his head and offered thanks, annoyed when he heard sniffles across the table. With a hasty "amen" he looked up to see her wiping her eyes with the back of her hand.

"By the mass! What?!" He slammed his serviette on the table and thrust his hands heavenward. Gabrielle's lower lip began to tremble.

Charlotte glanced at Anatole and Gabrielle, contemplating whether to broach the subject in their presence. She decided they were too young to understand.

"Doesn't it bother you to see a good man treated this way?"

"Who? The schoolmaster?" Thomas dipped a large chunk of bread in his pottage and grimaced when it touched his tongue. "Did you burn the garlic?"

"Are you listening to me?" She shook her head with a snort.

"I always listen." He spit the bread into his bowl.

"It's wrong, what they're doing to good people who simply want to practice their faith. Why should innocents be punished?"

"You're mistaken. Those whose minds the réformées corrupt are the innocents."

"Maman, do I have to eat all my pottage?" a small voice piped up. "It tastes funny."

"Yes, Gabrielle. Eat all your pottage and a piece of bread, and then you may go back to your play."

"Me too," Anatole copied his sister. "I want to play." He kicked his legs against the highchair, sloshing the pottage in his bowl.

"Stop kicking or you'll spill your pottage. Neither of you will get a snack later unless you finish your dinner." She hissed out a sigh.

"But I have to eat a piece of bread," Gabrielle whined. "Why doesn't Anatole have to eat bread?"

"Gabrielle, stop whining. You're bigger than Anatole, so you need more food. Would like to play after dinner? Yes? Then stop complaining and do as I said."

Gabrielle stared into her pottage, biting her lower lip, while Anatole worked on finishing his supper, swinging his legs back and forth.

Charlotte rested her spoon in her bowl and wiped her mouth before locking her gaze on Thomas. "Did Christ punish anyone?" she demanded. "No. Nowhere in the Bible is it written that Christ led anyone to prison, or to the stake, or to the wheel. How can the Pope claim to follow Christ's religion when he condemns innocents to death?" She lifted a spoon full of pottage to her mouth, blew on it, sipped, and spit it out. "Yes, burnt garlic." After swishing a sip of wine in her mouth she continued, "In Christ's day, the wicked put Christ's followers to death, not the other way around. Do you think it's any different now?"

Thomas ignored the hungry rumble from his stomach. "Perhaps you're misunderstanding the holy scripture. That's why you, and folks you sneak around with, shouldn't be reading the writings of heretics and trying to interpret the holy book for yourself. Look at us. We're hostages here, even in La Rochelle, refuge of heretics. Are you happy now? You have to worship in secret, and I'm surrounded by hereti—réformées in this village who detest the authority of both the church in Rome and King Francis. This is no better than Bordeaux. We could have kept silent and gone about our lives in peace there, and I wouldn't have had to leave my business. I'm worse off here than I was back in Dartford."

"Gabrielle and Anatole, you may go play now."

"But Maman, I'm not finished with my pottage and bread," the girl protested.

"Just go," Charlotte demanded.

Gabrielle gazed up at her father, confused. Thomas nodded. "The pottage is bad. You may go play, both of you." He lifted Anatole from the highchair and set him on his feet. Anatole scurried to retrieve his horse and blocks from the toy box. Gabrielle beat him there, pulling out her doll and clothes.

Sitting back down at the table with a huff, Thomas avoided eye contact with Charlotte. He picked up his bowl and took a sip of pottage, then spit it back out. Tapping his fingers on the table he glanced toward the door and mumbled, "Perhaps I'll go to the tavern and get something to eat."

"We call them Nicodemites—those who won't stand up for what they believe." Charlotte looked past him, ignoring his threat to leave. "If more of them had courage, perhaps we wouldn't find ourselves in this position."

"I'm tired of living this way. Tired of being suspect because of your association with the réformées, tired of you sneaking around in the dark to secret meetings, tired of worrying about the authorities watching my children. I came here for you, and where has it gotten me? You're no happier or safer here than in Bordeaux. Now, we're all miserable."

Charlotte plunked her spoon on the table and ripped a piece of bread from the heavy oblong loaf she baked that afternoon. "If I've made your life so miserable, perhaps one of us should leave."

Her words charged the air like a cannon shot. Several seconds elapsed before Thomas answered, his eyes cold and dark.

"What about your children?"

"What about 'my' children? Is that all you can say? No concern for me?" She started to dip a piece of bread into her pottage but caught herself and popped the dry bread into her mouth.

"You'll never be content," he complained. "We were happy until you mixed with the réformées in Bordeaux. You've been troubled ever since. You're not the woman I married."

She buried head in her hands. Gabrielle looked up, wide-eyed, and approached her mother, doll in hand.

"What's wrong, Maman?"

"Go back to your play, *Cherie,*" Thomas admonished. With a fearful glance at her mother, Gabrielle promptly obeyed. Thomas moved his face close to Charlotte's, lowered his voice and growled, "Get ahold of yourself—you're frightening them. You should be grateful I saved you when the authorities were hunting réformées in Bordeaux. Perhaps I won't be so well-disposed next time." Without stopping for his cloak or cap, he stormed out the door.

Knowing Thomas made no idle threats, Charlotte lifted her goblet of wine and took a sip, her hands trembling. She bowed her head and petitioned heaven for help.

London

"Lady Askew is back in London." After spitting out the news, Christopher leaned against the doorway to catch his breath. "I ran all the way from Smithfield to tell you."

"Who is it, Anne?" Victoria stepped away from the fireplace, where she'd been stirring a slab of sheep tallow into a hot iron kettle. She cursed under her breath when a drop of hot grease from the sizzling tallow landed on her arm.

"It's just Christopher." Anne joined him outside and pulled the door closed.

"'Just Christopher'? A fine welcome that is!" He sniffed the air. "Candle making?"

"Yes. I don't know why we don't just buy them. Victoria will spend a day to save a ha'penny." She peered over Christopher's shoulder to make sure they were alone. "Lady Askew in London? How could that be? The authorities ordered her husband to take her home."

Leaning forward to wipe a smudge of tallow from her cheek he replied, "She's like a hound that can't be fenced in. No matter how many ways they come up with to trap her, she finds a way out. I'm tempted to feel sorry for her husband. 'Twould be an impossible humiliation for a man to have an untamable wife." A wry smile crossed his face, then his expression turned somber. "We must speak with her."

Anne shook her head in protest. "'Tis dangerous and becoming more so. King Henry is in foul humor these days. He's in no mood to put up with a high-spirited young woman poking her finger in his eye. If she succeeds in ignoring the Six Articles, others will suppose they can, too. His Majesty won't allow the reformers to get the better of him. He'll have the last word. He always does."

The screech of cart wheels along an adjacent street made it difficult for them to hear one another. When the noise suddenly stopped, they froze. After a minute or so passed, Anne reached for Christopher's hand, her breathing shallow.

Christopher whispered, "Where does Lady Askew come by such courage? Doesn't she know what could happen to her?"

Anne put her forefinger to her lips, motioning him to shush. They stood silent, contemplating the perils of voicing forbidden opinions. A minute or so more passed, when Anne led Christopher by the hand to a bench in the garden. After they were seated, she lamented, "All of my life, I've seen myself as a loyal subject of my king, not as a rebel or a traitor. Yet now the king's laws have branded me a danger to the kingdom. The only safety seems to be in stifling one's convictions."

He noted with a twinge of melancholy that the lovely sparkle in her eyes had dimmed. "You're not a threat to the king. Neither am I. I've never been anything but a loyal son of England." He leaned forward to rest his face in his hands, appreciative at the soothing stroke of her fingertips on the back of his neck.

"One would think," she opined, "with the growing number of dissenters, that those in power might soften. But no, His Majesty is intent on silencing them. I don't blame those who are fleeing to Basel or Geneva. What is to become of a kingdom that snuffs out its most virtuous subjects? Sometimes I wonder, where is God? Why doesn't he step in to protect those who are standing for his word?"

"I suppose that question has riddled mankind since Adam and Eve were banished from the garden," he mumbled, watching a bee flit from rose to rose.

"I don't know if I want to be seen with Lady Askew. I'm ready to stop attending the meetings. I'll just attend mass and hold my peace."

He bolted upright. "But Anne, that is their aim. If they succeed in silencing the truth tellers, they will have won."

She shrugged her shoulders. "What will we gain by standing against a monarch? How can one man or woman overcome the power of a king and his officers? He has an entire navy at his disposal, as well as sheriffs, constables, bishops, and priests, to name but a few. We're but gnats— fragile, powerless gnats."

"I can't believe you're saying this. You helped open my eyes—although I don't know whether to thank you or curse you."

"Curse me?" she gasped. "How could you say such a thing?"

"Life is simple when all you live for is to eat, drink and be merry. Believe me, belching out obscenities in a tavern beats watching over your shoulder to see who might be taking note of every word you say. But I can't stop thinking about the topics we discuss at our meetings, such as whether folks should follow their conscience, or injunctions and rituals they don't believe in. The reformers speak with such boldness and conviction, I can't ignore the things they say. Whether we win or lose is in God's hands, but choosing sides is in our own. Does heaven reward a coward?"

"But standing against a monarch is futile. He has all power, power over life and death."

"Stop." He placed his palms on her cheeks and held them there until she met his gaze. "There is but one who has power over life and death—one alone—and 'tis not King Henry."

"You know what I mean." She pulled back. "The king gives no thought to executing his closest advisors. You and I are but flies to him. If we disobey, he has the power to smite us as mere pests that flit about creating trouble."

Victoria peeked her head out the back door, her lips taut. "There's a man at the front door," she whispered. "He's asking for you, Christopher. I don't recognize him."

Christopher's heart skipped a beat. "Do you have a back gate?" he asked, his voice trembling.

Shaking her head no, Victoria stepped outside to keep Anne company while Christopher made his way to the cottage door. With a fearful look over his shoulder, he disappeared inside.

Anne crossed her fingers.

"Are you Mister Wade?" The inquiry came from a middle-aged man with thinning salt-and-pepper hair. His bushy sideburns reminded Christopher of squirrel tails. The stranger stood slightly slumped over, as if he'd been pushing a cart his entire life and become stuck in that position. Christopher looked past him to a cart with large wooden wheels parked on the street, the bed loaded with skeins of thread.

"Yes." Christopher's heart raced. "Have I met you?"

The man removed his hat with stubby, arthritic fingers and fanned his brow with the brim, drawing Christopher's attention to unruly eyebrows that protruded outward at least a half-inch. "Saint Bart's Fair, just shy of two years ago. You don't look like the Mister Wade I remember. 'Twas an older gentleman. Not older than me, mind you, but older than you."

"Tell me why you're seeking him. Perchance I can help you."

"I met Mister Wade at Saint Bart's Fair. He was a linen weaver, he was. Said he was lookin' to purchase embroidery thread for his wife to use on her needlework. Told me to look him up, but I never got 'round to it. He gave me the address of a Mister Nathan Wade, where he stayed while in London. I just came from there. Was told I might find you here."

"The man you're speaking of is my father, William Wade. I'm sorry to tell you, he passed on a few months ago."

"Oh, a pity 'tis. A right kind gentleman, he was. A linen weaver like your father, are you?" Christopher shook his head while swallowing a lump in his throat.

"No? What do you do, lad, if I might be so forthright?"

Christopher felt his face flush, as if he were standing too close to a fire. "A pin maker. Only temporary," he added, "until I find something more suitable."

"I see. A pin maker. I'm sorry, lad." The man turned toward his cart, then stopped and pointed his crooked forefinger at Christopher. "'Tis a shame your father passed. He seemed to be a fine man." Slapping his hat atop his head, he grasped the cart handles and started down the street, the cart screeching and rattling as he pushed it along the cobblestone.

Christopher returned to the garden to find Victoria and Anne waiting in tense silence.

"Who was it?" Anne inquired.

"A fellow looking for my father. They met at the fair a couple of years past. He said my father inquired about purchasing embroidery thread. You'll be happy to know I solved the mystery of the squeaky cart we heard earlier."

"Thank goodness." Anne exhaled her tension. "Truth be told, I'm a bit skittish, of late."

"A bit?" Victoria chuckled as she strolled to a flower bed to pick a pink rose. "I dare say, you're much more than a bit skittish."

"With good reason," Anne retorted.

"I'd better be on my way," Christopher sighed, rolling the tension from his neck. "I never thought I would envy someone working at the meat market, but when I sit making pins and consider Nicholas up to his arms in entrails, I think of how much better off he is. Speaking of Nicholas, he should know Lady Askew is in town. I wonder if he'll speak with me yet?"

"It wouldn't hurt to try." Anne stood and crossed a stone walkway to sniff the roses. "I'm sure he would want to know."

"I'll look for him. I haven't seen him for a few days."

"Perhaps he's ill." Anne bent a rose toward her, then pulled back when she saw a bee.

Swinging his cloak around him Christopher complained, "Off to paradise I go. Are you sure you wish to marry a pin maker? A beautiful maiden like you could do much better." He leaned down and gave her a peck on the cheek.

"You're a linen weaver, and always will be." She hugged him tightly, then raised her right index finger. "Wait." After a minute inside the cottage she returned with two large wedges of fresh scone. "This will give you something else to think about on your way to work. I included an extra as a peace token for Nicholas."

He examined the wedges. "Currants? My favorite. I can't guarantee that the second will make it to Nicholas, but I'll do my best. G'day to you both."

"A fine lad you've found yourself," Victoria commented as she watched Christopher turn the corner away from view. "You've made yourself a good catch."

Anne smiled. "I believe so. If only he can find suitable work, we'll be on our way."

"Something will come along; you'll see. There's something about that lad I like. He'll rise to his challenges."

"I agree," Anne nodded. "If we can only get through the present obstacles."

"We always do," Victoria replied. "Do we have any other choice?"

June, 1546

———

La Rochelle

Adjusting her shopping basket on her left elbow, Charlotte hurried along the street known as Rue des Merciers, past the turreted town hall, to the grand clock tower guarding the northwest corner of the harbor. Under ordinary circumstances she would be delighted to be out of her cramped rental cottage, visiting with townsfolk and enjoying the sights, sounds, and smells of the market, with its intoxicating variety of products from near and far. She barely noticed the aromas of exotic spices, roasting meats and fresh-baked breads; the rainbow hues of colorful textiles; the first fruits and vegetables of summer; and the hum of exchange between merchants and shoppers.

It wasn't foods, or spices, or textiles she came for. She was seeking a specific person, one who had been carefully described to her. At the harbor, guarded by two towers known as the Chain and Saint Nicholas, near the water's edge, she was to look for a well-built man in his early thirties who stood about 6'4", with shoulder-length, sandy blonde hair.

She checked the inside bottom of her basket to make sure the token was still there to present to the English merchant, so he would know she had been referred to him. Her stomach growled, reminding her she skipped breakfast that morning despite Thomas pestering her about needing to eat for the child she carried. It wasn't the nausea of pregnancy robbing her appetite; it was the fear and anticipation of what she must accomplish. Despite weeks of careful planning, Thomas suspected nothing. This was her ordinary shopping day. She left the cottage to visit the market at her usual time, carrying no extra provisions other than a few sols saved from her grocery allowance.

The tension between them had grown unbearable. He no longer allowed her to attend the meetings, after a parishioner told him the réformées held secret trysts in caves near the seaside. *Cursed lies!* she thought. He forbade Gabrielle and Anatole from playing with réformée children, afraid that doing so would bring danger upon the family and disapproval from his peers. He had enough of living a lie, he said, and doubled down on his devotion to the Roman church after they came to La Rochelle. Sometimes she wished she'd surrendered herself to authorities in Bordeaux the night Nicole came to warn her, and gotten her ill fate over with.

After passing under the clock tower's pedestrian archway to canvass merchant ships dotting the port, her eyes scanned the water for a ship with the name *Saint Thomas. How ironic*, she thought, that both her captor and her means of deliverance could bear the same name. But the name of a ship wasn't her primary concern. She must find the man to whom the ship belonged. Her life depended upon it.

*La Santa Maria, Margaret, The Rose…*she read the names, the sound of her heartbeat pounding in her ears. Amid the press of ship workers, towns-people stopping to gab about the latest news, and market shoppers, what if she failed to find the gentleman? He wasn't aware she sought him, so he wouldn't be looking for her. With a prayer in her heart, she walked along the harbor's edge.

Dock workers hustled and bustled about, loading and unloading barrels and crates, shouting words to one another that made her blush. A thin man sporting a large, red moustache hoisted a sack of salt over his shoulder, the veins on his temple protruding. She expected him to stumble under the weight until a muscular lad in his mid-twenties ran over and took one side of the sack. They carried the precious commodity to the ship where it was being loaded. Charlotte continued along the water's edge, searching in vain for the *Saint Thomas* and the tall gentleman with sandy blonde hair.

A ship worker with olive skin and greasy black hair looked her up and down as if he were perusing a piece of merchandise. She avoided eye contact and continued on her mission. He lunged toward her and grabbed her wrist, spouting out gibberish she couldn't understand, the strong smell of alcohol wafting in the air about him. The men around him scolded him in a language she didn't understand. She shook her wrist free and pushed him away. He cackled and returned to his work.

Battling a growing sense of hopelessness, she finished reading the names of the last few ships and felt compelled to look back. A man with sandy-blonde hair and a pale complexion, standing near a vessel on the opposite side of the port, caught her eye. He wore a red shirt with small buttons from neck to waist, a skirted black and red doublet adorned with gold brocade, and a flat black cap with a flamboyant, cream-colored plume. White hose and black leather turn-shoes completed his ensemble. He possessed an authoritative air as he spoke with a bald, portly man in the process of unchaining the ship from its mooring.

She hurried toward him, wanting to call out to get his attention, but not daring to lest she draw unwanted attention to herself. No one who knew her must see her speaking to the gentleman. A stone's throw away from the *Saint Thomas*, she heard her name.

"Madame Nix!" She pretended not to hear. "Madame Nix!" As she turned toward the voice, her heart sank. It was Thomas' priest, Father Jean, a man who loved to talk. With her right hand wrapped around the token in her basket, she stopped to exchange pleasantries.

"Father," she smiled. "How are you?"

"I'm well, thank you. The market has a fine assortment of fruits and vegetables today." He showed her his basket, brimming with fresh produce, and lifted up a bundle of asparagus. "Look at this. You must hurry before it sells out." Seeing her basket empty, he frowned. "No purchases today? Poor Thomas will starve." He chuckled at his clever comment. "What brings you to the water's edge?"

"The press of the crowd was suffocating me, and I love watching the ships," she answered, keeping an eye on the English gentleman.

"Yes, it seems the entire kingdom has come to market today." He eyed her basket again, noting her fisted hand inside. The gentleman with the plumed cap made his way toward the plank. Shifting her weight from one foot to the other, she screamed inside for the priest to leave.

"Could you tell Thomas when you get home that the parish is raising money to clean and repair the statues of the saints in the St. Barthélemy church? I'm sure he would like to participate."

"Yes, I would be happy to tell him."

"Thank you."

She expected him to bid farewell, but the priest hesitated, fixing his gaze on the man she had come searching for. Her heart skipped a beat when he pointed with his nose and lowered his voice.

"The English merchant there—I've seen him here before. He's trouble. Last time he showed up here, two réformée families disappeared. No one has seen them since."

"Oh, no. Is that so?" Charlotte feigned shock.

"You haven't heard?"

She struggled for a response, staring helplessly at the man Father Jean confirmed was the one.

"Father," a feeble voice called. An elderly woman hobbled over, her snow-white hair pulled back tightly enough under a coif to smooth her forehead wrinkles. "Oh, thank God, I have found you. My knees are aching, and my basket is too heavy. I pray you, lend me a hand."

"Of course, Madame Plouffe. Here—lend me your basket. Are you going home?" The priest pushed his own basket up to his bicep, then slid Madame Plouffe's below it and linked his free elbow in hers. With a wink at Charlotte, he shuffled away. Charlotte wanted to hug Madame Plouffe.

"Be sure to get some of that asparagus," he turned and shouted.

"Thank you, Father," she waved. Charlotte waited until they were lost in the crowd. She turned. The man was gone.

Where he'd been standing, two men stood conversing. She took a few steps forward and tapped one of them on the shoulder. *"Pardon, Messieurs."* The men turned, their pupils enlarging at the sight of an attractive woman trying to get their attention.

"*Madame.*" One of the men removed his cap. His jerkin and breeches looked to be strangling him from his neck to his calves.

"I'm looking for a tall gentleman with blonde hair. I saw him here just moments ago."

"Sir Winston, Madame?"

"I don't know his name. I was told to look for him here, and to show him this." She took the token from her basket and extended it toward the stranger.

The man inspected the token, eyed her suspiciously and returned it.

"I don't know the meaning of this thing, and Sir Winston is aboard the ship preparing to depart. You're too late, Madame. He'll be returning in three or four months. Perhaps you'll have better luck then."

Her eyes moistened. "Please, sir, is there nothing you can do? I must get on this ship. I simply must."

"This ship will take us to a larger cargo vessel outside the port, Madame. There's no place for you."

"Mister Cooke," the second man elbowed his shipmate. "Perhaps she's a Lutheran. Remember the last ones? They told of entire villages of their countrymen being slaughtered in the south of France. Do you think Sir Winston is expecting her?"

"He's not expecting me," she corrected, "but I was told he would give me passage. Please, you must understand. I can't stay here. I have to board the ship."

The ship listed. Charlotte's eyes grew wide with fear.

"Are you a Lutheran?" Mister Cooke inquired bluntly.

"Call me what you will, I'm not safe here in my country." With growing panic, she watched the main sail lift. Dropping to her knees, she pleaded, "My husband will turn me in to the authorities. I have nowhere else to turn. Please, have pity on me."

Moved by her plight, Cooke shouted to a worker on deck. "John, call Sir Winston."

"Eh?" John yelled back, his hands tangled in rope.

"Make haste! Call Sir Winston," he yelled. John disappeared and returned with the tall Englishman. Piers Winston acknowledged the men on the quay with a wave. Cooke pointed to Charlotte.

"She says she must board," he shouted.

Charlotte stood. "Please, Monsieur." She held the token high. Sir Winston squinted. She waited, holding her breath. He nodded.

"Row her out," he shouted.

"Looks like your lucky day, Madame." Mister Cooke escorted Charlotte by the elbow to a rowboat. Lifting her skirt above her ankles, she stepped into the boat and sat on a bench seat, holding on to the sides with both hands.

"Thank you, sir," she panted, with a nervous glance over her shoulder toward the clock tower.

Just before passing under the tower into the central village, Father Jean took one last look over his shoulder at the harbor. In the distance, he saw a rowboat moving toward the Chain and Saint Nicholas towers. At the sight of Charlotte, his heart churned with rage.

London

"This can't be happening," Anne Cooper whispered under her breath. She wedged her middle finger between her teeth to chew the fingernail, but discovered the nail was already down to a stub.

Rocking back and forth from his heels to his toes, Christopher studied the crowd gathered in front of Saint Bartholomew's church. Some folks shouted words of encouragement, some stood in quiet disbelief, some wept, and others jeered as two men carried Anne Askew on a chair into Smithfield. From the chair, they lifted her to a seat attached to the stake, where she joined her friend John Lascelles, a gentleman of King Henry's court, and two others.

Christopher elbowed Anne. "Why isn't she walking?"

Her bottom lip quivering, Anne whispered, "When they questioned her at the Tower, they stretched her on the rack until her limbs were torn. She can't stand on her own."

A shiver crawled up Christopher's spine. "'Tis fortunate for Nicholas that he returned to Dartford. Better to not witness this day."

Anne stood mute, her eyes fixed on Lady Askew in an ankle-length white gown, and the other three heretics, surrounded by large wood faggots.

Thomas Wriothesly, the king's representative, stood before the condemned with a small stack of papers in his hand. With raised voice he declared, "I hold here the king's pardon, if ye will recant your heretical opinions."

Lady Askew shook her head. "I'm not here to deny my Lord and Master."

Red-faced, Wriothesly shook the documents in front of her. "I implore you, foolish lady, recant and save yourself."

"I will stand forever with my Lord, not with the heretical doctrines of popery."

A lump formed in Christopher's throat.

"You can't stand at all, foolish maid," a man shouted. Laughter rippled through the crowd.

"On the contrary, Goodman, this day I will stand in the presence of God," she shouted. Lascelles nodded, appearing strengthened by Lady Askew's boldness.

The former Bishop Nicholas Shaxton, tasked by the king to preach to the crowd, stepped forward. He scanned the vast congregation, raised his chin and proclaimed, "I was also blinded by the seduction of Luther and Tyndale, by what some call the new learning. By His Majesty's grace, I turned from my error." He waved his hand toward the four at the stake. "Shun the heresies of these folks. They preach the fables of deranged minds."

"Coward!" The scolding came from a printer who worked on Cheapside, standing directly across the crowd from Christopher and Anne. Wagging a finger at Shaxton he shouted, "You once professed the same doctrines as these innocent folks who stand before you."

Shaxton's eyes narrowed. Waving his index finger at the man he countered, "King Henry's is the only true religion." Raising his voice to a fevered pitch, he proclaimed, "Embrace the king's religion. His Majesty is God's anointed, the head of the church in England." Returning his focus to the detractor, he declared, "Recant, foolish man, or you'll be next." He turned to Anne Askew. "Woman, do you recant of the heresies you insist on spreading to the good folk of this realm? Our merciful, sovereign lord has taken every measure to save you. He'll yet spare your life, if you but recant."

"I will not," she declared. "Do with my body what you will, for you only send me to join my Lord in paradise."

"I can't look." Anne wiped her eyes with her sleeve and turned away.

"Don't weep for me, good folk." Anne Askew's gaze met Christopher's. "Weep for those who don't embrace the truth." His heart fluttered. Her words pierced his soul as if he were the only person in the crowd.

"You leave no choice." Shaxton nodded to an officer holding a torch. Thick smoke dispersed around the base of the encircling faggots, gaining momentum until flames licked at the feet of the four martyrs. At the sound of coughing, Christopher closed his eyes. Lady Askew cried out. A shout rose in the crowd. Suddenly, a series of explosions thundered in his ears. The astonished crowd stampeded backwards. A merciful bystander had thrown gunpowder into the fire to shorten the duration of suffering. A loud clap of thunder nearly rattled Christopher out of his skin. He opened his eyes, glimpsed the grisly scene, and closed them again, salty moisture trickling down his cheeks. As he clasped Anne's hand in his, he felt her body shudder.

"The thunder—'tis God speakin' from heaven," a woman behind him shouted.

Weep for those who do not embrace the truth. Lady Askew's words played over and over in Christopher's mind, muffling the jeers and cheers of the surrounding crowd. *Weep for those who do not embrace the truth.*

He opened one eye for a split-second, then covered his nose with his elbow, choking on the overpowering stench of charred flesh. Anne Askew's breath was gone. They had destroyed her body but, somehow, he knew they had not destroyed her soul.

London

The tantalizing aroma of fresh poppy seed cakes—Piers Winston's favorite—wafted down the hall from the kitchen. Piers followed Molly toward the source of the smell, admiring the waist-length, wavy red hair she hadn't yet pinned up under her coif for the day.

Equally at ease on land or sea, Piers was one of five brothers born into a long line of London shippers. When he married Molly, the daughter of an Irish wool merchant, he combined his shipping experience with her connections in the wool trade. Piers' business sense and a bit of luck enabled the Winstons to prosper shipping raw wool to the Continent.

Hearing a *tink-tink-tink* sound coming from the kitchen, he tapped Molly's shoulder. She turned.

"Agnes is already working this morning?

Molly nodded. "She wanted to get off early today."

"I wanted to ask you privately, have you spoken with the French maid yet?"

With a pained look in her eyes, she shook her head. "It's been three days, and she hasn't come out of her room. I often hear her weeping. She doesn't touch the food I leave her, and she's had barely a sip of ale. Something unspeakable must have happened to her."

"At sea, she was the same. For hours at a time she stood beside the ship's rail, gazing across the water, repeating two names over and over—Anatole and Gabrielle. Seasickness seemed to get the better of her. She heaved over the side rail several times."

Molly searched her husband's eyes. Although the plight of reformers on the Continent roused her compassion, she worried about Piers putting his life and livelihood at risk to rescue them. Entering the kitchen, she pulled her apron from a peg next to the fireplace and greeted Agnes, while Piers stole a warm poppy seed cake from a silver tray on the table. As he raved about how delicious it was, Agnes looked up from the mortar and pestle with which she was grinding fresh sage and thanked him with a warm smile.

"Would you like me to check on the boys?" Agnes asked, her Spanish accent thick.

Molly nodded. "They should be working on their rhetoric." Tying on her apron, she waited for the sound of Agnes' footsteps in the hallway to fade before she resumed her conversation with Piers. "I'll offer the woman some fresh ale and poppy seed cakes this morning. Keep your fingers crossed. She has to eat, or she'll waste away. Have you considered putting her in touch with the others you brought from France—the ones that came a few months past?"

Piers shook his head. "I hadn't thought of it. Would you propose it to her, if you get a chance to speak with her?"

"Yes, of course. Does Master McMillan know of her? With his connections in London, perhaps he can help us find a safe place for her—unless she can stay with us?"

"I'll be meeting with the Christian Brotherhood later this week and inform them of her situation. We've helped several flee France and Flanders in the past few months. Oh, Molly, unspeakable acts are happening across the sea in the name of God. In answer to your second question—she could stay with us, although I would imagine she has her own plans for the future."

"Poor woman!" Molly lamented. "What plans could she have? A stranger in a strange land. She's clearly mourning someone she left behind. Where will she go from here, alone?"

"All we can do is pray for her, and trust God to direct her steps." Piers took a long sip of ale from the mug Agnes placed next to him before she left the kitchen. "I'm off to check the progress of my wool shipment. Headed to Antwerp tomorrow morning."

"Wait—I'll walk you to the door." In the parlor, Molly wrapped her arms around her husband's neck and complained, "I hate it when you leave me. I spend every second afraid you'll get caught. And the boys—they turn into rascals. Should I continue with my list of grievances?"

With a flash of mischief in his eyes he teased, "You should have thought twice before marrying me. Who was the lad—the street performer who had his eye on you?"

She rolled her eyes. "David Plott."

"Molly Plott—sounds like a burial site. He would have left you alone even more than I do, crisscrossing the kingdom to entertain strangers."

"He became a traveling fire-eater," she smirked. "I saw him at the fair one year, when he called me over to…" A stampede in the hallway interrupted her.

"Mother!" Seven-year-old Mark barged into the room, holding something in his right hand. "Simon broke my hornbook. He smashed it against the bedpost."

"You see, Piers," Molly lamented, "you haven't even left us, and they're at it already."

Piers examined the hornbook, his lips pursed. Half of the mica overlay was broken off and missing. "Simon!" Piers shouted. A freckled twelve-year-old lad with curly red hair trudged into the room trying to suppress a guilty frown.

"Did you do this?" Piers demanded.

Neither confirming nor denying, Simon glared at Mark and barked, "He called me a maggot-pie."

"Simon, look me in the eyes," Piers demanded. "Did you?"

Lifting his gaze to his father's chin, Simon muttered, "Yes, sir."

"Mark, fetch the switch." Both boys grimaced. The dreaded birch switch consisted of several branches bound together at one end to form a handle. It left lacerations in the skin that made sitting uncomfortable for several days.

"But Father," Simon protested. "He started it."

"Mark, you were wrong to call your brother a maggot-pie, and Simon, you were wrong to break Mark's hornbook. Your tutor will be here any minute. You're causing your mother grief, and you've delayed my leaving. Apologize to one another." Scowling at the floor, the two boys muttered half-hearted apologies.

"Simon, you'll have to share your hornbook until you can earn the money to purchase Mark another one."

His face reddening, Simon protested, "But…"

"No 'buts,'" his father cut him off. "Molly, I believe you would prefer to leave the room while I take care of this."

Avoiding eye contact with her sons, Molly turned and hurried down the hallway to the kitchen. She winced at the crack of the switch, followed by her youngest son's wail. Biting her lower lip, she arranged two poppy seed cakes and a half-filled mug of ale on a ceramic tray. With a silent prayer, she approached the guest chamber. After a gentle rap on the door she inquired, "Madame?" Several seconds passed in silence. She knocked again and had just crouched down to place the silver tray on the floor next to the door when it creaked open.

"*Merci, Madame.*" Charlotte's voice was raspy, her complexion ashen.

Astonished, Molly took a deep breath and lifted the tray from the floor. "I beg you, take some nourishment, Madame. Fresh ale, and Agnes made the poppy seed cakes this morning."   Charlotte opened the door and bid Molly to enter. After placing the tray on a bedside table, Molly sat on the bed.

"You and your husband have shown me such kindness," Charlotte whispered. "Please, forgive my poor manners."

"You have nothing to apologize for. If you should ever like to speak about it, I would be interested to know what brought you here."

"You and Monsieur Winston have a right to know." Charlotte crossed the room and sat on the blue coverlet next to Molly, the tiny slits in her puffy, swollen eyes betraying hours spent weeping.

"Shall I fetch you a cold compress?" Molly offered. "To soothe your eyes?"

"Thank you." Charlotte offered a weary nod. When Molly returned with a damp rag, Charlotte pressed it against her eyes with a relieved sigh.

"You speak English very well," Molly remarked.

"My husband is Englich."

"I see." Molly studied Charlotte's face, struck by a certain beauty beneath her grief and fatigue. "Do you have children?" Molly inquired.

Covering her mouth with the rag, Charlotte choked back a sob.

"Anatole and Gabrielle?"

Charlotte nodded.

"I'm sorry," Molly whispered. "Perhaps my husband could arrange to pick them up next time he sails to La Rochelle."

"He would never let them go."

"Who, Piers? Piers would certainly let them go."

Dabbing at her eyes, Charlotte sniffed, "No, my husband. He wouldn't let them play with my friends' children or go with me to meetings. He threatened to turn me in to authorities. That's why I fled. I didn't want Gabrielle and Anatole to see me imprisoned." She paused for several seconds. "Or worse."

Averting her gaze to the floor, Molly whispered, "I see."

"This is no better," Charlotte sniffed.

Molly reached for Charlotte's limp, cold hand and gave it a warm squeeze. "You mustn't lose hope. My husband helped two families escape from France several months ago. I wonder if you're acquainted with them."

"From La Rochelle?"

"Yes. Let me see if I can remember their names—Moreau and Rivoire, I believe. I didn't meet them, as they went to Canterbury. Piers tells me they were silk weavers. He said their silk is much finer than ours in England."

"I didn't know any silk weavers in La Rochelle. Perhaps they came from another village."

"Perhaps," Molly answered. "But at any rate, he did get them safely out."

"Mother?" A child's voice echoed in the hall.

"Come in," Molly called. Four-year-old Grace raced in and scrambled up on her mother's lap. "What is it, Grace?" Molly wiped a stream of tears with the ruffle on her sleeve.

In staccato, Grace choked out, "Si…Si…Simon b…b…bit me." She lifted up her forearm to reveal a red oval mark.

Running her fingers over the tooth imprint, Molly complained, "What's gotten into that lad? A lashing from his father isn't enough?" She stroked back Grace's dampened hair with a sigh. "I could use help tending the children. My husband is away much of the time." She strode to the door with Grace in her arms, then turned and added, "I'll pray for you."

Charlotte studied Grace. A faint smile softened her countenance. "She reminds me of Gabrielle."

"I'm sure Gabrielle is beautiful, like you," Molly smiled. "Now, let us help you get your strength back. We won't intrude, but we're here for you. Things have a way of working out. They always do."

"Yes, Madame."

"You may call me Molly."

"Thank you, Molly. And you may call me Charlotte."

"If I can get you more cakes and ale, Charlotte, or anything else, please let me know."

Listening to the thump of Molly's footsteps on the stairs, Charlotte picked up a cake and nibbled it halfheartedly, hoping Madame Winston was correct. Somehow, things would work out.

London

Trapped in darkness, with the rapid pounding of his heart resonating in his ears and chest cavity, Christopher tensed his fists. His hands were sticky with moisture. Rivulets of perspiration ran from his forehead down his temples. Feeling as if an anvil were on his chest he gasped for breath, but life-giving oxygen refused to enter his lungs. A cold, driving rain pierced his body like hundreds of pin pricks, while a female sprite pushed her twisted, grotesque face into his, moaning over and over, "Weep for those who do not embrace the truth." He thrust his arm forward to push her away. After blinking several times, he made out the outline of a window. Patting the area around himself, he felt the coarse wool texture of his coverlet. With a sigh of relief, he realized he was in his bedchamber, on his pallet.

It was the dream again, the one that had haunted him since he witnessed Lady Askew's fiery death. He rolled from his back onto his right side, then returned fitfully to his back, willing away the image of Anne Askew surrounded by flames. Determined to replace the dismal picture with a happier one, he pondered her striking beauty, and the way she had captivated him at first sight. But even more impressive than her physical beauty was her intangible beauty of soul, the fearless strength and courage that animated her every move. Where did she come by those qualities?

With a dreaded day of pin making looming ahead, he needed sleep. He closed his eyes and transported himself to his kitchen table in Dartford, where he pictured his mother frying pancakes. Inhaling deeply, he filled his lungs with the comforting aroma of batter sizzling in sweet cream butter, anticipating the sweet-tart taste of lemon and sugar sprinkled atop. How was Elizabeth faring without William? *I'm a terrible son,* he thought. *What kind of son abandons his mother and father?*

He rolled over, cursing his thoughts. Determined to chase away the demons tormenting his mind, he relived his excitement at Bartholomew's Fair—the merchants, the performers, the fragrance of roasted pork suspended in thick summer air—and into the picture drifted Anne Askew, on a chair in front of Bartholomew's church, flames licking at her feet.

By the mass, he cursed, pounding the straw pallet beneath him with clenched fists. *Will I ever find peace?* Precious peace eluded him in Dartford. It eluded him in London, and out at sea, and in the kingdom of France. To be sure, the world offered fleeting moments of happiness, but those moments never lasted. An endless supply of vexations sprung up, like noxious weeds, to choke out any hope of lasting well-being. He contemplated Anne Askew's serene countenance, her resolute steadfastness despite the hardships she endured. Where did one come by such peace? If anyone had reason to be bitter, Anne did. A line she often recited entered his mind: *I would sooner read five lines of the Bible than hear five masses in the church.*

An idea nudged him. Nathan kept a Bible hidden in a barley sack in the kitchen, with a standing invitation for Christopher to read it. He pulled his nightcap down over his ears, slipped out from under the covers, and fumbled for his slippers. Stepping lightly down the staircase, he skipped the stair that always creaked, almost losing his balance in the dark. Across the courtyard and into the kitchen he tiptoed. Immersing his arms up to the elbows in the cool barley, he fished in vain for the book. A wave of disappointment washed over him.

Just as he plopped on a stool to contemplate his next move, a flicker of candlelight appeared in the window. He watched the door handle lift, his heart racing. Screech by screech, the door inched open to reveal Nathan in his bed clothes. At the sight of Christopher, Nathan slipped inside, set his candlestick on the windowsill, and exhaled a relieved sigh.

"I thought perhaps we had a thief on the premises. What brings you to the kitchen at this hour?"

"I couldn't sleep. Thoughts of Lady Askew were haunting me."

"She's not easily pushed out of mind." Nathan cinched the belt on his robe tighter and sat on a stool next to Christopher.

Searching Nathan's face in the candlelight, Christopher asked, "Where did she come by her strength?"

"I've asked myself the same thing more times than I can count." Nathan studied the flickering candle. "I wager such strength can come only from God."

Christopher nodded. "I thought I might find your Bible, but 'tis not in the sack. I would have asked you, but at this hour…"

Nathan interrupted, "I moved it to a safer place. A sack of barley is one of the first places they look these days. I'll…" he hesitated, searching Christopher's eager eyes for any hint of insincerity. "I'll get it for you, if you promise to guard it with your life. Don't let anyone see it—no one! Follow me back to my chamber. I'll loan it to you for the night."

An inexplicable sense of warmth tickled Christopher's soul. "Thank you, Uncle Nathan. I don't believe I'll be sleeping tonight."

By the light of a tallow candle on the wood crate next to his pallet, Christopher nestled under his coverlet clasping the precious book. His soul hungered for something he knew he lacked, but wasn't sure where to find.

'Tis a curious work, this book, he mused. He perused the ruddy front cover, flipped it over, and studied the back, taking note of scratches and scrapes perhaps sustained on its clandestine journey from Antwerp to London. Engraved in gold lettering on the spine he read the words, "New Testament. Tyndale. 1536." If the book could speak, what tales would it tell? Did it sneak into England buried in a barrel of wheat, or tucked in a bale of cloth? Did its smugglers consider the risk if they were caught? *What is it about this book*, he wondered, *which leads intelligent men and women to go mad?*

An image of Lady Askew speaking to a street crowd came to mind. She was arrested, imprisoned, released, arrested again, and finally tortured on the rack in the Tower in the hopes she would inform on others. Through it all, she held firm. Some folks said she behaved like a dog returning to its vomit, running away from her husband, preaching on street corners and defying the king's authority. Christopher would never see her as anything but an angel. The book in his hands was the lifeblood coursing through her veins.

He contemplated others with the same passion that energized Lady Askew. Her martyrdom came ten years after Tyndale himself suffered death at the stake. Some painted Tyndale as an ignorant man, but Nathan told Christopher Tyndale spoke eight languages fluently—including Greek and Hebrew—and studied at both Oxford and Cambridge. He held a variety of elevated positions in the church, and published treatises of religious philosophy many considered brilliant. Why did this book Christopher clutched in his hands lead a man with so much worldly potential to suffer imprisonment, exile, and death by burning? *No book on earth is like this one*, he thought. A warm sensation quickened him, starting at the top of his head and working its way down to his toes.

Flipping through the Bible's pages, he stopped at the words, *The Gospel of Saint John, the Apostle and Evangelist.* To the right of a woodcut illustration, in elaborate calligraphy, he read:

In the beginning was the word, and the word was with God; and the word was God.

The same was in the beginning with God.

All things were made by it, and without it was made nothing that was made.

In it was life, and the life was the light of men,

And the light shineth in the darkness, but the darkness comprehended it not.

The last phrase gave him pause. *The light shineth in darkness, but the darkness comprehended it not.* Lady Askew's words resonated in his soul, *Weep for those who do not embrace the truth.* Could it be that folks fought against the truth even when it was presented to them plainly because darkness filled their minds? He'd never considered such a thing and contemplated it now only because of the words on the page.

Into the wee morning hours he read, drinking in the words like a man who had stumbled upon a life-giving spring after years of wandering in the desert. He read of folks who struggled as he did, with doubts and fears; of folks rich and poor healed of infirmities of all kinds; of the humble and proud. He read words Christ himself uttered, and he couldn't recall ever feeling the power of those words as he felt them now, reading them for himself in the English tongue.

Come unto me all ye that labor, and are laden, and I will ease you. Take my yoke on you, and learn of me, for I am meek, and lowly in heart: and ye shall find ease unto your souls. For my yoke is easy, and my burden is light.

A seed of hope sprouted in his heart. *That is what I seek*, Christopher thought. *Ease to my soul.* Peace distilled upon him as he read the passage again and again, until his head bobbed and his eyelids flickered closed. A soft rap on the door startled him upright. The Bible fell from his chest to the floor.

Nathan slipped into the chamber, wrinkling his nose at the unpleasant smell of the tallow candle that had been burning all night. "The morning bells are sounding," he said, eyeing the Bible on the floor. "I have to hide the book away." Christopher picked it up and extended it before rubbing his eyes with his fists. "It appears you fell asleep reading," Nathan said. "What is your opinion of the book?"

Christopher replied, "When might I borrow it again?"

Nathan smiled. It was exactly the response he hoped for. "A small group of us is having Bible study tonight in the kitchen. Would you like to come?"

Cocking his head, Christopher replied, "Bible study? I thought you'd done away with them."

"Only so far as the authorities suppose." Nathan flashed a mischievous grin.

Playing with a loose thread on his blanket, Christopher contemplated the offer. It was one thing to admire Lady Askew's courage, but entirely another to risk attending forbidden meetings.

"Would you be willing to lend me the book to study on my own?" he asked, fearing Nathan would decline.

"Of course. But I thought you might enjoy meeting and learning from others."

Christopher tugged on the loose thread and mumbled, "I'll think about it."

Headed for the stairway with the book tucked under his arm, Nathan stopped when he heard his name.

"Why do you do this?" Christopher asked, his gaze fixed on the Bible.

Turning, Nathan scratched his chin. "Do what?"

"Why do you hide a Bible and hold cottage meetings, knowing how dangerous it is?"

"Keep reading the book. I think you'll find out for yourself."

Disappointed with his uncle's answer, Christopher returned a polite nod. As soon as Nathan closed the door behind him, he dragged himself out of bed, groggy from lack of sleep, and dressed for the day.

July, 1546

———

Dartford

Amy Coppinger nudged her husband, Tom, with her elbow, bursting with pride over her good instincts. Tugging down on the waist of her rust-colored Sunday frock, she prayed for the side seams to hold. The dress kept riding up to her knees, and goodness knows she didn't want folks questioning her modesty. She took a deep breath of the floral-infused air drifting from floor vases brim with daisies and lavender, where Father Garrett stood facing the guests in attendance.

The past few weeks she'd spoken with as many townsfolk as were willing to share their opinions, and not one of them had an inkling. Most thought her prediction preposterous, but Amy spotted it a mile away. She knew William's "leanings" had been a thorn in Elizabeth's side the couple's entire married life, so why shouldn't the poor widow finally be equally yoked to a devout man? Elizabeth deserved it, after enduring the shame of William's proclivities toward the new learning and the public humiliation of her son running away to London. Her smile beamed upon the happy couple.

Following a loud thunder clap, the outside rain turned to hail. To Matthew's young son John, the hail sounded like an army of giant archers pelting the roof with arrows. He couldn't focus on the nuptial ceremony, too busy imagining that the thunder represented a giant cannon retaliating against the archers. Besides, he wasn't enthused about a bossy woman marrying his father and invading his home.

Just as Father Garrett pronounced the couple man and wife, sunlight broke through the clouds and streamed through the church windows, casting a rainbow of colors across the somber stone walls. The priest considered the light a good omen. More than anything else, he felt relief. At last Elizabeth had a good man, one who wouldn't be sowing seeds of heresy in the parish. *Elizabeth Cooper.* The name sounded as if it were always meant to be. A new name for a new start, and one less widow for him to deal with.

After declaring the words, "I plight thee my troth," Elizabeth turned and flashed a dimpled, ear-to-ear smile at the guests. Christopher couldn't recall ever seeing her smile that way—radiant, joyful. His stomach churned as a whirlwind of emotions clouded his mind. On one hand, seeing his mother so happy with a man who detested his father made him uncomfortable; on the other, he felt relieved at the chance to finally get out from under the curse of being a Lollard's son. Folks in Dartford were already treating him better.

The sun returned to its hiding place behind the clouds. Wedding guests braved a ten-minute sprint in a torrential downpour to the Cooper cottage on West Hill, where Elizabeth's friends had laid out a feast of roasted pigeon and pork, fresh rye bread, beans, and Amy's famous ale. Of course, Abby Wellington provided a heaping tray of taffaty tarts.

With Nicholas Hall and John Whitfield both in attendance, and feeling that luck was on his side, Christopher thought about trying to make amends with his lifelong friend. As Nicholas and John shared pleasantries across the room, he whispered in Anne's ear, "Do I dare try to speak with Nicholas?"

She frowned. "This is our parents' moment to celebrate. I wouldn't want you to make a scene."

Nicholas spoke into John's ear and both men looked in Christopher's direction. *What are they up to?* Christopher wondered. To his surprise, Nicholas started toward him, with John close behind.

Extending a hand, Nicholas smiled, "Congratulations. I wish your mother every happiness. And you've gained four siblings. You're a big brother!"

"Putting up with me won't be an easy task, as you know," Christopher replied, grateful Nicholas made the first move.

"You were insufferable for awhile, but I suppose you had your reasons. I've had plenty of time since I returned to Dartford to think about what happened in London. I owe you an apology."

"*You* owe *me* an apology? I'm the one who should apologize."

Nicholas shook his head. "I bear no grudge, and hope you feel the same."

"If you were standing in my shoes, with England's most beautiful maiden, I would hate you." Christopher wrapped his arm around Anne's waist and pulled her close. "But the past is behind us."

John stepped up to offer his hand. "I hope you'll forgive me for tormenting you when we were young."

Rubbing the back of his head, Christopher teased, "Feel this permanent lump on my skull from the rocks you and Edwin threw at me."

With a chuckle, John flexed his arm. "My aim and strength are nothing to be trifled with."

"That's the truth," Christopher smiled. He turned to Nicholas. "Are you back to laying bricks?"

Nicholas nodded. "With the king's Manor House finished, work in Dartford has been hard to come by. My father and I are working in Maidstone."

John elbowed Nicholas' side. "Tell him your news."

"My news?"

"You know, your *news*."

"He doesn't care to hear that," Nicholas balked.

"Tell us your news," Christopher coaxed.

"Pray, do tell," Anne chimed in.

"He met a maiden," John poked Nicholas in the bicep, "and she actually fancies him. Imagine, a canker-blossom like him."

"Stop," Nicholas blushed. "You'll start the rumors flying."

"She's from Maidstone," John continued.

"Do I hear wedding bells?" Christopher squeezed Anne's hand.

With a vigorous shake of the head, Nicholas protested, "I'm a sworn bachelor. John, wipe that smirk off your face."

"He'd ask for her hand in a minute if he thought she would say yes," John countered.

As the cottage emptied of guests, Elizabeth's friends busied themselves picking up platters, wiping tables, and throwing scraps in a slop bucket for Matthew's hog.

"Things look to be winding down," Christopher remarked, watching his mother giggle and guffaw with guests, her hand in Matthew's. He blinked twice and shook his head, still struggling to digest his mother's choice of a marriage partner.

Nicholas plopped a morsel of rye bread in his mouth with a sideways glance at Matthew and Elizabeth. "Where will the young couple honeymoon?"

Cracking his knuckles, Christopher answered, "Abby Wellington is going to tend the children while Matthew takes Anne and I back to London. They'll spend a night there and return to Dartford."

"A night in London—not too shabby." Nicholas lowered his voice, focusing on Anne. "How are Bible studies in London going?"

A pained look darkened her eyes. "Lady Askew is gone. Did you hear?"

"They sent her back to her husband again, did they? She'll free herself and return to London again. They might as well give up."

"No—they—at Smithfield, a huge crowd gathered and—it was terrible." She averted her gaze to the straw-strewn dirt floor.

Ashen-faced, Nicholas whispered, "What? God help us. Did you witness it?"

"Yes. She went praising her Maker, as you would expect. They tried to convince her to recant, but she would have none of it." Nicholas gulped.

"Folks," John interceded, stuffing a piece of taffaty tart in his mouth, "this is a wedding. Let's speak of more cheerful things."

"Actually, I need to be on my way." Nicholas glanced about the almost empty room. "Let's catch up before you return to London. You *are* returning to London?"

Christopher nodded. "Yes, tomorrow."

"Have you given any thought to returning to Dartford? Weaving would have to be better than any work you've found in London."

"Anne and I will discuss it when we return to London to prepare for our marriage." He waited for a reaction.

Unfazed, Nicholas replied, "I figured the news was coming. Congratulations to both of you."

Nicholas and John bid farewell to Anne and Christopher, wished the newlyweds well, and left.

"I need to get some sleep," Christopher yawned. "It'll be strange, staying at the old cottage alone."

"Wait." Anne squeezed his elbow. "I want to get something for you." She intercepted two taffaty tarts just as Elizabeth's friend, Dorothy, reached to wrap them in a cloth for herself. With a roll of her eyes, Dorothy spun around to find another task.

"Take these with you." Anne's eyes twinkled. He gazed into those eyes, sure he would never tire of the way they made his heart skip a beat. "A breakfast to look forward to."

After thanking her with a kiss on the cheek he whispered in her ear, "On the morrow."

"Sweet dreams." She squeezed his hand.

"Sweet dreams." Christopher stopped to wish Matthew and Elizabeth well before he stepped out into the pleasant summer night air, relishing the unexpected surge of optimism that swelled within him.

Tripping over the threshold, Christopher steadied himself just in time to prevent a collision with the kitchen table. He set his lamp on the table and scanned the room. Not much had changed except the position of the loom. Pushed into a corner, covered with a thick layer of dust and cobwebs, it looked forsaken. He thought of the countless hours he'd spent perfecting his craft, and of his foolish decision to walk away.

William's tawny wool cloak hung on a hook next to the door, as if it were waiting for William to show up any minute and slip it on. The delicate fragrance of lavender bundles, hanging upside down next to the fireplace, freshened the dank, humid air while the empty rug in front of the fireplace reminded him of Dart. Poor dog! Elizabeth informed him his four-legged friend ran away a week after he went to London and was never seen again. The bed stood where it always had, with his straw pallet tucked beneath it, dusty but welcoming after an emotionally exhausting day.

Stifling a yawn, he pulled out the pallet and crossed the room to get a bed sheet from the cupboard, lingering to gaze at the loom as if he were beholding an old friend after a long absence. He made up the pallet and borrowed a feather pillow from the bed, praying for a good night's sleep. Too weary to fold his clothes, he tossed them on the bed and slipped his nightshirt over his head, eyeing the loom. In his mind's eye, he saw William standing next to it, beckoning him. He crossed the room and wiped his forefinger across the dusty crossbeam, then blew the dust off his finger and watched it float through diffused rays of lamplight.

"'Tis yours."

Goosebumps erupted on his arms. The voice—his father's voice—was so distinct, he turned to make sure he was alone. Returning his attention to the loom, he pictured himself wheeling a loaded cart to High Street on Market Day. What a fool he'd been. How low he had stooped!

With a whisk broom he started at the top of the loom, sweeping off cobwebs and dust, stopping to sneeze every few seconds. Once finished, he stood back and smiled. There. The machine had regained its dignity. He felt it smiling back at him.

"'Tis mine, Papa?" he whispered, caressing the breast beam. As he inspected the heddles, a stack of cloth on the floor behind the loom caught his eye. He sorted through the pieces with a feeling of reverence, first a tabby weave, then a satin—one sample after another his proud father saved to document his progress. Running his fingers across each piece of fabric, he felt the sensation of touching his father's hands.

When he reached the bottom cloth, his heart skipped. It was a sample of the diaper weave he was working on when he broke William's heart with the announcement he had no intention of being a weaver. Regret racked his conscience. His father toiled day in and day out, with never a complaint, to prepare him for this inheritance. How disappointed William must have been when Christopher threw all of it in his face.

Falling to his knees, he pleaded for forgiveness, and prayed to know whether he should return to Dartford. After pouring out his soul, he slipped between the coverlet and the sheet. Sleep came instantly.

Saintes, France

Father Jean slapped his right palm on the heavy oak table that ran the length of the meeting room. The loud *bang!* rattled a crucifix hanging in the middle of one wall and jolted a priest from Cognac into sitting up straight. Fathers Antoine and Jacques flinched with a sideways glance at one another.

Father Jean's probing eyes scanned each priest's face, his demeanor mild but authoritative. "We have to do more. They're weeds. Just when you think you've pulled them all up, more sprout in their place."

As he tapped his plume on the table, Father Jacques wished he were more like his colleague from La Rochelle. Father Jean was as reliable as the rising and setting sun, pleasant in the midst of the current crisis, yet as firm and unflinching as a steel sword in carrying out his duty to rid the church and kingdom of dissenters.

The constant *tap-tap-tap* of Father Jacques' plume was wearing on Antoine's nerves; he hissed out a quiet sigh of relief when the priest stopped tapping to speak.

"I thought they had quieted down," Father Jacques declared. "When we visited La Rochelle with Bishop de Bourbon last October, we left no uncertainty as to how the réformeés would be dealt with. The schoolmaster was excommunicated. That alone should have gone a long way toward halting the spread of devilish doctrines. To think of all the young minds he polluted—it's infuriating."

While the clergy gathered from around the region murmured amongst themselves, Father Jean raised his right hand, waiting until each pair of eyes was fixed upon him. Antoine wished he were sitting across a tavern table listening to Father Jean's jokes rather than suffering as a hostage in the stuffy room to discuss heretics.

"Don't be fooled, brethren," Father Jean warned, pacing the length of the table. "They may have quieted, but few have recanted. They've gone underground. They still circulate forbidden writings. They teach their children these heresies at home. Removing the schoolmaster didn't solve the problem."

"Given their stealth, how do you know these things?" Father Jacques dipped the plume in ink, not bothering to look up from his note-taking.

Father Jean stopped pacing and combed his fingers through the silver beard that covered his cheeks and chin. "The innocents—the children. They betray their parents. One of my flock came to me, complaining that she caught her daughter singing réformée hymns. This child often played with children of parents who supposedly recanted."

Father Antoine, who had taken his eyes off Father Jean to watch a wasp crawl in circles on the bookshelf across the room, returned his gaze to the speaker. "Short of taking their children away from them, how can we stop them from teaching their own offspring? We would need to put soldiers in every home, to watch their every move."

Jean nodded. "It may yet come to that." A startled look flashed in Antoine's eyes. Eager to motivate his fellow brethren, Father Jean spoke louder, shaking his forefinger for emphasis. "We have to get names. The bishop has asked that we double down and insist that the faithful inform on their réformée neighbors. I take no joy in it, brethren, but it's for the greater good." He leaned forward, resting both palms flat on the table. "Listen to this. A member of my parish, who fled here from England because he could no longer practice the holy faith without persecution, lost his wife to these heretics. She disappeared on an English merchant ship last month, leaving her children behind. Think of it!"

Lifting his right brow, Father Antoine responded, "Where is Bishop de Bourbon this morning? Does he know of this incident? We should have his opinion on the problem."

"He said he had other affairs to take care of this morning." Father Jean strode to the door and looked down the hall in both directions. Returning to the table, he lowered his voice and continued. "Did you know the bishop has family members who are réformées?"

Father Jacques nodded. "Everyone knows." The priests sat in silence, Jacques tapping his plume, Jean pacing in front of the table, and Antoine dabbing beads of perspiration from his forehead with a kerchief.

"What counsel would you give this parishioner whose wife ran away?" Father Jean probed. "His heart is shredded. The children cry for their mother day and night. He doesn't know what to tell them. How do you tell a child his mother loved fables more than him?"

Fanning his face with his perspiration-soaked kerchief, Father Antoine suggested, "He should seek an annulment and find another wife, one who will raise his children in the true faith. Pray it's not too late for the children; the seed of heresy may have already taken root."

Father Jacques scribbled a line and looked up. "An ox should not be yoked with an ass. This man is an ox. His wife is a she-ass."

Laughter broke out around the table.

When the levity died down, Father Jean wiped his brow and continued. "This man—his name is Thomas Nix—carves and sells pilgrim souvenirs. His faith impresses me. He fancies if he could make a pilgrimage to Saint James that he might atone for anything he did to bring this calamity on his family."

Rolling the plume back and forth between his middle finger and thumb Father Jacques remarked, "He should be grateful she left. His mistake was to marry a réformée in the first place."

Father Jean stopped to glare at a priest from Rochefort who had been gazing out a window during most of the meeting. "Father Renaud, is our topic too dull for your taste?" He strode to the window and peered out to the churchyard. An attractive young woman sat on the grass with a basket of flowers, while a child played nearby with a papillon puppy. Renaud peeled his eyes away from the scene with a guilty blink and fixed them on Father Jean.

"It wasn't his fault," Father Jean continued. "She wasn't a réformée when he married her in Bordeaux. A few months ago, he discovered she'd been secretly attending a study group. When an insider from the group informed the authorities, she fled to her parents' estate. The parents aren't réformées but, understandably, they helped their daughter escape to La Rochelle. Monsieur

Nix went along with it for the sake of his children, until protecting her grew too cumbersome. He's done everything he feels feasible to hold his marriage together. When he told her he could no longer live in the shadows or support the endangerment of his children, she disappeared. He's wondering if he should go after her and force her to come back."

"I wish I knew what to say." Father Jacques jotted a few notes. "I feel for the man. This plague is biting even the clergy. Friar Goymoult is in episcopal prison for embracing the heretics. A monk, brethren, following the fables of Calvin! Let it be a lesson, no one is immune."

"I would never follow after such fables," Father Antoine stated, clapping at the wasp as it passed in midair. The insect fell to the floor.

"I trust that none of us would," Father Jean responded. "But beware, for Luther was of the same order as Friar Goymoult—an Augustinian—and you know what happened with Luther. Beware, brethren!"

Antoine swallowed hard. "This Englishman's wife—you say she left with an English merchant?" The story piqued his interest.

"Yes," Father Jean replied. "Scandalous. These réformées, they're adulterers. Leaving her own family and going off with a strange man." He looked at the floor and shook his head in disgust.

"They're possessed of demons," Father Jacques declared. "I recall the story of the devils entering the bodies of swine and running them off a cliff to destruction."

Antoine turned to Jacques. "Where did you hear that story?"

"It's in the New Testament," Father Jacques replied, doodling a pig. He held up his drawing. Father Antoine looked perplexed, Father Jean amused.

"A very apt description," Father Jean remarked. "Swine possessed by demons, running to their deaths. Very apt indeed."

Father Antoine breathed out an impatient sigh. "We could pass the day discussing grievances against heretics, but we came to discuss a solution."

"Is there a solution?" Father Jean paced again, playing with his beard. "We've been following instructions the lieutenant of Poitou passed along from the king, enacting maximum punishments with the goal of striking terror into their breasts." He looked out the window at the woman and child. "In my opinion, we're accomplishing nothing, except to drive them into hiding. In fact, I daresay too many spectators who watch a heretic suffer at the wheel or stake are moved more to sympathy than repentance. We can't afford to create new converts as we put away the old ones."

Fathers Antoine and Jacques nodded in agreement.

Encouraged, Jean continued. "We have to penetrate into their inner circles. Do you brethren suppose you could find members of your parishes willing to pose as réformées?"

"I can think of one or two in Essarts," Jacques nodded, his hand gliding the plume back and forth over his paper. "Perhaps more."

"I don't believe it would take more than one or two in any town," Jean said. "Enlist your sheep to bait the wolves. Reward those who help you generously, brethren, as they deserve to be rewarded. Many of the réformées have much property, for they're nothing if not enterprising. Divide the spoils."

"Father Jean, you have the English gentleman in La Rochelle," Antoine observed. "It seems to me he might be a perfect candidate to help in our cause."

"Hmm." Jean's eyes brightened. "You may have a point."

"We might be able to use him on a grander scale, beyond La Rochelle," Father Antoine continued. "You say he is a carver?"

"Yes, and a damn good one."

"And he speaks English. Perhaps we could use those things to our advantage." A self-satisfied smirk crossed Father Antoine's face.

"I don't understand." Father Jacques studied Antoine's expression.

"I'm not sure I see where you're going with this either," Father Jean admitted.

"Let me explain." Father Antoine stood to address the group, a diabolical smile on his face. "It would work like this…"

August, 1546

———

London

It was the worst possible job in England, and he didn't know if he could tolerate it for even one more day. Sitting on a hard stool in a dimly lit, smoke-filled shanty making pins sank lower than cleaning animal entrails, collecting leeches or sweeping chimneys.

An odd assortment of humanity surrounded Christopher—thin young children with nimble fingers and hollow eyes, dressed in little more than rags; bony-fingered elderly men and women barely able to see or hold on to the pins they were charged with making; indigents too healthy to beg, but lacking the skills to do anything else. Christopher tried not to stare, but he found himself stealing glances at the curious figures surrounding him. *I don't belong here*, he thought, studying the elderly woman next to him, a trembling skeleton covered with sagging skin and veins.

He recalled the sense of destiny that distilled upon him when he laid eyes on the loom during his visit to Dartford for the wedding. Since that night, the realization lingered that his father had only wanted him to succeed. William had tried to offer Christopher the best pathway in life that he could provide. *Here I sit*, he thought, *a hostage in a dark room, breathing toxic air from the soldering forge.* He glanced at a sliver of light struggling to penetrate the shack's lone, dingy window. *All because of my stubbornness and pride.*

He leaned toward the old woman hunched over on a stool next to him, her eyes only a couple of inches away from the one pin she had been working on the entire time it took him to make four. "I'd rather be a leech collector," he whispered.

She lifted her head to reveal a prune-like face, with shriveled lips that framed a few teeth clinging to her gums for dear life. Speaking with a lisp, she replied, "A pox on that notion, lad. Me husband was a leech collector. Right killed 'im, it did. Went from pond to bog and came home nights with leeches on his legs to sell to the apothecary. Sucked the blood right out of 'im, they did. The leeches, not the apothecaries." A feeble smile crossed her lips before she continued. "The spots bleed for half a day after ye pluck the leeches off. Did ye know that?" Christopher shook his head, repulsed by the image of a man's legs covered in leeches.

"Perchance ye meant to say gong farmer?" It seemed to Christopher that the elderly man with a wheezy voice suddenly awoke from the dead. He sported a full head of unruly white hair and permanently alarmed eyes, as if he'd been repeatedly struck by lightning. "Nothin' could be fouler than gong farming. Up to the neck in gong, ye are, lucky if the stench doesn't kill ye. Up all night in the witchin' hours, shovelin' up what comes from the backside of a Londoner. 'Twould make a man right mad, if he wasn't already. Why, I knew a gong farmer who had to be committed to Bethlem; went out of 'is mind going from privy to privy, shoveling the foul refuse and hauling it away in a barrow."

Christopher pricked his finger on the brass wire he was sharpening. "By the mass!" he hissed. A small droplet of blood welled up in the pinprick. He rushed the finger to his mouth to suck the salty liquid from the wound. "Gong farmer, leech collector, pin maker—a pox on them all," he spit. "And a pox on this place, and a pox on London." Inspecting his finger, he discovered another droplet of blood about to drip onto the table. He rushed his finger to his mouth and sucked on it.

A pale, bright-eyed girl named Jane who would soon turn eleven stared at him quizzically through the smoke the forge belched out. "Why are you so cross?" she inquired, brushing away from her soot-stained face a few strands of thin brown hair that escaped from under her bonnet, leaving black finger marks on one temple.

"Why aren't you angry? Look at us, in these detestable circumstances." He stopped sharpening the wire and leaned toward to her. "I had good fortune and I threw it away, like so much rubbish," he answered.

"What good fortune?" she pressed.

"Linen weaving. My father was a linen weaver in Dartford, and I was an apprentice to him. 'Twould be mine now, if I hadn't left."

"Dartford? Where is Dartford?"

"Have you seen the London Bridge?" he asked.

"Of course, silly." She rolled her eyes.

"Well, you cross the bridge into Southwark, and continue on Watling Street until you arrive in Dartford. You can walk there in a day."

"Is it pretty there?"

"I suppose I've never thought about whether it is pretty there. But yes, it is. 'Tis a comely village that lies between two hills, named East and West, with a church built by Bishop Gundulf, the same man who built the Tower. You've surely seen the Tower of London?"

She giggled. "Everyone has seen the Tower. If you've seen London Bridge, you've seen the Tower."

"Well, Holy Trinity Church in Dartford was built by the maker of the Tower. And the village has a wonderful market each Saturday, where folks come from all around to sell their wares. The valley is full of orchards with blossoms that smell heavenly in the spring—sweet cherries, and apples, and fat artichokes…" he drifted off, his eyes glazed. "And you'll find some of the best taffaty tarts you've ever eaten there," he said, wistful.

"Better than Mistress White's on Bread Street?"

"I'm sure of it," Christopher answered. "And the warblers flit from the gorse bushes to the heather, while the sheep call to one another on the heath."

"It sounds lovely. I should like to see Dartford." Jane's expression turned from pensive to sad. "But I suppose I'll never leave London. We're too poor."

Christopher sat sullen, deep in thought and nursing his pinprick. "Actually, I would like to see it again myself," he said, fighting a surge of homesickness.

"They like to use us because our fingers are nimble," Jane remarked, changing the subject. "Mother tells me without children, the pin sellers would be out of business."

"Then what use 'ave they for corpses like me?" the old man teased.

Smacking her lips, the old woman inserted, "We're filling the empty stools until they can find better."

Jane held up the pin she was working on. "I wonder where this one will end up? On the queen's ruff?"

"Or on His Highness's duff?" The old man snorted, pleased with himself for making a rhyme. "His arse is so fat a blind archer could hit it from a mile away. Heard tell, takes four men to haul His Corpulence around, and every one of them is nursing a hernia."

"Not so loud, old man. 'Ol Henry doesn't take kindly to mocking. Off with your head!" Christopher said bitterly.

"Fie on the smelly, pustulant old tyrant," the old man barked. "'Twould be doing me a favor to put me out of my misery, by my faith. Today I labor to earn a loaf of bread I can scarcely eat because I'm losing my teeth. While the king is so plump, he sits on his rump, hey diddle dump."

A young boy across the room giggled.

The old man dropped the pin he was working on. "By Saint John's head," he cursed. Jane hopped down from her stool to pick it up and handed it to him.

"Thank you, my child. Would 'ave taken me a week to find it with these eyes." He turned to Christopher. "Say ye could 'ave been a weaver lad? By my faith, ye must be repentin' of your folly now."

"Why are you here if you hate it so much?" Jane asked.

"A few weeks past, I was cleaning up for Barnard Johnson, a butcher in Smithfield," Christopher explained. "He told me of this pin shop. I thought anything would be better than cleaning up after the slaughter. Little did I know."

"Maybe your father would take you back," Jane said matter-of-factly.

Shaking his head, Christopher countered, "My father died a year ago, and I left because everyone in Dartford hated me."

"Everyone?" Jane persisted. "No one is hated by everyone. You've a mother, don't you? Your mother loves you."

Christopher smiled. Jane showed extraordinary wisdom for her eleven years.

"You should at least go back and try," Jane insisted. "You can't give up. You never know until you try."

Try. The word stirred something within him. It was a simple word, loaded with possibility.

Dartford

Something about a dead fish's eyes made Elizabeth squeamish. She could swear the creature was watching her. Avoiding eye contact with the salmon, she pressed open the gutted pink flesh and ran a filet knife under the skeleton to separate the meat from the bone.

A housewife waited on the other side of the table for the morning's freshly fileted catch from the Thames. The well-proportioned maid, with a button nose and inquisitive brown eyes, shifted her weight and moved her shopping basket from one elbow to the other. Carrot and beet tops peeked over the basket's edge.

"I do beg your pardon. I'm quite sure I must be slower than what you're accustomed to." Elizabeth bit her bottom lip, focused on her task.

"'Tis no bother. A lovely morning, it is. Not a cloud in the sky." With a soft sigh, the woman pushed a strand of hair under her coif.

"You're not from Dartford, I gather?" Elizabeth felt she needed to be sociable while she fileted the salmon. Matthew had drilled into her that friendliness was good for business.

"Crayford, actually."

"Crayford? My son used to play football against Crayford—against my will, mind you. As a good Christian woman, I detest that barbaric game."

"My Howard still plays." With her nose slightly elevated, she continued, "He's been team leader the past two years."

"Oh?" Elizabeth looked up just as she was positioning the salmon for the last cut that would sever the skeleton from the flesh. The knife slipped. "Zounds!" She rushed her thumb to her mouth.

"Oh my," the woman exclaimed. "Are you bleeding?" She pulled a handkerchief from her basket, shook it open, and extended it to Elizabeth.

Elizabeth pulled her thumb from her mouth long enough to inspect the cut. "Bleedin' just a bit. Perhaps the creature is gettin' revenge. I swear by God's teeth, 'twas watchin' me."

"Please, use my kerchief."

Taking a glance at the pretty white cloth embroidered with intricate black-work, Elizabeth politely declined. "I thank you, but I wouldn't wish to soil such a lovely piece."

The woman folded the kerchief and tucked it back in her basket.

"I do say," Elizabeth continued, "it appears I need more practice before I can chat and filet at the same time. Please bear with me." She flinched when church bells chimed the twelve o'clock hour.

The woman's eyes flitted from the nearby market stands, to an egg-soaked thief in the stocks, to a cluster of folks chatting near the chandler's shop. She rearranged the carrots and beets in her basket, obviously restless. "Howard will be looking for me. He accompanied me today so I wouldn't have to travel alone. There've been reports of highwaymen on the Roman Road."

Elizabeth recalled Christopher speaking about a football player from Crayford named Howard—a skinny, whining sort of a runt who never stopped complaining. A milksop, as he told it.

"There he is now." The woman pointed to a striking young man approaching from Market Square. He stood just north of six feet tall and sported a head of thick, brown hair cut chin length. His muscular physique, accentuated by a well-fitted burgundy jerkin, gave him the look of a noble. Elizabeth's pupils enlarged.

"Mother, I can't find the linen cart you described. I've been up and down High Street, and I even checked some of the side streets."

His deep voice left Elizabeth thinking anything but milksop. Wiping her hands on her apron, she turned to Howard. "Perchance I can help you. You say you're lookin' for a linen cart?"

"Yes," his mother interjected. "'Twas a year or so past, when I came to market and stopped at a linen cart on High Street, a stone's throw from the church. A kindly gentleman sold me the kerchief I showed you. I so fancied the fine weave and the blackwork embroidery, I wanted to stock up on them, and use some as gifts." She retrieved the kerchief from her basket and held it out for Elizabeth to examine. "You see? 'Tis lovely."

Elizabeth's breath caught in her throat. "That looks like my husband's workmanship. If so, that would be my blackwork. He had a cart on High Street, not far from the church. Yes, I'm quite sure 'tis our work."

"Your husband no longer has a cart?"

"He passed away just shy of a year ago."

The woman covered her mouth with her fingers. "I'm sorry."

"Thank you." Elizabeth didn't know what else to say.

"Might you still have a few that weren't sold?"

"I'm afraid not. They're all gone."

"Oh, what will I do? I had my heart set on them."

"I'm sorry. I hope you'll find somethin' you like equally well." She glanced at the kerchief again, a flood of memories moistening her eyes, and pushed the salmon toward the edge of the counter. "Here you are."

Tucking the cloth in her basket the woman replied, "'Tis doubtful." She wrapped the salmon in a thick cloth and placed it in a separate tote. "At any rate, we must be on our way. I certainly don't wish to be traveling the road after dusk. Godspeed."

The customer had almost reached Market Square when Elizabeth waved an arm and shouted after her, "My son is a weaver." The woman turned, one eyebrow raised. "He lives in London," Elizabeth continued, "but I'm hopin' he'll return to Dartford and take over the weavin'. Check back next time you're here at the market, will you? Perhaps he'll be here then."

Her countenance brightening, the woman shouted, "Yes, it would please me very much. G'day, Goodwife."

Howard tipped his cap. Charming lad, he was. *They do grow like weeds,* Elizabeth thought.

September, 1546

———

London

“Make sure the nose bag doesn't bunch up, would you?” Nathan thrust the reins into Anne's hand when Christopher—teeth clenched and veins bulging from his temples— stumbled through the cottage door lugging Anne's leather-trimmed, oak trunk onto the porch. Christopher pulled a rag from his belt to wipe the perspiration from his brow before plopping onto the trunk with a groan.

Anne wrapped the leather reins around her right hand and scratched the animal's dappled neck, happy to stay out of the men's way. *Men become ill-tempered when they're moving a woman's things*, she thought to herself.

She scratched behind the pony's ears, unable to shake the image of the French maid she met at the study group the night before. What kind of monster would threaten his wife and drive her away from her children? How did a French woman sympathetic to Calvin's doctrines end up married to an Englishman loyal to the mother church? Did the man sweep her off her feet, only to show his true colors after the nuptials?

Nathan slipped his fingers under one side of the trunk while Christopher picked up the other. With grunts and groans, the two men heaved it over the cart rail. The pony shifted her weight with a snort.

“Is this all you have?” Christopher asked, hopeful.

“No, I have two more.” Anne combed her fingers through the pony's coarse white mane. “They're in the front room.”

“I'll have to see an apothecary for the pain,” he moaned, exaggerating his discomfort. "Mother said there's a new one in Dartford—Doctor Bartholomew, I believe she said. I hope he's skilled at handling strains."

Anne swatted at him with one of the reins and scolded, "After a few years in London, one acquires some things. Besides, we'll be setting up our own household soon. You'll be grateful for the few things I collected."

He leaned against the cart with a huff. "I'll have to take you at your word. Will the pony be able to pull the weight, Nathan?"

Fanning his face with his cap, Nathan took stock of the cart's contents. "She'll do fine. The hackneyman assured me both pony and driver are reliable. I'd take you myself, but I need to be here to help Master McMillan protect the Bibles when the cloth shipment comes in from Amsterdam."

Christopher wiped his forehead with his sleeve. "Speaking of Bibles, I wish I could get my hands on one."

Anne interrupted, "Nathan, do you remember the name of the French maid at the study group last night?"

After a moment's reflection he answered, "Charlotte, I believe it was."

"Charlotte," Anne repeated. "How could a man threaten to turn in his own wife?"

"Why should it surprise you?" Christopher replied. "It happened to Anne Askew."

"What will Charlotte do?" Anne said. "She has no family or friends here. My heart aches for her."

Nathan spoke up. "She's had offers of work and lodging through the brotherhood. At the moment, the Winstons are helping her. Her plight pains me as well, but she'll be able to make a life for herself. As for leaving behind her children in France, I wish I could help her. Anyone attempting to smuggle her children away from their father will be putting himself at great risk."

"We could invite her to come to Dartford to embroider linens," Anne suggested, "or help my father in the Shambles."

Christopher shook his head. "We can't take care of ourselves at the moment, much less invite another to join us. Besides, she'll have better opportunities in London. You heard Nathan. Something will come along for her."

"But we could at least offer." Anne scratched the pony's shoulder, dejected.

"I wouldn't want to bring her to a village hostile to reformers, when she's trying to escape such things," Christopher stated with an air of finality.

Anne bit her lower lip. "I suppose. But London isn't friendly, either."

"She'll stay better hidden among the throngs in London, should someone come looking for her." Christopher peered into the back of the wagon. "The other two trunks aren't going to move themselves. Shall we?"

Nathan slapped his cap on his head. "One down, two to go."

They had almost reached the front door, when Christopher felt a tug on his elbow. Nathan pulled him to a stop.

"About you wishing you had a Bible. I can fix that." Surprised when Christopher frowned, he added, "I thought you'd be happy."

"I can't pay you until I'm earning money."

"I want to give you a Bible as a parting gift."

"I can't let you do that. I'm already forever in your debt, what with everything you and Aunt Lucy have done for me."

"Nothing would bring me more joy. I can come by another easily enough."

"But…"

Nathan raised his forefinger to stop Christopher's objection. "You can repay me by enjoying the book."

"That, I can promise." Christopher patted his uncle's shoulder. "Thank you, Uncle Nathan."

When the cart was finally loaded, Christopher stepped back to take in Honey Lane, with its narrow cobblestone streets and timber-framed buildings. His heart flooded with memories, but like the pony harnessed to the wagon, he chomped at the bit to move forward.

La Rochelle

Seated in a dim corner of The Two Towers tavern, overlooking La Rochelle's harbor, Thomas took a sip of red wine and licked his salty lips. King Francis' move to sharpen the sword of inquisition was bearing delicious fruit. Just a few days earlier, the king ordered sixty-two heretics to be arrested outside of

Paris in Meaux, after officials discovered them having secret meetings in one of their homes. Their pastor, Pierre Leclerc, had the audacity to celebrate Holy Communion with his flock of heretics. Thomas shook his head. Holy Communion, administered by a wool carder. They might as well hold mass in a pig sty. He smiled. Death sentences were sure to follow.

A month earlier, two faithless monks met their deserved fate at a stake in nearby Saintonge. Iron balls stuffed in their mouths stopped them from spewing their Calvinist dung to onlookers. *Why should heretics have an audience?* he told himself. It wasn't as if they hadn't been duly warned. Official church doctrines were published to the kingdom's subjects three years earlier, and everyone understood that no other interpretations—not in public, print or private—would be tolerated. Persistent sowers of sedition knew better. They deserved their "reward."

The opportunity to help inquisitors catch heretics filled Thomas with a deep sense of purpose. He felt a smug satisfaction in the advantages he had over his prey. For one, réformées perceived the English to be sympathetic to their cause. Those who didn't know him trusted him, just because he was English. Gullible fools! He chuckled inside. Second, his marriage to Charlotte gave him insight into their ways, their thoughts, and their secret comings and goings. Marrying her had not been a mistake, after all; it had turned out to be a fertile training ground.

Cracking his knuckles, he glanced about the tavern and contemplated the task at hand: smashing two flies with one blow. Today's work would earn him a generous reward. A wicked smile curled up the corners of his mouth. The réformées were nothing if not industrious, and it was they who paid his wage with their confiscated goods. How wonderfully ironic! A growing collection of confiscated goods only whet his appetite for more—silver works, tools, dishes, fine linens, guns and swords, furniture. Finding a larger home had become a priority, but—he combed his beard with his long fingers while refocusing his mind—today he had other business to take care of.

Savoring the oysters, goat's cheese and brown bread that comprised his midday meal, Thomas watched and calculated. Across the tavern, near a window, a stocky fellow with bright, intelligent eyes sat up straight, sipping an ale. A large pack rested on the floor next to his stool. Noting that the man was wiping the gravy from a bowl of pottage with his last chunk of bread, Thomas washed his final bite of cheese down with a swig of wine, paid his tavern bill, and ventured out into pleasant air that was neither too warm nor too cold. The lapping water and cries of gulls swooping over the harbor invigorated him. He hurried to the parsonage and knocked on the door. Father Jean opened.

"He's here," Thomas whispered, not multiplying words. Father Jean's eyes smiled.

"Ah, I was waiting for you," the priest whispered. "I'm ready."

"I'll be a few paces from the harbor—by the oak tree near the clock tower."

Father Jean nodded. He knew what to do next.

Thomas hastened back to the quay and perched his back against the tree, holding a carving knife in his right hand and a partially completed statue of the crucified Jesus in his left. Every few seconds his eyes scanned the line of three- and four-story white limestone buildings, focusing on the tavern door. He pretended to carve, but adrenalin made his hands too shaky to do any real work.

Father Jean appeared in the pedestrian archway of the clock tower and moved in Thomas' direction. Their eyes met. Thomas shook his head—*no, not yet.* The priest occupied himself watching a male bluethroat in the rushes near the water. As the bird lifted its head to whistle and chatter, the sun broke from behind scattered clouds and illuminated a cornflower-blue throat and rust-colored collar stripe. The palette of complementary colors struck the priest as the work of a master artist. He studied the bird until, from the corner of his eye, he saw the tavern door open. He glanced at Thomas. Thomas nodded.

Emerging from the tavern, Thomas' subject leaned upon an exquisitely carved walking stick with the pack over his right shoulder. His beard—sandy in color—extended to the middle of his chest, accompanied by a bushy moustache and sideburns that gave him a lion-like appearance. Before descending the tavern porch onto the street, he looked first to his left, and then to his right.

To his left, a priest stood a few paces away staring at the rushes; to his right, a carver leaned against a tree, whittling. Others came and went along the quay, including a young couple strolling hand in hand, a boy chasing after a brown and white spaniel, and an older woman carrying a basket of brown eggs.

The man stepped onto the street and turned left. Thomas pretended to whittle, keeping a careful watch. The spaniel burst past Thomas, toward the rushes where the bluethroat sat precipitously perched atop a blade. Chattering an alarm, the bird lunged forward on a low flight path past Thomas, skimming the water along the harbor's edge. With an air of amusement, the pack-toting man stopped to watch the bird before he continued along the quay. The spaniel brushed against his walking stick as it chased the bird, with the boy close behind shouting, "Lili! Lili!"

Thomas followed twenty paces behind the peddler and wiggled his hand behind him as a signal for Father Jean to follow. The priest kept pace an equal distance behind Thomas. Suddenly, the peddler stopped, lowered his pack to the ground and knelt down in front of it. He glanced around him, rearranged some books, and then hoisted the bag on his shoulder, not stopping to look behind him. When the peddler started forward, Thomas resumed following.

The peddler made his way around the shoreline and toward the shipyard. In the distance, rows of masts, like a forest of branchless trees, marked the destination. As soon as the man reached the yard, Thomas ducked behind a group of barrels while Father Jean concealed himself around the corner of a merchant's home.

A well-dressed shipbuilder offered the peddler a warm embrace. "Jean-Luc," the peddler smiled, "I hope you're doing as well as you look."

Jean-Luc returned a chuckle and a warm smile. "You're always the flatterer." He removed his cap to scratch the greying hair behind his ear with stubby, calloused fingers. "I take each day as it comes. And you, Pascal? How was your journey?"

Pascal set his pack on the ground with a groan. As he stretched backward, his knees popped. "Does that answer your question?" he snickered.

"You're on God's errand," Jean-Luc remarked. "And paying a price, it appears. Annette and I insist that you join us for dinner this evening. As the master said, the laborer is worthy of his hire. It's the least I can do, to nourish God's servant."

"God pays a handsome wage," Pascal replied. "I only wish he would keep my back from hurting. And, by the way, I wasn't joking. The passage of time is treating you well."

A muscular man with greasy brown hair eyed them from the ship's deck.

"I can't guarantee that unfriendly eyes won't watch us here at the shipyard." Jean-Luc bobbed his head toward their one-man audience, his chestnut eyes flashing a warning. "We must be on our guard."

"I've learned to always be on my guard," Pascal nodded. "Unfortunately, the wolves are as well. I noticed a priest outside the tavern, staring into the rushes."

"They watch and wait like vultures, ready to sink in their talons. Did he follow you?"

"Yes, but I didn't let on that I noticed."

"Very wise." Jean-Luc looked up to the deck and shouted, "Lazare, time for your break. Fifteen minutes, eh?" The man nodded, turned his back and disappeared across the deck. "He's harmless," Jean-Luc said. "There are others I'm not so sure about. At any rate, we would be wise to wait until evening, over dinner, to speak about matters. Annette and I customarily dine at seven o'clock. Do you have business to occupy you until then?"

"Yes, I have many books of general interest to peddle." Pascal pulled a book from his pack and flipped through it to reveal several black and white illustrations. "Have you seen this one, about a maiden named Flammette and her troubles in love? Translated from Italian."

"Oh, you can't be serious," Lean-Luc moaned, throwing his hands up in mock disgust. "My wife might read this, but me? Does this look like a dress I am wearing?"

With a sheepish grin, Pascal eyed Jean-Luc's perspiration-stained leather cap, the expansive chest filling out his tan vest, and the calf muscles bulging beneath his hose. "Of course not. I think this one, with words of advice about *chevalerie* from Olivier de la Marche, would fit you better." Pascal pulled another book from his pack and put the romance book back. "But as for your wife, should I save *Flammette* for her?"

"You're a born salesman; that I can't deny." Jean-Luc pointed to the ship with his chin. "We're refitting this merchant vessel to accommodate a privateer—adding munitions and such. *L'Étoile—The Star*—beautiful, isn't she? She's going to intercept the Spaniards as they cross the sea with their galleons full of gold and jewels from the New World. We can't sit back and twiddle our thumbs while they build their Babylonian empire."

"Hmm." Pascal stroked his beard. "That reminds me, when I was a young man, a couple centuries ago," he winked, "I heard a tale of a privateer named John Florin. From Normandy, if I recall. He intercepted a small Spanish fleet coming across the sea loaded with gold bullion. I fancied the reports were exaggerated, because the story stretched with every telling. It was said he went back and forth, and brought back savages and beasts, carved jade statues, exotic masks covered with precious stones—wild stories, I thought."

Jean-Luc's sea-green eyes brightened. "No, it's true. The Spanish explorer, Hernan Cortés, followed in Columbus' footsteps across the sea, to a world populated with non-Christian tribes. Florin intercepted Cortés and gave the spoils to King Francis. Florin traveled many times to this New World and brought back shiploads of riches and curiosities. And why not? Should Spaniards be allowed to build their empire with the spoils from these faraway lands, while they claim to take the Christian religion to savages? They take nothing but popery and threaten us with their expanding power and wealth. We must stop them. You should have these adventures in your book bag—they're much better than *Flammette*."

"Indeed, I should. But for now, I'll leave you to your work; the fate of empires rests on your shoulders. Thank you for the dinner invitation. I'll see you at seven this evening." Pascal lifted his bag over his left shoulder.

"I look forward to seeing you then." Jean-Luc tipped his hat and returned to the task of overseeing the ship work, while Pascal meandered along the quay toward the clock tower, enjoying the hustle and bustle of the busy port. He'd been walking no more than five minutes when he felt a tap on the shoulder. The priest who had been watching the bluethroat outside the tavern confronted him with a scowl.

"I noticed you're a book peddler." Father Jean stood a head taller than Pascal with his hands on his hips, his eyes slanted toward the book bag.

Tipping his hat Pascal replied, "Yes, you're correct. I say it most humbly, you're fortunate to have found me, Father, as I'm in La Rochelle only once a year. May I interest you in my newest reading material?" He put his pack down on the wooden boardwalk and fished out a book. "See here, I have the recently printed, 'Apology in Defense of the King,' by François de Sagon. The writer is a priest. Perhaps you know him?"

Father Jean crossed his arms, his lips taut.

"In the tale, the priest compares our King Francis' visit to the Ottoman Empire to the parable of the good Samaritan. I find it refreshing to see our monarch defended in such an able manner by one of his loyal subjects. Please, take a look." Pascal extended the book. Father Jean tucked it under his arm with a scowl.

"I'm interested in everything in your pack," the priest remarked stiffly. "Please, show me all of your offerings."

"I was just on my way to the market to set up." Kneeling, Pascal closed the flap on his pack without pulling the drawstring taut and hoisted the books onto his shoulder. It sagged open. "It would be quite inconvenient for me to pull out all my books here, and then have to repack them," he said, gazing squarely into Father Jean's steely eyes. "I pray you, Father, keep the book I gave you to see if you like it, and let me know later if you would like to own it. I'll be on Rue des Merciers. Won't you find me there and look at the rest of my books?" Succumbing to gravity, a book tumbled from his pack.

"Here, let me get that for you." Nearly pouncing on the book, the priest read the cover silently, biting his lower lip, and growled, "I'll accompany you."

"No need, Father. I know the area well. It's kind of you to offer, though."

"I'll accompany you," the priest growled.

Pascal swallowed hard and extended his right hand. "I'll take the book, if it please you." Father Jean obliged. Pascal removed his pack, placed the book inside, and pulled the drawstring tight before swinging the pack over his shoulder.

"Shall we?" Pascal chirped, despite his sinking heart.

The two walked in tense silence, side by side, passing under the clock tower into the central village. A breeze brushed across Pascal's perspiration-soaked skin. He shivered.

"He must be caught up with a customer. He's very popular in the village," Jean-Luc chattered, pacing in front of the door. "People love to talk to him, to hear his tales. I know folks who save up the whole year to be able to purchase a new book from him."

"The roast duck is cold." Annette leaned against the stone archway between the kitchen and parlor, sour-faced. "And the poached pears as well." She sighed and straightened her apron. "It's rude for a dinner guest to be so late."

"Perhaps he doesn't know the time. Pascal is a well-mannered man."

"He could have checked the clock on the belfry or asked someone." She turned her back and disappeared into the kitchen. The loud clatter of dishes accentuated her displeasure.

Jean-Luc lit a lantern and hung it on an outside porch hook. There was nothing more to do but sit in his chair and wait. To occupy his mind, he pictured himself as commander on L'Étoile, intercepting a Spanish galleon returning from the New World, losing track of time until a *tap-tap-tap* on the door brought him to his feet.

"Annette," he shouted, "our guest is here."

"I'll ready the table again," she sighed.

Jean-Luc threw open the door. His knees buckled.

London

"There, there," Charlotte cooed, stroking Grace's rosy cheeks while gently rocking her. The young girl's long, red lashes fluttered as her eyes closed.

A cherub, Charlotte thought, gazing upon the innocent face. "Oh, *ma petite*. What lies ahead for you?" Charlotte pictured her own daughter, across the sea in La Rochelle. Tucking a blanket around Grace she hummed "Une Jeune Fillette," a tune her mother had often sung to her.

> *There was once a young girl, noble of heart,*
> *Charming and pretty and of great worth.*
> *Against her will she was made a nun.*
> *This didn't please her at all, so she lived in great pain.*

As she hummed, waves of grief like a rip tide carried her soul to deep waters of despair. How much longer could she endure the pain of feeling broken beyond repair? Would she ever know happiness again, the sort of happiness she experienced when she first met the handsome Englishman and gave him her hand, or when she gave birth to her children, or when she first read the Master's words in her own tongue and felt heavenly light expanding in her soul?

A guilty longing for death to release her from the suffocating dungeon of circumstance teased her thoughts. She replaced it with images of Gabrielle and Anatole. To think of never again feeling their chubby arms around her neck, never hearing the music of their laughter, never running her fingers through their silky hair was unbearable.

After Piers Winston raised the possibility of smuggling out the children on his next trip to La Rochelle, she began saving every penny and shilling he paid her for household help in a rough wooden box tucked under her bed, to be prepared in case she returned to France. It was a risky venture, he stressed, requiring immaculate planning. If anyone could help, he said, it was a réformée Piers knew in La Rochelle, a well-respected shipbuilder by the name of Jean-Luc Mercier. Dared she hope? Clinging to hope was, in itself, a form of suffering.

The ruckus of a human stampede approaching the bed chamber jolted her out of her melancholy trance. Mark darted in, followed by Simon and Simon's friend Tommy. Grace's eyes blinked open. She whimpered and settled back to sleep.

"Chut! Chut!" Charlotte scolded the boys. "Your sister is napping."

"Simon won't let me play Nine Men's Morris," Mark tattled.

"Only two can play, and I'm playing with Tommy. Mark keeps knocking my men off the board." The whiney edge in Simon's voice grated on Charlotte's nerves. Tommy stood in the background, staring at the floor.

"Go outside and play at jousting," Charlotte said, rubbing her eyes.

"Why are your eyes so red?" Mark blurted.

"Never mind that," she whispered.

"Mother never allows us to play at jousting," Mark revealed.

Casting daggers with his eyes at his brother, Simon hissed, "You little maggot-pie."

"Boys!" Charlotte interjected. "I'm sure you can find a game everyone can play. You mustn't disturb Grace's nap, or she'll be cross for the rest of the afternoon."

"Let's play at jousting," Simon suggested. "Madame Nix said we could."

"Mother would tell father if she found out," Mark countered.

"No, you can't play at jousting if your mother doesn't allow it," Charlotte said, tensing when a clap of thunder shook the ground, followed by the deafening rattle of rain against the roof. Grace stirred, but her eyes remained closed.

"We can't play outside anyway," Simon moaned. "Mother doesn't like us to track in mud."

Tommy brightened. "Let's play Nine Men's Morris again. You and Mark play first, and I'll play the winner."

"I suppose," Simon sighed, wishing to be rid of his younger brother. They raced out the door, through the hallway and down the stairs.

Charlotte placed a hand on her abdomen. She would soon be showing too much to keep her condition secret. How she wished for the baby to be born into happier circumstances. Closing her eyes, she imagined a joyful reunion with her husband and children. She pictured Thomas throwing his arms open to greet her, whispering in her ear how glad he was to have her home. She savored the thought of Gabrielle and Anatole's arms around her legs. But then, a haunting image crowded in. It was Thomas, on his way to mass with Gabrielle, Anatole, and another woman whom the children called *maman. That's my name*, she protested, her chest tightening.

I can't let that happen, she thought. *I can't leave my children to a stranger.* Bowing her head, she pleaded in the anguish of her soul to know how to go forward. An idea formed. She pushed it away, but it came back, stubbornly insisting to be considered.

"Dear Lord, anything but that," she whispered. "I can't do that."

"I will give you strength," a gentle voice coaxed. She swallowed hard, tilted her head back, and stared at the beamed ceiling, wondering if the answer came from God or her own imagination. It must be from God, she reasoned within herself. Such an answer never would have come from her own mind.

With a knot in her stomach, she carried Grace to bed and tucked her in. Adjusting her own skirt and apron, she left the room and passed through the upstairs hallway. The Winston family expected supper on time, and Agnes was off to take care of personal matters. Charlotte descended the stairs and entered the kitchen. The thought of what she must do nudged her once again. She checked the spit in the fireplace and poked at the coals. They were still aglow from the morning fire.

Fresh, skinned pigeons that Molly bought from the Smithfield market rested on a platter on the counter, ready to be cooked. After threading the birds onto a spit rod, Charlotte secured the rod over the fire. Deep in contemplation, she sat on a stool slowly turning the spit. Fat from the birds dripped onto the coals, sizzling and feeding flames that jumped and licked at the flesh of the roasting fowl. She blinked back beads of salty perspiration burning her eyes.

"I will give you strength." The voice spoke to her heart again, insistent. Turning the spit, she wondered what awaited her if she followed through with the prompting. Somehow, she knew with a knowing beyond her own that she must put her trust in God and step forward into the darkness.

November, 1546

———

Dartford

Anne glanced across the room at Christopher every few seconds while she chopped turnips, carrots and parsnips for a pottage. They had been married two months, and life couldn't be more perfect. Even the cold, soppy weather outside couldn't dampen her cheer. The rain and fog only made the hearth's warmth all the more comforting, and it reminded her of her wedding day—rainy but joyful, nonetheless.

Although Christopher made the case there was nothing unusual about exchanging vows in a tavern, or a barn, or anywhere, for that matter, he let her have her way. She was set on the idea that they had a better chance of starting married life on the right foot if he didn't draw attention to his reformist sympathies. So, on their wedding day, Father Garrett greeted them in front of Holy Trinity with a few friends and family gathered to the side of the door. Anne wore a bottle green gown she'd purchased in London, and her hair in a braided crown woven with yarrow flowers, styled by Nicholas' friend Rachel. Christopher sported his best tawny wool breeches, a black leather jerkin, a white linen shirt and eyes full of panic. Everything went smoothly until—she giggled just thinking about it—they exchanged vows, and Christopher stuttered, "I plight thee my cloth." Oblivious to his mistake, he demanded, "What?" when a few of the guests—notably Nicholas and John—snickered.

She called her thoughts back to the present, admiring him as he worked on a sailcloth. *My handsome man,* she smiled.

After plopping a dab of butter in her kettle along with a spoon of lard, she hung the pot on a tripod in the fireplace. With a long-handled spoon, she stirred in the vegetables. Soon, a tantalizing aroma warmed the cottage.

"Smells delicious." Christopher didn't bother to look up. "What's for supper?"

Pleased that he noticed her effort she answered, "Just a pottage with a bit of fish."

"One of my favorites," he replied, gliding the shuttle up and down, over-under, across the warp. "Can't wait to try it."

His skill at the loom filled her with pride. She loved to watch various weaves materialize under his hands. In addition, Elizabeth was teaching Anne how to spin and embroider so she could add to their income, something Anne discovered she much preferred to fishmongering.

"Your father's former customers seem anxious to purchase your cloth," she said.

"I'm happy about that," he nodded. "I still need to find more customers, but slowly and steadily it will build."

She sprinkled a handful of oats into the pot for thickening, poured in a couple pints of vegetable stock, and dropped in the chopped fish her father gave her that morning, along with a sachet of dried parsley, sage and rosemary.

"Sage?" Christopher wiggled his nose like a hare.

"And rosemary," Anne beamed. "Your mother gave me some herbs she picked and dried from the garden. She invited me to plant my own herb garden next year."

"I'm glad the two of you are getting along." As he reached the end of a row, Christopher stopped to look up. "She can be quite…" he hesitated, searching for an appropriate word. "Well, folks have been known to call her an ox—behind her back, of course."

Shaking her head, Anne countered, "Well, I haven't noticed. She's a wonderful help. I'm grateful to have her close by." She rested the stirring spoon on a wooden trencher, covered the kettle with a lid, and moved to the table, where she had set out oat flour and eggs for cakes. The kettle lid rattled with the pressure of the steam.

Starting a new row, Christopher remarked, "Have you noticed how superstitious Mother is? I find it rather funny, to be honest. She thinks the wise woman—what's her name?—is a witch. To Mother's way of thinking, the wise woman might have killed my father by means of some strange potion or spell."

"Agnes Hubbard? Yes, Elizabeth told me of her concerns about Agnes. The woman does have a witch's mark. Have you seen it? 'Tis right up here on her arm." Anne pulled up her sleeve and patted herself on the forearm, leaving behind a dusting of oat flour. "The marking is strange indeed. She also keeps unusual potions and ointments, and strange creatures in jars."

"You believe Mother?" A corner of his mouth curled up.

Defiant, Anne retorted, "I saw the mark with my own eyes."

"I need to work harder on keeping the two of you separated."

She looked up from mixing the dough, miffed to see a smirk on his face.

"Actually," he continued, "at least Mother's teaching you something useful. If you could sell herbs and vegetables at the market, and perhaps embroidered towels, we'd have a good living—enough to support a growing family." At his mention of a family, her heart skipped a beat. "Are we obliged to anyone this evening?" He shifted on his stool and circled his head to relieve his stiff neck muscles.

"No, not this evening. Tomorrow Joan Fanner is holding a bride ale at the Fanner barn to raise money for her marriage to Walter Gybbyns. Why that couple needs to raise money for their nuptials is a mystery to me, but we should attend. I've heard Joan brews a good ale, well worth the price."

"I suppose I can make a showing, but I can't afford too much time away from the loom. I need to produce as much as I can for next week's market. I'd like to invite John and Nicholas for a Bible study tomorrow eve, if you're agreeable to the idea." He held his breath.

"Bible study?" She pounded the oatcake dough with her right fist, as if she were suddenly angry at it. "Are you sure you want to start down that pathway so soon after we've been welcomed in Dartford? I thought we agreed to keep quiet for now."

"No one needs to know of our Bible study here." He exhaled his frustration.

She stopped kneading and glared at him. "Holding such meetings is dangerous. Bible-reading by the common folk has been forbidden for three years now. You, of all people, should understand the risk, after witnessing what happened to Lady Askew and all the turmoil we saw in London."

"We're uncommon folk," he teased. "We're just friends gathering for an evening of mirth. No one will know otherwise. But if you're uncomfortable with the idea, I'll respect your wishes." He waited a few seconds and added, "For now."

His curt tone when he said "for now" infuriated her. Was he making a threat? She slapped the cakes into shape, put them in an iron skillet and turned her back to place the skillet over hot coals, her heart pounding. She tried to bite her tongue, but the words tumbled out. "I'd rather we bide our time. Why put at risk the life we're working to build here? Besides, you and I read together every morning. Can't that be enough?"

"Very well. But mark my words: now that the door has opened and folks have God's word in the English tongue, no one will be able to close it again—not even the king."

Anne rubbed her hands together over the rubbish bin to remove the sticky dough before wiping them on a rag, and crossed the room to massage Christopher's shoulders. "Along with you, I look forward to a day when we can read and speak openly about these things. But is it worth risking your livelihood—even your life—when you can just as easily worship in private? Isn't it written in the Bible to pray in your closet?"

He turned, searching her eyes. "Tell me it doesn't bother your conscience to follow the ways of popery, such as attending the Romish church with its idolatrous mass, when you consider it blasphemy."

She pulled back. "You misspoke. 'Tis no longer the Romish church, 'tis the king's church."

"Yes," he quipped, "'tis the king's church—but not Christ's church."

"But the king has made changes, and perhaps in time the church will be purified. We need to have patience."

Christopher clenched his jaw. He found the Bible delicious and had an insatiable hunger to learn more. Nathan was right. Once Christopher read the book for himself, he understood why folks were willing to go to such great lengths to defend it.

"Come here, Milady." He rested the shuttle on the loom and pulled Anne onto his lap. "You gave me a reason to keep going when I wanted to give up. Your faith led me to wonder if the reformers knew something I didn't. Now I know the popish church has gone clean astray. So explain to me why, now, you're the one holding back."

The honest, penetrating look in his crystal blue eyes pricked her conscience. Looking past him, she replied, "Are you willing to be branded a Lollard again? It was the very reason you went to London and were afraid to come home."

Averting his gaze to the fire, he spent several seconds in quiet contemplation. "I suppose you're right," he sighed. "I don't want to put our future at risk."

She nestled her face against his neck and whispered, "I love you, and I never want to be without you." As he leaned forward to kiss her, she stiffened and sniffed the air. "The cakes!" Racing to the hearth, she grabbed a potholder and tugged the skillet out of the fire. Using both hands, she carried the pan to the table and set it down, blowing at the smoking cakes.

Christopher opened the front door to allow fresh air to circulate, but promptly closed it when a wind gust scattered rain and dried leaves inside the door.

"I suppose we won't be having cakes for supper," she moaned. Fetching two clay bowls from the cupboard she asked, "Are you ready for pottage?"

"Yes." He filled two cups with cider and placed them on the table. "Say, after supper, I do need to pay Nicholas a visit."

One of the bowls slipped from her hands and crashed to the floor, sending shards in all directions. Red-faced, she stammered, "Isn't Nicholas working in Maidstone?"

He squatted down and began picking up the largest pieces of broken shard. "No, I saw him yesterday when I went to speak with Simon Nix about my cart location on High Street. Nicholas just returned from Maidstone. He and his father will be working in Dartford to repair the livery from a fire that damaged two of the walls a fortnight ago."

After retrieving her twig broom next to the front door, she swept the remaining shards into a pile and knelt down with the dustpan in hand. "You spoke with Simon Nix, and lived to tell?"

"Amazing, isn't it? He says he hasn't had word about Thomas since the night Thomas ran away. That makes seven years."

"Seven years? My word. Wasn't Simon hostile toward you?" She swept the shards into the dustpan and tossed them in the rubbish bin before lifting the pottage from the tripod. "Could you put a pad on the table, please? I forgot."

Christopher folded a towel into a thick square and placed it in the middle of the table.

Seating himself, he cracked his knuckles and continued, "I would describe him as coldly cordial, but I wanted to extend an olive branch. I don't think he'll cause any problems." After sipping a spoonful of the hearty bowl of pottage she set in front of him, he declared, "Delicious."

"I'm happy you like it. Simon Nix should be apologizing to you for false accusations."

"I'm just glad he spoke with me."

She fetched another bowl from the cupboard, ladled some soup for herself, and joined him at the table. "You say Nicholas will be working in Dartford—just across from you?"

"Yes, at the livery."

An awkward silence ensued. He lifted the bowl to his lips to sip the last few drops of pottage, then set it on the table and rested his spoon inside. "You'll manage without me this afternoon?"

"I'll manage," she sighed, staring at her steaming bowlful of pottage.

"You seem hesitant." He eyed the skillet. "Those cakes might be salvageable." After retrieving a cake, he tore off a burnt edge and stuffed the entire thing in his mouth. She held her breath until he forced a smile and wiped his lips on his sleeve. "Not bad."

"Christopher—there is…something concerns me…" she trailed off.

"What is it, Milady? Tell me."

"Promise me you're not meeting with Nicholas today to study the Bible or plan a study group."

He shook his head. "Rumor has it the king is ill. We're going to chat about it."

"I just can't bear the thought of you making enemies—not now."

"I would never break my word to you. But do you realize if King Henry dies, the world will be turned on its head?" He looked toward the door. "Have you seen my cloak?"

"The world is already on its head. Your cloak isn't hanging on the peg?"

"No. I suppose I'll have to wear yours." His eyes twinkled with mischief.

"You'll do no such thing," she scolded. Scanning the room, she spied his cloak in a heap on the floor next to the loom. "There," she pointed. "Surely your mother taught you to hang up your cloak?"

"Shame on me." He hung his head in mock humility, scooped up the garment, and gave her a peck on the cheek. "See you later, Milady."

After he closed the door behind him, she shook her head. "My handsome man, indeed." Placing her elbows on the table, she rested her face in her hands with a frustrated sigh.

La Rochelle

A boisterous crowd milled about on the rain-splattered square in front of Notre Dame des Cougnes church. Folks from all walks of life paused in their daily routines to be present for the occasion. Some huddled in large groups, others stood alone, while others congregated in clusters of two or three. Angry thunderheads had just rolled over leaving in their wake damp, frigid afternoon air charged with human emotion.

Thomas shivered beneath his wool cloak, making a mental of note of folks who appeared distressed or stood apart from the crowd. Twisting his moustache, he studied facial expressions and mannerisms while folks caught up on the latest news of the village and exchanged opinions about the spectacle about to take place. Gabrielle watched it all as well, perched on her father's shoulders. Her brother, Anatole, was safely tucked away on the other side of the village at a friend's cottage.

Thomas' heart flip-flopped when a horse-drawn hurdle screeched to a stop in front of the church, bearing two men. Each was barefoot, wearing only a calf-length white chemise. A hush fell over the multitude.

"Papa, why are the men in their nightgowns?" Gabrielle asked.

"So they can be comfortable," he lied.

"Why do they wear a cord around their necks?"

"Chut." Thomas tapped his lips with his finger. "They're bad men. They must be punished for their misdeeds."

"What did the men do, Papa?" she pressed. A kindly, auburn-haired woman next to Thomas, a faithful parishioner who ran a bakery on Rue des Merciers, shot him a glance that conveyed sympathy for the difficulty of handling a child's tough questions.

"That one there," he pointed to Pascal. "He peddled books full of devilish lies. And the other," he nodded toward Jean-Luc, "he's a shipbuilder. He's friends with the book peddler, and he helped criminals escape from the kingdom. They both lied and tricked people," he explained, "and they must not be allowed to trick people anymore."

"Oh," she replied, trusting her father's answer.

Pascal and Jean-Luc were led to separate wooden scaffolds and instructed to kneel down, while the throng filed past them into the church. Thomas pressed his forefinger against Gabrielle's lips, gloating with satisfaction as he passed the men on his way into the church. "We must be quiet," he whispered. "The mass is beginning."

After mass, he found a place in the square with a good view and swung a giggling Gabrielle up on his shoulders. Following an impassioned discourse about the evils of heresy, the Bishop of Saintes faced Jean-Luc and asked, "Do you demand pardon from God and the very sacred Virgin Mary, and the saints, male and female, and the King and Justice for your erroneous blasphemies, and for troubling the public repose of the faithful?"

Several moments of silence elapsed while Jean-Luc scanned the crowd, his chest rising and falling rapidly, and beads of perspiration glistening around his hairline. Raising his voice loud enough to echo through the square and bounce off adjacent buildings, he cried, "Would that you would worship the true and living Christ, rather than the false idols of Babylon." The bishop's facial expression contorted in displeasure.

"No! Please God, no!" a sob rose from the back of the square. Thomas turned to see Jean-Luc's wife, Annette, dressed in black, her face red and blotchy, her eyes nearly swollen shut. She fell to her knees and raised her hands to heaven. Thomas heard a chortle, followed by heaving sobs that would have pricked the sympathy of even the most heartless criminal. Jean-Luc stretched his neck and moved his head to the left and the right, trying to spot her over the crowd.

"Take heart, my good wife," Jean-Luc choked. "We will meet again in paradise. Until then, heed the errors of Rome!"

"Silence him!" the constable shouted.

"You may silence me today," Jean-Luc shouted, "But God will have the last word." He bowed his head.

"And you." The bishop glared at Pascal, his eyes narrow. "Do you demand pardon from God and the sacred Virgin Mary, and the saints, both male and female, and the King and Justice for spreading malicious and erroneous doctrines, peddling forbidden books, and troubling the public repose of the faithful?"

"I wish all could read the words contained in the books this kingdom has forbidden," Pascal declared, "that they might resist the doctrines of Babylon."

A pocket of folks near the front hissed. Thomas chuckled when a raw egg hit Pascal's cheek and oozed down the heretic's neck. Another cracked against the side of Jean-Luc's head, and then another. The bishop nodded to an officer standing between the scaffolds. At the officer's approach, Jean-Luc shouted, "Beware the devils of Rome! Flee Babylon and embrace the true gospel."

"He speaks the truth," Pascal added. "Heed the truth!"

"Si-lence! Si-lence! Si-lence!" The chant began at the back of the throng and worked its way forward.

"No more will you devils trouble the faithful," the bishop proclaimed.

"You've been found guilty of high treason against God and mankind, and are obstinate in your refusal to recant." Jeers erupted as the crowd began to flow like a river toward City Hall, pulling Thomas with them.

"Where are we going now, Papa?" Gabrielle squeezed her father's hand as they shuffled along.

"To City Hall, *ma chérie*. They'll spend a short time in prison, then come outside to receive their punishment." Father and daughter walked along in silence until he tugged on her hand. "Here we are." He pointed to City Hall, a beautiful white building resembling a small castle with two narrow turrets and crenelated walls.

"Why are the horses bringing wood?" She pointed to a horse-drawn cart, laden with faggots, standing in the town square. Two ebony draft horses swished their tails and stamped their hooves, feeding on the crowd's energy.

"The officers are going to build a fire, *ma chérie*." Thomas squeezed her hand.

"Then we can warm ourselves," she clapped, hopping up and down. "I'm cold." Thomas swooped Gabrielle in his arms, tightened her green wool cloak around her, and encircled her tiny cold hands with his large, warm hands.

Jean-Luc and Pascal emerged from the town hall. After forcing an iron ball in each man's mouth, an officer slid the book pack on Pascal's back, and attached faggots to Jean-Luc's.

"I see the men!" Gabrielle waved her hand in their direction.

"Yes, they're ready." Thomas shuddered with adrenaline, watching drool drip from the corner of Pascal's mouth. Officers fastened them securely to the stake, back to back.

"Papa, what are they doing to the men?"
"Warming the men with the fire," he answered, his legs quivering.
As torches touched the base of the faggots, Thomas felt Gabrielle stiffen in his arms.

"Papa!" she cried, "they're lighting the men on fire! Stop them!" Twisting and writhing, she struggled to get down. Thomas turned her head to block her eyes.

A loud wail erupted from the midst of the crowd. "*Mon Dieu!*" the woman sobbed. "No! No! No!" Thomas recognized Annette's voice.

"Papa, they're hurting them!" Gabrielle's voice cracked. "Why is the woman crying?"

"They're bad men. Bad men must be burned. That is what God would want."

Thomas strode away from the scene with Gabrielle in his arms, turning down a side street where she couldn't look back to see the men or the bonfire. The stifling smell of burning flesh assaulted his nostrils, while cheers from the crowd echoed down the street. He had hoped to meet with Father Jean after the event to arrange his payment, but his personal affairs would have to wait until the morrow.

"We must get home, my sweet." He lifted her off his shoulders and balanced her on her feet. "Shall we race?" Her face brightening, she sprinted under an arcade. Thomas stole a last look in the direction of the town square. Eerie firelight flickered on the white limestone walls, while putrid smoke billowed up above the three- and four-story rooftops.

"Papa! Come!" Gabrielle demanded, seeing that her father had not yet started in her direction.

"I'm coming." He trotted toward her, pretending he wanted to catch up, but deliberately letting her win. She looked back every few seconds to make sure he was still following, until she reached the door of their cottage, panting.

"I beat you!" she exclaimed, laughing.

"Yes, you did. I'm no match for you." Thomas opened the door. They entered and warmed their hands in front of the fireplace.

February, 1547

———

Dartford

That's odd. Anne cocked her head. *The church bell?* After crossing the room to the window, she peered left, then right. Except for a few chickens pecking at the ground under the neighbor's cherry tree, all was quiet—a typical Tuesday morning.

The church bell tolled again. Several seconds passed. It tolled a third time. She held her breath and counted—one, two, three, four, five. On cue, the bell rang. The somber, plaintive peal could signal only one thing. Her heart skipped a beat. *The death knell!*

Breathless, she stood on her tiptoes, straining to see further down East Hill toward the village for a clue about what might be happening. The front door burst open and slammed against the plaster wall with a thud, rattling her nerves as well as the pots, pans and utensils hanging near the fireplace. She spun around, her heart in her throat.

"He's dead! King Henry is dead!" After spitting out the news, Christopher leaned forward with his hands on his knees, gasping for breath. Beads of perspiration trickled down his forehead.

"You scared me to death!" Anne crossed the room to close the door, frowning at flakes of plaster scattered on the floor where the door hit the wall. "You look as if you've run all the way from Crayford. His Majesty is dead? When did that happen?"

"A few days ago. Word is just getting out." His breathing still labored, Christopher plopped on a stool and removed his cap to reveal a damp mess of matted blonde hair. "I just came from High Street. The papists are already in an uproar. 'Tis a precious sight." He bounced to his feet, wrapped Anne in a tight embrace and spun her around. While landing her on the floor he exclaimed, "Do you realize this could change everything?"

"You're this giddy about a nine-year-old prince?" she stammered, out of breath.

Christopher pranced to the window and peered down the hill. "Yes. He'll get the papists off our heels. We'll be able to read the Bible freely. He'll strip the church of popery—at least that's what folks on both sides are saying."

"I think you've lost your mind."

"No, trust me." Pacing in front of the window he explained, "Prince Edward has been surrounded by reform-minded folks his entire life. The day we've been praying for is finally here! I came home to tell you the news and see if you want to join me in celebrating at the Crown & Anchor. I don't want to miss a minute of the end of the papists' reign of terror. *And there shall be weeping, and wailing, and gnashing of teeth.* Ha! I can't wait to see Amy's face."

As he moved toward the door, Anne grabbed his elbow and pulled him back. "Slow down. Do you think the papists will sit back and twiddle their thumbs? What if they mount a resistance?"

"Let them. The king has his armies and God to protect him." Like a flash of lighting in a clear blue sky, defiance lit up his eyes. "Come with me to the tavern. It will be priceless, trust me."

Against her better judgment, Anne retrieved her cloak and gloves.

Reverberation from the commotion inside the Crown & Anchor seeped outside the tavern walls into the bone-chilling afternoon air. Nicholas, Christopher and Anne exchanged glances as they approached the door.

"Sounds like a jousting contest is going on in there," Anne whispered, her breath leaving a puff of white steam in front of her.

"It's a jousting contest all right," Christopher grinned, "a jousting of ideas. *En garde!*" He and Nicholas were slicing the air with imaginary daggers when the unmistakable silhouettes of Edward Bartholomew and Father Garrett darkened the bay window at the front of the tavern. Edward raised a fist toward the priest. Nicholas and Christopher exchanged wide-eyed glances.

Elbowing her husband, Anne whispered, "Promise me you won't do anything foolish."

"Me, foolish? This is going to be even better than I thought. I think I'll dance a jig on a tabletop to celebrate. Ready?" He winked at Nicholas.

"Don't you dare!" Anne gasped.

"Well, Christopher," Nicholas smirked, "you did dance on that table at The Anchor in Southwark."

Rolling her eyes, Anne moaned, "I wouldn't put it past him."

Christopher stretched his hand toward the door handle while Anne and Nicholas held their breath. Without warning the door flew open, knocking Christopher sideways as the tavern spewed out Edward Bartholomew. The baker landed on his rear-end several feet from the tavern porch.

"And stay out, you filthy babbler!" Tom Coppinger bellowed, the slamming door putting a final exclamation point on his anger.

Edward looked up sheepishly at his astonished audience. Before reaching for Nicholas' extended hand, he wiped the blood from his scraped palm on his breeches.

"I wouldn't go in there, if that's what you were intending," Edward grumbled, dusting off his clothes.

"What happened?" Christopher asked, noting the front of Edward's jerkin was soaked.

"It seems all the papists in Dartford are in the tavern conspiring to destroy us," Edward sighed. "I raised my fists to defend myself when Father Garrett threatened to douse me with his ale. You can see what good that did. Amy told me in no uncertain terms that 'my kind' are not welcome in her tavern. And her husband made good on her threat."

"But...but they lost. King Edward is in charge now," Nicholas asserted. "They have no right. We can't let them get away with it. I'm going in. Who's coming with me?"

A sideways glance from Anne warned Christopher he would face her wrath if he joined Nicholas. A shrug of the shoulders was all he dared offer as she kept her eyes on him.

"I'm not saying I'll never challenge them," Edward said, the veins on his thin, long neck bulging, "but I've had enough for one evening. Trust me, you'll be vastly outnumbered if you go in there. You might as well dance on a hornet's nest."

"Very well," Nicholas sighed. "But you won't find me surrendering to the papists like a scolded puppy. And I saw that." He was referring to Christopher's eyeroll.

"I'm certainly not surrendering," Edward countered. "Let's fight them with all we've got, but let's go about it the right way. With the king on our side, we have nothing to fear." He paused for a moment, then smiled. "Come over to my place. My wife just made a batch of fresh cider and rye bread."

London

Weary of staring at the backs of people's knees, her eyelids heavy and her teeth chattering, young Grace whimpered, "I want to go home."

"Perhaps you need a better view," Piers chirped, swooping her up on his shoulders.

Forgetting her complaint, she shrieked at her view over the heads of the crowd. Folks tall and short, thin and round, young and old crowded in to witness the gala procession honoring Prince Edward, about to be crowned king. Curious faces peered from behind latticed windows of three- and four-story timber-framed buildings, while onlookers tottered precipitously on rooftops. The multitude on Cheapside represented only a small sampling of the folks gathered throughout the city, stretched between the Tower and Westminster Abbey.

Piers wiggled his toes, numb after four hours of standing in the cold. "Do you see anything, muffin?" he asked.

Her eyes wide with wonder, Grace screeched, "I see a tightrope walker, and minstrels, and a man with a monkey!" After allowing her a couple of minutes to view the festivities, Piers lowered her to his bosom. She nestled her head against his chest, shivering.

Standing on her tiptoes, Molly hoped for a better view up and down the street. "'Tis after three o'clock," she noted. "The prince was to have left the Tower at one. His procession should be along any moment."

Piers stifled a yawn. "He must have been delayed with the entertainments folks prepared for him." He stretched to see over the crowd when a slow-moving ripple of shouts moved in their direction.

"I hear trumpets!" Charlotte exclaimed, her heart bursting with joy as the crowd broke into a chant:

Sing up heart, sing up heart, sing no more down,
But joy in King Edward that weareth the crown!

"I see him!" Charlotte pointed. "He's riding a white mount and wearing a gold gown. Two men in armor flank him, and several yeomen are walking in front and behind. He glitters like a god, covered in jewels." She paused to drink in the sight and sighed, "He looks so young."

Lifting her head from Piers' bosom Grace muttered, "I want to see, Father." He hoisted her up on his chest, only to hear her complain when a tall man in front of them blocked the view.

"I'll take her." Charlotte extended her arms.

Piers frowned. "Have you forgotten?"

Glancing down at her protruding belly, Charlotte relented. "Let me trade with you then." They shuffled places, and Piers lifted Grace once again.

"I see him!" Grace pointed in the direction of the oncoming procession.

"I see him too," Molly exclaimed, precipitously stretched on her tiptoes. "A lovely sight, he is. And he does sparkle as the sun."

"Only nine years old," Piers mused. "A boy king, like Josiah of Israel."

A lad sporting a costume to represent Truth sprang from the crowd to bow in front of the procession. Shouting above the noise he exhorted the new king, "Embrace God's truth, as your father has done. Then shall England, committed to your guard, rejoice in God, which hath given her nation, after an old David, a young king Solomon." With a wave and a nod, the prince acknowledged the young man.

Charlotte placed her hand over her heart, feeling it might leap from her chest. Would folks now embrace truth? Would God's lambs cease to be hunted as prey? Did God send this boy king, as King Josiah of ancient Israel, to destroy the idolatry and tyranny of the bishops of Rome? Piers and Molly were convinced of it, as were many of Charlotte's new friends in London.

Watching Grace's face light up at the passing king, Charlotte wished her children were by her side to witness the monumental event. She endeavored to soak in every detail so she could one day tell them, when a flutter within her womb reminded her at least one of her children was present.

"Charlotte." Molly's voice pulled her out of her trance. "Charlotte, you look pale."

"Thank you, Molly. I'm well enough." As soon as Charlotte spoke, a sharp pain shot through her abdomen. She clasped her belly with a moan.

"Let's get you home and fetch the midwife. All this revelry is upsetting the baby." Molly leaned close to Piers to explain Molly's predicament.

"Here?" he frowned.

Molly nodded.

"But she assured us it wasn't her time yet," he protested, incredulous.

"Look at her," Molly insisted. Seizing an opening in the crowd, she linked elbows with Charlotte on one side and took Grace's hand on the other and proceeded down a side street, stirring up glares and murmurs from disrupted onlookers.

"The wench should be in her chamber," snarled a woman with long, grey hair who looked like a witch. "Imagine, risking her babe to the noise of horns and cannons."

Charlotte's knees buckled in another wave of pain.

"We have to get her to Nathan and Lucy's house," Molly panted. "We'll never get home in this crowd."

"What if she delivers?" In Piers' mind, it was the worst of all possibilities imaginable.

"You and Nathan need to fetch a midwife, while Lucy and I stay with

Charlotte," Molly directed.

"But all of London is watching the procession," Piers protested.

"Piers, listen to me. You have no choice. The mother and child are at stake."

When they reached the Wade home Molly knocked on the door, waited a couple of seconds, and knocked again. She jiggled the door handle. It was unlocked.

Reaching past her, Piers covered her hand with his and shook his head. "We can't simply barge in as thieves."

"They'll understand. We have to get her out of the cold."

They entered the cottage and settled Charlotte on the floor next to the fireplace, where glowing coals offered welcome warmth. Molly fetched a blanket while continuing to plead for Piers to find a midwife.

"The entire city is along the procession route," he argued.

"Speak with folks. God will provide." She hissed out her frustration. "I'll try to keep her comfortable."

"Very well," he sighed. "Hopefully, I won't be too late."

When the door closed behind him, Molly found a kitchen towel and knelt next to Charlotte. "Fine time for him to act so stubborn. How are your pains?"

"They seem to have quieted." Charlotte leaned back against the wall while Molly dabbed beads of perspiration from around her hairline.

"Perhaps we'll have time to get you home," Molly said.

"I'm sorry I ruined the day. It's the grandest spectacle I've ever witnessed. Your husband mentioned King Josiah?"

"Yes, many expect that he'll purge idolatry from the land, like King Josiah in the Bible. They say Prince Edward is wise beyond his years. We're praying that God will use him to do a mighty work in England. How I hope we might become a true Christian nation."

Averting her gaze to the wall across the room, Charlotte began to massage her abdomen.

"More pains?" Molly stiffened.

"No, I'm thinking of my child. I hope the baby can live in a true Christian nation."

Their conversation ended abruptly when Nathan and Lucy burst through the door, followed by Piers and a petite, grey-haired woman wearing a peasant's frock. Introducing her to Charlotte, Lucy explained, "Mother Cecily delivered our children and grandchildren. She's a fine midwife."

Motioning for Piers to follow him Nathan told the women, "We'll be in the kitchen. Lucy, is there something I can do—heat pottage, or make tea?"

"Put some water on for tea," his wife nodded. "We'll be over shortly."

"I don't believe the baby's comin' just yet," Cecily said, smoothing the blanket over Charlotte's torso. "Do you have other children?"

The question stung. "Yes, two others. I didn't have this sort of pain with them."

"My advice is to take to your chamber and stay there 'til you're delivered. The activity and noise must have upset the baby."

Offering her hand to help Cecily to her feet, Lucy said, "I'm sorry we interrupted your viewing of the procession."

"It's all my fault," Charlotte frowned, moving to her knees to stand.

"Stop! Don't strain!" Cecily lurched forward. With a firm hand on Charlotte's shoulder she said, "The prince is young, with a long life ahead of him, God willin'. I'll have many chances to see 'im."

"He sparkled like the sun," Charlotte mused as she closed her eyes and leaned back against the wall.

"Yes, he did," Cecily smiled. "I managed to catch a glimpse of him. 'Twas a sight to behold. Long live King Edward."

A rap on the door interrupted them. Peeking his head in Nathan smiled, relieved to see the women calmly conversing. "The pottage is hot, and water is ready for tea. Cecily, you're welcome to join us."

"I must run along," Cecily replied. Shaking a finger at Charlotte she admonished, "Heed my advice."

"I will." Charlotte forced a smile.

Molly and Lucy linked arms with Charlotte and helped her to the kitchen where, over warm pottage and tea, the group speculated about King Edward's future. Several minutes passed in joyful camaraderie when suddenly, Molly raised a finger and cocked an ear toward the door.

"Did you hear that?" she whispered. Piers and Nathan paused briefly, then continued conversing. "Shh," she insisted. "There it is again." She hurried to the door, peeked out, and thrust it open with a moan. "Oh, my dear Grace! You were so quiet, I forgot you were with us. We closed the door before you could come in."

"My fingers and toes froze," Grace stammered, making a beeline for her father.

"I'm sure they did, my dear," Lucy sympathized. "Let me get you some pottage, and you'll be thawed in no time." Lucy dished up a half ladle of the soup and set it in front of Grace, now seated on her father's lap.

Noting the dimming light outside the window, Molly turned to Piers. "We need to get Charlotte home where she can rest—and Grace too."

"Revelers will be out all night," Nathan interjected. "The streets are already glowing with bonfires and running with ale. You're welcome to spend the night here, if you'd like. We have two extra chambers."

Molly rushed her hands to her cheeks.

"What is it now?" Piers said, blowing on his mint tea.

"What kind of mother am I? We forgot about Simon and Mark. We can't have them roaming the streets of London like stray hounds."

Piers sent Grace to sit with her mother and crossed the room to retrieve his cloak. "Thank goodness tomorrow's the Sabbath," he mumbled. "I'll definitely need a day of rest after today."

"I'll come with you," Nathan offered.

After donning their cloaks, the two men slipped outside.

March, 1547

———

Dartford

Barren. Cursed. A garden where nothing would grow. After several months of marriage, still without child, Anne jumped at Elizabeth's invitation to spend the morning learning of herbal remedies and other cures. It was no secret that Elizabeth wished for a grandchild as much as Anne wished for a child.

Given Elizabeth's penchant to talk, Christopher figured he had at least until the noon bell tolled before Anne came home, and he intended to put the time to good use. Hungry to learn more about King Josiah, and since the story wasn't in his Tyndale Bible, he'd borrowed John's Matthew's Bible and didn't dare keep it too long. He stretched out on his bed, opened to Second Kings chapter twenty-two and read,

> *Josiah was eight years old when he began to reign, and he reigned thirty and one years in Jerusalem…and he did that which was right in the sight of the Lord, and walked in all the way of David his father, and turned not aside to the right hand or to the left.*

Eight years old. A year younger than King Edward. Apart from their ages, Christopher wondered why people were comparing Kind Edward to King Josiah. Reading on, he learned that the ancient Israelites' temple had fallen into disrepair as the Israelites pursued idolatry. When King Josiah hired workers to repair the temple, a high priest named Hilkiah discovered within the temple ruins the book of the law given to Moses. Hilkiah passed the book to Shaphan, a scribe, who read it and brought it to Josiah.

And Shaphan the scribe shewed the king, saying, 'Hilkiah the priest hath delivered me a book.' And Shaphan read it before the king. And it came to pass, when the king had heard the words of the book of the law, that he rent his clothes…

Rent his clothes? What message in the book did the king find so distressing? Christopher wished he could discuss this with John and Nicholas; it tortured him that they held Bible discussions without him. He resolved to find a moment to talk about the story with Nicholas the next time they were both working on High Street.

He continued, reading King Josiah's instructions to Hilkiah:

Go ye, inquire of the Lord for me, and for the people, and for all Judah, concerning the words of this book that is found: for great is the wrath of the Lord that is kindled against us, because our fathers have not hearkened unto the words of this book, to do according unto all that which is written concerning us…they have forsaken me, and have burned incense unto other gods, that they might provoke me to anger with the works of their hands…

Staring at the flickering fire, Christopher wondered how a people so favored with miracles—deliverance from Egyptian bondage, the parting of the Red Sea, manna from heaven, water from a rock—could have strayed so far from their God. Did wicked kings become their downfall? Or was it their love of pleasure, and the allure of gold and fine things?

They forsook my law. The words popped into his mind. Of course, he thought. Neglecting God's word led to the downfall of a once-favored people—just as the Roman church's practice of withholding God's word from folks led to idolatry.

Reading on, he learned that King Josiah gathered all the elders in the land and caused the book to be read to them. In like fashion, Nicholas, John, and other reform-minded friends said King Edward would have the English people instructed in the Bible. *I hope so*, he whispered.

His stomach rumbled, but he hungered for truth more than food and read on. King Josiah covenanted to follow the Lord and keep the commandments in the book of the law, then exhorted his people to do the same. Intent on cleansing his kingdom, the king ordered objects used to worship the false god Baal destroyed. He removed idolatrous priests, punished wizards and soothsayers, and tore down images and altars used to worship false gods. *Like the reformers now*, Christopher thought.

He closed the Bible and rolled onto his back, contemplating the war of opinions raging about him, in England and lands across the British Sea. Pilgrimages banned; statues and altars removed; monasteries closed. Did these royal reforms parallel King Josiah's actions? As his eyelids fluttered closed, he pictured King Josiah reading from the book of the law for the first time as he, himself, read the Bible for the first time at Nathan's house. From kings to linen weavers, he mused, God's word roused souls and changed the courses of nations. With the story of Josiah on his mind, he drifted off to sleep.

The screech of the front door hinges startled him awake.

"Napping, are you?" Anne placed on the table a basket brimming with goods from her mother-in-law and proceeded to remove its contents. "Two Richard Crispe artichokes, first of the season. Your mother assures me we should eat artichokes as often as possible." After plopping the artichokes on the table, she retrieved a cloth bag closed with a drawstring and took a deep whiff. "Dried leaves of nettle and raspberry. I'm to make a tea and drink it every morning and evening—to warm my humors." Leaning the bag against an artichoke she explained, "And she told me you must eat oysters, which is easy since Father will supply us." Next, she pulled a piece of paper from the basket and waved it in the air. "A recipe for oyster pie." Christopher smirked. Her hand rummaged around the bottom of the basket until she produced a small trinket. "A Saint Thomas badge from Canterbury Cathedral."

Bolting upright, Christopher barked, "No! I draw the line there. The badge is a false idol. I've just finished reading about how false idols brought down ancient Israel. Mother should have done away with it years ago. She's a rebel, I tell you."

"An idol?" Turning the pewter image of Saint Thomas back and forth in her hand, Anne retorted, "She didn't ask us to worship it; she suggested I wear it under my shift for good luck. She also recommended a pilgrimage to Walsingham. Did you know almost five hundred years ago the Virgin appeared to a woman there, and instructed her to build a house to honor the holy family of Nazareth? A holy relic—a vial of the Virgin's milk—was kept there before the dissolution. Your mother claims that destroying the shrine didn't destroy its power."

Red-faced, he slid off the bed, took three long strides to the table and slapped his open hand against the wood, rattling the objects of Anne's hope. "What are you doing?" he demanded. "You know better than this. My mother is steeped in popish ways." Defiant, she tightened her grip on the trinket and averted her gaze to the floor. "Besides," he continued, "when would we ever find the time or the means to travel to Walsingham? 'Tis even further than Canterbury. It would take a fortnight to travel there and back."

She inched her gaze up to meet his. "Aren't you willing to do anything to have a child?" she stammered, tears pooling in her eyes.

"Anything short of popish superstition," he jeered. "Artichokes and oysters and herbal tea, yes. But I won't be calling upon the powers of charms or traveling long distances to worship idols, and I forbid you to even think of it."

She glared at him, her bottom lip twitching. "You're starting to sound like your father."

Impervious to her display of emotion he retorted, "And you like yours. You attended the meetings in London even before I did. You admired Lady Askew. Now, all of a sudden, you're blind to popish traditions?"

White-knuckling the figure of Saint Thomas she asserted, "I'm willing to do anything to be a mother."

Christopher stomped to the bed, closed the Bible and pushed it under his pillow. Hissing out an annoyed sigh he quipped, "I suppose we'll be having oyster and artichoke pottage for supper tonight?"

He watched her face turn crimson as she narrowed her eyes and drew back her arm. Just in time, he ducked to avoid the Saint Thomas badge hurled in his direction. She stormed out the door. He shook his head. Her volatile behavior sometimes mystified him.

April, 1547

———

"**P**iers tells me he hopes to set sail for La Rochelle in May or June." Plunging a staff up and down in the butter churn, Molly puckered her lips and blew upward to force a ringlet of red hair out of her eyes. "Has he spoken with you?"

"No, he hasn't said anything," Charlotte replied, pouring barley into a large ale vat. "Did he mention whether he'll be able to take a passenger?" She crossed the kitchen for water to add to the vat.

"I didn't ask him, but I will if you would like," Molly said. "He's been occupied more than usual with the Clothworker's Company. He's looking into a new wool market." After a long pause she complained, "The boys should be doing the churning. With Agnes ill, the work is piling up. I hope she'll be over her catarrh soon."

"I believe the boys are working on their grammar." Charlotte chose a long-handled spoon from a hook next to the fireplace to stir the barley and water mixture. "I saw them with their hornbooks. Would you like me to fetch them?"

"If they're occupied with study, let's leave them be. Those boys will be the death of me, I tell you. They're nothing but mischief, from sunup to sundown, and they ignore my correction."

Thinking Molly should be grateful to have her boys with her, Charlotte changed the subject. "Does Agnes speak of her days at the Dartford Priory?"

"No. I've learned to avoid that topic. She came from France, you know? Many of the Dartford nuns were French."

"Yes, I spoke with her about it. She seems terribly bitter about King Henry dissolving the priory. Her sympathies clearly lie with the Roman church."

Molly stopped churning to rest against the plunging staff. "As do the sympathies of many English folks. The practices of the church are changing, but until the hearts of the people change, I see trouble ahead. I can't blame her for being angry. All she ever wanted was to be a nun, yet she had to make a new life for herself."

Following Molly's lead, Charlotte stopped stirring to rest her aching arms. "What do you think of the riots in the city last week? Master Winston told me a statue of the virgin was found in front of St. Paul's decapitated, with her arms and legs broken off. He said a group of lads roaming the streets broke out all of the windows and smashed statues in a private chantry on the outskirts of London."

Molly nodded and resumed churning. "They used the excuse that since King Edward is going to do away with idolatry, they're simply helping him out. I think this growing violence and lawlessness is terrifying. The papists won't sit idly by forever." She opened the churn to check the progress of the butter. "Ah, yes. It looks perfect." Scooping the creamy spread into three stoneware crocks, she cocked her head. "Do I hear the baby crying?" Both women hushed for several seconds.

"I hear him," Charlotte replied. "Excuse me." She scurried upstairs and returned a couple of minutes later with the infant in her arms. "If it please you, I need just a few minutes to nurse him."

"Of course," Molly smiled. "You really should accept my offer to hire a wet nurse. 'Twould free you from the burden of constant feeding." The infant smiled and cooed at her. "Hello, little Joseph," she waved. "Oh yes, you are precious." Joseph wiggled his arms and legs.

"Thank you for your kindness, but I prefer to feed him myself." Charlotte moved toward the door until Molly's voice stopped her.

"Please, stay here. No one will bother us. Besides, I'd like to speak with you about some pressing matters."

Charlotte's heart dropped. She hated discussing her situation. It was too desperate, too painful, too complicated, but she managed a polite nod and sat on a stool in the corner of the room with a blanket over her torso while the infant suckled.

"What is on your mind?" Charlotte asked.

"I heard tell that your king—King Francis—died last month. Can you believe he died just two months after King Henry? Do you suppose the two of them are jousting in heaven?" While she spoke, Molly scraped every last bit of butter from the churn and divided it among the three crocks.

"More likely dancing over flames in the other place," Charlotte snorted. "*François au grand nez.*"

"François who?" Molly asked.

"Francis with the big nose." Charlotte waited for Molly to stop chuckling and explained, "It's his nickname."

"Perhaps we should call our former king 'Henry *au grand arse,*' Molly winked. She rushed her hands over her cheeks. "Oh, my. I'm a Christian woman. I can't believe those words slipped from my lips. But everyone speaks of how fat he was the last few years."

"Sometimes kings aren't so easy to love." Charlotte's eyes flashed in anger. "I wish France could have an Edward."

"Do you know anything of King Francis' successor?" Molly moved toward Charlotte to admire the baby.

"I don't know for certain. Most likely his son, Henry."

"Will Henry be sympathetic to reformers?"

"I don't know that either, but I intend to return to France for Gabrielle and Anatole. We'll build a new life here. Your husband promised to help me."

"Piers has connections everywhere. If anyone can help you, he can."

"He mentioned a shipbuilder in La Rochelle. I believe the name was Jean-Luc something."

"My husband knows many réformées in La Rochelle. He's been going there for years. He delivers books about the new learning to believers. He may have even given some to this Jean-Luc."

At Molly's words, Charlotte felt a surge of hope. She placed baby Joseph over her shoulder and patted his back while Molly stepped back, studying Charlotte as if she wanted to say something.

"Is there something else?" Charlotte asked, giggling when Joseph let out a loud burp.

"Oh, precious boy," Molly chuckled. "Will you—I don't know how to ask this, so I suppose I'll just blurt it out. Do you plan on taking the baby with you to France?"

The thought of leaving Joseph behind lacerated Charlotte's already wounded spirit, but she'd considered the problem from every angle. Traveling with a baby posed too great a risk, both for mother and infant.

She replied, "If I take him, I'll risk losing all three of my children to their father in France. Thomas mustn't have him." She blinked back the moisture pooling in her eyes.

"Here." Molly reached for the baby. Joseph whimpered for a moment, then calmed down and babbled as Molly paced in front of Charlotte. "Piers and I discussed it, and we'd like to keep Joseph for you. I can assure you he'll be in good hands, if that's any consolation. Agnes will be a great help as well."

Dabbing at her eyes with the corner of her apron, Charlotte sniffed, "I have no words to thank you. God brought me here, I have no doubt."

Molly stopped pacing and gazed tenderly at the strong, resilient woman she'd grown to deeply admire. "I've never had to be in a position like yours, thank God, but my heart has grieved for you from the moment you came. Piers and I pray for you every day."

"Thank you. I'll never be able to repay you."

"Don't be silly. I'll speak with Piers tonight, if I have the chance, and let you know what his plans are. I'm sure he'll speak to you himself at some point." Molly slipped Joseph, now sleeping peacefully, into his mother's arms, and whispered, "Take a break. You've been working hard all day."

"You'll excuse me while I go upstairs with Joseph for a few moments?"

"Take all the time you need." Molly listened to Charlotte's footsteps on the stairs, then bowed her head and prayed, "Bless her, Father. She needs a miracle."

July, 1547

———

La Rochelle

Charlotte strained to hear the goings-on above deck as the harbor master boarded to inspect the ship. She licked her fingers, tucked a few stray hairs under her cap, then smoothed the hose and breeches Piers purchased for her in London. The tan leather jerkin proved to be a bit roomy, but at least it somewhat concealed her womanly shape. It wasn't a perfect disguise, but she hoped it would get her to the shipbuilder's home without being recognized.

"You make a right pretty man," one of the ship hands winked as he passed by.

"Let us pray I'll get where I need to go," she blushed.

From her position below deck, she heard shipmen crisscross the vessel, doors creak open and closed, and inspectors make the rounds to remove all munitions, to be returned when the ship departed. She could just discern Piers' voice and the low, gravelly voice of the harbor master as they discussed the ship's cargo and intended length of stay.

When an inspector stopped to look her up and down, her heart pounded so hard she feared he might hear it. With a thick French accent, he inquired, "You're one of the crew?"

She swallowed hard and nodded.

He continued on, stopping once to take a second look at her over his shoulder. She heard his footsteps tap up a flight of stairs and across the deck. After a shout from the inspector to the harbor master, the ship listed and jolted forward. Charlotte ran up the stairs and crossed to the deck rail to watch the approach. A wave of emotion swept over her as she laid eyes on the bustling port, framed with luminescent limestone buildings that earned the village the nickname "The White City."

Her wonderful, terrible country—nursing mother and merciless captor! A lump caught in her throat as the *St. Thomas* passed the Chain and Saint Nicholas towers, standing as sentinels at the mouth of the port. The Bay of Biscay's salty air tickled her nostrils, while screeching gulls and the familiar banging and clanging of workers along the water's edge reminded her of the past she couldn't escape.

Rallying her courage, she vowed to remain stoic and allow nothing to distract her from her purpose. The words echoed in her mind, spoken to her heart weeks earlier by the still, small voice: *I will give you strength.*

After docking, Piers directed his men to unload the cargo before allowing them shore leave. Mingled with the sailors, Charlotte slipped off the ship carrying only a shoulder-sack stuffed with a nightshirt, gown and the money she'd managed to save. A wink and a nod from Piers communicated his well-wishes.

She'd committed to memory the directions Piers gave her, and had no trouble finding the shipbuilder's dwelling, a two-story apartment adjacent to the seaside rampart. Charlotte knocked and waited, admiring the skill of the mason who had carved lily flowers and a Zeus-like head into the limestone post and lintel door frame. The oak door, like the door frame, reflected the shipbuilder's wealth. It was the work of a master craftsman, carved with elaborate diamonds, circles and scrolls. She knocked again and heard footsteps pounding down a staircase. The door creaked open.

"Yes?" Standing a head above Charlotte, the woman peering down with wide, bulging eyes looked nothing like Piers' description of a petite, reserved shipbuilder's wife.

Suddenly insecure, Charlotte cleared her throat. "Pardon. I'm looking for Monsieur Mercier."

"Mm-hmm." The woman's probing gaze crawled from Charlotte's cap downward, stopping at her chest. Charlotte crossed her arms. As the woman scrunched her nose like a rabbit, her eyes rose to meet Charlotte's. "He's no longer here, but you'll find his wife living near the rampart on the other side of the village."

"Oh?" Clearly, Piers had not been up-to-date regarding Jean-Luc's where-abouts. "Could you tell me how to get there?"

"Of course. Are you familiar with the village?"

Charlotte nodded.

"Take the Rue du Temple to the Rue des Merciers. Continue along that street until you come to its end. A short way ahead you'll see a small shack next to a stone cottage. She lives in the shack. Anything else?"

"No. Thank you." The heavy door screeched closed. Charlotte adjusted the bag over her shoulder and started through the village, her heavy boots clicking on the stone streets. A curious glance here and there prompted her to pick up her gait and avoid eye contact.

Upon reaching the end of Rue des Merciers she stopped in her tracks, confused. Had Piers thoroughly misled her? A stone's throw away, on a plot of weed-infested ground, stood a shanty barely fit for animals, much less a home for a wealthy shipbuilder. She high-stepped through the weeds and lightly tapped on the door, concerned if she knocked too hard the rotting door would break loose from its rusty hinges.

A woman about five feet tall, slightly hunchbacked, emerged from behind the building, clasping a bundle of mint in her left hand.

"May I help you?" Annette inquired.

Charlotte swallowed hard. The woman's charcoal-brown eyes oozed pain, as if more sorrow had been poured into her than she could absorb.

"I'm looking for Monsieur Jean-Luc Mercier. Piers Winston sent me."

Annette's mouth twitched as she averted her eyes to the ground. "Jean-Luc no longer lives in La Rochelle." Her lips barely moved when she spoke, as if speaking were a task requiring too much energy.

After several seconds of awkward silence, Charlotte pressed, "Could you direct me to where he lives? I have very important business with him."

Annette pursed her lips, still staring at the ground. "He is dead."

Dead. The word struck Charlotte like a cannon ball to the stomach.

"But—you must be mistaken. Piers Winston told me Monsieur Mercier is a shipbuilder in La Rochelle."

Slowly raising her gaze to meet Charlotte's Annette croaked, "I'm his wife, Madame. I assure you, I'm not mistaken."

Charlotte's heart skipped a beat. "Not alive?" She leaned forward and lowered her voice. "I must speak with you privately. It's urgent."

Annette shook her head. "I'm weeding my garden. Perhaps another time."

"Please, Madame, give me just a few moments. I won't have another chance. I've come a long way—all the way from England—to meet with your husband." Uttering a silent prayer, she added, "I'm in grave danger."

Annette studied Charlotte for several seconds, her demeanor softening. "Very well, but I have only a few minutes. Come around." Once inside, Annette demanded, "Why are you seeking my husband?"

"I was told he might help me get my children out of La Rochelle."

"Who are you?"

Charlotte removed her cap and pulled out hairpins one by one, her auburn hair falling in sections to frame her face.

Annette's eyes widened. "Have I seen you around the village?"

"I used to live here, but I've been in England the past year. I left my children here when my husband threatened to turn me in to authorities. I'll have no peace until I get them out."

"You're a réformée?" Annette asked, her voice raw.

Charlotte nodded.

"Then you'll understand," Annette replied, the muscles around her mouth twitching. "The papists arrested Jean-Luc. Then they burned him. I'll never forgive them."

"I'm sorry," Charlotte whispered, averting her gaze to the dirt floor.

"You came for your children?"

Charlotte nodded.

"You'll never leave with them, trust me. The authorities will kill you unless you recant, and perhaps even if you do. They'll take everything you own. They took my husband and our beautiful home near the port. They took our furniture, linens, tools and jewelry—everything we spent our lives working for. Look at me now, living like a pig," she spit, eyeing her surroundings with derision. "Who is your husband?"

"I doubt if you know him. Thomas Nix." Charlotte held her breath, waiting for a reaction.

Annette gasped, "The Englishman?"

"Yes. Do you know him?"

With a flash of hatred in her eyes Annette responded, "All the réformées know him. He's a cruel man—a monster. We can't prove it, but we think he's an informer for the clergy. If I were you, I would turn around and sail back to England while you have a chance." She set the mint sprigs on a wood crate that functioned as a table. "You'll never save your children, not with this man in the way."

Charlotte felt a gnawing pinch in her stomach.

"I'm sorry to give you this bitter news, but it is better for you to know the truth. The réformées have been silenced. No one dares to speak up. Many have recanted to save their lives." Annette waited for a response, but Charlotte managed only a blank stare. "Jean-Luc was to help you, was he?"

Biting her lower lip, Charlotte whispered, "Yes."

"He would have, I am sure. He was that sort of man. They burned him in the town square, along with a book peddler who sold him forbidden books. I suspect your husband had a hand in their arrest."

Feeling weak-kneed, Charlotte stammered, "I don't know what to say."

"You look pale. May I get you a drink?" Annette motioned for Charlotte to sit on a rough-hewn, three-legged stool.

"You're most kind." Discovering that one leg of the stool was shorter than the other two, Charlotte rocked back and forth to find a stable position.

Annette returned with white wine in a teacup. "A poor substitute for a chair, isn't it?" she complained, handing the cup to Charlotte. "And this is a poor substitute for a goblet. Tell me, how did you come to be married to this monster, this Nix?"

In no mood to relive her past Charlotte offered an abbreviated version, telling of how her father rescued Thomas from the estuary outside Bordeaux, and of his change when she began to study the reformed faith.

"That's how it is with some men," Annette observed. She pulled the top wood crate from a stack and sat on it. "Gentle as a lamb to win your hand. After the nuptial ceremony, a tyrant takes over. Thank God, Jean-Luc was not like that." She studied Charlotte for several seconds and asked, "Where will you go if you don't return to England?"

With a shrug of her shoulders, Charlotte replied, "I don't know what to do now. I'm stuck. They'll arrest me here."

"You're welcome to stay with me while you think things through." Annette looked around the room apologetically.

"But I'm a stranger to you." The stool wobbled, causing Charlotte's wine to slosh over the brim of the cup.

"It's what Jean-Luc would wish me to do. Excuse me." Annette disappeared for several seconds and returned with a folded rag. She invited Charlotte to stand while she slipped it under the short stool leg. "There, that will help. You just came off a ship; you don't need more rocking. At any rate, you came expecting to find Jean-Luc. I can't offer you much, as you can see, but you may stay here. If I were you, I would return to England."

Charlotte shook her head. "I wasn't prepared for this. I only know I can't leave my children with Thomas."

"One is rarely prepared for life's bitter turns. Perhaps a good meal and a night's rest will help you think more clearly."

Despite wanting to protest that her problems were far too great to be solved with a night of sleep, Charlotte decided the complexities of one's circumstances could never be adequately explained to another person. She simply thanked Annette and looked about the room, wondering where Annette kept an extra bed.

"I'll make a pallet for you, on the floor there in the corner. I'm sorry I can't do better. I used to have a fine chamber to offer guests."

Charlotte nodded, finding herself at a loss for words.

"Help yourself to more wine. You'll find the cask outside the door. Put your things there, in the corner." Annette picked up a twig broom and swept a conglomeration of spider webs from the corner. A panicked spider scurried across the floor, making little progress before Annette smacked it with the broom and swept it against the wall. She balanced the broom against the door frame and restacked the crate she had used for a chair. "I need to finish weeding my garden. I'm preparing my produce to sell at the market. After you rest from your journey, perhaps you would like to join me outside?"

Running her hands across her jerkin and breeches, Charlotte replied, "I brought nothing else to wear but a nightshirt and a robe."

Annette chuckled. "Wear what you have on. Seeing a man in my garden will give the neighbors something new to gossip about." Noting the confused look on Charlotte's face she added, "I'm joking. Just a moment." She disappeared into the adjacent room and emerged with a linen tunic. Handing it to Charlotte, she excused herself to go outside. Just before her exit, she turned and asked, "Have you considered throwing yourself at your husband's mercy?"

"I—I—I hadn't," Charlotte stammered.

"He's a powerful man." With that, Annette went outside, leaving Charlotte to grapple with the unexpected turn of events.

Clutching the tunic in her right hand, Charlotte dropped to her knees to pray.

Morning sun seeped through cracks in the walls and ceiling. A dog's bark mingled with the pounding of footsteps as folks made their way to Sunday mass. At the melodic laughter of children running by, Charlotte brooded over how lovely the morning might be if she weren't on such a grave errand.

After combing and braiding her hair in the style Thomas liked best, she slipped into the form-fitting black robe she brought from London. As she laced the bodice and sleeves and tied a white cap over her hair, she considered the risk of venturing out in public undisguised.

"Are you ready?" Annette's voice rang from outside the shanty door.

"I'm coming." Charlotte emerged, double-checking the laces on her bodice.

At the sight of her guest, Annette expressed a genuine smile for the first time since Charlotte's arrival. "You make a much better woman than a man. I can't understand why any man would let you go. Are you nervous?"

"So nervous I can barely breathe." Charlotte inhaled through pursed lips and exhaled slowly, holding out her trembling right hand to demonstrate.

"I wouldn't want to be in your shoes." Annette offered Charlotte a reassuring squeeze of the hand.

"I don't want to be in my own shoes," Charlotte sighed. "Shall we go?"

The two women made their way to mass, Charlotte's heart pounding more violently with each step. When the church came into view she froze and watched townsfolk file into its open doors. Turning her back, she buried her face in her hands and mumbled, "I can't do this."

With a reassuring hand on Charlotte's shoulder Annette coaxed, "So often, one must choose between two bitter cups, and you—leaving your children or facing your husband…" Her voice trailed off. "Speak of the devil," she whispered. He had an imposing presence, this tall Englishman striding toward the church façade, linked arm-in-arm with a blonde woman a head shorter than he. A young boy and girl trailed behind.

Glancing over her shoulder, Charlotte gasped, "Anatole! Gabrielle! Oh, my babies." Motherly instinct compelled her to run and scoop them up in her arms, but prudence held her back. "He has a mistress! And it appears he's come into money." Garbed in finery befitting Parisian courtiers, Thomas and his mistress carried themselves with all the confidence the trappings of wealth offered. Charlotte glanced down at her gown, feeling suddenly inadequate.

Annette's eyes narrowed. "Blood money," she hissed.

Turning her back to the painful scene, Charlotte lamented, "Now what will I do? Everything is going wrong. I intended to submit myself to him, to beg his mercy, but I can't allow him to see me, now that he has another woman." She closed her eyes for several seconds, then whispered, "Could you tell Father Jean I would like to meet with him privately?"

Annette nodded, keeping her gaze locked on Thomas. "I'll speak with him after mass."

"Would you mind if I returned to your cottage?"

"Of course not. I'll bring you word from Father Jean." With a squeeze of Charlotte's hand Annette added, "I'm praying for you."

Charlotte glanced at the church just in time to see the blonde woman enter hand-in-hand with Gabrielle while Anatole squatted down to pick something up from the cobblestone. Trudging the lonely streets back to the shack, Charlotte felt as if her heart were an iron anchor dragging behind. The church bell's toll sounded lonely and far away. She slipped through the rickety door, threw herself face down on the pallet and surrendered to despair.

With heaving sobs, she choked a bitter rebuke to the force that betrayed her—the still, small voice that had whispered to her spirit all would be well. *My soul is weary of living*, she groaned, struggling for breath in staccato gasps. *You've stripped me of everything—my husband, my children, my homeland, my hope.* A low, primal moan escaped from the depths of her soul. *God, you're a terrible father! What kind of father allows such suffering? I hate you!*

Salty tears stung the tender skin around her eyes. She rolled onto her back and noticed, for the first time, thick wooden beams that prevented the sagging ceiling from collapse. Staring at the rough, splintered wood, she imagined gazing into Father Jean's steely eyes. He would demand to know why she fled to England. How would she justify her decision to leave France, her husband, her children? Would he sympathize when she explained, with utmost sincerity, why the doctrines of the reformers stirred her soul? Father Jean would be only her first hurdle; her greatest hurdle, Thomas, would show absolutely no mercy.

Suffocating in the harsh reality of the circumstances that had her cornered, she picked herself up and trudged outside to retrieve a long, thin rope hanging on Annette's garden fence. Back inside, with trembling hands she tied a knot on the rope's end. After carefully positioning the three-legged stool under one of the ceiling beams, she stepped onto it. The stool wobbled precipitously. Cursing under her breath, she stabilized the stool with the rag and mounted again. With arm drawn back, she hurled the knot toward a small gap between the ceiling and beam. The rope missed its target and tumbled to the floor. She remounted, stretched onto her tiptoes, and tossed the knot toward the gap. The stool wobbled back and forth before slipping sideways, throwing her backward. Her head hit the corner of a crate before slamming against the dirt floor. The ceiling blurred, and all went black.

"Charlotte. Charlotte, wake up." A gentle hand patted her cheek. Charlotte's eyes blinked open to see Annette hovering over her. Behind Annette stood Father Jean, with a curious expression hovering between contempt and pity. The priest tugged Annette's elbow and traded places, kneeling down in front of Charlotte. He made the sign of the cross.

"How long have I been out?" Charlotte cried, her heart pounding in her ears. Before anyone could answer she focused on Father Jean's eyes and choked, "Bless me, Father, for I have sinned. I've come home to recant of my heretical opinions."

November, 1547

—

Dartford

"Have you got a deck of cards?" Father Garrett licked gravy from the front and back of his pewter spoon, slipped the utensil into his pouch, and pushed his wooden trencher to the table's edge. "A jolly game of Primero would take the edge off my melancholy. And by the way, Amy, the pigeon pie was delicious."

"Thank you." Amy flashed the priest a smile on her way from the counter to the table. "Let me fetch the cards." She took his empty trencher to the kitchen, trotted upstairs, and returned with a deck of cards. "Deal me in," she said, handing the deck to the priest as she seated herself. "'Tis a slow afternoon. I'll be able to manage between patrons."

"The question is, do we wish to compete with you?" Father Garrett winked. "Put in your ante, folks." Each player slapped a ha'-penny in the center of the table. Garrett took a swig of ale, shuffled the deck, licked his fingers and dealt four cards, two by two, to each player. He then arranged the cards in his hand, glowering.

Amy had noticed a melancholy air about the priest of late, but didn't dare pry into his private affairs, so she was thrilled when he cleared his throat and began to divulge his thoughts.

"Are we imps needing to be checked up on?" he sneered, peering over his cards at Elizabeth, Matthew and Amy.

"What do you mean?" Elizabeth probed.

"The king's council sent out a delegation to pry into every parish in the kingdom," Garrett sighed.

Amy jumped at the chance to discuss the topic for she, too, had suffered unshakable malaise since the installation of the new king. "Everything we feared is coming upon us," she stated, flicking the corners of her cards with her thumb.

Father Garrett nodded. "Their so-called Josiah is nothing more than a puppet. His counsel should wait until the king comes to the age of majority, when he can make up his own mind about reforming the church." Biting his lower lip, he studied his cards for several seconds before releasing more venom. "Edward Bartholomew had the audacity to call the holy sacrament 'Jack in the Box' to my face. 'Twas all I could do to not put my fist to his jaw." He glanced at Matthew, looking for sympathy.

"I pass," Matthew sighed, discarding a card and drawing a replacement. "I've heard him say that as well. God help us with the blasphemies we must endure."

"I bid a ha'-penny." Elizabeth placed her coin in the pile. The other players quickly followed. "A pox upon Edward Bartholomew," she said. "'Twould serve him right."
Amy stared blankly at her cards, her lips taut.

Matthew leaned forward, his eyes narrowing. Lowering his voice, he said, "Clergymen are fleeing to France and Italy. A London wool merchant at the market last week told me a priest in London jumped from the bridge into the Thames to take his own life, despairing of King Edward's reforms. The reformers will have our religion clean erased if nothing stops them." He sat up straight and in his normal voice said, "What's your fancy, Amy? Pass?"

"I pass." She turned to Father Garrett. "You won't leave us, will you, Father?"

"I have no plans to do so," the priest replied, "but I can't say I won't change my mind. It depends on where this king leads us."

"I fear we won't recognize our merry England by the time they're done." Elizabeth shook her head. "They're pushing to destroy every memory of miracles and saints. I intend to take my rosary to the grave, so help me. And tell me, how do they expect to root the sacred relics from our very homes? Are they going to search our cottages?"

Scratching his chin with his cards, Father Garrett reassured her, "They'll never be able to visit every home in the realm. Besides, they're done with their visitations for the time being. Keep your sacred objects—in a safe place, of course—but keep them. We must keep the true religion alive."

"What concerns me," Matthew inserted, "is that they're just getting started. The king is nine years old. What if he reigns fifty or sixty years?"

"Happily, I'll be dead by then." Father Garrett scowled at his cards.

"'Tis not only myself I'm concerned with—I fear for my grandchildren."

Elizabeth had barely gotten the words out when Matthew interjected, "If we have grandchildren. But that's another matter altogether. Elizabeth's remedies aren't working."

Elizabeth wagged her head. "Perhaps William bein' a Lollard cursed Christopher. The curse of the fathers is to be visited upon the children—isn't that written in scripture, Father?" The priest responded with a perplexed look. Elizabeth continued, "Would that I could make a pilgrimage to Canterbury on their behalf."

"Pilgrimages—yet another part of our ancient worship they've stripped from us," Matthew lamented. "If ever we needed miracles, 'tis now." He took a sip of cider and closed his eyes while Elizabeth massaged his shoulder.

"Despite my frettin', I always come back to the thought that we must hold on to our hope," she declared. "The tide will turn. It must, for the true church of God is at stake."

"I wish your confidence would rub off on me," Matthew muttered, turning the opposite shoulder. "Could you get this side?"

"Let me tell you this," Amy interjected, wagging her index finger. "Mary Tudor is waiting in the wings, and mark my words—"

The tavern door swung open. Edward Bartholomew barged in, astonished to see his enemies gathered at one table. He averted his eyes and lumbered to a table across the room.

"All hail!" Matthew muttered under his breath. "The lofty bread baker who fancies himself a preacher."

Smiling at the comment, Amy set her cards down to attend to Edward, then stopped herself. She picked up the cards and cooed, "Whose turn is it?"

"I believe it was mine." Father Garrett studied his cards. "I'll throw in a penny."

"Ah, big spender, are you?" Matthew teased, pitching in a penny. Elizabeth and Amy followed.

Glaring at Amy, Edward cleared his throat and tapped his fingers on the table.

"Your turn, Matthew." Amy spoke loudly to spite her guest.

"I fold." Matthew laid his cards face down.

"I'd like a cider, please." The disgruntled request from across the tavern fell upon deaf ears.

"Fold?" Amy exclaimed. "Well, that is no way to start."

Cupping his hands around his mouth Edward shouted, "A cider, if you please, and a bowl of stew."

"Can't you see, we're playing at cards?" Matthew raised his hand high for Edward to see.

"If I'm not mistaken," Edward retorted, "folks come here for food and drink."

Rolling her eyes, Amy slapped her cards on the table and disappeared into the kitchen. A couple of minutes passed before she re-emerged, stomping across the tavern with a mug of cider and a bowl of stew, broth sloshing over the rim. Stone-faced, she placed the victuals in front of Edward, then returned to her seat with a huff.

As he sipped the cider, Edward stared daggers in Amy's direction.

"Watch this," Matthew whispered. "Ho, Edward." Matthew lifted his mug in mock salute. Blowing on a spoonful of stew, Edward stared past his tormentor. Matthew persisted. "Ho, Edward. Is it true some of the townsfolk are holding a regular Bible study?"

After swirling his mug in a circular motion, Edward put the vessel to his mouth, cocked his head back, swallowed and burped. "His Majesty King Edward encourages all of his subjects to read the English Bible. You might try it." Spurred on by priest's sour expression, he added, "How else will the English people recognize and throw down the idolatry in our midst?"

The veins his temples bulging, Garrett snorted, "Why, look at you. A loyal subject, you are. Seems you know the injunctions well."

"As all good Englishmen do," Edward quipped. "In fact, 'tis my understanding that the Lord's servants aren't supposed to be haunting taverns, drinking and dicing, playing cards and such."

"Would you fancy joining us in a game of Primero?" the priest taunted, relishing the flash of resentment in Edward's hazel eyes.

Edward shook his head, his curly, red locks dancing with the motion.

"I suppose you're too holy to play with us," Father Garrett persisted. "Self-appointed preacher that you are, you wouldn't want to disobey the injunctions." Edward glared at him while the priest continued, "It figures you would prefer to sit in a corner and read your English Bible while we play."

"I work hard for my money, and don't wish to waste it on gaming." Edward blew on another spoonful of stew.

With a wink at his table mates, Father Garrett continued. "Perhaps you would preach to us on the evils of gaming, per His Majesty's injunctions? Would you like to take my place at Sunday morning mass?"

Amy elbowed him. "Father, please," she whispered.

"Shouldn't the preaching come from you?" Edward retorted. He rested his spoon in the bowl, straightened his back and sucked in a long, deep breath. "And shouldn't that preaching come not only from your pulpit, but also from your conduct?" Father Garrett pursed his lips while Edward continued, "Why isn't your bastard son here to play Primero with you? Everyone knows why Widow Willoughby had to leave Dartford."

His eyes bulging, Garrett pushed himself up from the table.

"I pray you," Amy whispered, digging her fingers into Father Garrett's meager bicep.

To the astonishment of everyone in the tavern, the priest strode across the room, his footsteps heavy on the oak floor. Matthew jumped up from the table, following close behind. Without a word Garrett clenched Edward's tunic with both hands, pulled the startled patron off the bench where he was seated, and thrust him backwards to the floor.

"Speak to me that way again," the priest growled through clenched teeth, "and you'll live to regret it."

Amy and Elizabeth exchanged glances. "Should I get help?" Amy whispered.

Elizabeth shook her head. "Let them work it out. 'Twill ease their tensions."

Edward pushed himself to his knees and rose slowly to his feet, keeping his eyes fixed on Garrett. He stretched his arm across the table, cradled his fingers around his woolen cap, and inched it toward him.

At the sound of the front door creaking open, Amy turned with a start. It was her husband. He stepped inside, amused at the startled looks that greeted him.

"Did I interrupt something?" Tom removed his rain-soaked cap and cloak before hanging them on a peg next to the door. He eyed the glowing coals in the fireplace and poked a log into the fire. After rubbing his hands together in front of the fireplace, he crowded next to Amy at the table while Matthew and Father Garrett returned to their seats.

With a pinch on his wife's arm Tom said cheerfully, "Amy, the largest mug of your goodly ale and a piece of meat pie, please. I just hunted down a sheep thief in this dreadful weather. A warm meal and a game are just what I need." Amy fetched his food and drink and settled in next to her husband. The five friends proceeded with their game as if Edward weren't there.

The baker took advantage of the opportunity to slip out. A loud clap of thunder, followed by a torrential downpour, sent him sprinting toward the Jolly Miller in hopes of better company.

<h1 align="center">*January, 1548*</h1>

London

"Hmm." Piers turned a piece of cloth back and forth in his hands while carefully studying the texture. "This worsted wool is said to be the future of the wool trade. Manufacturers are springing up all around London, so I could easily find a supplier." When Molly didn't respond, he looked up to discover her gazing out the parlor window. "A penny for your thoughts," he said softly, resting the cloth on his knee.

She blinked out of her trance and mumbled, "What? Oh, pardon me. My thoughts are far away this evening."

"I noticed. Is something troubling you?"

She crossed the room and nestled next to Piers on the settee, reaching for his hand to find reassurance. "I hate to even speak of it, but last night I had a terrible dream. I saw Charlotte, surrounded by flames and crying out for help, but I couldn't reach her. When I called out, her face faded into the fire. It was terrifying. Then I woke up to Joseph's screaming. He's been up several nights in a row. Do you think he senses something with his mother?"

"He's cutting teeth. Have you tried massaging ointment into his gums?"

"Yes, but I think something else is disturbing him. I fear for Charlotte. This malaise won't let go of me."

Tickling the back of Molly's hand, Piers searched for words to comfort her. "Jean-Luc is skilled at helping folks escape," he said. "I don't know of a single soul he's lost. We've no reason to suspect Charlotte will be his first."

"But you must admit, reports of the new French king are troubling. He's a tyrant like his father. In fact, I've heard King Henry might be worse than King Francis. You know those two refugees that just arrived in London from Paris, the husband and wife? I believe his name is…"

"Claude," Piers interjected. "And Marguerite."

"Yes, Claude and Marguerite Rivière. Monsieur Rivière told me King Henry passed a law last October, creating a court in Paris to try the réformées. They call it the *chambre ardente*—the fiery chamber. Folks who are sent there are almost certain to meet their death by fire. I can't help myself, but to think our Lord must weep! The Rivières said prisons in Normandy can barely hold all the reformers imprisoned there. The timing of Charlotte's return to France was unfortunate. I'm afraid she walked straight into the fiery furnace, like Daniel of the Bible."

"God protected Daniel. I trust he'll protect Charlotte. Don't forget, I'm returning to La Rochelle this spring, and I intend to bring Charlotte and her children back to London with me. God led her to us the first time. He'll safely lead her back to us."

"I hope you're right. With your connections, isn't there a way we might learn of her whereabouts sooner?"

"I don't know how that would be possible," Piers replied. "We can only wait and pray."

Seeing the confidence in his eyes, Molly hoped her troubled dream was nothing more than the product of a worried mind.

La Rochelle

Charlotte shifted her weight from the right buttock to the left. The frigid stone floor numbed the flesh where her thigh made contact with the floor. She tightened a blanket around her that was too threadbare to keep her teeth from chattering. A shiver, starting from the depths of her soul, racked her body as it worked its way to the surface. She longed for death to rescue her. To live was to suffer. She had suffered enough. Shelter inside the prison offered little advantage over exposure to the winter elements outdoors.

In the eyes of kingdom and church officials, her list of crimes—furnished to local authorities by Thomas—was long. It included possessing forbidden writings, promoting them to others, and participating in heretical meetings that blasphemed the mass. Recanting to Father Jean had saved her from immediate condemnation to the martyr's flames, but Thomas had no intention of letting her off easily. Hoping a few months in prison would cure her of her sympathy for church reform, he had used his friendship with law enforcers to influence her sentence, assuring her the discomfort of prison was miniscule compared to the discomfort of the hell fire awaiting her if she didn't mend her ways.

At the tap of approaching footsteps, Charlotte stiffened. The *clink-clank* of metal keys drew her eyes to the corridor that led to the prison cell. She glanced at the three women sharing the frozen hell with her. No one spoke. Inserting a key into the cell lock, the prison guard pulled the iron door open. The high-pitched screech of rusty hinges resonated off the stone walls.

"Madame Nix. Come with me."

Her teeth chattering, Charlotte eyed her cell mates.

An elderly woman named Miriam struggled up to her full height of four-feet, eleven inches, her knees nearly buckling under her. Two years earlier, Miriam's own son, intent on getting his mother to recant, informed on her for organizing a study group in her parish in Saintes. Charlotte wondered if the son ever regretted misjudging his mother's determination.

Miriam thrust her knobby, arthritic right fist toward the ceiling. In a defiant voice, weakened by hunger and cold, she proclaimed, "Let God arise. Let his enemies be scattered. Let them also that hate him flee before him."

Miriam's declaration came from Psalm 68—the réformée battle cry. With a lump in her throat, Charlotte thought of how God rescued Daniel from the mouths of lions, and David from Goliath. He spared Meshach, Shadrach and Abednego from burning in the king's fire. Yet here stood tiny Miriam, frail and wasting away but giant in courage, in the place where she would likely meet her death. A tear escaped and wobbled down Charlotte's cheek.

"God be with you, Charlotte." The encouragement came from Noelle Godet, a carpenter's wife from Essarts, who spoke often of missing her three children. Noelle sat hunched over with a persistent cough, too weak to rise. A third cellmate, who kept the others awake each night with her sobs, lay in a heap in a corner, shivering under her cloak.

The young guard sneered at the spectacle of the old woman raising her fist. Charlotte acknowledged Miriam with a nod but dared not speak. Taking a deep breath to calm her racing heart, she followed the guard along a narrow corridor lit by torches. The two emerged into a room with high, arched windows that let in more light than she had seen in months. Thomas and Father Jean stood in the center of the room. At the sight of his wife's protruding cheekbones and hollow eyes, Thomas swallowed hard.

She lunged at his feet and dampened his soft Italian leather boots with her tears. "Please, forgive me," she choked. "I do embrace the true and most Holy Mother Church and, I promise, I'll never again allow myself to be led astray." Desperate for a show of mercy, she lifted her gaze to meet his. He pulled his boot away.

"Stand up," he grunted. "I didn't come to see you grovel at my feet like a dog." Swallowing her bitterness, she rose to her feet, her children's faces dancing through her mind.

Thomas glanced at the guard. "She may come with us, then?"

With a nod from Father Jean, the guard confirmed, "Yes, her release is cleared." Turning to Charlotte he said, "We'll return to the cell for your things." She followed him down the corridor, cursing the painful contact between her thin-soled slippers and the rough, cold stone. After placing her comb and the few other personal items she brought to prison with her into a pouch, she choked a tearful farewell to her cellmates and followed the guard back to the room where Thomas waited.

"Where are your shoes and cloak?" he barked.

Shivering, she looked down at her feet. "These are my shoes, and I have no cloak."

With a shrug of the shoulders, the young guard reacted to Thomas' icy glare. "We provide a blanket."

"She can't go out like this." Thomas removed his cape and draped it around Charlotte's shoulders. "I need something to wrap her feet, or they'll freeze. Go get the blanket." The guard disappeared down the corridor and returned with the threadbare excuse for warmth.

Marveling at her husband's authoritative demeanor, Charlotte experienced a pulse of long-buried feelings when he lifted her off the floor and cradled her in his arms. After a moment's hesitation, she relaxed her head into his neck, finding comfort in the warmth of his skin against hers. They emerged from the dreary prison into brilliant light, blinking against the blinding reflection of the sun on the thin crust of sparkling snow that fell the night before. The sun's warmth filled Charlotte with wonder. After five months inside a prison cell, to emerge into the outside world was to be reborn.

Gently, Thomas set her on Bijou's back—*yes, gently*, she noted—the harshness he displayed inside the prison gone. He pulled his dagger from its sheath and made a small cut on the edge of the blanket, then tore it in half. Working quickly, he wrapped a piece around each of her feet and tied them securely. A split-second gaze between them betrayed the unspoken pain on both sides. Gathering the reins in his hand, Thomas acknowledged Father Jean, who had followed them out, with a pained smile.

"I suppose you won't need me now." Father Jean patted Thomas on the shoulder. "Her penance appears complete. Go with God."

With a nod, Thomas clicked his tongue and led Bijou forward.

"Wait!" The priest removed his cloak. "Take this. I have another one." Against Thomas' protest, he insisted, "You'll need it for your journey home."

"Thank you, Father." Thomas swung the cloak around him, relieved for the warmth, and tugged on Bijou's bridle. As soon as they were out of earshot, he remarked, "You've grown thin."

She tightened his cape around her, a whirlwind of emotion churning in her breast. "The prison food was meager. I had no appetite."

"You haven't seen the children for a year and a half. They may not remember you."

"I've tried to prepare myself." She stroked Bijou's mane to calm her nerves.

They left the city ramparts behind and continued for twenty minutes along a bumpy, narrow road riddled with holes, past sleeping vineyards and fields, until the crunch of Bijou's hooves on the frozen snow stopped. The mare whinnied, steam from her nostrils hanging in the air.

"This is it." Thomas pointed to a side road lined with chestnut trees.

Charlotte's heart caught in her throat. On a spread of gently rolling landscape rose an impeccable estate dotted with oak, chestnut and sycamore trees. Gracing one corner of the property stood a small but impressive thirteenth-century château constructed of grey stone, with a massive square keep on one side and a circular tower on the other. Well-groomed gardens, lying fallow for the winter, stretched in front of the central living quarters. Numerous stone outbuildings dotted the grounds. A twelve-horse stable a stone's throw from the keep sheltered horses of different sizes and colors. The animals stamped and blustered at Bijou's approach.

A stable hand, wearing a heavy wool cloak and holding a shovel full of steaming manure, lifted his eyes in greeting. Thomas waved.

"Is all of this yours?" Charlotte gasped.

With a smug smile, he nodded. "God is a generous employer." He led Bijou to the stable, handed the reins to his stable hand, swooped Charlotte off the horse, and carried her to the gatehouse. Stopping at the gate, he held her gaze for the first time since they left the prison. "I've been wanting to ask you since I first saw you. Why did you come back?"

Shivering, she stuttered, "I saw the error of my ways, and realized I couldn't live without you and the children."

He surprised her with a long, tender kiss. "I'll make you happy you returned. All that you see will be yours, and more. Fine clothes and entertainments, rich food, servants, and company with the finest folks in the kingdom. I no longer have to work long hours carving or traveling to sell my work. You'll work in partnership with me."

Hope swelled in Charlotte's bosom. Her decision to return was the right one after all.

As they passed through the gate Thomas remarked, "Your first task will be to help me catch the Englishman who took you to England."

May, 1549

———

Dartford

Drowsy after stuffing their bellies with oyster pie and asparagus, Christopher, Nicholas and John stared at the coals in the fireplace. The *cheerily-cheerily-cheerily* of a robin on the apple tree outside offered a joyful reminder of spring's advent.

Christopher dislodged a piece of oyster from between his teeth with a fingernail and broke the silence. "This Thomas Bilney—tell us more of his story, John."

"I'd like to know more as well," Nicholas chimed in, debating whether to stoke the fire. Fickle spring weather had brought a string of warmer-than-usual days, but Christopher's cottage held a chill from the night before. Leaning forward on his stool, Nicholas pulled a log from a bucket next to the fireplace and poked it into the fire.

The lazy Sunday afternoon lent itself to just such a discussion. Supper had been served, the spoons and trenchers were washed, and Anne was gone for the afternoon to help Nicholas' betrothed, Rachel, finalize plans for the couple's upcoming wedding.

John eased up to a standing position from the rocking chair where he had almost fallen asleep and stretched his arms toward the timber-framed ceiling with an exaggerated groan. "I'd be happy to tell you what I know," he yawned, smoothing his gray woolen breeches before sitting back down. Christopher smiled at John's tendency to assume a professorial demeanor when he spoke of religious matters.

John watched the log in the fire pop and ignite while he cracked his knuckles and cleared his throat. "'Little Bilney' they called him, because he was short in stature. Folks at Cambridge knew him well, as he studied law there. Bilney began to feel anxious about his standing before God. Even after he took orders in the church and followed the priests' instructions, he felt like something was missing. You both know what that's like." Christopher nodded. "At great risk," John continued, "he secretly purchased a copy of Erasmus' Greek New Testament and smuggled it into his private chamber. As you know, reading the Bible was forbidden."

Christopher caressed the cover of his Bible. "I'm so grateful King Edward is letting us freely read the word of God again. Now Anne can't object to our study group. It took some doing to convince her to stop fretting about what her father thinks, but with the king on our side, Matthew can't stop us."

"Heaven is smiling upon us now," John agreed. "But it wasn't so for Bilney. As it happened, he was reading privately in his chamber when he came upon a passage in 1 Timothy 15. The words pierced his heart like an arrow."

"What did it say?" Christopher leaned forward.

"Here. I'll read it." John flipped through his Bible to a page he'd bookmarked. *"This is a faithful saying and worthy of all acceptation, that Christ Jesus came into the world to save sinners; of whom I am chief."*

After mulling over the words, Christopher remarked, "Bilney felt the message applied to him?"

"Precisely. He believed that if Jesus was willing to save Paul, who had persecuted the followers of Christ, surely there was hope for him. That simple message filled him with joy—a joy he never found in his papist rituals." John selected a piece of candied apricot from a bowl on the table next to him and popped it in his mouth.

As he reached for a piece of candied fruit, Christopher remarked, "With so many folks—Bilney, Lady Askew—'twas the simple word of God in the English tongue that changed their hearts." He slipped the treat in his mouth and rolled it around on his tongue for several seconds before continuing. "For me, the night I read from Nathan's Bible for the first time, something came alive on the inside. Reading the words of Christ for myself, it was like—like—" he gazed at the soot-stained ceiling, searching for just the right words. "Nicholas, remember when we set out to London from Dartford, that morning the sunrise lit up the whole sky, and life felt new and full of promise?"

Nicholas nodded. "That's why the papists fight it so fiercely. The word of God opens folks' eyes to idolatry, to tyranny, and to all sorts of mischief. The word of God is power and light. Light is what the devil fears."

"Precisely," John agreed. *"The word of God is quick and powerful, and sharper than any two-edged sword, piercing even to the dividing asunder of soul and spirit, and of the joints and marrow, and is a discerner of the thoughts and intents of the heart."*

"Where would I find that?" Christopher held up his Bible.

"In the book of Hebrews. Here, lend me your book." John flipped through the pages and returned the book to Christopher.

Christopher read the passage and exclaimed, "You committed the entire thing to memory."

John nodded. "In case the Bible is ever taken away from us again, I intend to have as much of it memorized as possible."

"I'd like to do that too," Christopher said.

"We could work on memorizing next time we meet," John suggested, reaching for another candied fruit.

"Good idea," Nicholas nodded. "So, what happened with Bilney after he read the passage about Christ forgiving sinners?"

"He started a Bible study group—like ours, I imagine," John explained. "And even though he was shy by nature, he overcame his timidity and preached in the open air. In 1527—when I was a mischievous lad throwing rocks at the back of your head, Christopher—he was arrested and tried before the Bishop's Court at Westminster. A few of his friends spent two days pressuring him to recant. Fatigue finally got the better of him."

"He recanted?" Disappointment darkened Christopher's eyes. "He was no hero, then."

"I reckon he only did what many of us would do," John countered, "but the story doesn't end there. They threw him in the dungeon of Saint Paul's Cross. The shame of recanting tortured him more than the imprisonment. Two years later they released him, and he returned to Cambridge. Those who knew him—including Hugh Latimer, King Edward's current chaplain—noted a change in him. They described it as if he rose from the dead. Bilney later preached in Norfolk against the Roman church, and authorities arrested him."

"I would never recant," Nicholas said, stretching his legs. He stood and poked the coals. "Fortunately, we'll never be in such a position. King Edward is rooting out popish superstition once and for all. Why do you have that look on your face?" He was referring to John's smirk.

John shrugged his shoulders. "How can you be so sure you wouldn't give in under pressure? Peter said the same thing, yet three times he denied knowing the Lord. He had even walked and talked with Christ in the flesh."

"Yes," Christopher inserted. "But Peter repented, like Bilney. I hope I would have the courage to stand, but I can't say what I would do if it came to that."

"I suppose none of us knows, faced with the ultimate test," John said. "But back to Bilney— the night before he was to be executed, he ate his last meal with his friends, and then did something curious. He stood up and put his finger in a lamp flame."

"Why?" Christopher asked.

"His friends asked him that very question. He said he was only trying his flesh, but the next day God's rods would burn his whole body in the fire. He removed his finger from the flame and quoted Isaiah 43:2 from memory."

"My Bible doesn't have that book." Christopher glanced at Nicholas. "Is it in the Matthew's translation?"

"Yes." Nicholas handed his Bible to Christopher. "Go ahead, read it."

After flipping to the page, Christopher read out loud, *"When thou walkest through the fire, thou shalt not be burned; neither shall the flame kindle upon thee."* Several seconds of silence followed as Christopher mulled over the words. "But—he did burn," Christopher finally objected. "And so did Lady Askew and countless others. Doesn't that make the promise untrue?"

"Why don't we take up that question next time we meet," John proposed, wrapping his fingers around a candied fig.

Entranced, Christopher watched flames dancing in the fireplace. "Christopher? Christopher?" John teased, "Have we lost you?"

Christopher blinked. "What did you say?"

"Your question about the promise in Isaiah—why don't we take it up next time we meet?"

"Of course." After closing the Bible, Christopher leaned over and pinched Nicholas in the side. "Now, about your nuptials. Took you long enough. I don't know how Rachel put up with the wait."

Nicholas blushed.

"You're betrothed to be marred," John quipped.

"You mean married," Nicholas rebuffed.

"I said what I meant," John insisted. "You won't see me running to the altar. 'Make haste when you are purchasing a field, but when you are to marry a wife be slow.'"

"Could he have been any slower?" Christopher hooted.

Taking umbrage at the insult, Nicholas retorted, "I'm well-established and ready to care for Rachel."

"Lighten up. I'm only teasing." John made his way to the window and watched a woman with a stick broom prod an uncooperative hog down a dirt pathway toward town. "Truth is," he sighed, "I envy both of you."

"You'll be the only bachelor remaining." Christopher winked at Nicholas. "A menace to society."

"Ah, yes." John groaned. "It's time for me to make my escape. Remember the question we'll take up at our next study."

"I will." Christopher stood to see John off.

"I need to be going as well." Nicholas helped himself to the last piece of candied fruit and joined John at the door.

"Enjoy your last week of bachelorhood," Christopher teased, waving good-bye. "See you at your funeral next Saturday."

August, 1549

———

London

The golden glow of dusk illuminated the parlor's lead-paned windows, signaling yet another day with no word from Piers. Molly ran the frightening possibilities through her mind, as she had hundreds of times before. Had pirates attacked the *Saint Thomas*? Did foul weather blow the ship off course? Did the vessel sink? With each passing day, hope wore thinner as fear loomed larger. Molly's middle-of-the-night pacing had worn a trail in the Persian rug.

"Mother, when is Father coming home to us?" Mark stormed into the parlor with a bow in one hand and two arrows in the other. "I want him to take me outside the city walls for archery practice."

"We have to keep praying that God will return him safely to us." Molly stepped to the window and watched the light on the three-story home across the street dim by degrees, weary of reassuring her children their father would return when she, herself, struggled with doubt.

"I do pray, and he's not home." Mark strung an arrow and pulled back the string.

"Not in the house!" Molly scolded, catching his action from the corner of her eye.

"I'm only pretending." He lowered the bow with a guilty frown.

"You mustn't even pretend to shoot an arrow in the house." Turning to face him, she continued, "You could put someone's eye out. No matter what, we'll keep praying and believing God will bring your father safely home."

Mark plopped down on the green velvet bench and let out an exaggerated sigh while holding an arrow to his eye to determine whether the shaft was straight. "Why did he have to go to France, anyway? Charlotte wanted to go there. Why should we lose Father because of her?"

"You haven't lost your father, and he wants to help her. It's very difficult in her country. God blessed us with a Godly king, who lets us to practice our faith. It isn't so in France."

"If God is over the whole earth, why doesn't he bless everyone with a king like King Edward?"

"When you're older, perhaps you'll understand." Molly resumed pacing in front of the window, feeling hypocritical. Although she was older, she certainly didn't know the answer to Mark's question.

Mark hated when adults lectured with the words *when you are older*. He shuffled his feet, fighting a growing sense of restlessness. "May I go outside to play?" Because it was growing late, he expected her to say no.

"You may, if you remain close to the house and come inside as soon as it is dark. Use prudence with your bow."

Afraid she might change her mind he hurried outside, bow and arrows in hand.

Molly trudged to her chamber, her heart heavy. She peeked in on Joseph as she passed his room. Asleep on his back, arms over his head, he took deep, even breaths. *Nothing is so angelic as the face of a sleeping imp,* she thought, lingering for several seconds to drink in his innocence.

With Grace and Simon visiting an aunt across the city and Mark outside, Molly retired to her chamber to steal a few moments of rare silence. She stretched out on her bed under a light coverlet and picked up her Bible from the nightstand. Opening to the gospel of John, she began reading where she left off the night before. Her eyelids flickered closed.

Pulling back his bowstring, Mark aimed at a pigeon grooming itself on the branch of a chestnut tree in the yard. The tips of his fingers relaxed to release the string when something flew past his ear and cracked against the black iron fence surrounding the house. Startled, the pigeon cooed and took flight. Mark turned around just in time for an egg to hit him squarely on the forehead. It cracked and oozed down his face.

"By the mass!" he cursed, spitting egg from his lips and wiping his face on his sleeve.

A trio of voices called from the street, "Mark is an orphan! Mark is an orphan!" Mark dashed to the fence in front of the house and peered through the bars, finding himself face-to-face with Julian, Griffin and Oliver, three neighbor boys who roamed London's streets like a litter of feral puppies.

Clinging to his bow, Mark hissed, "Am not!"

"Are too!" eleven-year-old Julian taunted. "My father says your father ran away because the sheriff is after him, and he won't dare show his face in London again."

"He did not run away. And your father is a lazybones, good-for-nothing rogue."

Julian scrambled over the fence, taking care to avoid snagging his breeches on the sharp fleur-de-lis post tops, and landed on his feet directly in front of Mark. "My father is not a lazybones. He's a shoemaker, and he could whip yours with his hands behind his back."

"Get out of my yard," Mark ordered, his knuckles white. Julian held his ground while Griffin and Oliver scrambled over the fence to join their partner.

"My father says your father helps heretics escape, and he had to run away to save himself. Heretic! Heretic!" Julian chanted.

"Not so," Mark shouted. "My father is coming home. Just wait and see. Your father is the heretic. Papist! Papist!"

"Mark is an orphan, Mark is an orphan," the two other boys chanted, dodging Mark's spittle. Mark set his bow and arrows down and charged at them, his fists swinging wildly. The three boys piled on top of him, rolling and punching, cursing and kicking, too distracted to hear the gate screech open.

"What have we here?"

Eight astonished eyes looked up in unison.

"Father!" Mark scrambled to his feet and threw his arms around his father's torso. "I knew you'd come." Piers set his bag down to give Mark a heartfelt squeeze before addressing the three boys gawking at him.

"The curfew bell will be sounding any moment, lads. Hasten along home. I'll take this up with your fathers later." The boys hustled out the gate, eager to escape, while Piers bent down to inspect Mark's face. "Let's get you inside. Looks like you'll need some doctoring." Piers rested a hand on Mark's shoulder as they strode to the front door.

"Julian said you ran away," Mark tattled.

"Does it look like I ran away?"

"No. I told them you would come back."

"And I did. I'm glad to be home, though I would have preferred finding you in more favorable circumstances."

Mark burst into the house shouting, "Mother! Mother! Father is back!"

The pounding of Molly's footsteps on the stairs shook the knick-knacks in the parlor bookcase. "Praise God! You're home." She threw her arms around her husband, breathless.

"Yes, thank God. And what a tale I have to tell you." He cast a sideways look at Mark.

"Did pirates hold you up, Father?"

"No, worse than pirates. I'll fill you in, after you run along and clean up."

Mark's pupils expanded. "Worse than pirates? Zounds!"

Molly peeled her eyes away from Piers long enough to take note of Mark's disheveled clothing and soiled face. She groaned under her breath. "Listen to your father—run along and clean up, and I'll bandage you when you return." Mark did as he was told, leaving his parents alone.

Molly wrapped her arms around her husband's neck, searching his eyes. "I've been sick with concern over you."

"I knew you would be." After a warm kiss, he continued, "I have so much to tell you."

She stepped back so she could drink in the sight of him. Her normally impeccably groomed husband appeared roughed-up, with a two-inch scab on his neck, several days' stubble on his face, and dark circles under his eyes.

"I can't wait to hear about it," she said, "but I'll wait for Mark to finish washing up. Simon and Grace will be beside themselves when they see you. Do you have news of Charlotte?"

"I wasn't able to find her, but I met someone who knows of her whereabouts." He led her by the hand to the parlor and pulled her next to him on the settle. Leaning close, he whispered, "I have word that she recanted, and lives with her husband on an estate outside of La Rochelle. He's enriched himself informing the clergy and local authorities of the whereabouts and activities of réformées."

"Oh, no." Molly covered her mouth with her hand.

"Would to God that it wasn't true. He's a despicable man. While Charlotte was here in London, he took a mistress and fathered a child."

"Does Charlotte know?" Molly whispered.

"I have my doubts. She spent several months in prison to pay for her heresy. A tavern owner not fond of Mister Nix told me that when Charlotte returned to France, Thomas sent his mistress to a nearby village. He secretly supports her and the child."

"How dare he!" A shadow on the wall alerted her to drop the topic. She looked to the doorway. "Mark?" He slipped into the room, holding Joseph's hand. The imp toddled to Molly and reached up with both arms. Lifting him onto her lap she turned to Mark, her eyes narrowing. "Have you been listening?" Mark shook his head vigorously.

Perusing Mark from top to bottom, Piers declared, "You look much better. How are you feeling?"

"Julian punched me in the stomach."

"Let me have a look," Molly said, lifting his nightshirt. Her son's torso had several scratches, and a bruise the circumference of a turnip had formed over his right rib.

"What was this tussle about?" Piers inquired.

Averting his eyes to the Persian rug, Mark mumbled, "They called me an orphan."

"A silly matter to fight over, isn't it?" Piers asked.

"They said you ran away because you help heretics."

"Is that so? I hope you straightened them out."

"Piers!" Molly interjected, "the boy needs no encouragement in rogue behavior."

Patting the settle next to him, Piers smiled. "Come, sit down and hear my story." Mark cradled his head against his father's side while Piers continued. "After my ship landed, I went into the village of La Rochelle, and wandered through the market to see if I might find Charlotte there. No respectable French woman would miss the chance to buy fresh food for her family on market day."

"Did you find her?" Molly asked, tightening her arms around Joseph. He cuddled into her chest with his thumb in his mouth.

"She wasn't there, so I spoke with a tavern owner, a réformée. The state of affairs in the country is frightful. I fear Charlotte will never get out."

Molly kissed Joseph's downy head, her heart heavy. "Do you believe her recantation was sincere?"

"No, I think she feared for her life, and would do anything to reunite with her children."

"We must pray for a miracle. We worship a God of miracles," Molly said.

Piers nodded. "She'll need a miracle. In fact, 'twas a miracle that the authorities released me from prison and allowed me to return to England— although I was told they're usually easier on foreigners."

Mark tilted his head, his eyes wide. "You were in prison?"

Piers nodded.

"Were you in a dungeon, with wild beasts?"

"No dungeon, praise be to God. But it wasn't pleasant, I'll tell you that." Piers' stomach rumbled.

Molly eyed him. "When did you last eat?"

"Not since daybreak."

"You must be starved. Let's go to the kitchen so I can fix you something to eat." She winked at Mark. "We want to hear your story, not your belly."

February, 1550

———

Next to Dartford's stone market cross stood a tower of books encircled by villagers of all ages—from wiggling babes in arms to wobbling elders on canes. Father Garrett paced next to the pile hollow-eyed and pink-nosed, his arms folded tightly across his chest. He shivered and looked up. Moisture-impregnated clouds hovered just over the tops of the buildings. The afternoon sun was a faint disk barely visible through the clouds.

Huddled on the outer edge of the throng, Amy and Elizabeth stood with arms linked for moral support. Matthew stared at the cobblestone, sympathetic to his wife's grief as she repeatedly dabbed her eyes with her sleeve.

Christopher, Nicholas, John, and Edward Bartholomew were on the front row of the crowd, shoulder to shoulder, watching a flock of children dance around the pile of books as if it were a maypole. Edward's wife had retreated to the riverbank where her two children could run and play, and not pester her with questions about why some of the men looked angry and why many of the women were crying.

A thick, black cloud entirely shadowed the sun just as Father Garrett lifted his voice to address the villagers. Fixing his gaze on Matthew Cooper he announced, "On Christmas Day, His Majesty King Edward sent a letter to bishops ordering the burning of all catholic books and primers." Chatter rumbled through the crowd. He waited, adamant that folks understood this was the king's idea, not his. When the murmurs hushed, he continued, "He intends that the reformation of the church will continue forward with all due speed. I must fulfill the king's orders."

A low rumble of disapproving boos that sounded like lowing cattle arose from the back of the crowd. Christopher felt a sharp sting on the back of his head and spun around, unable to discover the culprit who threw a rock at him. He returned his focus to the burning of catholic books, not wanting to miss a delicious second of it.

Wearing a bitter scowl, Garrett nodded at Luke Tisdale. The justice of the peace held a torch to the base of the pile while Elizabeth fingered the rosary under her chemise, blinking back tears as she watched a hungry bonfire lick at and then devour the printed doctrines of Rome. Parchments and books writhed and twisted as they gave up the ghost. A cold gust of indifferent wind swept across the square, fanning the flames and sending ash swirling through the air. People ducked and darted to avoid inhaling black smoke and getting hit by sparks. Cristopher rubbed his stinging eyes and coughed.

Emboldened, Edward Bartholomew piped up, "King Edward rightly called the pope the true son of the devil, a bad man, an antichrist and abominable tyrant. As the king said, if the poor lambs of God don't do the Pope's bidding to offer to idols and devils, he burns them and makes them bear a faggot." He flashed a self-satisfied smile, his oily complexion and mottled teeth reflecting the fire's glow.

"The devil fancies himself a preacher," Matthew growled through clenched teeth to Amy and Elizabeth. Oh, to put the arrogant young man in his place, but he knew he had no choice except to hold himself in check.

"Good riddance to popish rubbish," Christopher chimed in. Anne shrunk inside, not wanting him to draw any attention. Oblivious to her embarrassment he added, "Our Josiah is cleansing the land of idolatry." With the toe of his boot, Christopher nudged a smoldering book back into the fire that had tumbled down from the top.

Anne glanced at her father. The reflection of flames danced on his face as he glared at the fire. Her arms erupted in goosebumps.

After whispering, "I can't watch," Elizabeth turned to make her way toward the bridge. Matthew followed on her heels. When they reached the river, her anguish spilled out. "I lost my husband to Lollardy, and now my son to Luther. If that weren't enough, I'm losing my country as well. God has given me a bitter cup to drink."

Reaching for her hand, Matthew said, "Alas, I drink from the same cup. I couldn't have imagined this day. Do my eyes see what I think they see? Is this horror truly happening?"

Elizabeth squeezed his hand, finding a small measure of comfort in the warmth of his touch. "I tried to teach him, to save him from his father's clutch, but to no avail. I've failed."

"You haven't failed where you've tried your best. Forces swirl about us that we can't tame. Don't flagellate yourself. It won't solve anything."

"I suppose you're right, but I would give my life for my son to embrace the Holy Mother Church. I would give it now." Elizabeth glanced over her shoulder at the blazing bonfire. "After tonight, I won't dare wear my rosary, even under my shift. They've turned me into an offender for my faith. Even King Henry didn't torment us so."

A pained sigh arose from deep within Matthew's being. "Had I known how good life was then, I might have appreciated it more fully." The two watched the river meander along its route, finding solace in the ancient rhythm of the water's flow. "I would find it insufferable to face these times alone," he continued. "For this—for your companionship—I know God hasn't forgotten me."

A surge of defiance welled up inside Elizabeth. "No one can take our faith away," she declared. "Let them shatter every statue, remove every feast day from the calendar, and burn every book. They can't destroy the faith in my heart and soul."

"Well said." His teeth chattered. "Some things can't be destroyed by man."

"You're shiverin'. Shall we return to the fire?"

With a glint of mischief in his eye he teased, "I thought we might return to our own hearth, to warm ourselves by our fire."

She looked down at the wet grass and shook her head with a smile. If there was one trait about Matthew Cooper that had taken her by surprise, it was his ability at the most unexpected of times to bring lightness to heavy situations. She was grateful for it. Hand in hand, they strolled along the river-bank and turned on the path homeward, away from the noise and commotion on Market Square.

June, 1550

Dartford

“C hristopher, prithee, come inside the cottage for a just a moment.”
Christopher stopped hoeing between the turnips and looked to the cottage door, squinting to make out an object cradled in Anne's hands.

“Just a moment,” he called. “Could you wait for me to finish weeding this row?”

“I suppose.” The unmistakable disappointment in her voice unnerved him as he heard the door squeak closed.

Making a note to grease the door hinges, he wiped his brow with a kerchief, tucked the cloth into his belt and decided to do her bidding. Hoeing would wait, and he could use an ale break. Leaning his hoe against the old apple tree, he wondered what Anne was up to. He opened the door to discover her standing next to the table, staring at two earthenware pots.

Red-faced, she straightened. “Oh! I thought you would be awhile.”

“Where did you get those?” He studied the two pots, amused.

“I purchased them at the market earlier.”

“They're lovely. Is this why you asked me to come in?”

“Yes, to see the pots.” She twiddled her fingers and rocked from heel to toe with a nervous twitch of her mouth.

“What will you use them for?” Her unusual behavior piqued his curiosity.

“They'll help us determine where the fault lies—whether with you or me.”

“Fault?”

“The fault of conception.”

Sensing that he was trapped, he fought the urge to flee outside and instead leaned back against the wall, arms folded. "I pray you, Milady," he declared, "be at peace and let nature take her course." Immediately, she averted her eyes and turned her back to him. Regretting his words, he stepped in front of her, took her hands in his and pleaded, "Forgive me. Please, tell me about the pots."

With less enthusiasm than she first displayed, she backed away and held up one of the pots. "Each of us must make water in a separate pot, and I'll mix a small measure of wheat bran in them. They'll rest on the mantle for ten days and ten nights. If worms—small, living worms—appear in one pot or the other, the fault lies with that person. If worms appear in neither pot, we will most likely have children, if it be God's will."

With all his might, he fought the urge to roll his eyes. "What if worms appear in both pots?"

"Then I suppose the fault lies with both of us."

"Did you learn this from Mother?" He turned one of the pots back and forth in his hands. Her silence answered his question. "Very well. I shall participate, but may I finish weeding the garden?

"Of course."

"And you must draw me a mug of ale. Deal?"

"Deal." She threw her arms around him. "Thank you, Milord."

"'Tis the least I can do, and the ale will move the process along nicely."

"You're mocking me," she complained, filling his mug from a cask that stood in the corner near the loom. He guzzled it and gave the mug back to her. "Before you go back out…" she stopped.

"Yes?"

"'Tis your mother. I'm worried about her. Since the king outlawed the rosary, she's speaking with ever more anger about him. She's doing a dangerous thing, I think."

"This king is nothing like his father. He won't put folks to death for speaking ill of him."

"But both she and father have grown so bitter, I'm afraid they'll join in a rebellion against the king."

"I doubt your father or my mother would do any such thing. You have to understand my mother. She's all bark and no bite. You have nothing to fear."

"I hope so." Brooding, Anne set the pot on the table.

"Is there something else?"

She slumped down at the table and buried her face in her hands.

"Tell me what's wrong," he said softly, moving behind her to rub her shoulders.

"You're trying to get the garden hoed." She dabbed her eyes with her apron hem.

"It'll wait. What's the matter?"

She choked out, "Some of the women of the village say God has cursed me with barrenness. What have I done for God to punish me? Tell me! I've searched my heart, and I can't find the answer." Her words fueled his own frustration with their situation, something he kept closely guarded, even from Anne. "Look at Denise Twisden, or Leticia Barnam. Why do they deserve a baby more than I do? And even widow Willoughby—why didn't God curse her union with Father Garrett? What have I done wrong?"

Christopher stroked her shoulders, feeling helpless to comfort his grieving wife. "I don't understand why God hasn't blessed us. But we mustn't lose hope. Perhaps he's testing our faith."

"'Tis not fair. I have faith."

"No, 'tis not fair. But we mustn't lose heart. Think of Sarah and Abraham. God promised them offspring as the sands of the sea, yet Sarah passed the age of childbearing with the promise unfulfilled. She had times of doubt and laughed at the promise that in her old age, she would bear a son. Do you remember what the angel asked her?"

Anne nodded through her tears. "'Is anything too hard for the Lord?'"

"Perhaps our time hasn't come. Nothing is too hard for the Lord. You must remember that."

"'Tis so easy for others," Anne complained. "They give it no thought, while I bear the shame and reproach of wagging tongues and empty arms, trying strange potions and desperate measures. Pitiable orphans wander about

London, bastard children are born to harlots—yet God is withholding a child from us."

Feeling like a failure, Christopher shrugged his shoulders.

"Go ahead, hoe the turnips," she stammered. "I'm sorry for burdening you."

Taking pains to close the door softly, he crossed the yard and pounded at the weeds with his hoe, his mood soured.

September, 1550

—

Dartford

As he deliberated speaking his mind to Elizabeth, Matthew transferred oysters from a thigh-high barrel into a crock. He placed the crock on the counter for the day's customers. Shading his eyes from the morning sun, he shuffled next to the table where she stood fileting salmon to assess her mood. He cleared his throat and watched her jaw stiffen.

"You've gotten quite good at fileting," he remarked politely.

"Thank you for noticin'," she mumbled, not looking up.

He observed her for several seconds, struggling with his thoughts.

With a sideways glance she asked, "Is somethin' on your mind?"

"Well, yes actually. The rogues who study the Bible together are getting more obnoxious. Don't you agree it's time to do something?"

Elizabeth rolled her eyes and added a huff for good measure. "Can we stop them? They have the king on their side. Perhaps it's a youthful phase. You know how young folks chase after newfangled ideas." She slid the filet knife along the salmon's skeleton.

He sighed. "I didn't reject the Holy Mother Church. Did you? No! These young folks are a wild lot, and our lawless monarch is feeding their rebellion. I wish Christopher hadn't pulled Anne into this new learning."

She slammed the knife on the table. Pointing a forefinger at him she growled, "I knew it. You're blamin' Christopher? Anne's the one who led him to the new ideas in London. You know how it is with men—they'll do anythin' to woo a woman. He did what he fancied he had to do. He doesn't believe that stuff."

"Woman, put that finger down and take your blinders off. He doesn't act like he's pretending. He's upsetting the whole village with his bleating and braying about "popish" traditions. Stubborn as a mule, just like his father."

She tossed the salmon bones in a rubbish barrel and faced him with her hands on her hips. "What you want to say is he's as stubborn as his mother."

"Don't put words in my mouth. I said what I meant." He turned his back to scoop mussels with his hands from a large barrel into a smaller tub.

Elizabeth pushed her fileted salmon aside and slapped another one on her cutting board, tight-lipped.

As he set the mussels on the counter, Matthew continued his rant. "A pox upon this boy king for making our children bold in their heresy. A pox upon the council of Lutherans making his decisions. The world is turned on its head. I fear it will never be upright again."

Elizabeth pursed her lips and said nothing.

"Giving me the silent treatment now, are you? Very well. A bit of quiet never hurt a man." She cast him a contemptuous glance. "Don't look at me that way with a knife in your hand," he taunted. "Are you sure Anne and Christopher studied the new learning in London?"

She continued to filet while answering his question. "I was helpin' Anne unpack when they first arrived in Dartford, and noticed they each had a Bible. The book was forbidden at the time. They had to have gotten them in London."

"They deceived us, then."

"They never said they don't believe in the new learnin'. They were mum about it."

When Matthew slapped a sea trout on the counter, Elizabeth flinched. "All my effort to keep Anne from heresy did no good," he complained. He pulled another trout from a barrel and laid it next to the first, eyeing them in comparison. "To think I once wished she'd marry John. Now he's the ringleader, with his damnable Cambridge education. What they learn at the university these days!"

"When all is said and done, they choose their own way. You did the best you could. Isn't that what you told me?"

He stacked the two fish and picked up a cleaver. "Damn the heretics," he hissed. "A pox on the whole lot of them, filling our young king's head with fables, stealing our children away from us and turning the kingdom upside down." He whacked the fish heads off in one coup while Elizabeth watched, wide-eyed.

"Give me those." She nodded at the trout heads. "I'll use them in a soup for supper." She slipped the heads into a small bucket with the edge of her knife and set them under the counter. "I swear they're watchin' me," she shuddered, pushing the bucket away from sight with her toe. "Mary Tudor is holdin' strong and waitin' in the wings. Despite all the pressures the king and his ilk have put on her, she hasn't buckled."

"Mary will never be queen," he groaned. "Give up that notion. His Majesty is a child. He'll be king long after we and Mary Tudor are in our graves."

"The Almighty has power to bring down the king and place Mary Tudor on the throne. You'll see. Her Majesty, Queen Mary, will restore old England to its rightful worship. I pray for it every day."

"Believe what you must to console yourself. As for me—well, I don't know anything anymore." He pushed the sea trout aside with the cleaver and looked up to see Father Garrett approaching, carrying something in each hand.

"Look at this!" The priest stormed up to the counter. "Our Lady, desecrated at the hands of barbarians. What has the devil unleashed?" As if he were handling baby birds that had fallen from a nest, Father Garrett extended a headless statue of the Virgin in one hand, and the head in the other. Matthew set his cleaver down to reach for the pieces while the priest continued, "I know who did this and, so help me, they'll pay. Nicholas, Christopher, and John, along with others—it had to be them."

Matthew inspected the pieces. "I think you're right. I was passing by the church the other day. John Whitfield was loitering outside the Crown & Anchor and happened to see me. He had the audacity to cup his hands over his mouth and shout, 'All the popish superstition in the world won't save you.' *Shouted it out*, mind you, in front of a large group of folks. They all looked up to see what the commotion was! These young men are sowing discord in the village."

With a flash of anger in his eyes the priest replied, "We'll hold them accountable for wanton destruction of property. Otherwise, what is to stop them from more vandalism like this?"

Elizabeth wilted onto a crate.

"What is it?" Matthew cast her a sideways glance. "Did you see a ghost?"

She shook her head. "Worse than that."

Handing the statue pieces to Father Garrett, Matthew stepped to Elizabeth's side. "What is it?"

She covered her face with both hands and leaned forward. "I can't hold up," she muttered. "I'm not feelin' well. I need to lie down." Reaching for the counter's edge to steady her, she struggled to a standing position.

"Do you need help getting to the cottage?" Matthew asked.

"No, I'll manage."

"Very well." Matthew shrugged his shoulders. Once she was out of earshot, he spoke up. "The lad, Christopher, is following in his father's footsteps. I fear the sorrow of it all will be the end of her."

Father Garrett looked at the broken statue in his hand and wagged his head. Sorrow was a state he knew all too well.

October, 1550

———

La Rochelle

Charlotte glanced out a window to check on Anatole and Gabrielle playing in the apple orchard. She looked at them, but didn't really see them; rather, in her mind's eye, she saw a blonde woman.

She turned away from the window, massaging a troublesome pinch in her stomach, and slumped into a black leather chair. An image haunted her thoughts, something she witnessed at the market the previous week near a table with baskets of turnips and apples. It was the blonde woman standing near Thomas, looking ridiculously out of place in a blue velvet gown and elbow-length white gloves, her face powdered white, her lips red.

Thomas—*the serpent*! *No*, she corrected herself. To label him a serpent insulted serpents. He was a shriveled apple lying in the dirt next to the tree, covered with dung, infested with worms, brown and rotten to the very core. If only spitting him out of her life were as simple as spitting out a mouthful of rotten apple.

Charlotte wouldn't have connected the woman with Thomas had he not been at arm's length away from her shopping for carved ivory jewelry boxes from Italy. Hiding behind an archway Charlotte watched the two lovers giggle, flirt and fawn over one another. Thomas acted like an adolescent fool. To think she believed him when he told her he was going to Rochefort that day on business. The duplicity of the man!

He carried a toddler in his arms who looked to be about two years old and bore a striking resemblance to the woman. Charlotte doubted that Thomas bothered to tell his mistress he had a wife. She knew what his excuse would be: *You ran away without telling me—was I supposed to wait for you to come back? I'm a man. I have needs.* Whatever the case, Charlotte had discovered her husband's secret, and had no idea how to deal with it.

Now she understood why he used his influence to secure her prison release: to keep her, like a servant, to care for his home and children so he could pursue his "pleasantries." Twice, his charm had fooled her—first, when she met him in Bordeaux, and second, when he brought her home from prison. She should have known better. Thomas lived for himself. Like a master chess player, he moved folks into position for his own strategy. She was nothing more than a pawn in his game, and he had her cornered. She'd been released from one prison, only to enter another.

All hope of returning to England had evaporated the moment Thomas demanded she inform on the man who helped her escape. She warned Piers of the danger by way of an informant, a tavern owner in La Rochelle, but her warning arrived too late. Authorities caught Piers, held him in prison, and finally released him with a stern warning to never set foot in France again upon threat of death. She had no reason to believe Piers would defy the order.

The bitter irony of it all was unbearable. After she left England, King Edward had issued a royal charter granting religious freedom to French refugees. A church was established in London for their safe gathering. Some of her réformée friends had already fled France or were preparing to do so, yet here she remained, trapped. She massaged her stomach again.

An urgent *rap-rap-rap* at the door jarred her from her tormented musings. Butter-making occupied her housemaid in the kitchen, so she approached the door herself. Passing a window, she noted the sun high overhead. Midday visitors were rare with Thomas away. She cracked the door open.

"Madame Nix?"

At first glance, the visitor appeared to be a farmhand seeking employment. He wore a loose tunic cinched with a leather belt over wool hose and smelled as if he'd been working long hours in the fields—a mixture of soil, horses and perspiration. Perhaps Thomas hired him without her knowledge. The stranger kept his head low, but when he glanced up a kindly light in his piercing blue eyes put her at ease. Looking past him, she spied a chestnut palfrey tied to a post in front of the manor with a saddled jennet behind, attached by a lead rope.

"Yes, I am she." She scratched her chin. "Do I know you?"

He glanced left, right, and over his shoulder before leaning forward to speak just above a whisper. "I've been sent to help you. If you choose to leave, you have to come with me immediately." Pointing his nose toward the orchard he asked, "Anatole and Gabrielle?"

"Who are you?"

"Piers Winston sent me."

Her heart flip-flopped.

Marc emerged from behind the stables and looked uphill in the direction of Charlotte and the stranger. She cast a discrete glance in the stable hand's direction and whispered, "He's watching."

"He won't bother us. If you choose to come, you must call your children and come now."

"But—my things. And my husband—he'll kill me this time. I know he will."

"There's no time to pack. Your needs will be taken care of." Charlotte stared at the stranger, paralyzed. "You must come now," he repeated in earnest.

"But…" She glanced at the stable hand.

"Trust me, he'll cause no problems. We need to be well on our way before your husband comes home. What is your decision?"

"I can't take anything?"

"Nothing. You must call your children immediately."

She searched his face for several seconds until, as if prodded by an unseen hand, she trotted toward the orchard. "Anatole! Gabrielle!" she shouted. Digging at the roots of a tree with a stick, Anatole looked up. Gabrielle sat perched on the lowest branch of the tree, her feet dangling. "Come!" Charlotte cried. "Hurry!" Gabrielle slid, feet first, into her mother's arms. With one hand Charlotte tugged Anatole, stumbling, across the knobby terrain toward the château.

"What is it, Maman?" Gabrielle asked, resting her soiled hand across her mother's cheek.

"The man is taking us on a voyage. We have to hurry," Charlotte panted. To her astonishment, the children didn't question. The stranger whisked Anatole onto his palfrey, instructing the child to hold on tight while he helped Charlotte mount the dappled jennet.

He positioned Gabrielle in front of her mother, pinched the girl's elbow and winked. "Hold on tight and don't let go. We'll be running fast, as if in a race. It will be fun." Then he scooted Anatole to the front of his palfrey's saddle and mounted. With a glance over his shoulder he admonished Charlotte, "Hold on as if your life depends upon it, and keep up at any cost. Are you ready?" Charlotte nodded and tightened her grip on the reins, squeezing her elbows into Gabrielle.

With a click of his tongue and a gentle kick on his palfrey's sides, the stranger led the way down the driveway with the jennet trotting behind. Upon reaching the main road, he pulled to a stop and again looked over his shoulder. "Ready?"

Charlotte felt Gabrielle tense in her arms. "Hold on, *ma petite*," Charlotte reassured her.

"I am, Maman."

They were off. A rush of adrenaline shot through Charlotte at the sound and feel of the horses' hooves pummeling the road at a full gallop, past salt marshes and vineyards and an occasional traveler. They eased into a saunter and continued at that pace until they arrived a safe distance on the outskirts of La Rochelle, where only an occasional dwelling dotted the landscape.

The muscles in Charlotte's arms and legs began to complain. Relieved when the stranger slowed his horse to a walk, she guided her jennet alongside him and stammered, "Who are you?"

"I can only tell you Piers Winston sent me."

"But I'd like to have something to call you."

"Call me whatever you would like," he chuckled.

"You're like a heavenly messenger. You showed up out of nowhere to help me." She thought for a moment. "May I call you Angel?"

A corner of his mouth turned up, as if he found something amusing about the name. "I'm no angel, but you may call me that if you wish."

Several minutes passed before Charlotte spoke up again. "Where are you taking us?"

"If all goes well, you'll end up in London."

Her heart leaped. "London?"

"Yes, London." He patted his palfrey's neck. "Our animals are rested. Are you ready?"

She nodded.

He tapped the reins against his horse's shoulder. The animal lurched forward. Eager to keep up, the jennet jolted, nearly spilling Charlotte and Gabrielle onto the dirt road. Charlotte centered herself and Gabrielle on the animal's back and squeezed her knees into the horse's sides, gripping the reins with white knuckles.

The lowering sun cast long shadows across the ground. Thickening oak, ash and maple trees signaled their entrance into Benon Forest. She watched a lark in a maple tree fluff its feathers and take flight. *I'm like the lark*, she thought. *If God wants me to fly, He will give me wings.* She smiled. For the first time in years, it was a heartfelt smile, as opposed to the sort of smile one forces in polite company. As her thoughts formed into a tune, she hummed softly,

I know if the Lord wants me to fly, he will give me wings.
He has given every bird a song, the song it sings,
And when I look and see a bird in flight, a symbol of a soul so free
I look to God and thank him for the wings that he is giving me.

"What are you humming, Maman?" Gabrielle asked, mesmerized at the beauty of her mother's voice.

"I'm thinking of a song, *ma petite*." Charlotte sang her new song in Gabrielle's ear.

"God is giving you wings?" Gabrielle scrunched her nose. "People don't have wings, only birds do."

"I can't explain it now, but someday I will." Charlotte kissed the top of Gabrielle's head.

At the edge of a valley with a rocky hill in the distance, the stranger pulled to a stop. He dismounted and lifted the children off their horses. They raced to a marshy spot a few paces away and began to throw pebbles in the water. Charlotte remained mounted, her discomfort building as the sun sank below the horizon.

Angel approached her and scratched behind the jennet's ears. "This is a good place to stretch your legs, Madame. You may not be able to see it," he pointed across the valley, "but that cottage at the base of the hill is where you'll spend the night." Charlotte made out a faint, flickering light through the trees. "From there, you'll be taken to Poitiers where you'll lodge with another family, and so on until you reach Calais. You'll be safe in Calais; it's ruled by the English king. From Calais you'll sail to Dover, where an escort will take you to the Winston family. The names of those who are helping you will be kept secret, for your safety and theirs."

Charlotte reluctantly dismounted and surveyed the darkening forest that surrounded them. "Will anyone follow us?" she shuddered.

"It depends on how your husband reacts when he learns of your departure," the stranger replied, stroking his freshly-trimmed beard. "Your stable hand will tell him a courier showed up demanding your immediate leave because of an emergency with your parents. Monsieur Nix is a ruthless and vindictive man, but I can't tell you how he'll react. I wager you can predict his behavior better than I can."

She shrugged her shoulders.

He led the horses to a nearby pond. Charlotte called for her children and followed closely behind. The jennet took a long draw of water, then suddenly raised her head, laid her ears back and twisted her lips into a shrill whinny. Vibrating ground beneath them signaled the approach of riders.

Terrified as three men on horseback reached the pond, Charlotte nudged Anatole and Gabrielle behind her. She breathed a sigh of relief upon seeing they were law officers.

"We're searching for two highwaymen—brothers," one of the officers declared, gripping a pike at his side. "They robbed two travelers this afternoon and left them for dead outside La Rochelle. A witness in Courçon saw them head this way on white mounts."

"We've seen only a few peasants," Angel replied, unruffled.

"They're armed and dangerous." The officer eyed Charlotte and the children. "Take special care with your lady and children. They have no regard for the weak."

Charlotte gulped.

"They could be taking cover in the woods anywhere in the area. They're a head shorter than my palfrey here, with brown eyes and black hair to their shoulders. One has a cut above his left eyebrow where I slashed him before he got away."

Angel nodded. "We'll be on alert."

Satisfied, the officers turned and resumed their pursuit, the thundering of hooves fading into the distance.

"Highwaymen?" Charlotte's voice quivered.

"We'll be on our way now. We're almost to our destination. With officers in the area, we should be safe." Angel lifted Anatole and Gabrielle onto the horses. He and Charlotte mounted and continued toward the cottage.

A high-pitched scream in the trees ahead sent spasms of fear down Charlotte's spine. She tightened her grip on the reins. Two more screams and a chuckle echoed through the forest. She narrowed the space between her jennet and the palfrey.

"Maman, I'm scared," Gabrielle whimpered.

"Monsieur?" Charlotte shouted. When he didn't respond, she maneuvered her horse next to his and cleared her throat. "Angel?" she pleaded.

He pulled back on the reins.

"I heard a scream." With a quivering hand she pointed to a cluster of oak just ahead. "Over there." As if on cue, another scream echoed through the trees.

Avoiding eye contact, he wiped a smirk from his lips. "A tawny owl.

They're common in these woods."

Feeling foolish—and rattled—she rode in silence to their destination. As they approached a stone cottage with a thatched roof an elderly couple emerged and held a lantern high. After helping Charlotte dismount, Angel reached into his purse and extended a small fabric pouch to her.

Hearing the jingle of coins, she protested, "I can't repay you. I don't even know your name."

"There's no need," he smiled, his eyes twinkling in the lantern light. "God is a generous master."

The elderly man stepped forward. "You won't spend the night?"

"I have to be back in La Rochelle before sunrise," Angel replied.

After handing him a bundle of cloth tied at the corners, the woman kissed Angel on each cheek. "Cheese, sausage and bread for your journey. Be careful. Two highwaymen have been in the area. We'll be praying for your safety."

"Yes, we were warned." He turned to Charlotte. "Godspeed, Madame. And don't fear. You'll be cared for along the way."

She kissed his hand, choking back her emotion. "You're an angel, sent by God."

Working quickly, he helped Gabrielle and Anatole dismount and tethered the second horse to the first. After mounting, he tipped his cap and disappeared into the forest.

"Come in, dear." The woman extended a hand. "What are your children's names?"

"Anatole and Gabrielle."

She patted Anatole's head and motioned for Charlotte and the children to follow her. "Beautiful—the names and the children."

Inside the cottage, a table set for five greeted the travelers. The aroma of roasted chicken and fresh bread wrapped around Charlotte's weary soul like a warm blanket. Every detail of her escape seemed to have been considered, from the moment Angel showed up at her door. Who were these people? How had things been so perfectly planned?

"Are you hungry, Madame?" the woman asked.

"Yes, very." Charlotte patted her stomach. Gabrielle and Anatole stared at the couple, wide-eyed. The woman chuckled.

"After the meal, I'll show you to your bed prepared in our upstairs loft. My husband will take you at daybreak on the next leg of your journey. We have provisions packed for you—coats, food, and all else you will need as you continue on."

Charlotte bit her lower lip.

"Is something wrong, Madame?" Like a mother comforting her child, the woman placed a calloused hand against Charlotte's face.

A tear trickled down Charlotte's cheek as she cradled the woman's hand with her own. "People whose names I will never know are risking their lives to help me."

Her countenance bright, the woman responded, "My bones are too feeble to make the journey to see the English king the réformées speak of, this Josiah. My husband is able but, God bless him, he won't leave my side. I'll never worship my Lord without fear, but you and your children will. In that, I find joy. It's my way of serving God."

Charlotte choked a *merci* and took a seat at the table.

After dinner she slept fitfully, fearing a knock on the door would seal her doom.

January, 1551

———

"Piers, are you expecting a visitor?"

"No one I can think of. Why?" Piers slid a place-marker into the book he was reading and joined Molly in peering out the parlor window at a carriage parked in front of the house. Large puffs of steam billowed from the horses' nostrils, mingling with thick chimney smoke trapped in the narrow streets. A woman emerged from the carriage, her identity concealed by a heavy winter cloak and hood.

"I can't tell who it is," Molly squinted.

The woman unwrapped her wool head covering while waiting for the driver to set a small wooden trunk, bound with leather straps, in the snow next to her.

"Charlotte!" Molly gasped. She dashed out into the frigid January air with no thought of stopping for her cloak. After embracing the weary traveler, she drew back with a frown.

"Are you unhappy to see me, Madame Winston?" Charlotte asked.

"Your children—they're not with you?"

The driver lifted Gabrielle from the carriage and placed her next to Charlotte, followed by Anatole.

"Your little ones! Praise be to God." Arms open wide, Molly approached the children. Gabrielle backed away, while Anatole slid behind his mother's legs and peeked around to eye the stranger.

"Of course—they don't know me." Molly took a step back to give the children their space. "They're beautiful."

"Thank you. I can't believe we finally made it." Charlotte squeezed Molly's hand and held tight for several seconds, while Piers emerged from the house to investigate the commotion.

The young carriage driver set a leather a knapsack on top of the trunk and approached Piers expectantly. After Piers placed a couple of pennies in the lad's hand the young man mumbled "good day," mounted the carriage and shook the reins.

"By God's grace, you made it," Piers said, gazing upon Charlotte with tenderness.

"Carried on the wings of angels." Charlotte managed a weary smile.

"Let's go in, and not stand here freezing." Molly reached for Gabrielle's hand. The child buried her head in Charlotte's cloak. "I suppose she'll get to know me soon enough," Molly lamented. She picked up the knapsack and led the way. Once inside the door, Molly took Charlotte's cloak, then squatted eye level to Anatole and Gabrielle and offered to take their coats as well. The children looked at their mother with panicked expressions. Charlotte slipped off their coats and handed them to Molly.

"How long have you been traveling?" Piers inquired, depositing Charlotte's trunk near the parlor doorway. "Come, have a seat." He led her to the settle, haunted by her gaunt appearance. "You must be exhausted." Piers leaned against the doorframe studying Gabrielle and Anatole, his eyes moist with emotion.

"I am. We all are." After she seated herself, her children scurried to her side like chicks to a mother hen. "We left La Rochelle at the end of October. Almost three months ago."

"I wish I could have arranged for your departure earlier. The middle of winter obviously wouldn't have been my first choice."

"Don't apologize, Monsieur Morgan. We were well cared for along the way."

A ruckus in the hallway interrupted the conversation. Mark, Simon and Grace barreled into the room, with Joseph close behind.

Pointing at Gabrielle and Anatole Simon blurted, "Who are they?"

"We don't point at people," Molly scolded. "Do you remember Charlotte speaking of her children who lived in France?"

Simon nodded.

With her rag doll tucked under one arm, Grace approached Gabrielle. "Would you like to play?" she asked, gawking at her visitor's tattered dress and soiled stockings. "Are you poor?"

"Grace!" Piers and Molly shouted the reprimand in unison. The girl's eyes widened in bewilderment. "Find one of your dresses for her to change into," Molly demanded, casting an apologetic look at Charlotte.

Gabrielle pressed against her mother for security, overwhelmed by the foreign surroundings. "She wants to play with you," Charlotte explained in French. Immediately brightening at the prospect of a playmate, Gabrielle allowed Grace to lead her by the hand out of the room.

"Simon, Mark," Piers directed, "show Anatole the new bows you received for Christmas."

Jumping at the chance to show off his prized possession, Simon led Anatole and Mark out of the parlor, with Joseph tagging behind.

"Joseph, just a moment," Piers said. The four-year-old boy stopped and lifted his gaze to Piers, confused. "You may join the boys in a moment." Piers motioned toward Charlotte. "Your mother is here."

Rather than running to his mother's arms, Joseph stiffened and averted his gaze to the floor. Charlotte swallowed hard. "You don't remember me?"

Panicked, Joseph looked at Molly for rescue.

"Don't force him," Charlotte whispered. "We'll have time."

With a wink and a smile Piers set the boy free. Joseph ran from the room as fast as his legs would carry him.

After an awkward silence, Charlotte cleared her throat and remarked, "My little lad is an Englishman." Smoothing the threadbare fabric of her dress over her legs she continued, "It's been three and a half years—of course he doesn't remember me."

"He'll warm up to you quickly, I have no doubt." Molly stood. "I have your room prepared. I wager you would welcome a few moments of quiet. Piers will bring your trunk."

Accepting Molly's outstretched hand, Charlotte breathed a sigh of relief. "A few minutes to refresh myself would be wonderful."

"We have so much to catch up on," Molly chattered as Charlotte followed her up the stairs. "I'm impatient to hear what you've been through since you left us, but I'll let you rest and get settled before I riddle you with questions." When they reached the chamber, she gave Charlotte a warm embrace, swallowing her alarm at the feel of Charlotte's protruding shoulder bones. "'Tis so good to have you back safely."

After setting her knapsack on the floor, Charlotte plopped on the bed. Running her hand across the coverlet she sighed, "Miracle of miracles—we're here. It hasn't soaked in."

"I'll go check on the children," Molly smiled. "Come down for supper when you're ready. Take all the time you need." She reached the doorway and turned. "May I get you an ale or cider?"

"A cider would be wonderful." Charlotte stood to follow Molly to the kitchen.

With a wag of the finger, Molly stopped her. "Stay put. I'll send Agnes up."

As soon as she heard Molly's footsteps on the stairs, Charlotte stretched out on the bed and closed her eyes, oblivious when Agnes tiptoed into the room, set a mug of cider on the nightstand and tiptoed out, leaving the door slightly ajar.

"She's asleep," Agnes reported upon entering the kitchen. "I wanted to ask her about her journey." Breathing in deeply she declared, "The sparrow pie smells delicious. Nothing beats bacon, sage and pastry to warm the soul on a cold winter's day."

"It smells divine," Molly agreed, setting the butter crock on the table. "Could you fetch the salt cellar? We'll let Charlotte sleep as long as she needs to," she remarked, "although I'm anxious to hear her story as well. I'll call Piers and the children for supper."

<h1 align="center">*July, 1551*</h1>

———

"Molly! Molly, can you hear me?" Frantic, Piers patted his wife's cheek. Rivulets of perspiration, glistening in the candlelight, trickled from her hairline, down her jaw and onto the damp bedsheet.

Dr. Whitsun stepped forward, blowing his nose into a kerchief. "When did her symptoms begin?" he asked, while Piers shuffled sideways to allow him to examine the patient.

"At bedtime, three or four hours ago. She complained of a pain in her shoulder." Piers rubbed his eyes with his fists. "Soon she was complaining of aches all over, and then bouts of flushing and wind set in. I don't understand. Just yesterday, she was running her errands in London with no sign of illness."

After several unsuccessful attempts to coax a sip of ale and whey posset between Molly's teeth, Whitsun set the posset on a nightstand and pushed a few strands of oily, chin-length hair away from his bloodshot eyes. "Sweating sickness is all over the city. I don't know what else to do. She's too delirious to drink from the cup." He pulled a soiled kerchief from his satchel, wiped his brow and continued, "I brought along a concoction of sorrel and sage to help her sweat the sickness out, but she's too weak to drink the posset. I see no point in trying."

Piers blinked back the moisture in his eyes. "Do you know of any survivors so far?"

The doctor slumped into a chair next to the bedside, laid his head against the backrest and closed his eyes. "I lost my own son and a daughter yesterday," he mumbled, barely intelligible.

Placing a hand on the beleaguered doctor's shoulder, Piers whispered, "I'm sorry. You should be home." He'd known Whitsun for more than a decade, and until this night he'd never seen the man's quick wit and cheerful disposition succumb to despair.

Piers sat next to Molly on the bed, took her hand in his as if he were cradling an injured bird, touched his lips to her ear and whispered, "Molly, you have to get well. For me. For the children." Her eyelids fluttered open. She stared vacantly past him for a few seconds before they fluttered closed again. "No. Molly! Wake up!" he cried, shaking her arm. It was limp and unresponsive.

Doctor Whitsun sprang up to check Molly's wrist for a pulse. A few seconds later he lowered his head, placed Molly's arm on her chest and whispered, "I'm sorry. Hundreds of Londoners have lost their lives in the past week alone. I wish I could sit with you till morning. As it is, I'll barely get to a fraction of the folks waiting for a visit." With a sympathetic squeeze of Piers' shoulder and an understanding nod from Piers, he trudged out.

Several minutes passed in haunting silence, when a whimper drew Piers' attention to the chamber doorway. He pulled the sheet over Molly and swallowed hard.

"Grace," he straightened. "What is it?" In tears, she ran across the room and curled up on his lap, violent shivers racking her small body. He felt her forehead, cradled her in his arms and stood, turning her face into his chest and away from the bed where her mother's lifeless body rested. Stepping lightly through the hallway to her chamber, he laid Grace in her own bed and covered her loosely with a sheet. "Rest, my love," he whispered. With a kiss on her forehead, he added, "Doctor Whitsun left a potion with me. I'll go fetch it."

"Father," she stammered, her eyes glassy. "Where is Mother?"

"I'll be back in a moment." He hurried out of the room and returned with the herbal potion, posset and a wet cloth. Holding the posset to Grace's lips, Piers urged her to drink. She took a sip and fell back, too weak to sit up.

"I feel as if I'm on fire," she quivered, beads of perspiration dripping down her temples. He dabbed her face with the cloth and laid it across her forehead, unaware that Simon had entered the room and was standing behind him until the boy cleared his throat.

"I didn't hear you come in," Piers mumbled, not looking up.

"What's wrong with Grace?"

"I'm not sure. How are you feeling?"

With a shrug of the shoulders he replied, "Fine, I suppose."

"And Mark—how is he?"

"Sleeping."

"I need you to Fetch Agnes," Piers commanded, his voice raw. He glanced over his shoulder to the window. Pale morning light illuminated the curtains. "I'll need her help today."

"Yes, Father." Simon was more than happy to make the trek across London to Agnes' apartment in Bishopsgate. It would give him the opportunity to catch a glimpse of the pretty young pastry seller who had recently started working at a stand on Cheapside. He hurried to his room to change out of his nightshirt, bounced down the stairs and slammed the front door.

Under better circumstances, Piers would have found Simon's behavior amusing. He stroked Grace's cheek, feeling as if an anvil were on his chest.

"Father, am I going to die?" Grace wheezed, shaking the bed with her shivering.

"No. Doctor Whitsun left this potion to help you sweat the sickness out." He cradled her head in his hand while coaxing a trickle of the liquid into her mouth. She choked, spewing liquid into his face. Undeterred, he held the cup to her lips and encouraged, "Drink, love."

"I can't," she whimpered.

Piers set the cup on a nightstand and dabbed Grace's forehead, softly mouthing his favorite hymn.

Our God is a defense and tower,
A good armor and good weapon;
He hath been ever our help and succor,
In all the troubles that we have been in.

He hummed the verse again, then bowed his head and prayed as he had never prayed before. Grace's body grew limp.

Within the hour, Simon burst into the room. He glanced at Grace, assumed she was asleep, and panted, "Agnes can't come. She's ill."

"Sweating sickness?"

"The mistress of her house believes so."

"Go into your chamber with Mark, and don't come out under any circumstance until I tell you to do so."

"But don't you have more errands I can run for you?"

"No, you and Mark will have to stay inside until the danger has passed. Make some posset for the two of you and take plenty of food into your chamber. I'll let you know when it's safe to come out."

Struck by a sudden realization, Simon's countenance fell. "Where's Mother? Why isn't she caring for Grace?"

"Your mother succumbed to the sickness."

"But Father…"

"We'll discuss it later. For your safety, get to your chamber."

As Simon left the room, Piers returned his gaze to his daughter's angelic face, framed by long, red curls. She lay perfectly still, wearing a half-smile, her cheeks still rosy. He felt for a pulse, lowered his head, and wept.

Across the city, church bells tolled a mournful dirge, accompanying the cries of grief-stricken souls whose loved ones had been full of life one day and were gone the next. Piers, Simon and Mark stood, ashen-faced, at a mass grave where workers shoveled soil over the corpse of Agnes and countless others. Unlike Agnes, Grace and Molly would have proper burials.

Sensing a warm presence next to him, Piers glanced sideways.

"I came to offer my condolences." It was Charlotte, dressed in a black robe and clutching two yellow roses.

He blew his nose, raw and red beneath the nostrils, and tucked his kerchief away. Making brief eye contact before returning his focus to the gravesite he said, "I would feel better if you stayed inside until the sickness passes."

"I had to come. I'll miss them terribly."

Biting his bottom lip, he met Charlotte's sympathetic gaze and asked, "How is your household faring?"

"So far, we've escaped. It could change without warning."

"It very well could. Please, get yourself home. God didn't bring you this far to succumb to the English sweating sickness."

After handing the two roses to Piers Charlotte patted his shoulder, nodded farewell to the two boys and hastened toward Threadneedle Street, where she was lodging with a Parisian family who had escaped to London a few months earlier. Piers watched her turn the corner before returning his attention to the death-filled trench in front of him.

"Father, I don't feel well." Mark tightened his cloak around him. "I feel like I'm standing next to a bonfire."

Piers took a deep breath, willing himself to carry on. He trudged home with his two sons, wishing he could block from his mind the haunting toll of the bells.

March, 1552

———

La Rochelle

Too preoccupied to think of offering a drink to his mistress, Thomas poured himself a goblet of claret and paced the floor in front of the fireplace. "I hope she died during her escape," he vented, taking a long sip and swishing the wine around in his mouth as if to wash the bitter taste of Charlotte's memory away. "She deserves no less." He set the goblet on a beautiful mahogany desk he'd confiscated from a réformée furniture maker in Saintes and plopped down on his favorite leather chair.

Thomas' contempt for Charlotte gave Joelle a small measure of comfort. At least Joelle wouldn't have to live in another woman's shadow or raise the two children who served as a reminder of Thomas' past. She snuggled onto his lap and drew squiggly lines on his bicep with her right forefinger.

"Now we can marry, *mon chéri,*" she cooed.

"Yes. We'll marry soon. I promise." He gave her a lingering kiss, stared into her questioning eyes and teased her by tugging and releasing one of the blonde ringlets that framed her impish face. "Until then," he whispered, his lips working their way across her cheek to her ear, "you'll let me warm myself by your fire, won't you?"

To his surprise, she slipped off his lap and faced him, hands on hips, red-faced. "I'm nothing more than a plaything that you use at your convenience," she snapped.

"No, that isn't true," he objected, scooting forward to the edge of the chair. "You're my all, my everything." He stood and reached out for her. She backed away. Blowing out a frustrated sigh, he picked up a gilded mirror from the desk and proceeded to primp his moustache and beard. Satisfied, he set the mirror down, grabbed her hand and pulled her toward him, enjoying her resistance. "I'm a busy man. I don't want to marry you and disappoint you with my frequent absences. You don't want to be a widow, in essence, do you?"

She jerked her hand free and backed away, glowering at him. "Our son needs a father, one who will be there to teach him the arts of men. You're always away. He's desperate for your attention."

Taking a step toward her, he argued, "I'll settle down soon. Trust me."

"I trusted you in the beginning," she insisted, "but now I see this devil that drives you. I fear it will consume you. You'll never plunder enough to satisfy your greed or desire for revenge on the unfortunates."

His jaw dropped. "Plunder? Unfortunates? These 'unfortunates' are wrecking our empire and defiling the church. We're their victims, not the other way around. And yes, you're right. I won't be satisfied until every last one is gone from the face of the earth. What you call 'the devil that drives me' is righteous indignation, the same thing Jesus felt when he cast the money changers out of the temple."

Anger flashed in her eyes. "I believe you on one count. You'll never be satisfied." She stormed out of the room.

He hurried down the hall after her, stretching his hand toward the back of her robe. The soft, indigo velvet slipped through his fingers. "Stop," he demanded.

She turned, choking back her tears. "For more than four years, you've led me along. At first, I didn't know you were married. I forgave you when I found out, because she left you, and I believed it wasn't your fault. But she showed up in La Rochelle, even though you assured me she never would. When you split your time between us, I felt I would die knowing you were with her. Now she's gone, and your other children with her. Nothing is standing in our way of getting married and still, you make excuses. I'll hear no more of your excuses. You're a selfish madman." She pirouetted and trotted down the hallway, her gown swishing around her ankles.

"The whole world is mad," Thomas shouted, watching helplessly, his words ricocheting down the narrow hall. He lifted his hands toward the ceiling, mumbled an expletive and returned to his desk to plan his next catch.

La Rochelle

"It's rumored the English king is a sickly lad." Awaiting Thomas' reaction to the news, Father Jean tapped his fingers on the greasy tavern table in a manner that set Thomas on edge.

Swallowing his irritation, Thomas nodded. "We can only hope the king's weak nature will speed his downfall. His betrothal to the French princess Elisabeth would spell disaster for us. Imagine him becoming our ruler. If King Edward were to force the doctrines of Luther upon the French people, as he does upon the English, I would be a fugitive twice over."

Thomas offered to refill Father Jean's goblet, hoping to busy the priest's fingers so he would stop tapping. The priest accepted. Pouring the sweet red wine, Thomas continued, "God raised up Joan of Arc to deliver your people from the English. How can King Henry even think of betrothing his daughter to a wretched English Lutheran? It would be akin to slapping God in the face."

"I don't control the affairs of the royals," the priest sighed. "Alas, I only do their bidding. Perhaps God will have to send another Joan to liberate us from the Lutherans."

"Let's hope that won't be necessary." Thomas eyed an attractive young wench across the tavern who had just begun strumming a lute. His pupils enlarged.

"Thomas, your wandering eye is a deadly sin." Wearing a smirk, the priest shook his head and began tapping his fingers again.

"Why did God make them so beautiful to behold—and to hold?" Looking the woman up and down Thomas added, "And so difficult to keep."

"To tempt and afflict man," the priest replied, admiring the maid's nimble fingers and pouty, rose-hued lips. "In England, the clergy may now marry," he sighed.

Thomas grinned when he imagined Father Jean with the lute player. "Just for today, don't you wish you were an English priest, and she an English maid?"

The priest closed his eyes and listened to the music, tapping his toe on the oak floor to keep time with the melody. "Perhaps," he replied, letting his eyes caress the black, wavy hair cascading down her back. "Just for today."

"That reminds me of a matter I've been meaning to discuss with you." Thomas took another sip of wine. "Could a man who already has a wife marry another?"

Father Jean snapped out of his guilty fantasy, a look of disgust on his face. "And practice bigamy? You're even worse than I imagined. What makes you think that maiden over there would marry you? Besides, just for today, her hand belongs to me." He pointed to himself with his thumbs. "*Moi*, John. *Je suis* Englishman."

Thomas chuckled at Father Jean's sense of humor. "No, not the maiden playing the lute, but Joelle. Charlotte is gone, yet I'm still bound to her. Joelle is begging me to make her my wife. We're fighting more and more about it. What shall I do?"

"Flee as fast as you can?"

Thomas sobered. "I'm earnest."

"Very well. I can work to get you an annulment on grounds of heresy. Everyone knows your wife was an unrepentant heretic, despite her pretense of recanting. It was you alone who stood between her and certain death."

"I'm loth to take another wife. The first one left a bitter taste in my mouth."

"Why did you marry Charlotte in the first place?"

"She was beautiful, and I believed she was devout, like her parents."

"I could spend all my days listening to the woes of men who allowed a pretty face to woo them to the altar. In fact, I take back my wish to be an Englishman for a day. She's beautiful," he cast a wistful glance at the musician, "but at least I'm free from the troubles of matrimony."

"Will you help me secure an annulment, Father?"

"It's the least I can do for you, in light of your loyal service in the cause of Christ."

Combing his moustache with his fingers and tapping his foot in rhythm with the music, Thomas breathed a sigh of relief. At last, Joelle would stop pestering him, and he could go about his business in peace.

December, 1552

—

London

"**Y**ou!"

At the brash outcry, Charlotte's heart skipped a beat. She turned in the direction of the voice, wondering if the shout was directed at her. Sure enough, a woman standing behind a table of neatly stacked linens wagged her finger in Charlotte's direction. Coarse grey hair poked out in all directions from beneath a coif which sagged forward on her pocked and wrinkled forehead. The maid definitely missed the line when God bestowed feminine charms, Charlotte thought, but she immediately reprimanded herself for the uncharitable intention.

Narrowing her eyes, the woman brayed, "Got yourself a good catch, didn't you? Perhaps a bit too good." She looked Charlotte up and down, her lips pursed. "Many a maid would have relished the hand of Master Winston. Fancy him choosing a stranger from across the sea—a maid of no consequence. A heretic, no less, chased out of your own land and come to take ours."

Charlotte bristled at the verbal lashing. "I've no intention to take anything from anybody," she retorted, putting back the damask tablecloth she might have purchased were it not for the woman's rudeness. Rattled, she didn't bother to wish the woman a good day and continued along Cheapside. Suddenly self-conscious, she wondered how many others saw her as an unwelcome intruder, the illegitimate wife of a successful man who could have had his pick from among many respectable Englishwomen.

God brought me here, she repeated to herself over and over. *And God brought me to Piers. What God hath joined together, let no man—or busy-body—put asunder. 'Tis none of that woman's affair.* She hurried forward, arguing with the woman in her mind while growing angrier and more insecure with each step. *The woman is right. Why did Piers choose me? He could have had anyone he wanted.* Staring at the cobblestone street just in front of her feet, engrossed in thought, she ran headlong into a solid obstacle.

"Pardon me," she gasped, face-to-face with a middle-aged man sporting salt-and-pepper hair and a friendly grin. He tipped his cap.

"'Tis a good idea to keep one's chin up while traveling this busy street," the stranger quipped, his eyes twinkling. He extended his hand. "Nathan Wade, weaver."

"Do forgive me, good man," she replied, offering her gloved hand. "Charlotte Winston."

"*Madame*," he bowed his head. "'Tis a pleasure. You're the wife of Piers Winston?" She nodded reluctantly, wondering if rumors about her had spread to this man as well. "I'm well acquainted with Master Winston. We work together with the Christian Brotherhood. I believe you came to our fair city to enjoy the liberties afforded by our goodly king?"

She curtsied. "Yes, sir. Thanks to the efforts of your good brotherhood."

"It warms my heart to see the fruits of our labors." Nathan smiled. "Is London treating you fairly?"

"For the most part," she replied, with a slight waver of her voice.

"Don't let the few who don't get under your skin." Nathan cast a glance toward the woman at the linen stand. "We haven't altogether eliminated the papists, and some resent the competition your able countrymen bring to England. A talented lot, and well-mannered as well. You're a boon to this realm."

"Thank you." Charlotte blew out a relieved sigh. "Your timing couldn't have been better."

Leaning closer, Nathan cupped one hand against the side of his mouth as if he were telling a

secret. "I must let you in on another tidbit, good lady. Not a few widows and spinsters in the city had an eye on Master Winston after his wife died. Don't let their jealousy get under your skin."

"Oh!" Charlotte blushed. "It is as if God sent you to be a messenger."

"London is a large city, but not so large that news doesn't spread. Cloth workers are a chatty bunch." He winked. "Say, perchance you and Master Winston would join my wife and me for Sunday dinner on the morrow?"

"I'm not sure what Piers has planned, but I'll ask him."

"He knows where we live. On Bread Street, just over there." He swept his right hand in the direction of his home. "Send a messenger to let us know, if you will—one of the children, perhaps."

"I will," she nodded, extending her hand again. "I'm enchanted to have met you, Mister Wade." He kissed her gloved hand.

"Good day, Madame. I hope we'll have the pleasure of supping with you tomorrow. I would love to hear the tale of how you came to London."

Nathan Wade continued forward, leaving Charlotte with a smile. She completely forgot the woman's rudeness, anxious to tell Piers about her encounter with a member of the Brotherhood.

"The roast pork is delicious. And I couldn't help but admire your damask tablecloth. I looked at one yesterday on Cheapside and thought to buy it, but put it back." Charlotte cast a sideways glance at Piers.

"Oh?" Lucy responded. "Why so?"

"The maid was so—" Charlotte guarded her words in case Lucy knew the woman.

"Sour grapes?" Lucy finished the sentence with a chuckle. "Nathan told me. Her name's Ruth Westover. She's a spinster. When Piers lost Molly, poor Ruth was convinced her time to marry had come. Alas, 'twas not to be. She's very jealous of you and will tell anyone willing to lend an ear that you stole London's most available bachelor from her."

Feeling his face flush, Piers took a sip of perry and changed the conversation. "Christopher, you say you're visiting London for the Christmas holy days?"

After swallowing a mouthful of roast pork, Christopher dabbed the corners of his mouth with a serviette and explained, "Yes. Anne's aunt lives nearby. We came from Dartford to spend a few days with her, and to see for ourselves how things have changed in London since we were here last. 'Tis a wonder to behold. So many of the popish idols that dotted the streets and churches have been plucked out."

Charlotte raised her eyebrows. "Dartford, did you say?"

"Yes, Anne and I are from Dartford. 'Tis a day's foot journey from here."

"My first husband fled to France from Dartford. It was many years ago—in 1539, if I recall."

"You don't say." Christopher leaned forward on his elbows. "What is his name?"

"Thomas Nix."

Christopher straightened. Anne's breath caught in her throat.

"Do you know him?" Lucy asked.

Christopher nodded. "He fled when King Henry sacked Canterbury Cathedral. One night—I remember it like it was yesterday—he spouted off in the tavern to the king's company, who were passing through Dartford on their way back to London with the treasures of the cathedral. The man he insulted happened to be one of King Henry's chief commissioners."

Charlotte cocked her head sideways, her eyes narrowing.

"The commissioner was charged with investigating religious houses for corruption. As my father and I sat in the tavern that night, trying to enjoy our ale, the commissioner boasted of looting the cathedral. He went on a rant about the shameful behavior of clergy, and mocked Saint Thomas Becket. In a fit of rage, Thomas Nix all but called him a donkey's arse. Nix stormed out of the tavern and hasn't been heard from since. In Dartford, that is. It appears you had the misfortune of finding him."

Charlotte gazed out a window for several seconds to process the astonishing information before responding. "He started out selling truffles, traveling between Sarlat and Bordeaux by river. His boat capsized in the estuary near Bordeaux. My father rescued him and brought him to our estate. For a time, he made a living carving pilgrim souvenirs. We married and had three children together."

With a snap of his fingers Christopher exclaimed, "Yes! I thought you looked familiar. I stopped in Bordeaux several years ago, when I worked on a Dutch ship. I believe you sold me a comb."

A look of recognition flashed in Charlotte's eyes. "You tried to talk the price down. I remember. And I also saw you at a cottage meeting in London. I don't believe you and Anne were married at the time." She stuffed a piece of bread in her mouth.

"I still have the comb," Anne interjected. "Amazing coincidence. How did it happen that you came to England?"

"In Bordeaux, I got my hands on a French Bible, and began to study with the réformées. Thomas tolerated it at first. As persecutions rose, we fled to La Rochelle. Finally, he threatened to turn me in."

Anne's eyes widened. "Your own husband threatened to turn you in?"

"Yes, it's happening quite often in France, children turning on parents, husbands on wives, friends on friends..."

Her eyes bright with admiration, Anne asked, "You fled to preserve your life, then?"

"Yes. The first time, I came to England without my two children. I was carrying our third. After I gave birth to Joseph, Piers took me back for Gabrielle and Anatole. I immediately learned that the man who was supposed to help me get my children out of France—Jean-Luc Mercier, a shipbuilder in La Rochelle—was burned as a heretic. But it was already too late."

"Oh, my!" Lucy gasped. "How did you get out?"

"At first, I resigned myself to stay. I pretended to recant. After several months in prison I went back to Thomas—for the sake of my children. Then I learned he had another woman, and another child."

"He sounds like riffraff," Nathan observed.

"Worse. He's a devil. He's enriched himself informing on réformées. Thomas gave me all the things money could buy, but he couldn't give me what I wanted most."

"What was that?" Anne blurted out, captive to Charlotte's every word.

"Truth."

A tingling sensation crept up Christopher's spine.

"Amen," Nathan said. "Truth. No amount of earthly wealth can substitute for it."

Christopher contemplated Charlotte's words. What price was he willing to pay for truth? This woman had paid dearly.

"Tell us, how did you finally get out?" Lucy repeated her question, impatient for the answer.

"One day, a stranger showed up at my door while Thomas was away. He told me I must decide then and there whether I wanted to go with him. And here I am."

"She gave you the short version." Piers placed his hand on Charlotte's. "The Christian Brotherhood had a hand in her escape. The man who helped her—Vincent Blanc—has risked his life to help many flee to safety. We must give credit where it is due." He offered a warm nod to Nathan. Nathan reciprocated.

"Charlotte," Anne asked, "do you suppose Thomas would ever try to follow you?"

"He's occupied with his mistress and his money—and with catching French réformées," Charlotte replied. "I doubt he'll ever leave his comfortable life."

"A remarkable story." Anne wondered how she would have measured up, given Charlotte's circumstances.

"I'm grateful to your king for inviting us to come here. Before, I had to worship in secret, fearing for my life, stalked like prey. Here, I read the word of God openly, and worship without fear."

"God save the king." Christopher raised his cup.

"May his days be long." Piers tapped his cup against Christopher's.

"Hear, hear," the others shouted.

Christopher downed his last sip of perry and smacked his lips. "I've been dreading it, but we must be on our way. Thank you, Aunt Lucy. Dinner was delicious."

"My pleasure," Lucy smiled. "Thank you for your company."

"May I help wash the dishes, Lucy?" Anne stacked Christopher's trencher on top of hers and reached for Nathan's.

"It won't be necessary, but thank you," Lucy replied. "I'll have them done in no time."

"We must be going as well." Piers offered his hand to help Charlotte up from her stool. "Thank you for a wonderful meal. You must join Charlotte and me for dinner soon."

"Yes, would you?" Charlotte folded her serviette in half twice and laid it on the table before accepting Piers' outstretched hand.

"We would be delighted." Lucy flashed her guests a gracious smile.

Nathan and Lucy ushered their guests to the door, returned to the kitchen to wash dishes, and finally retired to their chamber to discuss the wonder of Charlotte's escape to England.

May, 1553

—

London

Charlotte heard the front door slam and immediately recognized Simon's gait as his feet pounded heavily down the hallway. He peeked his head into the kitchen.

"What is it, Simon? You appear troubled." Clutching a damp dishcloth, she turned to offer him her full attention.

"Are you the only one home?" He removed his cap to fan his face, his cheeks and nose rosy from his run home from to tell about the exciting event he witnessed.

"Your father took the children with him on a river ride," she replied, noting an object in his hand.

"I suppose you're better than no one," he replied, leaning against the counter. "On my way home from the guild meeting this morning, I passed a man with his ear nailed to the pillory." The faint odor of perspiration wafted about him as he took a greedy bite of the poppy-seed cake he'd just purchased from the maiden on Cheapside.

"Nailed to a pillory? For what crime?"

With his mouth full he replied, "He declared King Edward dead." She cringed when he spoke with food in his mouth, but she didn't consider it her place as his stepmother to correct his manners.

"Such is the penalty for rumor-mongering about the king," she said, reaching for a cup to wipe dry and returning it to the cupboard. "Do you suppose there's any truth to it? Why would a man make up such a tale?"

He stuffed the rest of the cake in his mouth, wiped his hands on his wool breeches and replied, "By Jove, 'tis either true or not. One can't be partly dead."

Holding back the annoyance rising within her at his ill manners, she moved a couple steps closer. "Do you suppose the king is ill?"

He nodded. "I was having a drink with some friends in Southwark a few days ago, when we looked across the river and saw men carting ammunition and artillery from the Tower. Not an everyday sight. 'Tis also rumored that members of the king's council are buying up armor as if their lives depend upon it. The royal court is preparing for something."

Charlotte's chest tightened. "I pray for the king every day," she commented, turning to the stack of dishes waiting to be dried. "God simply must spare his life. Surely with so great a work to accomplish, he'll have divine protection."

Simon shrugged his shoulders.

"Did you purchase your cake from the fair maiden?" she teased, looking over her shoulder. The corners of Simon's mouth turned up. "I see where your thoughts are," she winked. Pity, she thought, that the young didn't grasp the gravity of events taking place around them. From painful experience, she understood the importance of having a God-fearing king. But Simon didn't know. He wouldn't know, she supposed, until he learned through his own suffering. Buying cakes from a pretty maiden was the most important event in his life at the moment. If only the wisdom of the elders could more easily be passed to the young. So much needless calamity could be avoided.

"Does your father know of events at the Tower?" she said, her back turned. Several seconds passed in silence. A glance over her shoulder revealed Simon staring into space. She realized pursuing the conversation was futile. He was love-struck, adrift in a fairy tale where the maiden of Cheapside's pastries pierced his heart like Cupid's arrows. She dried the rest of the dishes in silence.

"I'm going to my chamber to rest for a spell," she said, hanging the wet towel next to the fireplace to dry. Upon reaching her room, she opened the window and sank into her plump velvet chair. A fresh, rain-scented breeze wafted past, rustling her hair. Opening the Bible Piers gave her as a wedding gift to the eighth chapter of Romans she read,

Who shall separate us from the love of god? Shall tribulation? Or anguish? Or persecution? Or hunger? Or nakedness? Or peril? Or sword? As it is written: For thy sake are we killed all day long, and are counted as sheep appointed to be slain. Nevertheless, in all these things we overcome strongly through his help that loved us. Yea, and I am sure that neither death, neither life, neither angels, nor rule, neither power, neither things present, neither things to come, neither height, neither depth, neither any other creature shall be able to depart us from the love of God shewed in Christ Jesu our lord.

Sheep to be slain. How true the words rang! She had watched her countrymen hauled off to prisons and dungeons because of their longing to read, share and live by this newfound treasure, the word of God in their own tongue. The apostle Paul understood; he lived persecution as well. Some things would never change, she thought, across centuries of time. But one thing, most of all, would not change, and for that she was grateful: nothing could separate her from God's love. Not her first husband's betrayal, or imprisonment, or leaving her homeland—none of it, for God's love followed her everywhere and in all circumstances. She bowed her head, wrestling with a perplexing mix of joy and sorrow, when the door screeched open.

Piers stood in the doorway, his face pale, and closed the door behind him. A clap of thunder accentuated his downcast demeanor.

"What is it?" Charlotte asked, placing her Bible on the table.

He approached her, wringing his hands. "The rumors—you've no doubt heard rumors about the king?"

The tension emanating from his countenance alarmed her, especially after the news from Simon. She swallowed hard. "I've heard both that he is ill, and that he is dead already."

"The first one is true. The king is gravely ill. He's been ill for months and is wasting away. No one is to know, so please don't say a word outside of this chamber. The king's council was told to spread the rumor that the king is improving."

"It can't be," she gasped. She rose from the chair and crossed the room to close the window, taking a moment to watch folks scatter to find shelter from the pea-sized hail that began to pummel the ground. "How do you know?"

He joined her at the window. "A member of the cloth guild is kin to a member of the king's council. Word through the grapevine is that John Dudley is working with the king to amend the royal will, to designate Lady Jane Gray as Edward's successor. Dudley married his son Guildford to Lady Jane Gray in a rush wedding last Sunday. Some say Dudley is pursuing his own ambitions, and others that this is the king's idea, but regardless of Dudley's motives, the rumors about the king are true. He is ill, and movements for a successor are already in play." He crossed the room and slumped down in the chair Charlotte vacated.

"God help us." Mesmerized by the hail rolling off rooftops and bouncing on the streets below, Charlotte remarked, "I don't understand. Lady Jane has a right to succession? What about the king's own sisters—Mary, or Elizabeth?"

"I couldn't hear you over the hail," Piers shouted.

She approached him. "Why are the king's own sisters being bypassed?"

"The king declared them illegitimate. Jane is his cousin, and King Edward designated her to succeed him. She's reform-minded. He wants to make sure reform of the church continues to go forward." He laid his head back and stared at the ceiling with his mouth gaping open.

"What does this mean?" She plopped onto the bed with a pained sigh.

"The hail? Perhaps it's a sign from God that portends trouble."

"No, I meant the succession—what does it mean, that actions are being taken to make Lady Jane queen?"

"At best, the king, or Dudley—or both—are doing all they can to prevent Mary from undoing the reforms. She's catholic down to the last hair on her head."

"And at worst?"

"In my opinion, the worst that could happen is that Mary will insist upon her birthright to be the next queen. Then, God only knows how she would use her power."

"How could she make such a claim, if the will says otherwise?"

"Never underestimate the determination of those who are close to power to seize it by any means possible. Especially someone on an errand to right the perceived wrongs committed against her and the entire popish religion." Sitting up straight, he continued, "She has all the papists in the world behind her, including the Holy Roman Emperor. He fancies himself the defender of Christendom. Do you think the papists will be content to let England slip through their hands, when they consider it a holy duty to spread their tentacles even to the New World?"

Charlotte stared at the floor, agonized in spirit.

"What are you thinking?" Piers asked.

"I was thinking while I was reading the Bible just now, I've had times in my life when God felt close, as if he were holding my hand. Times when he worked wonders for me, and set things in motion with perfect timing, with such precision that only he could have brought it to pass. In those times, I couldn't question whether he is real, for to question would be to question the air that I breathe, or the sunshine that warms my face. I felt his love for me as if I were his only daughter, worthy of his personal care and attention. And then—" she slipped off the bed, strolled to the window and gazed out, struggling to find just the right words to express herself.

"Yes, and then?" Piers joined her at the window.

"And then, I've had times when no amount of pleading, no depth of suffering could reach him. Times when my poor cries for mercy echoed through the corridors of a cruel, dark sky and bounced back to me with a mocking laugh. At those times I wondered, why does he ignore me? Or even worse, does he know that I exist?"

Wrapping his arms around her Piers asked, "And what do you think of God now?"

"I know he showed his love for me by bringing me to England and placing me in your arms. For now, that's all I need."

The hail had subsided, and was replaced by a quiet, misty rain. As they gazed out the window together, he whispered, "What are you watching out there?"

"Hordes of folks with no idea what is coming their way. They dart to and fro, buying and selling, laughing and crying, while powers above them plot and scheme in ways that will affect their lives profoundly. God pity the poor folks, pawns in the hands of rulers for good or ill."

He squeezed her tightly and whispered in her ear, "You're proof that God smiled upon me."

"*Je t'aime*," she whispered.

"I love you too." He breathed out a long sigh. "Whatever comes, we'll get through it together."

Cradling her head against his shoulder, she whispered, "Yes. Somehow, we'll get through it."

July, 1553

Dartford

"Christopher!"

Anne slammed the door and leaned back against it. Her coif had slipped from her head and was dangling around the back of her neck. As she fumbled to tie it back up, Christopher looked up from the loom in alarm. "Make haste," she panted. "A heralder on Market Square is waiting for townsfolk to gather."

He put the shuttle down and hurried across the room to slip into his shoes. "'Tis evening. What's all the hurly-burly?"

"Princess Mary claimed the throne. Folks are dancing and shouting, throwing rocks—it's utter chaos."

With a vigorous shake of the head, he objected. "They're mistaken. Lady Jane is queen. It was announced just a few days ago. King Edward put it in his will." He buckled his shoes and the couple raced out the door, Christopher following closely behind Anne all the way to Market Square.

Christopher assessed the large crowd. Elizabeth and Matthew stood at the front, facing Father Garrett. Garrett's expression gave away nothing. Next to the priest, the bailiff waited to introduce the heralder.

"Keep silence, all!" the bailiff declared, motioning to a scrawny, greasy-haired adolescent.

Raising his raspy voice to a shout, the heralder read, "I hereby proclaim Mary…" He stopped to glare at a pocket of hecklers next to the market cross, lifted the proclamation in front of him, and started over. "I hereby proclaim Mary, by the grace of the God of England, France, and Ireland, queen, according to King Henry VIII, her grace's father. God save Queen Mary!"

A thunderous chant of "God save Queen Mary" spontaneously erupted. With tears streaming down her cheeks, Elizabeth lifted her skirt to dance a jig. She stopped to pull the rosary from under her smock, and proceeded to dance in circles, elbow-in-elbow, with Amy Coppinger. Matthew threw his hat into the air. He and Elizabeth jumped up and down and then embraced one another.

Christopher watched, dumbstruck. Had he heard correctly? As the bailiff led the crowd in *Te Deum Laudamus*, Christopher tried to force the words. No sound came out.

We praise thee, O God.
  We acknowledge thee to be the Lord.
All the earth doth worship thee,
  The Father everlasting.
To thee all angels cry aloud,
  The heavens, and all the powers therein.
To thee cherubim and seraphim
  Continually do cry,
Holy, Holy, Holy,
  Lord God of Sabbath;
Heaven and earth are full of the majesty
  Of thy glory.

A prickly heat warmed his chest and spread to his cheeks and forehead, as if someone were sticking him with a million hot pins. He turned away, intent on going home, until Anne grabbed the back of his tunic.

"You'll draw attention to yourself if you leave so soon," she warned.

"No matter. I have nothing to celebrate."

"Perhaps Queen Mary won't last long. Before you know it, Princess Elizabeth will be installed in her place. Princess Elizabeth will favor reform as King Edward did. We can bide our time."

He stared at her, expressionless.

"Strike up the bonfire!" Matthew yelled, waving his hands high in the air. Tom and Amy Coppinger disappeared into the Crown & Anchor and returned with armloads of wood. Other townsfolk scattered, carting back sticks and logs to contribute. Soon, a bonfire two stories high lit the square.

"Free ale!" Amy Coppinger bellowed, swinging her arm overhead. "Free ale at the tavern. Come folks. Long live Queen Mary!" She waddled toward the tavern, followed by a flock of townsfolk eager for free liquor.

Father Garrett disappeared into the church and emerged a few minutes later with a wooden crate he had cached in the cellar. "Children! Come here!" He placed the box, filled with bells, on the cobblestone a few feet from the fire. Children clamored around and crisscrossed Market Square wildly waving their bells.

"It does my heart good to see folks rejoicing once again," Elizabeth declared, clasping her hands across her chest. "Truly, God is in his heaven and has had the final say." She linked elbows with Matthew and joined others in dancing circles around the fire.

Christopher whispered in Anne's ear, "Do you see Nicholas or John?"

She shook her head. "I'm going to wish my father and your mother well. Come, join me." She tugged on his hand.

Casting her an incredulous glare, he jerked his hand away. "Do you find it so easy to accept a popish queen that you'll congratulate her supporters?"

"Of course, I'm not happy about it," she glared back. "But we have to bend with the times. The destiny of monarchs and kingdoms isn't in my hands, but in God's hands. Besides, we owe our parents our respect."

"You go ahead." He folded his arms across his chest, scowling. "I'm going to look for Nicholas and John."

"Fine, you go ahead. But trust me, your reaction is being watched."

Christopher worked his way through the crowd, feeling strange and alone, as if he were suddenly cast into the midst of a foreign people whose customs and manners he couldn't understand. He walked past the church and turned left on Overy Street to seek out his friends at the Jolly Miller. A faint light flickered through the pub windows. He pushed the door open and peeked his head inside.

"Christopher?" A despondent voice drifted from a dark corner of the pub. Christopher stepped inside, squinting in the direction of the sound. "Come in," John mumbled, lifting a mug of ale.

"Is anyone else here?" Christopher looked in all directions.

"They're all off celebrating," John replied. Christopher's footsteps echoed in the empty room as he made his way to a stool at John's table. They stared across the table at one another until the eye contact grew uncomfortable. Christopher averted his gaze to the fireplace.

"You're sitting in the dark," he muttered, unable to think of something intelligent to say.

"They made off with the wood," John replied flatly.

"For the bonfire," Christopher nodded. He cupped his face in his hands, then peeked through his fingers and moaned, "Josiah is dead. Idolatry has won."

"Perhaps she won't be such a bad queen." John guzzled the rest of his ale and set the mug on the table with a loud thud. "Princess Mary has been in many a tight spot. Let's hope she learned compassion in her exile."

"We can only hope," Christopher agreed, tapping his fingers on the table. "Where is Nicholas?"

"He was here just before you arrived. He and Rachel went home. She isn't feeling well."

"Expecting their third child in four years. I suppose they have other matters to occupy them."

"Nicholas would have stayed, but Rachel assured him she couldn't manage by herself."

"Did they hear the news?"

"Is it possible to miss? Folks running through the streets, dancing like madmen, ringing bells, building fires— by God's teeth, even ol' ha'-penny Harry was leaping about as if he'd been resurrected from the dead. You would think an angel trumpeted Christ's second coming, the way they're behaving."

Christopher shook his head. "I fear it's the coming of the antichrist."

"You got that right."

"We had the victory," Christopher sighed.

Drowning in a cesspool of despair, John stared at the wall behind Christopher.

"Doesn't it bother you to mope here in the dark, listening to revelers celebrate our return to Babylon?"

John picked up his empty mug and rolled it back and forth in his hands. "The darkness fits my mood," he said, his breathing becoming increasingly labored. Suddenly, he stood and drew back his arm. Just in time, Christopher ducked sideways before fragments of pottery and white plaster splintered in all directions on the other side of the room. "Damn!" John shouted, slamming his open hand on the table. "Damn the papists! Damn, damn, damn them all to hell." He sat down and buried his face in his hands, his words hovering in the air like living things.

Several moments passed before Christopher finally broke the heavy silence. "I couldn't have said it better myself."

November, 1553

———

La Rochelle

"Here—read this." Father Jean leaned forward, extending a pamphlet to Thomas. "I think you'll appreciate it." The priest crossed his arms with a smug smile and leaned back on the pew in Notre Dame de Cougnes church.

"Pray tell, what is it?" Thomas took the pamphlet in his hands and quickly scanned it, front and back.

"The final confession of John Dudley, the Duke of Northumberland. He's the fool who attempted to place Lady Jane on the throne. He spoke these words on the scaffold at the Tower of London, addressing those who gathered to watch his execution. The level of contrition one is capable of when his head is on the block is stunning. Go ahead, read it. He was executed on August twenty-third, just two months ago."

Thomas held the pamphlet in front of him and read silently, squinting in the dim light.

> *Good people, all you that be here present to see me die. Though my death be odious and horrible to the flesh, yet I pray you judge the best in God's works, for he doeth all for the best. And as for me, I am a wretched sinner, and have deserved to die…*
>
> *I pray you and all the world to forgive me: and most chiefly I desire forgiveness of the Queen's Highness, whom I have most grievously offended.*

And one thing more, good people, I have to say unto you, which I am chiefly moved to do for discharge of my conscience, and that is to warn you and exhort you to beware of these seditious preachers, and teachers of new doctrine, which pretend to preach God's word, but in very deed they preach their own fancies, who were never able to explicate themselves, they know not today what they would have tomorrow, there is no stay in their teaching and doctrine, they open the book, but they cannot shut it again. Take heed how you enter into strange opinions or new doctrine, which hath done no small hurt in this realm, and hath justly procured the ire and wrath of God upon us, as well may appear who so list to call to remembrance the many-fold plagues that this realm hath been touched with all since we dissevered ourselves from the catholic church of Christ, and from the doctrine which hath been received by the holy apostles, martyrs, and all saints, and used through all realms christened since Christ.

And I verily believe, that all the plagues that have chanced to this realm of late years since afore the death of King Henry the eight, hath justly fallen upon us, for that we have divided ourselves from the rest of Christendom whereof we be but as a spark in comparison: Have we not had war, famine, pestilence, the death of our king, rebellion, sedition among ourselves, conspiracies? Have we not had sundry erroneous opinions spring up among us in this realm, since we have forsaken the unity of the catholic Church? And what other plagues be there that we have not felt?

Thomas read a bit further before meeting Father Jean's gaze with a wry grin. "He admonishes the English people to return to Christ's body, or else they will experience utter ruin."

"Yes," the priest smiled. "Read to the end."

Thomas continued to mouth the words. "He says the words come from himself, and that he wasn't persuaded of anyone."

"Remarkable, hmm?"

Thomas nodded and continued. "He praises Queen Mary for granting him clemency, considering his grievous action of bringing troops against her. The law required that he should be hung, drawn and quartered, but she mercifully allowed him to be placed on the block." He read to the end. "He claims he died in the catholic faith."

"A repentant English heretic. These words are being circulated in Latin, German, French and Italian—all over the continent—to call stray sheep back to the fold."

"I hope it's accomplishing its purpose. Do you intend to share it with the flock here in La Rochelle?"

"I'll read it from the pulpit. What greater instance of a relapsed heretic have you ever witnessed?"

"I can't think of one." Thomas' eyes caressed the tract as if it were the most beautiful thing he'd ever seen. "It gives me hope for my country. Long live Queen Mary!"

"*Vive la reigne!*" Father Jean exclaimed.

"Can I take this home to show Joelle?"

"Of course," Father Jean replied. "It is yours."

"I learned something interesting today." Thomas handed Joelle a cup of white wine and eased next to her on the settee. "Father Jean brought me the written confession of John Dudley, the man who tried to enthrone Lady Jane Gray. Dudley went so far as to rally troops against Mary Tudor, with the intent of imprisoning her in the Tower. He reached her too late, and his plot failed."

"Oh?" She finished reading a prayer in the treasured *Book of Hours* Thomas had purchased for her in Paris. Placing it on a side table, she gave him her full attention. "What does his confession say?"

Holding the tract up for her to see, he explained, "He exhorts the English people to repent of listening to preachers of the new ideas, and claims the plagues and unrest that have visited England since the days of Henry the Eighth have come as a result of straying from the catholic church. His recantation is being translated and distributed all over the continent."

"Very interesting. How is it being received?"

"Well, I spoke with some English merchants in the tavern yesterday. They're very pleased with the new queen's reforms thus far."

Her interest piqued, Joelle leaned forward. "What reforms has she made?"

"The English parliament last month repealed all of King Edward's reforms. Queen Mary is working toward returning the church to its true catholic form. The merchants expressed astonishment at how rapidly the tide is turning. They don't doubt it to be the hand of God."

The melodic sound of a child's humming approached the parlor where Thomas and Joelle sat conversing.

"Papa, will you play with me?" Five-year-old Charles entered the room clutching a wooden knight in his stubby fingers. He walked the figure up Thomas' leg while continuing to hum. Thomas lifted the lad onto his knee and fluffed up the wild, curly brown hair that framed the boy's face like a mane.

"Well, *mon bonhomme*, let me have a look at this." Thomas recognized the carving; it had belonged to Jean-Luc Mercier. He swallowed a twinge of guilt and set Charles on the floor, then joined him on his hands and knees. Scooting the figure toward his son he roared, "Make way for Charles the Great—Charlemagne the Emperor!"

"Charles is my name too!" the boy squealed, his amber eyes lighting up.

"Yes, you are Charles le Petit, but one day, you will grow up and be great." Thomas stood and raised his hand from the top of Charles' head, higher and higher, to a height of about six feet. Charles jumped up and down, swatting at his father's hand.

"But for now," Joelle swooped in and lifted Charles in her arms, "you must get your sleep so you'll grow up big and strong."

The lad tried to wriggle out of her arms. "I'm not tired," he protested.

"Let me take him." Thomas held out his arms. "I'll tell you a story if you promise to rest quietly and listen."

"Yes, Papa."

Thomas carried Charles to his chamber and tucked him into a comfortable mahogany bed, a fine piece of workmanship that had belonged to a wealthy réformée family from Poitiers with four children. With Thomas' help the children were sent to Bordeaux to be schooled in the holy faith by priests and nuns, while the mother and father landed in prison, where they belonged. Thomas admired the bed's elaborate wood carving as he tucked Charles in.

Charles stared intently into his father's face, his breathing shallow with anticipation. Reclining on the bed next to his son, Thomas began, "Once there was a kingdom, grander and more beautiful than any other kingdom on earth. 'Twas a beautiful land, full of rolling green hills, covered with grazing sheep, great castles, majestic cathedrals and strong, brave lads and maidens. The people lived happily, celebrating and feasting, working and playing. Then, along came a monstrous king. He ruled the people harshly, and the people grew very sad. Some tried to fight back, but the king's soldiers killed them."

"Who was the bad king, Papa?"

"King Edward was his name. Edward was a very evil king, just like his father Henry, only worse. Wicked King Edward made his subjects rip all the beautiful things out of their churches, get rid of their candles and their rosaries, and stop ringing their bells and celebrating their feasts and holy days. He made them paint over all the pretty pictures in their churches with white paint, and burn their holy books. And you know the beautiful windows in the churches, the *vitrines*, which tell stories and cast lovely colors upon the walls when the sun shines through them?"

"Yes," Charles replied, holding his breath.

"The wicked king encouraged his helpers to break the windows from the churches. And he used stones from the altars to pave the streets, so folks were forced to trample the very things of God underfoot. All of this made the people very, very sad." Charles stuck out his bottom lip. "And that is not all. The wicked king melted the precious relics of God, and he used the gold and silver to pay for his evil schemes."

"What happened to the people?" Charles stretched his arms overhead with a yawn.

"Some of the people escaped to faraway lands, where the kings were kinder. Others hid their precious things and pretended to agree with the king, all the while hoping and praying that God would send them a good king who would allow them to ring their bells, and celebrate their feasts, and do all of the other things that made them joyous." Charles' eyes fluttered and closed. Thomas cut the story short. "And God answered the people's prayers, but he did not send a king, he sent a fine queen."

"What was the queen's name?" The inquiring voice belonged to Joelle. She approached from the doorway, where she had been eavesdropping, and squeezed next to Thomas on the bed.

"The queen's name was Mary. And lovely Queen Mary encouraged the people bring their treasures out of hiding, and celebrate their holy days and feasts, and the people rejoiced with great bonfires all over the land."

Joelle clapped softly. "A grand story. Do you miss England?"

"Sometimes, when I see a peasant carding wool, or hear lambs bleating to one another in a field, or watch a pilgrim traveling his route with excitement, I think of home. At least, how my home was before."

"It must be difficult," she stroked his forearm, "for so much time to pass without seeing your family, or your homeland or people."

"This is my homeland, and these—you—are my people," he replied.

"But a part of you will always be English, *n'est-ce pas*?"

He stared at the ceiling for several seconds before meeting her gaze. "I suppose you're right. One's homeland is always a part of his soul, just as one's blood will always be one's blood."

"Perhaps you should make a voyage to England, now that you have a catholic queen. What a joy it would be for you to see the church restored, after the pain of watching it being torn down."

The corners of his mouth curled up as he twisted the ends of his moustache. "I actually brought that up to Father Jean this morning," he smiled.

"And what did he say?"

"He encouraged me to go."

"Charles and I will go with you. I would love to see your homeland."

A wave of homesickness washed over him. "Yes," he nodded. "I think now is the time. I haven't seen my father for years. As far as I know, he has no idea where I am. I don't know how he managed after King Henry destroyed the souvenir trade. I wonder…"

Joelle interrupted him with a squeeze of the hand. "You have many questions. A trip could give you the answers."

Thomas flashed her a crooked grin. "Thank you."

"The twinkle in your eyes tells me a trip will be more than worth it." Joelle leaned her head on his shoulder. Together in the candlelight, they watched their son's chest rise and fall in peaceful slumber.

April, 1554

———

London

Gibberish, Piers thought, his mind wandering as he sat in the nave listening to the priest prattle on in a dead language. Latin had been reinstated; English tossed out. The statues, candles and other popish trappings surrounding him added to his melancholy, reminding him of exorcised evil spirits, returned to occupy the host body. *Images are the laymen's books*, the papists said. *Why not just give them the books?* Piers argued in his mind. *Give them the books and let them come to the truth.*

He lifted his gaze to the rood loft. The scripture verse painted there during King Edward's reign was recently whitewashed. Closing his eyes, he contemplated the monumental shift taking place around him. *This can't be happening*, he thought, his chest tightening. *The pendulum cannot swing this far, this fast. It's a bad dream.* He opened his eyes. It was not a dream.

The priest's chant became a hum of background noise as Piers' mind drifted to an event that took place in front of Saint Bartholomew church two months earlier. Wanting nothing more than to make the word of God available to all, John Rogers, a converted priest, had committed the crime of finishing Tyndale's work of translating the Bible into English. Piers could still see the look on the martyr's face as he faced the stake cheerfully, buoyed up by his children. The papists had denied him a last meeting with his wife. *Swine*, Piers thought. *Papists are lower than swine.*

And thus, Queen Mary's reign of terror began. Several reformers had been burned at the stake in the past two months. *The lambs of God*, he thought, glancing up at the priest. *The lambs of God sacrificed at the altar of the harlot.* Boiling with righteous indignation, he wanted to stand and shout "hypocrites!" But standing against Her Majesty's reforms would mean—*ask John Rogers what it would mean.* His forearms erupted in goosebumps.

Charlotte leaned over and whispered, "I feel like I'm attending mass in France."

"What did you say about mass in France?" Gabrielle interjected, speaking too loudly. A woman down the row leaned forward to scold the family with a sideways glance. Charlotte cast Gabrielle a look that warned, "Be quiet, or else."

After the service, Piers and Charlotte trudged along the street while the children darted ahead to chase pigeons.

"We should have escaped to the Continent last year, with the others," Piers sighed, breaking the silence. "Her Majesty won't stop until she turns England into a little Rome. She's arresting those who speak out against her and reinstating popish bishops, and has pawns everywhere to do her bidding."

"Is it true she's purging the married clergy from their posts?" Charlotte asked.

"Yes," Piers replied. "And most worrisome, she coerced Parliament to reinstate the heresy laws. That means death by burning, and we see she has no qualms about enforcing it." His hopelessness grew as he listened to himself describe the situation.

"Yet when she first took the throne, she assured us we could keep our ways of worship." Charlotte tightened her cloak around her as a bone-chilling breeze stirred the newly budding trees lining the street.

"Rather like the vixen telling the hens as she enters the coop with fangs bared, 'Don't be afraid. I'll protect you.'" Piers reached for Charlotte's hand, finding comfort in the physical contact.

"Did I step from the frying pan into the fire?" Charlotte lamented. At the sound of jeers and shouts in the distance, she stopped and tugged on Piers' hand.

Several paces ahead, Gabrielle spun around and waved her right hand high in the air. "Maman! Piers! Come, quickly!" she shouted.

"You go ahead," Charlotte urged.

Upon reaching Cheapside Cross, Piers stretched on his tiptoes to peer over the heads of the disorderly crowd. A sickening sight greeted him: a black and white cat, dressed in mock monk's garb, was hanging from a gallows. He turned to find Charlotte, and shook his head in a vigorous warning.

A tall, gangly woman with bright red hair screeched, "The heretics did this. We'll get the queen on you, we will. Hang the heretics!"

Folks joined in, chanting louder and louder, "Hang the heretics! Hang the heretics!" Piers sensed an eerie hunger for violence that sent a chill down his spine.

A booming bass voice echoed over the throng, "Come forward, cowards. Who did this? Come forward." The taunt came from a giant of a man who stood a head above the others gathered at the cross. Scanning the crowd for a culprit the giant shouted, "Do your deeds in the light of day. Show yourself."

An adolescent lad on the edge of the melee called to a priest passing by. The crowd parted for the clergy member. At the sight of the cat, the priest gulped and scuttled toward St. Paul's Cathedral, not bothering to look back.

Piers threaded his way through the crowd back to Charlotte. "Be glad you didn't see it," he reported. "Poor cat." She raised her eyebrows. "Some rogue dressed a cat as a monk and hung the poor creature."

"What will become of us?" she shuddered.

He shrugged his shoulders. "I'm afraid things will get worse before they get better."

As they resumed their walk home, Charlotte watched folks peer from second- and third-story windows to get a view of the goings-on near the cross. "See there," she pointed with her nose, "they can't get enough. We're living in a tinder-box. I don't want to live in fear again, or worship in hiding. I know what it's like to meet in a cave in the dark of night for the Lord's Supper. I know the panic of an unexpected knock at the door. I've looked out from prison bars like a caged animal, and watched good people stripped of everything they own, including their lives. I don't want to live through that again."

Piers squeezed her hand. "What would you think of building a new life in Geneva?"

She stopped. Searching his eyes, she whispered, "Geneva?"

One corner of his mouth turned upward.

"But last time we discussed it, you said you thought we were too late."

Behind them, the crowd noise intensified. He tugged her hand, pulling her into a brisk walk. "I've given it more thought. We have the Brotherhood. If they can't help us, no one can."

She savored the proposal like a delicious, sweet confection, until the thought struck her, "What would we tell the children?"

"That they're going to have a grand adventure in a foreign land?"

"I think all but Simon would be happy to go. The English children tease Anatole and Gabrielle because they're foreigners. Joseph is still too young to have an opinion, and Simon is so smitten with the pastry maiden—what's her name?"

"Maggie."

"Yes, Maggie. We may not be able to pull Simon away from her."

"He's of age. He can make up his own mind."

They hurried along, lifted by a flicker of hope as the noise from Cheapside Cross faded in the distance.

February, 1555

———

Dartford

A chestnut tree, devoid of its leaves except for a few brown, shriveled hold-outs from autumn, cast spindly shadows across the crusted snow on St. Edmunds church grounds. A spectacular sunset of violet and rose warmed the dreary landscape.

Engulfed in melancholy and unmoved by the stunning sky, Christopher stood facing John with his back against the chestnut tree, memories of the adventures he and his friends had shared on those very grounds flooding his mind. He blew warm breath on his hands and took a quick swipe at the moisture pooling in his eyes, hoping John didn't notice. Uncomfortable with the silence, Christopher kicked at John's boot.

Startled, John looked up. "Why did you do that?"

"I wish I could come with you to Venice," Christopher stated. "What if we never see you again?"

"Nonsense," John protested, tapping holes in the thin crust of snow with his boot heel. "You can bet I'll be back, and the first thing I'll do is call on you and Anne and your seven children."

Eager to join the conversation, Nicholas left his perch on the edge of East Hill and trotted over. "Mark my words, John," he panted, his breath lingering in the frigid air. "You'll come back with a Venetian bride who has you reined into submission, hunchbacked and walking with a cane, a henpecked old man before your time."

"Not so," John chuckled. "No, I'll come back to Dartford with a Venetian beauty on my arm. She'll be the envy of the village, young and old—including both of you." His eyes twinkled with mischief.

"No one could top Rachel," Nicholas stated matter-of-factly.

Christopher tightened his cloak and stomped his feet to encourage blood circulation in his numbing toes. "I hate to change the subject, but how about a song to warm ourselves? John, did you bring your hymnal?"

John nodded at the leather bag he'd hung from a broken tree branch.

"Since you're the one leaving us," Christopher suggested, "you pick the song."

Scanning the area, John whispered, "Do you think anyone will hear us? Plenty of folks already think we're heretics. The last thing we need to do is give our enemies fodder."

Nicholas scouted the churchyard while Christopher jogged past a cluster of pine trees to peer over the edge of the hill. They returned to report all clear.

Satisfied, John pulled Miles Coverdale's book "Ghostly Psalms and Spiritual Songs" from his bag. Flipping through its pages, he smiled. "Ah, yes, here it is. 'Let Go the Whore of Babylon.' Do you know it?" His question was met with puzzled looks. Holding the book high so Christopher and Nicholas could read the words over his shoulder, he hummed a verse and then broke into a pleasant tenor singing voice. The other two hummed along, managing to get a few words here and there.

> *Let go the whore of Babylon,*
> *Her kingdom falleth sore;*
> *Her wicked begin to make their moan,*
> *The Lord be praised therefore.*
> *Their ware is naught; it will not be bought,*
> *Great falsehood is found therein:*
> *Let go the whore of Babylon,*
> *The mother of all sin.*

"Sounds like a barnyard chorus," John teased, glancing over his shoulder.

Nicholas shrugged his shoulders. "This is the first time I've heard the song."

"John, I envy you," Christopher lamented. "You get to sail away from Babylon."

"Only because of my father's connections with the Venetian exiles." Feeling somewhat guilty about his favorable fate, John returned his attention to the hymnal. "Shall we cheer ourselves with another verse? I like this one—verse three."

"The tune is getting the better of me," Nicholas complained.

"It'll come with repetition." John lifted his voice and sang,

> *Of Christian blood so much she shed,*
> *That she was drunken withal;*
> *But now God's word hath broken her head,*
> *And she hath gotten a fall.*
> *God hath raised some men indeed,*
> *To utter her great wickedness:*
> *Let go the whore of Babylon,*
> *And her ungodliness.*

"So true," Christopher sighed. "She cuts down the men God raises to cry against her wickedness."

"But God will have the final say," John replied. "In the meantime, he draws his saints to his bosom, to dwell with him forever."

"Forever sounds dreadfully far off when we're fighting Babylon here and now," Christopher remarked, hearing a faint sniffle beside him. "Nicholas," he snickered, "was that you?" He punched Nicholas in the side, accidentally knocking the kerchief from his friend's hand.

"You maids aren't crying, are you?" John swallowed hard, fighting his own rising emotion. He pointed to the fourth verse. "I like this one."

> *Ye hypocrites, what can ye say?*
> *Wo be unto you all!*
> *Ye have beguiled us many a day;*
> *Heretics ye did us call,*
> *For loving the word of Christ the Lord,*

> *Whom ye do always resist*
> *Let go the whore of Babylon,*
> *That rideth upon the beast.*

"Take that, hypocrites!" Christopher lifted a fist toward the steeple of Holy Trinity Church.

"Take this, Babylon." Nicholas drew back an imaginary bowstring and released an arrow toward the church.

"I would be careful if I were you," John warned, with a quick glance in all directions.

Nicholas sighed. "You're right. And lucky. I can't believe you're leaving us in the morning. In Venice, you won't have to worry about folks spying on you."

"You're making me feel guilty. To be honest, I can't believe it myself," John admitted. "From Dartford overland to Dover, where we'll board a ship to Antwerp. From there, on to Venice."

"Venice! What an adventure. Do you know where you'll—" Christopher stopped at the sight of a human silhouette hurrying across the edge of the grounds and over East Hill. He blinked, wondering if his imagination was playing tricks on him. With his heart pounding wildly in his chest he whispered, "Do you think they heard us?"

"I'm not taking any chances." John slipped the hymnbook into his bag. He put a hand on Christopher's back and whispered, "You're a true friend."

Christopher gulped.

"And you." John embraced Nicholas. "Thank you, my friend."

Nicholas nodded, too emotional to speak.

"Stay strong and true in all circumstances, like the Apostle Paul," John admonished.

Dabbing his eyes on his cloak sleeve, Christopher felt the reassuring warmth of John's hand on his shoulder.

"I've never seen you this way," John said.

"It's just—I can't stop thinking about the night you told us the story of Bilney."

"Which part of the story are you thinking about?"

"How he placed his finger in the fire," Christopher continued, "and quoted from the prophet Isaiah. Do you remember that verse?"

"Of course. 'When thou walkest through the fire, thou shalt not be burned; neither shall the flame kindle upon thee.'"

"That's the one. And I objected that he did burn, and so did Lady Askew. It troubled me that the promise of God seemed of no effect. You suggested we make the question a matter of study."

"What did you find?" John shot a quick glance in the direction where they last saw the silhouette.

"Last night I was reading in the book of John, when I came upon these words spoken by Christ: 'Verily, verily, I say unto you, except the wheat corn fall into the ground and die, it bideth alone. Yet if it die, it bringeth forth much fruit.'"

Slipping his cap on his head, John replied, "That's your answer?"

"Yes. He allows the fires, that they may bring forth much fruit."

"I have to say, my friend," John frowned, "your words make for a very heavy farewell." He swung his bag over his shoulder.

"I can't tell you why, but that verse has lingered in my mind all day."

John responded, "I hope you're not having a premonition about my future."

Nicholas piped up, "How about we move to the Jolly Miller for one last ale together?"

"Best idea this afternoon." John raced ahead to the edge of the hill and knelt to pack a snowball. He lobbed it at Nicholas.

"Oh no you don't!" Nicholas protested. When he reached down for snow, John sprinted ahead.

Not in the mood for games, Christopher lagged behind. They arrived at the pub shivering and soaked, eager to warm themselves by the fire.

April, 1555

——

Dartford

Duke barked and pranced in front of the door, his claws clicking on the oak floor. The spaniel cocked his head to the left and then to the right, glancing at Simon Nix every few seconds to see if his master was paying attention.

"Was that a knock I heard, Duke?" The dog wagged his tail. At another *rap-rap-rap*, Duke planted his paws firmly, faced the door, and barked with a vigor that threw him off balance. After slipping a robe over his nightshirt, Simon picked up a candle and shuffled to the door.

"Who is there?" he called. Several seconds of silence followed when, finally, someone on the other side of the door cleared his throat.

"Father? 'Tis I, Thomas."

His heart pounding in his chest, Simon whispered, "My Thomas?" He cracked the door open to peek through the gap. Duke squeezed outside, sniffed around the visitors' ankles, and wagged his tail. Like sun rays breaking through a storm cloud, the truth flooded Simon's soul. He threw open the door and cried, "My son!"

Choking on emotion, Thomas dropped his bags and opened his arms.

After a long embrace, Simon stepped back to study Thomas' face. "When I saw you last, you were a lad of nineteen. Now you're a man. You're…" He scratched his chin.

"Thirty-six." Thomas grinned through his tears. "Seventeen years. I know, 'tis hard to believe."

Peering over his son's shoulder, Simon inquired, "And who have we here?"

"My wife, Joelle, and your grandson, Charles."

Forgetting his manners, Simon gaped at the attractive blonde and fidgety young lad. Self-conscious, Charles stepped behind Joelle.

"He's a bit timid," Thomas apologized, shocked to see how much his father had aged. Simon stood with a slight hunch; his once jet-black hair was white; his eyes appeared sunken and doubt-filled.

"I understand. You were like that," Simon replied.

Joelle pulled Charles in front of her and offered her hand. Simon kissed it.

"*Enchanté*," she blushed.

"We've come from France," Thomas explained.

"All the French I know could fit in a thimble," Simon confessed. "By Jove, what am I thinking, leaving you out in the dark? Come in." Simon ushered the three visitors inside. "Please, find a seat."

Three stools offered meager seating in the room that had been well-furnished when Thomas lived there. Barren shelves, once bursting with souvenirs and trinkets awaiting sale at The Pilgrim's Hat, appeared lonely, covered with dust and cobwebs. Charles plopped down on a stool and swung his legs, until Joelle scolded him to sit on the floor to make room for the adults.

"Pardon the seating," Simon apologized, wiping dust off a stool with his sleeve and motioning to Joelle to sit down. "Between Kings Henry and Edward, I sold off a lot of stuff to get by. But you don't need to hear about me. How is it that you're here, after all these years?"

Thomas positioned himself behind Joelle and gently massaged her shoulders. "Word of Queen Mary's doings has of course spread abroad. I wanted my family to witness England's restoration to the truth."

"Have you been in France all this time?"

"Yes, all seventeen years." Knowing he couldn't begin to do justice to all that had happened since he left England, Thomas left it at that.

Simon studied his son's face with wonder. "'Tis more than I could have asked for," he said. "To see God's church restored and my son, here in front of me. With a new daughter and grandson to boot."

Duke, who was sitting politely in front of Charles, lifted his paw. Charles shook it and scratched behind the dog's ears, then looked over his shoulder at Thomas to see if he noticed how the dog had taken to him.

Thomas smiled and crouched beside Charles to scratch Duke's head. "Speaking of God's church, how are the queen's reforms coming along?"

"God bless her." Simon stretched his age-spot speckled hands toward the ceiling, then covered a yawn and sat on one of the stools. "She's rebuilding the houses of God, rooting out heretical priests and bishops, and restoring Latin services. In just a matter of time folks will be making pilgrimages again, I'm sure of it. Then you'll see fine chairs here, rather than these rough stools, and my shelves full again."

"If we've learned nothing else, it's that God will have his way." Thomas gave Duke a pat on the head and moved to the empty stool to sit down. "In France, folks still make pilgrimages. For a while, I made a living carving and peddling souvenirs."

"Is that so? You look to have done well." Simon had noticed the young family's clothing. From boots to cloaks, it was definitely not the simple attire peasants wore.

"Yes, and quite well at that." Thomas looked about the room, disheartened by his father's circumstances.

With small talk exhausted, an awkward silence filled the room. Bored with his inability to understand or speak English, Charles began to hum. Suffering from the same challenge, Joelle watched a cobweb on a shelf dance on invisible air currents in the lamplight.

Simon leaned forward on his stool, fixing his eyes on Thomas as if he'd been rehearsing this moment for years. "What if I told you the king's men never intended to arrest you? Would you have stayed?"

"Come again?" Thomas raised his eyebrows. "Did I hear you correctly?"

After licking his lips, Simon replied, "Luke Tisdale told me himself. The king's commissioner actually found your behavior in the tavern quite amusing. They wanted to put a bit of fear in you, nothing more."

Thomas twisted his moustache while caressing Joelle and Charles with his gaze. "If I'd stayed in Dartford," he mused, "I wager I would have lost more than I gained."

Without warning Duke jumped to all fours, cocked his head, and barked at Charles.

"Maman!" Charles groaned, covering his stomach with both hands at the sound of a low rumble that lasted several seconds. Duke cocked his head left and right. The boy's face turned red.

"Why, where are my manners?" Simon rose stiffly from the stool. "You must be famished. Let me fetch some vittles. And please, hang your cloaks there, on those hooks by the door. Take off your boots and make yourselves comfortable." He disappeared through a doorway in the back of the room and re-emerged a couple of minutes later with a wood platter on which he'd arranged several chunks of hard cheese, a few slices of brown bread, and some pieces of ham. He tugged a small table into the center of the room and placed the tray there, grabbing Duke by the scruff of the neck when the dog lunged forward to sniff the food. After dragging the dog out the back door, Simon reappeared a few seconds later while Duke howled outside in protest.

Feeling more at ease, Thomas popped a piece of cheese in his mouth and asked, "What became of the Wade clan?"

"Ah, the Wades," Simon grimaced. "The father passed away several years ago. His son, Christopher, ran off to London, and came back after his father died. The lad married Matthew Cooper's daughter and works as a weaver. If you can believe it, the mother married Matthew Cooper." Simon slid a piece of ham between his teeth. "You look confused. I know, the truth is stranger than a fairy tale."

"Yes, I am a bit lost. Let me see if I understood. Christopher Wade's mother married Matthew Cooper, and Christopher married Cooper's daughter—Anne, is it? But Cooper is catholic—how can a Lollard's wife and son take up with a good catholic family?"

"'Tis not my business to meddle, but when the Wade lad ran off, 'twas rumored he rejected his father's Lollard ways. Now that he's back, he embraces the same heresies his father did—they call it King Edward's religion. Matthew Cooper isn't happy about it, nor is his wife, Christopher's mother. Did you follow all that?"

Thomas nodded. Joelle let out a long sigh and shifted her weight on the hard stool. Sensing her fatigue, he asked Simon, "Do you know the best place to lodge while we're here?"

"You're welcome to stay here. Your chamber is still as you left it."

"We don't wish to wear out your hospitality, but if we could stay at least for tonight—Joelle and Charles are weary from the long journey."

Simon stood, his knees popping loudly. "Let me show you upstairs. I was headed there myself before you showed up on my doorstep. Don't get me wrong—I'm happy for the interruption. Follow me."

After heaving his travel bag over his shoulder, Thomas followed his father up the stairs, trailed by Joelle and Charles.

"We'll catch up more tomorrow," Simon yawned. "You plan to attend Easter mass in the morning, I assume?"

"Yes. I wouldn't miss it." Thomas placed the bag in a corner and rolled his neck with a groan. "Church at Holy Trinity—I thought I would never set foot there again."

"Folks will be pleased to see you. You'll find extra blankets in there." He pointed to a weathered oak chest.

"Mother's chest." Thomas crossed the room to caress the box and thought of the Saint Thomas badge it once protected. He assumed the badge was still in the Medway River where he threw it for good luck on his way to France. "I'm happy to see you kept her prized possession."

"If I had done otherwise, your mother wouldn't let me hear the end of it when I pass Saint Peter's Gate, God rest her soul." Simon advanced to the doorway, turning to absorb one last image of his son before saying good night.

Joelle arranged a pallet for Charles on the floor with musty-smelling blankets from the chest before she slipped into bed. Thomas blew out the candle, closed his eyes and, with a knot in his stomach, wondered what awaited him at Holy Trinity Church the next day.

Anne entered the church without her husband and slumped into the pew beside her father, wishing she could dissolve into the wood.

"Where is Christopher?" Matthew whispered, noticing Anne's eyes were slightly red and puffy.

"He felt feverish and wished to rest," she snapped.

Leaning across Matthew, Elizabeth whispered to Anne, "He hasn't attended any of the holy week ceremonies."

"I know. His illness is lasting quite a spell." Weary of making excuses for her husband's absences, Anne stared at the cold stone floor.

Sitting further down the pew, Amy cast Anne a narrow glance oozing with judgement.

Elizabeth leaned in front of Matthew again and probed, "Is he well enough to attend our Easter feast after church? He's usually first at the table to break his Lenten fast."

"Would you like to trade me places?" Matthew let out a frustrated sigh at being sandwiched between the two women. Elizabeth waved him off.

"I can't say," Anne mumbled, aware that folks around them were beginning to stare. She lowered her voice. "I suppose I'll find out when I arrive home." Everywhere she went questions about Christopher surrounded her, like pesky flies that she couldn't swat away. She wished folks would mind their own business.

Maria Cooper leaned close to Amy's ear and whispered, "I saw him eating forbidden flesh last week."

Amy covered her mouth with her chubby right hand, then lowered her voice and said, "You mustn't tell anyone, especially not the church warden. 'Twould land Christopher in a heap of trouble."

"Oh, no. I would never tell," Maria promised. "But I dislike him, even if he is my step-brother. Nobody likes him. He's arrogant, and constantly criticizes the queen." She settled back against the pew with folded arms and a smug smile.

Elizabeth leaned across her husband for a third time and whispered, "Is Nicholas stricken with the same illness as Christopher?"

With a shrug of her shoulders, Anne took a deep breath, thinking, *pesky flies*. She pictured herself swatting Elizabeth and Amy away. To her relief, the congregation hushed and stood. As Father Garrett proceeded toward the chancel with his altar boys close behind, Anne pictured Christopher, home reading his Bible.

Thomas Nix, who was seated directly behind, pretended to pay no heed while scrutinizing the interaction taking place in front of him.

May, 1555

———

Dartford

"Are you quite sure?" Father Garrett leaned forward in his chair, the hunger in his eyes palpable.

Averting her gaze to the grey ragstone wall behind him, Amy Coppinger tinkered with a button on the front of her frock before making eye contact again. "Positive. I heard the lads, with my very own ears, singing a heretic song at the Saint Edmunds churchyard. 'Twas a shocking tune. It called the Holy Mother Church a harlot, and the pope an antichrist. I saw the Wade lad lift his fist toward the church, and the Hall lad pretend to shoot an arrow, while they called the church a—" she looked down at her lap. "I can't say the word."

Father Garrett licked his lips. "Go ahead, say it. God will forgive you."

She closed her eyes and swallowed hard. "Well, they called the church a…" Making the sign of the cross she whispered, "forgive me Father, they used the word *whore*." A shiver ran up her spine.

Father Garrett savored the revelation like a delicious piece of roasted flesh, while Amy continued, "I also have it on good word that Mister Wade ate meat during the Lenten fast."

Revealing no trace of outrage or surprise, the priest leaned back in his chair, interlocked his fingers and laid his hands across his belly. "The lads' leanings were no secret during King Edward's reign, but I attributed their behavior to the folly of youth."

Amy's eyes narrowed. "They're growing more obnoxious by the day.

I passed Christopher Wade's linen stand last week just in time to hear him shout to Luke Tisdale, 'Flee Babylon!' He said it in the most obnoxious way, over and over. Mister Hall is no better. In fact, I was in the Jolly Miller last week when both of them jeered at folks who were having a peaceful conversation in favor of the queen's reforms. I feared 'twould come to blows. They're not welcome in the Crown & Anchor. I have a reputation to keep." She leaned back with a self-righteous *humph.* "I tell you, Father, our good townsfolk are weary of their seditious and pestiferous words."

He nodded. "We can't have them disturbing the peace. 'Tis Master Tisdale's job to keep order in the village. I'll speak with him." Father Garrett pressed the tips of his fingers together, his lips taut.

"You understand, I take no delight in reporting this. My interest is the good of the townsfolk." Amy smiled sweetly.

"Be at peace. You've done the proper thing, by the Holy Mother Church, by the queen, and in behalf of our village. I had my suspicions. Both lads missed all of the Holy Week activities and failed to come to confession and mass. One can only be ill for so long."

"Yes. Well, thank you for listening, Father." When she stood to leave, Father Garrett rose as well. She took one step and turned. "Father, a canker must be lanced so the rest of the body isn't infected, mustn't it?"

He came around his desk to place a reassuring hand on her shoulder. "For the health of Christ's body, we must cut off heretics. You've played the physician today." Before she could get out the door, he tapped her shoulder. "Look at this." Reaching past her to a niche in the wall, he retrieved an ivory reliquary carved with images of the Virgin Mary. "Look what I rescued from the cellar." He lifted the lid.

At the sight of a lock of brown hair, she squealed. "You kept it? Through all the dark days of King Henry and King Edward, you managed to preserve Saint Margaret's lock?"

"I preserved it," he beamed. "And by reporting heresy, you're preserving the Holy Mother Church." He closed the lid.

"I would have come sooner, but I wasn't sure. I didn't know—"

The priest lifted a finger to stop her. "Be at peace and go with God." He placed the reliquary back in its niche. "You've done a godly work this day."

June, 1555

—

Dartford

Anne stirred hot coals from the previous night's fire and arranged a fistful of gorse branches on top. Within seconds, narrow tongues of smoke licked upward. A small flicker ignited. She blew softly to fan the flame. After crisscrossing several finger-thick sticks over the twigs and watching to make sure they caught fire, she knelt down in the firelight to pray.

Christopher stirred. She remained perfectly still, but it was too late. He rolled from his back to his side and squinted across the room, discerning her silhouette in the dim light. "What are you doing up so early?" he groaned.

"I couldn't sleep." She rose from her knees and brushed a few pieces of straw from her nightshirt.

"Again?" He yawned. "Come back to bed."

"I can't push the heaviness away."

"Don't worry about the queen. God holds us in the palm of his hand."

"I know, but it's not helping me sleep."

"Wake me up when the cock crows, would you?" He rolled over and closed his eyes. Within a minute she heard the soft cadence of his snore.

She knelt again, hoping to pray peace into her troubled spirit. After whispering *amen*, she glanced at Christopher and noticed the white nightshirt she recently made for him lying in a heap next to the bed. Tiptoeing across the room to retrieve a coverlet, she stopped to fold the nightshirt, placed it on a stool, and then curled up in front of the fire, desperate for sleep.

As she stared at the flames, her eyelids finally grew heavy and fluttered closed. Her sleep was short-lived, as a sharp jab in her side jolted her awake. She discovered herself surrounded by townsfolk, jabbing and taunting her with sticks while hurling accusations and insults at her. Against her frantic protests, two men dressed in armor set their pole axes down, then lifted her up to throw her into a bonfire.

"Heretic!" the mob chanted, dancing in a circle around her. "Burn her!"

Kicking and screaming with all her might, she could not break free. A creature with the body of a man and the head of a demon plucked Christopher's nightshirt from the stool and drew his arm back to hurl the garment into the fire.

"Stop!" she screamed, writhing and spitting. The demon called her name.

"Anne!"

Her eyes blinked open to see Christopher kneeling beside her, tapping her side.

"Anne, you're dreaming."

She bolted upright. "It was terrible," she panted, wiping beads of perspiration from her hairline. "A demon and men with pole axes were taunting me." A glance at the stool showed the nightshirt neatly folded where she left it.

With a squeeze of her hand he assured her, "You're safe. I wish these night terrors would stop."

"So do I," she yawned, rubbing her eyes. "I'm so tired. What time are you leaving today?"

"The cock is already crowing. I need to get an early start." He slipped his breeches on and laced up his jerkin, humming the tune, *Behold the Whore of Babylon*. "The market will be busy today. A troupe from Maidstone is performing. They always draw a large crowd."

"Does the troupe have a juggler?"

His crooked smile gave her the answer.

"Ah, then you will be entertained while you work." She pushed herself up to her feet and folded the coverlet, then busied herself buttering a piece of day-old bread. "Christopher…" she stopped and handed him the bread.

"Yes?"

"Never mind. 'Tis nothing." He caught the flash of concern in her eyes before she turned her back to him. Tugging her elbow, he forced her to face him. She averted her gaze to the floor.

"Anne, what's wrong? Why did you look at me that way?"

Slowly raising her eyes to meet his she asked, "Do you plan to meet with Nicholas today to discuss the new learning?"

He responded with the same sheepish grin he gave his mother years earlier, when she made him promise not to play football.

"Never mind," she sighed. "'Tis no use." She drew a cup of ale and handed it to him. "You wouldn't listen if I told you."

A rooster crowed just as sunlight broke over the eastern horizon and streamed through cracks around the door and through the window. Christopher gulped down the ale, wolfed down the bread and said, "Help me load the cart, would you?"

"Of course. That stack there?" She pointed to a large pile of folded linen in the corner.

"Yes."

Hoisting as much as she could over her shoulder she carried it outside, while Christopher followed her out with the rest. Invigorated by the brisk morning air, she placed the fabric in the cart and strolled across the dew-damp-ened yard to check the progress of apples on the tree.

"I've just a few more goods to load," Christopher shouted across the yard. He disappeared inside and returned with a large basket full of tablecloths, kerchiefs and other linens Elizabeth and Anne embroidered, then crossed the yard to the apple tree and kissed her good-bye.

"I'll see you later this morning when I come to fetch some things we need," Anne said. "Will you be there?"

"I don't plan to be anywhere else. Why do you ask?"

"I don't know." She held up a green apple the size of an apricot.

"A bit tart yet, I'd wager." Picking up the cart handles, he flashed a wide smile and winked, "See you later, Milady."

Tossing the apple aside she watched him disappear down the hill, listening as the cart's wheels screeched into the distance. She picked an apron full of peas and carried them into the house, noting that the garden needed weeding. As she busied herself making the bed, an inexplicable malaise gnawed at her. She whispered a prayer, then ate a piece of buttered bread before going outside to weed the garden.

The sun was high overhead when she realized she'd lost track of time. Retreating inside the cottage, she poured herself a mug of ale and had just lifted it to her lips when the church bell tolled the noon hour. Driven by an inexplicable urge, she plopped her half-full mug on the table and hurried out the door, lifting her skirt as she ran down East Hill and past Holy Trinity church.

A quick glance showed Christopher's cart parked in its usual spot, but he was nowhere in sight. She burst through the door of the Crown & Anchor. Startled, Amy Coppinger looked up from the counter, circled around, and put her hand on Anne's forearm. "You're out of breath, dear. Is something wrong?"

"I ran all the way to town," Anne panted, leaning against the counter to catch her breath. "Have you seen Christopher?"

"Not since this morning." Amy glared past Anne, out the bay window. "He was there earlier. I saw him speaking to the justice of the peace when I stepped out to shake my rugs."

Dabbing the perspiration from her forehead with her apron hem, Anne responded, "Master Tisdale? What business would he have with Christopher?"

"I have no idea. Perhaps Master Tisdale was looking for a witness to a cutpurse? You know how the market attracts questionable folks, and your husband has a good view of goings-on from his cart."

Stepping aside to allow a group of out-of-town patrons to enter the tavern, Anne inquired, "How long ago was it?"

"Two hours, perhaps."

Her heart sinking, Anne muttered a polite "thank you" and slipped out of the tavern, making a mad dash to Market Square. As Christopher predicted, a large group had gathered around the performing troupe. She weaved in and out of the crowd, hoping to spot her husband. No luck. Next, she raced to the livery where Nicholas had been doing brickwork. Her desperate pounding on the livery door was met with silence.

"Lookin' for someone?"

Startled by the voice behind her, Anne spun around. She looked the stern woman up and down before asking, "Do you know Mister Hall?"

"Yes, if you mean the obnoxious bricklayer who is always carpin' 'pope this' or 'Babylon that.' Tells me every time I see him to flee the whore and heed the words of the Bible. Avoid him like the pox, I do."

"Have you seen him today?"

"Earlier." The woman pointed toward Market Square. "He and the linen weaver had their eyes fixed on a juggler."

"Pray tell, do you know where they went?"

"I saw them with the justice of the peace a couple of hours ago. They didn't look happy, not a one of them. I heard a scuffle, a ruckus in the mob. Master Tisdale put your husband and Mister Hall in manacles." Anne's knees weakened. "What's wrong, maid? The color clean drained from your face."

Anne spun around, raced through the village and uphill along Watling, ignoring curious marketgoers, amused merchants, and gawking children. She stumbled over a pothole, lifted her skirt higher, and continued up the hill until she reached a timber-framed cottage set back from the road. With her chest pounding and her lungs stinging, she battered the door with her fists.

"Rachel! Rachel!" She gasped for breath and pounded again.

Rachel opened the door and surveyed the area for the cause of her friend's distress. She saw nothing but typical Market Day goings-on. Blocking the door with her body to keep her children from leaking out past her she asked, "What is it?"

"Christopher and Nicholas!" Anne panted. "Luke Tisdale led them away in manacles."

Rachel admonished her children to be good and wait patiently while she stepped outside and closed the door. Pressing their noses against the window they watched, like spectators at a play.

"What are you telling me?" Rachel asked, biting her lower lip.

"I just learned that Luke Tisdale arrested Nicholas and Christopher.

Someone informed on them—I'm certain of it. I haven't been able to sleep, with terrible nightmares, and—oh, Rachel. What have they done?" Anne glanced over her shoulder at a group of marketgoers leaving the village in a swarm.

"But Nicholas went to work this morning, as always," Rachel protested. "He didn't let on that anything was wrong."

Taking Rachel's hands in her own, Anne lowered her voice. "Rachel, listen! I just came from the market. The linen cart is vacant, and Nicholas wasn't at the livery. Christopher wanted to watch the troupe. He would be there if something weren't amiss. A maid across from the livery saw them in handcuffs, led away by Master Tisdale, perhaps two hours ago."

"Dear God," Rachel gasped. "Where would he take them?"

"Do they give no warning?" Anne cried, releasing her grip on Rachel's hands. "Like vultures, they scoop up unsuspecting folks and carry them off?" Pacing back and forth in front of the door, she glanced toward the road every few seconds as if she might see Nicholas and Christopher on the pathway to the cottage to share a midday meal, like any ordinary day.

Rachel slumped against the door, paying no heed when one her children tapped the window. "Our husbands have had warnings—plenty of them," she lamented, chewing the fingernail off her index finger and spitting it out. "I warned Nicholas, I did. I begged him to keep quiet, but he wouldn't listen. They know very well what the queen expects of her subjects." She fell silent while a rider passed by and then whispered, "We must speak with Father Garrett. He'll know where they are."

At the mention of Father Garrett, Anne felt a knot in her stomach.

July, 1555

———

Dartford

"I can't remember a July day this oppressive, as long as I've lived in Dartford," Simon complained, removing his cap to fan his perspiration-soaked forehead. "Let's find some shade." Spying some trees up ahead along the Darent riverbank, he led the way.

Thomas glanced upriver at Joelle. She was supervising Charles as he tossed rocks in the river. As he followed Simon along a narrow pedestrian pathway next to the river, he changed the subject. "Does it seem to you Father Garrett has a younger air about him, or is it just me?"

"No, the same thought struck me when I watched him conduct yesterday's evening service." Simon stopped at a cluster of pine trees. "Here?"

"He reminds me of a bird that has been let out of a cage and discovered its wings,"
Thomas commented. He sat on a boulder while his father tossed a stick into the river. The splash sent a spooked tabby cat zig-zagging through the tall grass along the bank. "I believe it's Queen Mary," Thomas remarked, watching the grass ripple as the cat bounded along. "She liberated him from the heretics."

Nodding his agreement, Simon pointed to Charles staring at his own reflection in the river. "You have a budding Narcissus there," he chuckled.

"I can't imagine where he picked that up," Thomas replied, twisting his moustache. "It's been difficult for him here. He's picking up a bit of English, but the customs and language have pushed him into a shell. Joelle's having a tough time of it as well. I planned to stay in England for a few months, but I think we'll return to France soon. The truth is, I've lived there for so long now, it's home. At least I can say I witnessed England's return to her holy mother. The prodigal nation is home."

A satisfied smile warmed Simon's face and brought light to his sunken eyes. "I wish you were here to stay, but I understand." A robust breeze swept past them, rustling the vegetation and providing welcome but short-lived relief from the stifling heat. With an affectionate pat on Thomas' back Simon said, "To see you again and know that you are well—'tis the best gift I could have."

Thomas smiled. As he watched a family of coots glide across the water, a wave of nostalgia washed over him.

"Is your work waiting for you in your absence?" Simon asked. While he waited for a response, he watched a coot dip its white face underwater, leaving only its black tail exposed.

Thomas took his time formulating a tactful answer to his father's question. "Let me put it this way," he said in a measured tone. "As long as France has heretics, I'll be busy."

Sensing he shouldn't pry, Simon steered the conversation in another direction. "Speaking of heretics, what do you think of Wade and Hall's arrests?"

"It was necessary for the public good. Pestiferous agitators have to be removed from the public so they can't keep spewing their poison. Long overdue, I'd say."

"Most of the townsfolk are relieved, in truth." Simon removed the leather cap Thomas brought him from France and scratched the bald crown on his head. "One grows weary of being the target of verbal assault. Will you at least stay long enough to find out what their sentence will be?"

"If I can convince Joelle. Nothing would satisfy me more than to see justice come full circle."

Simon plucked a sprig of wild barley and slipped the sweet stem between his teeth. "The possibility of recantation is there, I suppose."

Snorting his contempt, Thomas countered, "Wade, recant? When hell freezes over. He sealed his fate when he missed the Easter mass and avoided confession."

A shout interrupted their conversation. Joelle pointed to the water, where Charles was thrashing in panic. Thomas sprinted upriver, jumped in, and pulled the child out of the water to safety. Stretched on his back Charles gasped for breath, terrified but safe.

Rochester, England

Peering through the iron bars that separated him from the freedom he had enjoyed only a couple of weeks earlier, Christopher felt a sense of impending doom smother him like a heavy black cloak. From the moment Dartford's justice of the peace slapped shackles on his wrists, he'd rehearsed in his mind an endless stream of *if-onlys*. If only he hadn't risen up in the middle of Father Garrett's homily to protest the Latin mass. If only he and Nicholas hadn't met in Market Square more than once to publicly protest Queen Mary's policies. If only he hadn't chided Amy Coppinger, in front of everyone at the Crown & Anchor, about the foolery of praying with a rosary. If only he hadn't called the host a jack-in-the-box within earshot of Father Garrett.

But the *if-onlys* begged the question, *what if*? What if he'd buried the light that the word of God in the English tongue imparted to his soul? What if he remained silent while idolatry reclaimed the kingdom? What if he had to live forever with the shame of knowing he was a coward who denied his Lord?

At this very moment, he might be sipping an ale at the Jolly Miller, free in body, but a prisoner of his own guilty conscience. How quickly the tables had turned. If only King Edward could rise from the dead and right the wrongs of his ruthless sister, Mary Tudor. *If only*.

His cramped muscles stung; his hungry stomach churned; his troubled spirit groaned for justice. Staring at the cold, grey walls, he contemplated the price of freedom. He could confess that he had been deceived and pretend to conform. Anne begged him to do exactly that, suggesting he could bide his time and wait for the tide to turn again.

An inescapable truth had him cornered him with its fangs bared. He had only two choices: recant or burn. To complicate matters, he had not only himself to think about, but Anne as well. How would she manage without him? Would she forever be branded a heretic's wife? Would she marry another man and be happier, the way Elizabeth seemed happier with Matthew than she did with William? He recalled the raw angst in Anne's eyes the morning he was arrested. She ached to warn him, but she knew he wouldn't listen, so she no longer tried. How foolish he'd been! He didn't even get to tell her goodbye before they carted him and Nicholas off to prison.

Exhausted, he slumped onto his side, curled into a ball and closed his eyes. Hot tears streamed down his cheek and neck, dampening the floor beside him. An image of Lady Askew came to mind. He rolled onto his back and stared at the oppressive ceiling, contemplating Jesus' words,

Blessed are they which suffer persecution for righteousness sake: for theirs is the kingdom of heaven. Blessed are ye when men revile you and persecute you and shall falsely say all manner of evil sayings against you for my sake. Rejoice and be glad, for great is your reward in heaven. For so persecuted they the Prophets which were before your days. Ye are the salt of the earth: but and if the salt have lost her saltiness, what can be salted therewith? It is thenceforth good for nothing but to be cast out and to be trod under foot of men.

Ye are the light of the world. A city that is set on a hill cannot be hid, neither do men light a candle and put it under a bushel, but on a candlestick and it lighteth all that are in the house.

Let your light so shine before men that they may see your good works and glorify your father which is in heaven.

Rejoice and be exceedingly glad. The words flowed through his mind like the cheerful babble of a clear, refreshing brook, bringing a small measure of comfort. Drifting into a fitful slumber, he found himself walking along a jeweled pathway in a place of exquisite light and beauty. Flowers and trees, in hues and forms surpassing anything he'd seen on earth, glorified the landscape. He gazed in wonder upon fields of daisies surrounding him. Their white petals refracted light like crystals, while their centers glittered as cloth of gold.

Stooping to pick a bouquet for Anne, he relished the joy she would find in the magnificent flowers.

A company of men, radiant in countenance, milled about on the opposite side of a gulf that separated him from them. They beckoned to him. Christopher tried to step forward but found he couldn't move. Looking down at his cloak, he saw that the garment was covered with dirty spots. Suddenly ashamed, he looked in vain for a place to hide.

"What must I do?" he shouted across the gulf. One of the men smiled but said nothing. "Ho there! What must I do?" Christopher yelled. The man turned and walked away. "Ho, you there!" Christopher screamed, his heart pounding wildly, but the men paid him no heed. The sound of his own shout awakened him.

The spots, he thought, looking down at his tattered clothing. *No unclean thing can enter the kingdom of heaven.* He closed his eyes. Sleep refused to come.

Bishop Maurice Griffith of the Rochester Diocese glanced at his colleagues, first left, then right, twisting the amethyst-studded gold ring on his third finger. He rose from his velvet bishop's throne and narrowed his focus on the two young men—a linen weaver and a bricklayer—standing in shackles before him. The bishop licked his lips. Except for a fly buzzing near a small upper window, the cavernous room was silent.

With raised voice he declared, "We here, by the sufferance of God, proceeding in a cause of heresy against Nicholas Hall and Christopher Wade, of the parish of Dartford, of our diocese and jurisdiction of Rochester, do lay against you the following articles. To which, and to every parcel of them, we require of you a true, full, and plain answer, by virtue of your oath thereupon to be given."

Christopher wiggled his fingers. The shackles had grown heavy upon his wrists. His eyelids waxed heavy from lack of sleep. Nicholas shifted his weight from right foot to left and, with great effort, lifted both hands with the attached shackles to scratch his chin.

"Christopher Wade, linen weaver from Dartford parish, and Nicholas

Hall, bricklayer of the same." Christopher took a deep breath. "The charges of heresy are these." Bishop Griffith swooped his right arm upward, shaking his hand to emphasize each point while reading the charges from a sheet of parchment on the table in front of him.

"First: You claim to be 'Christian' men. Second: They which maintain or hold otherwise than our Holy Mother the Catholic Church are heretics."

Christopher glanced sideways at a priest who was dozing off.

"Third: That you hold and maintain, that in the sacrament of the altar, the bread and wine are not the very body and blood of Christ. You maintain that the body of Christ is in heaven only, and not in the sacrament, whereas the Holy Mother Church teaches that the bread and wine are the very body and blood of Christ."

After the third charge, Christopher's heart began to hammer within his chest. All at once, he knew beyond knowing that he wouldn't deny the accusations. His breathing grew shallow. His legs shivered like those of a cold, wet dog. His muscles softened, threatening to abandon him into a heap on the floor. He prayed that the physical symptoms of his distress weren't obvious. He didn't want his inquisitors to have the satisfaction.

"Fourth item: You maintain that the mass, as it is now used in the catholic church, is naught and abominable."

Yes, abominable. Christopher thought. *Yes, yes, yes* to all of your popish nonsense.

"Fifth item: You've been among the people of the jurisdiction in and around Dartford vehemently suspected of heresy." Griffiths glared at the accused with furrowed brows. "What have you to say to these charges?" Smoothing his scarlet robe under him, the bishop settled onto his throne.

Summoning his courage with a deep breath, Nicholas proclaimed, "As a Christian man, I cannot call the catholic church my mother, because I don't find it so called in the scripture."

With one eyebrow raised, the bishop turned to Christopher. "Mister Wade?"

"I have but one mother, and her name is Mistress Elizabeth Cooper."

The bishop scowled and turned to his colleagues. They leaned in to discuss the responses, while the scribe's plume raced back and forth across a piece of parchment. Licking his lips once more, Bishop Griffiths resumed his interrogation.

"Charge three. Is the sacrament verily the blood and body of Christ?"

Several seconds passed while Nicholas studied the arched ceiling. Then, allowing his gaze to meet the bishop's, he declared, "The body of Christ is in heaven, and the sacrament is a remembrance of his death. But the popish sacrament is neither a token nor remembrance, because it is misused and changed from the way Christ instituted it."

One of the priests mocked Nicholas' response with a roll of his eyes. Another groaned. The priest who had drifted into a light slumber sat upright. Bishop Griffith's pupils contracted, focusing raptor-like on the prey standing before him.

"Mister Wade, do you believe, as stated in the fourth article, that the mass, as used in the catholic church, is an abomination?"

Unflinching, Christopher met the bishop's gaze. Bishop Griffiths blinked and looked at the floor. A still, small voice whispered to Christopher's soul, *you are clean and unspotted from the world.* Unexpected courage surged within him, even as his legs continued to quiver. Looking Griffiths squarely in the eyes, Christopher replied, "Exactly as you have stated it."

Pursing his lips, the bishop turned to Nicholas for a response to the same question. Nicholas nodded.

"As to the fifth charge," Griffiths continued. "The people of this jurisdiction—those among whom you work and live—have strong reason to suspect you of heresy. How can you sow seeds of discord among the flock, yet claim to follow the Prince of Peace?"

Nicholas retorted, "How can you claim to follow the said prince, while you slay his lambs, as King Edward described?"

Christopher's heart soared with pride at the courage of the man standing next to him. He wanted to shout and slap Nicholas on the back, but his shackles kept him subdued.

"Exactly as he stated," Christopher added, stone-faced.

"You won't recant these seditious notions, and spare your lives?"

When thou walkest through the fire, thou shalt not be burned. The words that had once troubled him now took him by the hand and guided him along. Christopher understood them now. These men—impotent men—had no power to do him lasting harm. A sense of calm distilled upon him like dew from heaven. He took a deep breath and stared into the bishop's eyes. "'Tis you who should recant and spare your soul."

"You've done your best," a heavy-set priest barked, slapping his open hand on the table. "These dogs will not turn from their Lutheran vomit."

Bishop Griffiths stood, his jaw tight. "Christopher Wade and Nicholas Hall, you are hereby charged as heretics, to suffer a penalty of death by fire." He nodded to the guard. The raptor had his prey.

July 17, 1555

—

Dartford

Thomas Nix rose Sunday morning to find it, in many respects, no different than any other. All over the countryside, roosters crowed at the crack of dawn while sheep grazed peacefully in the heath. Here and there a dog barked at the clang of a bucket or a red squirrel scrambling up a tree. Folks slipped out of bed to milk their cows. Horses stamped and switched flies with their tails, munching their morning fodder. Children gathered eggs, and families ate their breakfast porridge. It was a typical Sunday, except for the multitudes streaming into the village. By the thousands, people packed the roads leading into Dartford and pressed forward, eager to get a spot at the Brent with a good view.

At the clip-clop of horses' hooves passing in front of The Pilgrim's Hat, Thomas jumped to the window and peered out. "A cart just passed by," he shouted. "It's carrying a stake and several bundles of reeds. Let's make haste to get to the Brent. I want a good spot." He waved his hand for Charles to come. "Are you ready, Joelle?" he called up the stairs. "Hordes of people are already on the way. I want a good place."

"Coming." She descended the stairs in her finest gown, tucking a strand of hair under her French hood.

"Father?" Thomas paced back and forth at the base of the staircase.

Simon showed up at the top of the stairs, fastening the top button of his favorite jerkin. "Let me fetch my coin pouch. There will likely be fruitiers about. And perhaps Widow Davis." He winked at Thomas.

The *bump-bump, bump-bump* of another cart passing by on the cobbled street drew Thomas back to the window. "This one is carrying broom-faggots and longer wood to stoke the flames after the reed bundles catch," he reported. "Come along—what is the point if we won't be able to see? Are we all ready?" Thomas lifted the door handle and herded his family outside. He followed Joelle and Charles along High Street, past the church, over the stone bridge, and up East Hill toward the Brent. Elbowing their way through the mob, they found a suitable place to view the gravel pit, an execution place for felons.

"Cherries, O! Fresh, round cherries! Two pence a pound. Ha'penny a twig." The crowd parted for a fruitier on horseback a stone's throw from the Nixes, pulling a cart laden with cherries.

"Get his attention. Thank goodness, we aren't too late." Simon raised his arm.

"Cherries, ho!" cried a lanky, dark-haired man a few paces away.

"Whoa." The driver, a baby-faced lad of about seventeen, pulled his horse to a stop and jumped to the ground to wait for Simon and the lanky man to approach.

"Four sticks and a pound, if you please." Simon handed the vendor an empty basket and waited, while Thomas watched men set up the stake. The driver handed Simon four sticks loaded with plump, red Kentish cherries attached with thread. Next, he measured a pound and poured the cherries into Simon's basket. Simon laid the cherry sticks on top.

"That'll be four pence," the lad smiled. "Fine day for an execution, eh?"

Simon gazed up at the blue sky and nodded, placing four pennies into the lad's scarlet, cherry-stained hands. The vendor dropped the coins into a pouch strapped around his waist, tipped his hat and served the man next in line. After distributing the cherry sticks to Thomas, Charles and Joelle, Simon kept one for himself.

"Papa, when will the her-tic be here?" Charles asked, struggling to detach a cherry from his stick. Joelle pulled off a piece of fruit and handed it to him. Charles popped it in his mouth, puckered his lips and complained, "This one is sour."

"It won't be long now." Thomas lifted Charles to see the preparations at the gravel pit. "See there, they must get ready first. Run! Get a piece of the gravel for a souvenir." Thomas set Charles down and watched him scamper toward the stake. One of the workers glared at the young boy as he approached the perimeter of the execution place.

"Stay back," the man growled. Charles' eyes opened wide. Keeping an eye on the worker, the boy squatted and snatched a piece of gravel before running back to his father, clutching the stone in his fist.

Thomas patted Charles on the head as Charles handed him the gravel. "Ah, yes." Turning the small grey stone back and forth in his hand, Thomas detected a faint odor of smoke from previous fires and smiled. "This will help us remember. Would you like me to keep it in my pouch?" The boy nodded and begged Joelle for another cherry.

A friar was supervising the installation of four poles, covered by a canopy, on a mound a few paces away from the stake, when a melodic sound drifting above the cacophony of the crowd caught Thomas' ear. He tapped Joelle on the shoulder and pointed in the direction of the noise.

"*Oui*, I see them, there." Joelle watched the sheriff approach, with a large number of gentlemen and their retinue.

"By God's wounds, there's the heretic now," Thomas pointed. Standing on his tiptoes he reported, "I see they have him bound, on horseback. He's accompanied by a maid—Mistress Margery Polley, I believe. I heard talk about the village she's to be burnt in Tonbridge following Wade's execution. The Hall lad will be burned in Rochester in the next day or two."

"Singing? How could it be?" Joelle cupped a hand behind her ear. Thomas did the same. The music that met his ears soured his mood.

> *Our God is a defense and tower,*
> *A good armor and good weapon;*
> *He hath been ever our help and succor,*
> *In all the troubles that we have been in.*

"The maggot-pies! It's the song of Luther, the one they all fancy. They hold it as some sort of battle cry."

Page 266

The sheriff's company stopped in the distance to survey the scene. At the sight of thousands gathered on the Brent, Christopher's heart caught in his throat.

"You may rejoice, Wade, to see such a company gathered to celebrate your marriage this day," Polley declared. He swallowed hard.

The company continued down the hill into the village and stopped in front of the White Horse Inn.

"Wait here," the sheriff told his female prisoner. "I'll be back to convey you to Tonbridge." He helped Christopher dismount.

"God be with you, good man," Margery encouraged, her voice kind and soothing. "Before long, we shall sup together with the Lord in paradise." With a nod, Christopher blinked back the moisture pooling in his eyes.

The sheriff escorted him inside the inn, where a friend of Anne's was waiting. She offered Christopher a neatly folded white bundle. Christopher mouthed his thanks and buried his face in the nightshirt Anne made for him, breathing in the soft aroma of lavender while stifling a sob. The sheriff led him to a chamber and unbound his hands, waiting outside the room as Christopher slipped into the nightshirt with the noise of the crowd thundering outside. Sheriff and prisoner emerged from the inn. The sheriff mounted his palfrey while Christopher proceeded on foot toward the Brent, surrounded by gentlemen carrying pikes and halberds to hold the mob at bay.

"Christopher!" The shout rose above the dissonance of the crowd, like a nightingale's song in the dark of night. He stretched tall and turned his head in the direction of the voice.

"Keep going, Wade," an officer prodded.

"Christopher!" His heart flip-flopped. It was Anne's voice.

"Master Sheriff, if it please you, I would like to speak to my wife one last time." Christopher managed a quick glimpse behind him and saw Anne standing on the old stone bridge, waving a white kerchief, her face damp and swollen. She appeared small, shrunken. If only he could break free of the bonds that held him and run to her, take her hand, and escape where the world would never find them. Ignoring his request, the sheriff prodded him forward.

Standing his ground, Christopher stretched tall, peering over the retinue until his eyes met hers. "I love you, Milady," he shouted, his voice hoarse. She touched her fingers to her mouth. He stared at her, transfixed, inhaling the scene as if he were breathing in pure gold.

"Move along." An officer poked his calf with a pike.

As he forced himself forward Christopher again heard Anne's voice, closer this time.

"Christopher!" she sobbed, thrashing through the crowd. "I am…" The ruckus around him drowned out her voice.

"Subdue his wife," the sheriff ordered. Two gentlemen fought their way back to Anne and held her arms.

"Milord," Anne cried, her voice raw. "I'm with child." The men pinned her wrists behind her back to keep her from moving forward.

"A fine gift your wife has given you on your execution day," the guard closest to Christopher quipped, prodding him in the buttock.

With child. I'm a father. Was he dreaming? Were the jeering crowds a figment of his imagination? Yes. He would shake off this nightmare, take Anne's hand and stroll home to celebrate the joyful news.

But it wasn't a dream. Cruel fate forced him reluctantly and mercilessly forward. He looked about, scenes of his life passing through his mind. Chasing Dart across the Brent as a young boy. Learning how to weave at his father's knee. Hurrying to the market on Saturday mornings to savor a taffaty tart. Playing Shrove Tuesday football against Crayford. He and Nicholas sliding down East Hill on a winter day, catching Father Garrett with Widow Willoughby. The fragrance of apple and cherry blossoms in the valley each spring. The first time he saw Anne at the market. Standing next to her at the altar, where she held a bouquet of daisies in honor of the time he tripped in front of her and spilled daisies across the walkway.

And now, a child he would never know.

All hope that a miracle might intervene evaporated when he arrived at the gravel pit. The sheriff directed him to step into a pitch barrel. Then, the miracle came. All at once, a power beyond himself enveloped him like a warm, comforting blanket. Christopher embraced and kissed the stake before setting his back to the post. A smith stapled a hoop of iron under his arms; it would support him when the greedy flames rendered him unable to stand.

Settling against the stake, he cried with a loud and cheerful voice, "Show me a token for good, that they which hate me may see it, and be ashamed because Thou, Lord, hast helped me."

"God give you strength," a freckle-skinned woman shouted. "I pray that you won't break."

"Thank you, good maid," Christopher shouted. "I will not."

"His father was a heretic as well," a wrinkled older woman snipped to an even more wrinkled elderly man standing next to her. "'Tis a shame they corrupt their children with such fables."

"May Her Majesty cleanse Christ's body of heresy!" Thomas shouted above the throng. Turning to a young woman who stood close by, weeping, he snipped, "Dry your tears, wench. He's getting what he deserves. 'Tis God's way of purging evil from our midst."

Christopher stood, praying earnestly, when the friar strolled to the mound near the stake where a canopy had been set up earlier. With a book in hand, the friar cleared his throat to speak to the crowd.

"Heed the gospel, and beware the errors of Rome," Christopher shouted before the friar could get a word out. "Believe the gospel preached in the days of King Edward. Shun the beliefs of the whore of Babylon that this man would teach you."

"Be quiet, Wade, and die patiently," the sheriff ordered, exasperated.

"I am quiet, thank God, and so trust to die," Christopher replied.

Seeing that he couldn't get the people's attention, the friar turned without a word and returned to the village.

As tall faggots were piled around the stake, Christopher found his view blocked. He pulled the faggots aside, creating a hole through which he could continue to speak to the crowd. "Be true to King Edward's teachings, good folk," he shouted. "Beware the whore of Babylon." A middle-aged man rammed a stick into the gap, cutting a bleeding gash into Christopher's cheek.

As an officer touched a torch to the base of the faggots, Christopher gazed heavenward. Raising his arms, he cried, "Lord Jesus, receive my soul!"

"The devil receive your soul," Thomas whispered, watching flames lick at the faggots and crawl from Christopher's feet, to his knees, igniting the nightshirt, and finally engulfing his body.

"Lord Jesus, receive my soul. Lord Jesus, receive my soul. Lord Jesus, receive my soul. Lord Jesus…" At last, with arms still raised, the charred body stood eerily silent.

Charles buried his face in Thomas' neck. "It stinks, Papa," he whimpered. "I want to go."

Amy Coppinger folded her arms over her stomach with a satisfied sigh and sent an approving nod in Father Garrett's direction.

Running his fingers through Charles' curly mane, Thomas stole one last look at the charred figure reaching in vain to heaven. He shook his head, spit out a cherry pit, and muttered, "'Tis a shame he chose not to recant. Father, Amy, will you join us at the tavern? Drinks are on me."

Geneva, Switzerland

Charlotte placed her hand on Piers' knee, taking a long, deep breath of fresh air. "The reflection of the mountains on the water is stunning this evening," she remarked, as their rented shallop sliced across Lake Leman's placid surface.

Squeezing her hand, Piers surveyed the lake, savoring the magical moment. "Far superior to any view in London. I could never tire of the beauty of this place." He considered the stately Château de Chillon on Lake Geneva's shore, compared to the oppressive Tower of London on the shore of the Thames; Geneva's fruitful vineyards bursting with plump grapes compared to London's plump priests bursting with perry; and Geneva's steep glacial canyons transporting clear alpine water to the green hills below, compared to London's murky waterways transporting sewage to the sea. The lofty mountains raised his spirit heavenward.

A crisp breeze swept across the lake and rustled Charlotte's hair. Illuminated from behind by glistening sunrays, she struck Piers as an angel wearing a halo of light. Moving to Geneva agreed with her. He could see it in the twinkle of her eyes, and in her gentle grace now that the burden of persecution had lifted from her shoulders.

He smiled. "The beauty around us is exceeded only by your own."

Nestling into his side, she sighed, "Pinch me! Am I truly here in this refuge with other like-minded folks? It seems too good to be true. Here we sit at Calvin's feet, feasting upon God's word. Tell me I'm not dreaming."

He kissed the top of her head. "You're not dreaming."

She wove her fingers between his, savoring the warmth of his hand. "Every trouble I ever had was worth it. Look!" she gasped, pointing to the sky. A golden eagle, with its powerful wings outstretched a full eight feet, circled overhead before swooping across the water toward the shoreline, where the city of Geneva spread like a nurturing mother with outstretched arms.

"Spectacular," Piers commented.

They watched the regal bird in silence for several seconds, when Piers declared: 'But unto them that have the Lord before their eyes, shall strength be increased; eagles' wings shall grow upon them: When they run, they shall not fall: and when they go, they shall not be weary.'"

"The prophet Isaiah?"

He nodded.

"Did you memorize his words?"

"Not the whole book, just a few favorite passages. Speaking of scripture, what did you think of Calvin's sermon yesterday—about God's providence in all that happens? Even a sparrow can't fall to the ground without God noticing."

"It was wonderful. Master Calvin has a gift—a power of expression unlike any speaker I've ever heard. And he uses no notes! I wish I could remember every word. I know our time here won't last forever. To think, we have opportunity to hear him preach twice on Sundays, and mornings during the week—it is glorious!"

He nodded. "When I'm in Saint Peter's Cathedral, surrounded by simplicity and the word of God rather than Babylonian idolatry, I find myself comparing it to Saint Bartholomew's in London. Truly God gave us the means of escape. You said it best. He gave us wings."

"I want to shout hosanna from the rooftops—but how would folks look at me if I did?" she chuckled.

"Most of them would probably join you." Her unabashed joy made his heart smile. The small vessel jolted to a stop. Piers stretched his stiff, lanky legs in front of him with a low moan. "Our ride ended too soon."

A heavy-set man with a thin moustache approached the vessel and caught a rope thrown by the shallop driver. Once the vessel was securely tied, the driver climbed out of the boat to extend a hand first to Charlotte, and then Piers.

The couple walked hand-in-hand toward the city wall, mesmerized as lights twinkled on—a candle here, a lantern there, a torch along a street.

A sense of peace warmed Charlotte's soul. "Lights in the darkness. Destiny hovers over this place. Do you feel it too?"

"Definitely. God has gathered a body of believers here to be taught, so we can return to our homelands to work for reform. I relish the thought of taking truth back to England."

She stopped, wrapped her arms around his neck and kissed him. "You're not the only one who memorizes scripture. Psalm 91—do you know it?"

He shook his head. "Why don't you recite it for me?"

She faced the lake, where the setting sun set the horizon ablaze with hues of purple and orange. Lifting her voice, she proclaimed,

Whoso dwelleth under the defense of the most high, and
abideth under the shadow of the almighty: He shall say unto
the Lord: oh my hope and my stronghold, my God, in who
I will trust. For he shall deliver thee from the snare of the
hunter, and from the noisome pestilence. He shall cover thee

under his wings, that thou mayest be safe under his feathers:
his faithfulness and truth shall be thy shield and buckler.

"Beautiful," he remarked, lifting her off her feet and spinning her in a circle. "The storm is past," he whispered. "We're safe at last."

END OF BOOK TWO

www.ingramcontent.com/pod-product-compliance
Lightning Source LLC
Chambersburg PA
CBHW050002070726
47592CB00018B/258